"READ THIS! READ IT <u>NOW!</u>
IT'S MARVELOUS!!"
—MARION ZIMMER BRADLEY

"I am totally enthralled. . . . One of the best fantasies I had read in a long time . . . worth rereading several times over . . ."
—ANDRE NORTON

"Hers is a world of intricate textures and brilliant visual imagery. . . . A fine poet she is!"
—KATHERINE KURTZ

Books by Nancy Springer

The Sable Moon
The Silver Sun
The White Hart

Published by TIMESCAPE/POCKET BOOKS

Nancy Springer

THE SILVER SUN

Based on her earlier novel,
The Book of Suns

A TIMESCAPE BOOK
PUBLISHED BY POCKET BOOKS NEW YORK

Another *Original* publication of POCKET BOOKS

A Timescape Book published by
POCKET BOOKS, a Simon & Schuster division of
GULF & WESTERN CORPORATION
1230 Avenue of the Americas, New York, N.Y. 10020

ISBN: 0-671-44244-9

First Pocket Books printing August, 1980

10 9 8 7 6 5 4 3 2

POCKET and colophon are trademarks of Simon & Schuster.

Use of the TIMESCAPE trademark is by exclusive license
from Gregory Benford, the trademark owner.

Interior design by Sofia Grunfeld

Printed in the U.S.A.

Bright shadows of an Otherplace
Pass across my sight, deflect
The turnings of my days. Above
The weaving trees, a tortured face,
A burning tower. Beyond the green-flecked
Fire, a sword, a dauntless love,
A gold-winged steed. What fey embrace
Of Otherfolk makes dreams direct
My ways? The raven and the dove,
The seer and his desire, grace
The circling seas and seasons. Chance
We shadows also join the dance?

—a song of Hervoyel

THE KINGDOM OF ISLE

at the time of Sun Kings

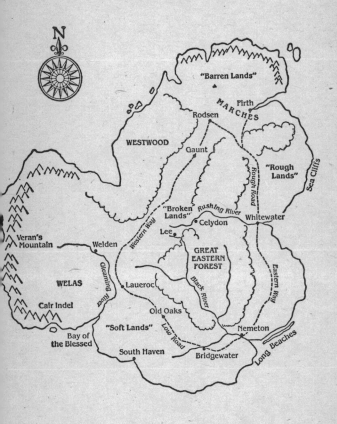

book one
THE FOREST

Chapter One

The Forest was the abode of warlocks, folk said, and goblins, and other creatures even worse. Still, Alan bent his staggering steps toward the Forest, as a desperate man will. Robbers had stripped him of everything—horse, weapons, even his clothing. The peasants could not spare him more than a beggar's crust. But within the Forest wilderness, Alan hoped, he might be able to find something to eat and a covering for his naked body.

He had not reckoned on his own dizzying weakness. The world swam before his eyes, and trees encircled him with a green blur. He sensed movement and angry shouting, but he did not care. Then the sting of a sword-flat across his back jolted him into full awareness.

Alan found himself facing a big, angry captain at the head of a mounted patrol. The next blow of the captain's sword knocked him to the ground. He lay sprawling, with no strength to flee or defend himself. Closing his eyes, Alan braced himself against the punishing blade.

But as suddenly as the blows had begun, they ceased. Alan looked up. What he saw was to remain clear in his memory for as long as he lived.

The burly captain had turned pale with fear. His chin quivered above a glinting blade pressed against his fleshy throat. But more fearsome than the sword's point, Alan thought, was the one who held the sword. He was a youth with the face of a warrior, straight of brow and strong of jaw—but there was more than a warrior's power about him. His eyes were steel gray, and there was some quality in his hard gaze that caused the captain to tremble and flinch, that caused Alan himself to struggle to his feet in hazy alarm. Yet he could not name the fear that he felt.

The gray-eyed youth spoke a few words that Alan could not understand, while his glance flashed with an eerie intensity of will that shocked Alan anew. Though the stranger had not moved, holding his sword to the captain's throat, the horses plunged away from him. The captain's men could not control them. Squealing and shying, they bolted into the Forest with their hapless riders on their backs. The stranger knocked the captain's sword from his limp fingers, slashed his reins and sent his horse careering after the others.

Alan stood watching, swaying with hunger and pain, vaguely thinking that he should leave as well. He did not have the strength to move a step. But the gray-eyed youth seemed to sense his hesitation. Quietly he dismounted from his big, gray horse and walked to face Alan. "My name is Hal," he said, "and I will befriend you, if I may. Will you come with me?"

Alan was absurdly glad that a choice was offered to him, though he could not have turned away without falling. He nodded and reached out toward the other, shaking with the effort. He could scarcely see. He felt a gentle hand take hold of him, and he gulped burning liquid from a flask. Hal wrapped him in a cloak and helped him into the saddle of his gray steed, then mounted behind. They sped away into the Forest.

"It will not take those ruffians long to come after us," Hal muttered, and Alan decided he liked the sound of that low voice.

The ride was a haze of pain for Alan. The horse was strong and swift, and the Forest whirled by. Alan barely noticed when they came to a rocky stretch of waste, but he did notice when they entered the Forest again, for his rescuer guided the horse slowly and carefully over the ground. Then they stopped in a dense stand of cover. Before long Alan heard approaching hoofbeats. The captain and his demoralized troop swept past. The big man had found his sword, and his face was as red as his red roan horse.

Hal chuckled, and Alan grinned in spite of his pain. They moved on, more slowly now. Alan lost track of time until at last they stopped and he felt himself lowered to the ground.

He needed another pull from the flask before he was able to sit up and look around. He was by a small spring which flowed into an open forest meadow. The horse was grazing, and Hal knelt, rummaging in the saddlebags. He drew forth strips of bandage, a dark little jug and a rather old hunk of bread. To Alan the bread was a vision of bliss, and he grasped at it with the impatience of a child.

"Eat slowly," Hal cautioned. His gray eyes were darker now, but softer, as gentle as they had been hard before.

Alan bit into the precious bread. He scarcely noticed as the blood-stiffened cloak was peeled away from his wounded back. Hal carefully washed the sword stripes, applied ointment from the jug, than laid on pads of cloth. He bandaged these on with strips of cloth around Alan's body and shoulders. Alan was surprised that he could not eat much of the bread, but it did not matter. A blanket was wrapped around him, and he slept.

It seemed only a few minutes later that he was awakened by a gentle shaking. But it was after nightfall. A small campfire was crackling nearby, and over it sat a kettle from which issued a delicious aroma of meat.

"Can you sit up?" asked Hal. "Here, lean against this tree." The blanket served as a pad for Alan's sore shoulders. The fire warmed his bare legs. Hal filled a battered metal dish with stew, and handed it to him, along with a spoon and a cup of water.

Alan spoke with difficulty. "Hal, have you eaten?"

The other shook his head. "After you. There is only the one bowl and spoon."

Alan ate eagerly. The venison, roots and berries seemed to him food fit for a king's board. But he could not eat more than a few mouthfuls.

"I have not yet thanked you for saving my life," he said as he rested against the tree.

Hal lowered his gray eyes, flushing, genuinely ill at ease. "Never mind that," he mumbled. There was no hint about him now of the power that had cowed the captain and his armed troops. Alan had never believed in warlocks; it was his hunger-fogged brain, he thought, that had imagined strange words and a stranger glance half a day before. Still, the horses had run away in spite of curbs and cuffs. . . . What sort of oddity was his new companion, that he could sow such fear with a glance?

"How did you come to be in such a pass?" Hal broke the silence. "Were you robbed?"

"Ay." Alan was still too weak for much speech.

Hal phrased his next question with diplomacy. In those days, when men could be outlawed for stealing a loaf of bread, it was not wise to pry. "Were you going anywhere in particular when you were robbed?"

Alan shook his head. Like Hal, he was a homeless wanderer. It was odd that two such youthful outcasts should meet.

"Will you travel with me, then, when you are better?" Hal poked at the fire, and Alan could not see his lowered eyes. "My horse is as good as a man in many ways," Hal added, "but rather quiet. Sometimes it is lonely. . . ."

"Certainly I will travel with you," replied Alan promptly. For Alan was brave, and inclined to deal generously with life. He saw a shy smile touch Hal's face, and then he went to sleep on his bed of moss without a doubt or a fear. He never afterward questioned his answer.

Alan felt much stronger when he awoke the next morning. He put on the patched tunic Hal gave him, and ate some leftover stew. He put a pinch on the ground, first, for the god.

Hal glanced at him curiously. "Whom do you serve, Alan?"

"No one!" Alan smiled sheepishly. "I am not bound by any god of grove or cave or temple. But a lifelong habit is hard to break. . . . My fathers worshiped the Star Son."

"Ah." Hal's face was unreadable. "He is not too demanding, this Star Son?"

"Nay," Alan answered grimly. "Not like the Sacred Son of the Easterners, who inflicts suffering worse than his own." He spoke harshly, for he was remembering someone he had once known. He could not tell that, behind the cloudy sheen of his gray eyes, Hal remembered as well.

After breakfast they scrubbed the pot in the stream, then wandered through the forest glade. It was late spring;

the trees were covered with bright leaf, and the grass sparkled like the water. Hal and Alan lay down and basked
in the sun. The warmth baked much of the stiffness from
Alan's wounds, and he stirred contentedly.

Hal spoke lazily. "I dare say we shall be having company soon."

"Company?" Alan was almost asleep.

"The outlaws that control this part of the Forest."

"Outlaws?" Alan was startled awake.

"From what I hear they are decent folk, though rough
in ways. . . ." A bird whistled from within the Forest.
"There they are now. Let me speak for us."

Alan nodded, his mouth dry. Then he froze in consternation as Hal whistled an answering birdlike call.
For a moment the Forest stood in shocked silence. Then
came a sharp spoken command, and from the brush
stepped eight men, from as many directions, each with
drawn bow. Their leader, a tall man whose deerskin cap
could not entirely hide his flaming red hair, strode forward.

"Get up," he ordered sharply.

Hal arose, keeping his hands in plain sight. "We are
unarmed," he said.

"And ye," the outlaw snapped menacingly at Alan.

"My companion is injured!" Hal protested. Alan struggled to his feet, wincing as a wound tore open. Bright
blood stained his tunic. Hal turned to help him, and he
hotly reprimanded the outlaw.

"Ket the Red, I expected better from you! Did I not
give you the signal of friendship?"

Ket's jaw dropped, his face a mixture of astonishment
and chagrin. "He speaks truth. Lower yer weapons," he
called to his men. And then to Hal, "How did ye know
my name?"

Alan's bleeding had already slowed, and Hal spoke
more calmly. "I lived a year with the band of Craig the
Grim, in the southern Forest. We heard much good of
you." He pressed a fold of cloth over Alan's wound. "I
beg pardon for my sharp words, but I feared for my friend.
May I care for him?"

"Ay, surely!" said the outlaw hastily. At the camp, two
outlaws stood watch while the others helped fetch water
and bandages. Only when Alan was attended did Ket
speak again.

"What are yer names?"

"I am Hal, and this is my friend Alan."

"Ye're not brothers, then?"

"Nay!" It was Hal's turn to be surprised. "Why do you ask?"

"Why, by the Lady, ye look alike!"

Alan and Hal regarded each other quizzically. Ket was right. Their light, sun-streaked hair, their high cheekbones and angular jaws were the same. Alan's mouth was a bit wider and more expressive than Hal's, but only at their eyes did all resemblance cease. Alan's were clear and open as blue skies, while Hal's were shadowy and full of mystery. What Hal's feelings were about this strange coincidence, Alan could not tell. He only shrugged as he turned back to Ket.

"I have no brother," he continued. "Alan and I first met yesterday."

"Yesterday? And how did Alan come to be hurt?"

Alan broke his silence, knowing that Hal could not very well recount his own exploit. "Let me tell you, Ket. I was not paying proper attention, I suppose, when that troop of lordsmen came along. I was far too hungry. . . ."

Alan described his predicament and his rescue, glossing over the fright of the horses; he did not know how to explain that. The outlaws listened intently, and laughed heartily when he mentioned the captain's red face.

"So that was how the big bastard came to be pelting through the Forest yesterday, with his britches soiled and his helmet askew, and his face red as a beet!" cried Ket. "We saw, but we little knew the reason. 'Twas sweetly done, lad." Then he sobered. "They'll be looking for ye, long and hard. Ye must be wary."

Hal winced at the praise, and he changed the subject. "Ket, if you are no longer angry with me, I would like to ask your help. I have shot a deer. Half is for you. And I would like to trade a haunch and the hide for bread and eggs and such, if you will tell me where."

"Ye shot a deer! But I see no bow, nor did we find the remains of a kill."

"Here is the bow," said Hal, drawing it out of a bag. It was less than half the length of the outlaws' bows, very thick and powerfully curved. Ket the Red whistled. "It takes a strong arm to draw that," he said, and eyed Hal narrowly, with mingled suspicion and respect. "But where is the deer, and how did ye hide the offal?"

Hal laughed. "I cannot give away the secrets of Craig the Grim, even to you," he said. "Let us say that it was well hidden. But as for the deer, it is here." He parted the bushes to reveal the hanging carcass.

There followed some argument. Ket maintained that it would be too dangerous for Hal to go to the village, because of the affair of the previous day, "and also," he added kindly, "because ye're far too young, for all that ye're of man's height, lad." He offered to go, or send one of his men. Hal would hear nothing of it.

"You are all well known in these parts, especially you, with your flaming hair," he retorted. "Every time you appear, you are in great danger. But who is likely to recognize me from any description our husky friend may have given? Since I must be a lad today,"—Hal took a significant pause—"I'll be just another farm lad. I shall leave the horse in the Forest, and walk. Only tell me where to knock."

"For the matter of that," asked the outlaw, mildly, "where is the horse?"

Alan knew by now that Hal's steed grazed loose. Hal whistled, a single low note. There were no hoofbeats to be heard, and the outlaws exchanged amused glances. But suddenly the horse was there, as if he had materialized from the gray trunks of the trees. Silently and gracefully he moved to Hal's side, an alert, questioning look in his fine eyes.

Hal smiled, and spoke to the horse in a low voice; Alan could not catch the words. "He thought something was wrong," Hal explained, turning.

Impulsively, Alan reached out to pat the beautiful creature, but the steed drew back with a snort.

"You have not yet been introduced," Hal said. "Give me your hand." He spoke to the stallion in strange words, and placed Alan's hand on the horse's neck. "He is trained to let no hand touch him except mine," Hal explained. "Otherwise he would have been stolen from me many a time."

Alan felt odd and at a loss for words. He was used to horses that did as he told them, not to great gray beasts that roamed at will and required introductions. "What is his name?" he managed to ask.

"Arundel. Arun for short."

It was not a familiar name. "Does it mean something?" Alan ventured. Names might have meanings, he thought, to Hal.

"It means 'dweller in the Eagle Valley.'"

Alan stroked the highly arched neck and looked into the deep eyes of the proud beast which looked down on him. He wondered what strange turn his life was taking. Ket broke in on his thoughts.

"We did not see that horse, or hear him, on our way here. Did he seek to avoid us?" the outlaw demanded.

"Ay. He is trained to do so."

Ket shook his head helplessly, then spoke with a countryman's slow, grave courtesy. "By my troth, now, I dare say that one who has entered my Forest without my knowing it—and who has shot a deer under my very nose with a bow the size of my forearm—and whose very horse goes with the stealth of a ghost in the night—might trade for a few victuals and stay clear of the gallows."

"I thank you," said Hal, grinning, "for your 'daresay.'"

Ket gave Hal instructions on how best to approach the village and where to go with the meat. Such meat was forbidden, since the Forest game was supposed to be preserved for noble sport. So Hal had to be careful on more than one account. Ket seemed to be restraining himself from reminding him of this fact. He set his outlaws as a guard around the Forest glade, and Hal left on his errand.

"And you, Alan," Ket admonished, "bide quietly, and tend to yer wounds." He strode away.

Left alone, Alan lay once again in the warm sun and dozed. It did not seem long before Hal returned. He was grinning as he entered the glade, and when he had dismounted he began to laugh heartily.

"Alan, such a jest!" he wheezed at last. "I met an old woman near the road, and also two cowherds, and they all told me the same tale. It seems that the lord's captain met a demon-ridden creature, a gaping idiot (yourself, Alan!) which he was bravely attempting to dispatch, when out of the forest rode a great black warrior, over seven feet tall, on a great black horse whose nostrils breathed fire, and this warrior wielded a flaming, blood-red sword. He put a magical spell on the brave company, so that they could not move, and off rode he and the evil creature, cackling curses. And when the lordsmen took pursuit, the sorcerer, horse and idiot all three disappeared in a puff of fiery smoke over the waste!" Hal paused for breath. "I was hard put to keep my countenance! Small wonder they did not recognize me at the village!"

Alan was glad that Hal laughed. The talk of sorcery made him uncomfortable.

"I should have known," a voice said, "that the lord's pride would outweigh his anger."

Hal jumped like a startled stag, crouching and reaching for his sword. Then Ket stepped from the bushes. A touch of red tinged Hal's cheekbones as he relaxed.

"I did not mean to startle ye, Hal," said Ket worriedly.

"I am not used to being taken by surprise," answered Hal, beginning to smile. "There's your revenge, Ket, for this morning. Will you eat with us?"

"Ay, gladly," replied the outlaw. "But first I have something for Alan."

He led from the thicket a horse loaded with all necessary harness and gear, including clothing. "He's for ye, and all he bears," Ket told Alan gruffly. "He came to our camp one day with a wounded man on his back. The fellow was tall, with a warrior's scars, but he died without telling us his name. The horse is of no use to us; we're countryfolk, not riders. He has grown fat and lazy, but nevertheless I think he will serve ye."

"I thank you greatly," gulped Alan, and reached out to touch a soft nose. He had felt worse than naked without a horse; he had felt bereft. Ket could not know the extent of his gratitude.

"And here is the fellow's sword," said Ket.

Alan took the weapon reverently. It was a fine blade, strongly made and carefully balanced. Golden scrollwork covered the scabbard and hilt, the end of which was in the shape of a lion's head, with peridots for eyes.

"This man," said Alan slowly. "Was he dark of face, with straight dark hair, and a hooked nose with a scar across the bridge, thus?"

"Ye knew him?" marveled Ket.

"Ay," replied Alan. "His name was Leon Aleron, a brave warrior and a good man. I am proud to wear his sword."

Hal seemed startled. He glanced at Alan with keen

interest and something like fear flickering in his gray eyes. But Alan did not notice, for he was patting his horse.

The beast was anything but fat. He was long-limbed and rangy, strong but not particularly handsome, dusty brown in color, with a humorous expression on his long face. He was equipped with a functional saddle and saddlebags, in which Ket had packed basic equipment: clothing, boots, a blanket, a few dishes, and a long hunting knife in a leather scabbard.

Alan tethered the horse to a stake while Hal cut the bread he had brought back from the village. Ket put eggs in the kettle to boil, then speared a slice of venison on the tip of his long hunting dagger and held it near the fire. Alan tried to do the same, but the heat in his face made him weak.

"Sit back," Hal told him. "I'll do yours. You are not yet well."

They ate bread and meat, then bread and cheese, then some spring onions. Alan could feel the strength welling back into him.

"Ye're new to the Forest, Alan?" Ket asked.

"Ay," Alan replied. "But I like it," he added.

"Ay? Ye'd make a proper outlaw, lad. There are some ruffians in the Forest, but most of our enemies fear it. Kingsmen and lordsmen; ye won't find them skulking much beyond the fringes. There is a power in the deep woods that keeps them away. We call it the Lady."

"You worship a woman?" Alan exclaimed.

Ket turned to him with a smile tugging at his weatherbeaten face. "Ay, lad, how not? The Lady is a good friend to us countryfolk, a far better friend than those Easterners and their cursed Fatherking and Sacred Son! To be sure, the Lady has her moods. . . . There are storms and hunger and freezing cold—"

"And wolves," suggested Hal, wryly.

"And wolves. But, angry or not, the Lady is always beautiful, and she feeds us well enough."

"Have an egg," Hal offered. "So you will not bow to the Sacred Kings, Ket?" Irony was heavy in his voice.

"Nay, not I!" But Ket hated to let go of his good humor, and his frown relaxed into a slow smile. "Now, if the Very King were to come, and take the Lady to bride—to him I might bow."

"The Very King?" Alan was puzzled again.

"An heir of Veran, perhaps, or of one of the ancient royal houses of Isle. May he come soon!" Ket turned to Hal and asked what Alan had not dared. "Who is yer god, Hal?"

"The One."

"One? What one? There are many gods."

Hal shrugged, looking uncomfortable. Alan turned the talk away from gods. At least, he thought gratefully, Hal had not mentioned the horned god of warlocks.

"How did you come to be outlawed, Ket?"

It was Ket's turn to look uncomfortable. "In truth, I'd rather not tell ye, Alan. . . . But I'll tell ye this, I would like to strike a strong blow against some proud lords some day!" Ket had given up his good humor now in earnest; his lean face looked dangerous. "Curse the Eastern invaders! There was peace and plenty in Isle before they came and drove the folk into servitude! Now, even our women suffer under their heavy hands. . . ." Ket calmed somewhat. "Though there is peace in the Broken Lands, of a sort," he conceded. "The lords are all wary of each other, and they all need their folk. Men are seldom killed out of hand, as they sometimes are in the south. But we countryfolk are often hungry and miserable. The winters are harsh this far north, and many of us sicken and die."

"Yet it is always winter in the south, near the King," Hal muttered.

By the time they were done eating, Alan's horse had pulled up his tether and was straying in the underbrush. Laughing, Ket helped to catch him, then took his leave. The horse swung his bony head into Alan's stomach and stepped on his foot.

"Ow!" Alan complained. "Hal, how is it that Arundel is so good and this beast is so very bad?"

"Arun and I are friends," answered Hal, smiling. "You must talk with your horse. How can you be friends when you have not yet named him?"

Half in jest, Alan sat in front of the lanky animal and meditated aloud on the subject of a suitable name. In all due respect, he concluded, the name should not be an openly disparaging one, such as Knobby Knees. But in all honesty, a romantic name, such as Destrier, was not in order. Aside from ungainliness, Alan decided, the prime characteristic of the beast was a well-developed sense of humor. He chose the name of an ancestral hero of his line, a valorous man of extremely bony build.

"Alfie is your name," he told the horse, feeling rather silly when the creature only flapped its ears at him. But Hal nodded soberly, and Alan saw that to him it was no jest at all.

Chapter Two

The following weeks were like a dream of deep peace for Alan. He began to understand Ket's feelings for the Lady. In spite of the frightening tales he had heard since his earliest childhood, the vast, leafy greenness of the Forest seemed to him like an embrace that shielded him from all harm. He rested on the bosom of this new-found lover, and as he grew stronger he began to explore the labyrinth of her shadowy paths. He learned to find the food she offered. He fished the brown streams and tended his snares and helped Hal search out the roots and herbs that flavored their meals.

He spent hours talking and working with Ket and Hal, and he liked what he learned of them. Ket treated his "lads" as equals now, and Alan found that the plain spoken outlaw was more subtle than he chose to appear. Hal brought out the statesman in Ket, and no wonder. Alan was often surprised, and sometimes irritated, by Hal's air of command. His clothing was only rough, common stuff, and all his gear was of the plainest sort, but there was controlled power in his every easy move, even in the lift of his head. Much was strange about Hal. In ways he seemed aloof, though he was evidently eager for Alan's company. There was some secret in his changing eyes.

14

Alan was skeptical of peasant terrors, not one to cry witch, and he thought no evil of the youth who had saved his life. But he often wondered what mystery might be hidden in those misty, sea-gray eyes.

One day, after his bandages were finally off, Alan wandered into camp to find Hal shaping a couple of hefty sticks into rough wooden swords. He tossed one to his friend, and Alan grinned as he caught it expertly by the hilt. This was one skill that Hal would not have to teach him.

They parried, circling each other. Alan soon sensed that Hal was at least his match. His reach was long and his responses were excellent. But Hal seemed to be holding back. Alan went into the attack, and ended up giving his partner a hard blow to the head.

"I'm sorry!" he exclaimed.

"Whew!" Hal cried, throwing his makeshift sword onto the fire. "You're ready to travel, Alan."

Ket came by as they were packing. "So ye're off," he grumbled. "Where are ye going?"

"North and east," Hal answered succinctly.

"There's nothing there but the Rushing River, and Whitewater town, which ye'd do well to stay away from," Ket complained. "And beyond that the Waste, and the northern Forest, and outlaws I know nothing of. Couldn't ye go west?"

"Some other time," Hal smiled. "Bide easy, Ket; we will keep to the Forest for a while yet." He swung up onto Arundel, and Alan mounted Alfie. Ket clasped hands with them both.

"Farewell. And Alan—take care."

The two of them rode eastward for days before they reached the fringes of the Forest. Then they turned northward and traveled along its rim, earning bread from time to time at isolated cottages. They learned to till and reap, and Alan found that Hal carried his herbs for more than cookery. With his potions and salves he could strengthen sickly children, heal hurts or relieve the aches of the elderly. Often, grateful cottagers offered Hal and Alan whatever hospitality their homes could afford. But they always returned quickly to the Forest. Outside of that protecting wilderness they felt endangered, and exposed. As much as they could, they kept to the Forest and lived on the takings of their snares.

After riding northward for nearly a month, they had become very tired of rabbit meat. One morning, when a deer flashed through the trees, they sent the horses after it. They ran the deer till past midday. At last they trapped it against the steep gorge of the Rushing River, and Hal made the kill with his bow. The carcass fell into the gorge, and swirled away in the swift, spring-fed water that ran out toward the sea and Whitewater town.

"Confound it!" Hal shouted, and Alan muttered something about the deer's lineage. Hot from the long chase, and out of temper from dodging trees, they cantered along the high riverbank, watching the dead deer bob through the foaming white water far below.

"It will never come ashore in that freshet!" Alan protested despairingly.

Just as he spoke, the deer suddenly stopped its jerky voyage, aground in midstream. Staring, Hal and Alan could see a faint, zigzag trail leading down the gorge on either side.

"A ford!" Hal exclaimed, and sent Arundel as fast as he dared down the steep path. Alfie clattered along behind. The deer was bumping about near the far side of the ford. Hal and Alan left the horses on the shore and went after it. They were soaking wet from falling down by the time they reached it.

"Why don't we just lift it out on this shore?" Alan sputtered.

Hal shook his head. "Back the way we came. This must be the Ford of Romany. On the far side the Forest ends, this far east, and there is no cover on the open Waste."

They hauled the deer to shore, slipping and splashing, and threw it over Alfie's rump. By the time they had scrambled back up the riverbank, they were hot and out of temper once more. Grimly, Hal gutted the carcass and began skinning. Alan knelt to lend a hand.

"I'll take a haunch," said a clear, young voice.

Hal grunted in sudden discomfiture. A knife was poised against his ribs. Alan's startled glance showed him a sturdy, towheaded youngster. The robber could not have been more than twelve years old.

Hal held up a hindquarter of venison, moving carefully. "Don't you want to steal the whole thing?" he asked the blond boy through tight lips.

"Nay, indeed, a haunch will be plenty. Thank you," the lad replied politely. He took the meat and disappeared. Alan and Hal could hear him rustling through the underbrush. For a moment they sat in frozen silence. Then Hal sprang to his feet and gestured for Alan to follow.

They stalked after the boy. Hal padded as quietly as a cat in the undergrowth. Alan tried to copy his movements. He made noise enough, even so, but the blond youngster was hurrying and heedless. His camp was not far from where they had first shot the deer. Some pine branches were pulled into a rude shelter, and under them a man lay softly moaning. As Hal and Alan looked, the boy went to him and moistened his fevered face with a wet rag. Then he cut some green sticks with his knife and made ready to spit his meat.

Hal walked out of his cover and straight past him to where the man stirred weakly on his hard bed. The lad jumped up with a gasp, but Alan caught his arm before he could raise his knife.

"You could have had the meat for the asking," he told him. "What is your name?"

"I will not beg!" the boy flared defiantly, with a flash of blue eyes. "And it's Corin," he added, suddenly subdued. "What is yours?"

Alan told him, and they both watched as Hal knelt by the sick man. The muscular fellow struck at the air, then calmed under Hal's touch, but he scarcely seemed conscious of his visitor.

"That is my father," Corin explained, "Col, son of Cadol. We're smiths by trade, from Whitewater. Lord Gar is planning another war. Taxes have been high and the lordsmen busy. Father could not meet the tribute, so they used his tools on him. Look." For a moment the boy's confident air left him, and he turned his head away.

Alan saw the welts and burns on the man's bared chest, red and oozing. Hal looked up in a kind of appeal.

"He will not be able to eat meat; we must make him some broth. Alan. . . ."

"I'm going," Alan answered, and strode off to get the horses. He brought them, and the half-butchered deer, to Corin's camp. Then he had to climb the steep bank to the river to fill the kettle for broth. Corin climbed it again to

get a basin of water for his father. Hal emptied his saddlebags, looking for herbs. His face darkened.

"Nothing," he muttered. "Well, here's a bit of bread for
him, Corin."

They set the kettle over the flames, and then they ate
half-cooked chunks of venison from the spit, burning their
fingers in the process.

"We are leaving Whitewater," Corin told them in a low
voice. "Not just because of the branding; my father has
been in trouble with Lord Gar before. But the lordsmen
almost took me for the garrison yesterday, because I am
big for my age."

"They must have been joking, or threatening!" Alan exclaimed. But Hal shook his head.

"Lord Gar has nearly deflowered his people, from what
I hear. He plays at war like some men play at dice."

"They would have taken me soon," Corin stated. "They
have taken every youth in the town."

"So where will you go?" Alan asked, still incredulous.

"North, to the Waste or the Barrens. Land is to be had
there, by those who are hardy enough to live on it. My father will serve no more lords. But we went south first, to
throw off the pursuit. They will pursue us, you know,"
Corin declared. "Smiths are needed persons."

"That smith is infected," Hal said grimly, "and not
likely to live long, unless I can find him some medicine."

"Father will not die," Corin told him fiercely. "He is a
smith, and he is tough."

"What kind of medicine?" Alan asked.

"Nothing that grows in these parts. I shall have to go
a-bartering."

"You are the healer." Alan rose. "You stay, and I'll
go."

"You wouldn't know what to get." Hal also rose.

"You can tell me what to get," Alan said in a hard
voice, but Hal shook his head impatiently.

"Any of a dozen things. Some cottage wife may have
some, but if not, I shall have to go to Whitewater." He
hid a chunk of meat in a saddlebag, for trade. "Is it far,
Corin?"

"Half a day's walk."

"So, an hour's hard ride. I can be in and out before
the gates close. . . . Keep bathing that fellow, face and

wounds." He vaulted onto Arundel and trotted away between the trees.

Corin went for water again. Alan muttered to himself and rather viciously finished butchering the deer. He was barely done when Arundel cantered back to their camp, riderless. Hal's sword, still in its scabbard, was protruding from his blanketroll.

"He is in trouble already!" Alan exclaimed. "Afoot, and weaponless. . . . Corin, good luck go with you. And you are welcome to the meat." He saddled Alfie hastily and sped away, with Arundel trailing after. In his dismay, Alan did not notice that Corin reached out a hand as Arun passed. Corin was left alone with his feverish father. But the boy smiled triumphantly, for he was armed, at least. Hal's sword was in his grip.

After Alan left the Forest, Arundel took the lead, cantering through the cover of scattered hedges and woodlots near the riverbank. Presently he slowed to a quieter jog, then to a walk. Alan caught glimpses of metal helmets off to his right, and after a while he sighted Hal. Mounted lordsmen held him prisoner, and he was afoot, being jerked along by the rope that bound his arms. Even from his cautious distance, Alan could see the blood on his face. His stomach knotted; he felt as if he himself had been struck.

He could think of no way to free Hal from that armed troop of nearly a dozen men. So he followed, aching. By late afternoon he had neared Whitewater, a walled town with three castle towers rising within. The place was heavily fortified and perched high above the river gorge. Beyond were masts of ships, and the Eastern Way ran below the walls, south to Nemeton.

Alan halted in the last copse of trees, and watched as Hal disappeared through the dark tunnel that was the town gate. For a long time he fixed the stone walls with his gaze, as if by desperate will he could pierce them with his sight and find the place where Hal had been taken. Finally, when darkness was falling, he dismounted and patted Arundel meditatively. He tethered Alfie, and patted him too, out of a sense of justice. Arundel did not need a tether, and Alfie was already attempting to eat his. Alan eyed his unruly beast with mingled affection and despair.

"For once in your life, Alfie," he pleaded in a low

voice, "try to behave tonight." Then, although feeling absurd, he added softly, "I need you. And I like you. Be here when I get back." Firmly, he refused to add, "*If I get back.*" He patted the horse once more, laced his sword tightly to keep it quiet under his cloak, and trudged down the road toward Whitewater.

The tired gatekeeper let him in without question. Alan strode through the narrow, smelly streets, hoping only to avoid the lordsmen until full dark had fallen. Then he must try to find Hal, but how? The castle was like a giant triangle, three strong towers with walls between. The barracks would be somewhere in the courtyard.

His thoughts were interrupted by hoofbeats. Alan dodged between the close-set house, but he had been seen. A shout rang out. Alan fled through a maze of twisting entryways where he hoped the horses could not follow. Then he hid, panting, behind some hogsheads. He could hear the lordsmen calling to each other not far away. He startled violently when a door creaked open nearby. A wrinkled face looked out, and a clawlike hand beckoned him into a narrow, clay-daubed house.

"Many thanks!" Alan gasped as he bolted through the doorway.

He had no need to say anything more. His ancient hostess had a tireless tongue. She sat him down at her smoking hearth and fed him well, gossiping all the time about hard times, high taxes and the plight of her neighbors.

"Time was, when a tower of wood or stone was sufficient for the keeping of a lord," she chattered indignantly, "but Gar must have a walled stronghold, no less, and the money to pay for it, and the men to build it, for the spoils of his wars do not come near meeting the price, and after five years it is not done yet! The old stone tower, the White Tower, the one nearest the sea, has only half-done walls, though to be sure it would not need any, for what army could climb the sea cliffs, I would like to know?"

Alan glanced up with interest. "Do they use that tower, then?"

"Ay, to be sure they do! 'Tis a stronghold in its own right, and the castle guard is good. The lord uses it for prisoners that he holds for ransom, and for his enemies, and malcontents, anyone who causes him trouble. . . .

Why, that is where the lordsmen put that lad they brought in this afternoon!" The old crone's face saddened. "I saw them go by with him. He was a right proper, spirited lad, fighting them all the way. Poor thing, he will learn better before long . . . or he is likely to die for it."

The good woman gabbled on, telling about the sufferings of other young men she had known. Alan became anxious to get away from her. He managed to say that he was going to visit a relative who lived near the castle, and he received very detailed and confusing instructions on how to get there without meeting more lordsmen. At last he succeeded in taking his leave. The gossip wished him well and charged him, on his next visit to town, to come see "old Margerie." Alan strongly hoped there would be no next time, but he promised nevertheless.

It was dark now, and the streets were quiet. Alan passed quickly through back lanes, coming at the castle from the less traveled side. He had no trouble recognizing the White Tower of Whitewater; it shone in the moonlight like a shaft of ice. From the shadow of a cottage Alan studied the walls and the movements of the castle guards. There were no guards on the rubble of the half-completed walls, but atop the nearer section there were many. Alan sighed. The moon had served him well so far. Now he begged it to go behind a cloud and stay there.

To his grateful surprise, it did. Silently he ran across the dry ditch which separated him from the castle, and scrambled up the embankment beyond. He crouched under the wall and crept along until he came to the edge of the sea cliff. Twenty feet above his head, he knew, a guard was standing with his back to the sea.

Through the hazy darkness Alan made out the form of the cliff. It was rough and uneven, offering purchase enough. But the stone was loose and treacherous. The surf pounded loudly below, the first sea surf that Alan had ever seen, and he did not like its cold, angry look. Slowly he lowered himself over the edge of the cliff.

Once over, Alan moved as quickly as he could, but with great caution. A loosened stone could alert the guard, or send Alan crashing to the rocks below. He lowered himself for several feet, then started to work his way across the cliff face. A large stone slipped from under his foot and left him hanging momentarily by his hands.

He scrambled for a foothold, too frightened to think of the guard. But, as he clung to the cliff, the only sounds he heard were the pounding of the surf and the pounding of his own heart.

After a while Alan went on, moving tensely to within a few feet of the top. He was past the guard now, and past the fortified walls, but the unfinished stonework rose smooth and sheer from the edge of the cliff. Alan inched along, with throbbing arms and stiffened fingers, until at last he found a wooden scaffolding where masons had been working. He hauled himself up and lay panting on the timbers, grateful to be alive.

Then he stiffened. Footsteps were approaching just beyond the stones. A guard was walking inside the wall; Alan could see the glint of his helmet. His head passed within feet of Alan's face. But he did not look around or shoulder any weapon. An evening stroller, Alan decided.

At first he thought only of slipping by the man, though he felt sure he would be forced to fight before the night was over. But then a desperate plan came to Alan's mind. He remembered the robber's fingers on his throat, the blackness which had quickly followed, and he felt certain that he could do as much. He crept forward on the stony rubble as his quarry wandered back in his direction. Then, when the man's face was only inches from his own, Alan struck like an eagle and gripped with all his strength. The guard gave a small, questioning sound, struggled a moment and then went limp. Alan swung himself down from the wall and sank to the ground beside his prey, thankful for the shadows and the silence of the night.

He hastily stripped the guard of his helmet, breastplate and gloves. He slipped them on, and the man's cloak, not daring to be more elaborate. Briefly, he wondered what to do with the guard. Slit his throat, like a downed deer? Cursing under his breath, Alan found that he could not bring himself to kill so coolly. He gagged the man with a strip of shirting, and bound him hand and foot with bootlacings.

In a few minutes a quaking guard entered the door to the White Tower, head down under his helmet and keeping well away from the torch stuck in a sconce beside the entrance. "Ah, Joe, feeling better?" cried the doorkeeper cheerfully. Alan gestured in the manner of one who is not feeling well at all, and fled into the inner darkness.

Furtively, Alan peeked into the cells on the ground floor. Groans greeted him; he could discern nothing but suffering. The stench of the place was terrible, and he hastily made his way up the spiral stairs to the next level. Near the top a door was ajar. Alan peered cautiously around the doorjamb. In a small, bare room was a table, and on the table stood a tallow candle. The candlelight shone on a heavy ring of iron keys which hung from the wall. But between Alan and the keys a burly guard sat at ease with his back to the door.

Alan flexed his hands, steeling himself to throttle another guard. Then he realized that even if he could find Hal, it would take him half the night to find the right key. There were perhaps a hundred on the ring. He felt for his hunting dagger, drew it from the leather scabbard and felt its razor-sharp edge. Then he moved.

Chapter Three

Hal sat in the filthy straw of his cell, chained to its clammy stone wall by leg and wrist irons. His face was swollen and his ribs ached where they had beaten him. But he scarcely noticed his injuries, for he fully realized that in the near future he was likely to face far worse. He could see only a choice between death and a fate worse than death: lifelong dishonor of a type Alan could not suspect. But Hal clung to hope. While life remained, there was a chance of escape, as he knew from his past. Though to escape from such a stronghold not once, but twice, was far beyond the bounds of what he thought his luck would bear.

He heard approaching footsteps, and stiffened in surprise and fear. Surely they would not be coming for him already! But footsteps stopped at his cell door, and a cold voice said, "Open it." Despair washed over Hal; he struggled to conceal it. Two guards were coming through the door, the first a stocky man with a candle and a strangely pale face, the second—Hal's jaw dropped; surprise and joy flooded him like morning sunlight. It was Alan, but an Alan he had never seen. His usually friendly, open face was set in ruthless lines. He spoke again in that voice Hal had not recognized: "Free him, or you die." His knife nudged the guard's ribs.

Hal felt his arms freed, then his legs. He rolled out of the way, rubbing his numbed limbs. He could not stand up, but he was able to hold the fetters while Alan locked them on his own prisoner. Alan gagged the guard before he slipped his knife back into its leather sheath.

Instantly he turned to Hal and grasped his hand in concern, all traces of the alien hardness gone from his face. They met each other's eyes in silence for a moment before Alan helped Hal to his feet. Pain shot through his legs as he tried to straighten himself. "There," Hal gasped finally. "I am all right. Did Arundel come to you?"

"Ay," said Alan. "Can you walk, Hal?"

"In a moment I shall be able to."

Alan divested the guard of his helmet, breastplate and cloak, then helped Hal buckle them on. The things were rather large. "Could you not find me a better fit?" Hal grumbled in mock displeasure, and for the first time that night Alan broke his tension with a smile. They took the candle and left the cell. The hapless guard glared after them. Alan locked the door and threw the keys through the grating into the straw of the cell, well out of reach of the prisoner.

"That might puzzle them for a while," he said, and smiled again.

"Keep your hands under the cloak," he instructed Hal as they moved down the corridor. "Keep your face in the shadow of the helmet, and do not let the torchlight fall on your legs." He left the candle in the guardroom, frowning with thought. "The doorkeeper we can silence, if need be, for he is alone. But the walls—it puzzles me what to do."

"How did you get in?" asked Hal logically.

"Climbed the cliff."

"Mighty Mothers!" whispered Hal. "We had better try the gate, since we are disguised."

The moon was darkened as they came to the door. Hal and Alan saw apprehensively that the doorkeeper was chatting with a guard. But, engrossed in their conversation, the two men gave them only a glance and a nod as they passed out. In the dark and the flickering torchlight, it was hard for them to see more than a flash of helmet and breastplate.

"So far, well enough," whispered Alan when they were halfway across the courtyard. "Pace like a guard, Hal."

It was by now well past midnight, and the watch was tired. The dozing sentries took no notice as they strode under the stone archway beneath the castle gatehouse. As quietly as they could, they unbarred the heavy wooden doors and spread them wide. The drawbridge was in place over the ditch, Hal noted gratefully; that unwieldy mechanism took many men to turn. Nothing stood in their way except the spiked, iron-shod portcullis. Alan ducked into the gatekeeper's room and started to winch it up. The noise quickly brought several surprised guards.

"What's afoot?" asked the first.

Hal blocked, without seeming to block, the gatehouse door. "Visitors," he said gruffly. "King Iscovar himself. Should be here any moment."

"You cannot be serious!" protested the guard. Most of his fellows headed back toward the battlements, chattering excitedly. Hal only shrugged as Alan, done hauling on the portcullis, stepped to his side.

"Come see for yourself," he barked, and moved toward the opening. Two guards, and Alan, followed.

But as they reached the outer arch, the fickle moon came out from behind her cloud and shone brightly on their faces. The guards jumped back and shouted an alarm. "Run, Hal!" cried Alan, whipping out his sword. But Hal had no intention of running, though he had no weapon. As a guard lunged at him, Hal slipped under his thrust and grasped his wrist, forcing the sword from his hand. Hal wrestled the man to the ground, picked up the dropped weapon and stunned him with the hilt. Alan had his man backed up against the wall, battling bravely but clumsily with his thick-bladed sword. As Hal watched, Alan's slender weapon worked its way through the guard's defense and stabbed him in the throat. He gurgled and fell.

Other guards were running toward them, shouting. Hal and Alan fled over the drawbridge toward the town. Some arrows followed them from the walls, and the guards pounded after them, but the fugitives ran faster. They gained the shelter of the houses and sped along the twisting streets, finally stopping in the shadows of an alley.

"Let us rid ourselves of this gear," panted Alan. "It does us no good now, but marks us."

His voice was tight. Hal touched his hand inquiringly.

"By the Moon Mother, I had to kill him!" Alan burst

out. "I had never killed a man, Hal. . . . Can you understand?"

"I understand," said Hal with new respect. It was a rare man, in those savage times, who did not take life lightly.

"Keep that sword," Alan added grimly.

Hal tucked the hacking sword through his belt, and they moved on. They ran softly in their deerskin boots through the tangled streets, choosing the darkest ways, heading toward the town gate even though they knew it would be closed. Twice they heard hoofbeats and crouched in the shadows until the riders had passed. At last they came near the gate. But as they approached the main street, they suddenly heard lordsmen, quite close, to their right. They started away, but then heard others approaching from the left and from behind. Too late they realized that they had been driven, like cattle, to be trapped against high walls. No shadow would now be left unsearched.

Alan bit his lip. "Come," he said. "Quickly."

He led Hal through a crooked maze of back entries, stopping at last at a door near some barrels. To Hal's astonishment, he knocked softly. "Grandmother!" he called under his breath. "Margerie! I have need of you!"

Presently the door was opened by the elderly dame, carrying a rushlight and blinking sleepily. She hurried them into the house, cackling with consternation, bustling to get cold towels and salves for Hal's injured face. The house was tightly shuttered, as Alan had been careful to note. No light would show. The old lady gabbled away, brushing off explanations and showing no interest in the lordsmen who passed close by the house. Hal eyed her narrowly over a bowl of excellent soup. Something in the quality of his gaze touched her composure, and her flood of gossip faltered to a stop.

"You are no fool, though you pretend to be," mused Hal admiringly. "I thank you greatly for your help."

"Almost anyone in this town would have done the same," she retorted defiantly. "We bear small love for our proud lord and his men. Our sons feel their whips, and our daughters their lust. It will be a great blow to their insolence, and the jest of the town, if you and your brother escape."

Alan was grinning in wonder. "I'll warrant you knew what I was about all the time."

"I had a notion," she acknowledged, smiling.

"But grandmother," Alan added, "I have no brother."

"I would have sworn from the first that you were brothers!" she insisted.

The two looked at each other, smiled and shook their heads. Hal changed the subject. "Grandmother, we must be over the wall before dawn. You have helped us till now. Help us in this."

She frowned. "They will still be looking for you. But if you are to beat the dawn, I dare say you must go."

She gave them directions, and they gratefully took their leave. "It may be that you will meet us again, if we live," Hal told the peculiar old woman. "Remember us, I pray you." And he kissed her withered cheek. Then they went out again, into the shadows.

The moon was low as they slipped away. A certain house, Margerie had told them, built against the town wall, could be climbed, and the occupants would not raise the alarm. Her instructions helped them avoid their pursuers, but nearly doubled the distance. Though they moved quickly, it was almost dawn when they came to their destination.

They climbed rapidly but as quietly as they could on the heavily thatched roof. They knew that not a quarter of a mile away, at the town gates, the castle guards and lordsmen were gathered. By the time they reached the peak of the roof, the black sky had turned to gray. Hal stood on Alan's shoulders and pulled himself up onto the wall, then hoisted Alan up beside him. Keeping low, they hastily slipped over the outer edge and dropped to the grass twenty feet below.

They could not take time to catch their breath after the impact. They ran, panting, to the copse where, they hoped, the horses waited. No alarm followed them; the gray dusk of dawn had served to hide them from sight. Arun welcomed his master with a joyful snort, and Alfie had not so much as pulled his tether. Both youths thankfully took saddle.

"My sword," said Hal.

"It was in the blanketroll."

"I know," Hal replied tensely. "They stuck it there when they were casting lots for it. But it's not there now."

Alan gaped. "It could not have fallen," he protested at last, "or not without my hearing it. . . . I never thought to secure it, in my hurry."

Hal said no more. Silently the pair turned their horses and drifted away like ghosts in the morning fog. They picked their way with care, keeping woodland between themselves and Whitewater. But once they were out of sight of the town, they touched heels to their horses and galloped toward the Forest.

"Did you get your herbs?" Alan asked, suddenly remembering Corin.

Hal only shook his head, looking grim. But when they clattered into the camp, before the sun was well up, they found it deserted. Some hunks of raw meat sat in Hal's kettle near the ashes of the fire, and the deer bones lay strewn where Alan had left them. Nothing else was there.

"Where is the smith who was sick enough to die?" Alan wondered aloud.

"He and his son can't have gone far," Hal said crossly. "Hide that offal—nay, I'll do it. Have a look around."

"Why?" Alan picked up the kettle. "We can't help them any more than we have already."

"Because the young rascal has my sword, Alan! Find them!"

But Corin and his father were nowhere nearby. Several circles told Alan that. He rejoined Hal, smarting inwardly because of the loss of the sword.

"There were traces near the ford," he reported evenly.

"They've gone north then, as the boy said. All right, let us be after them." Hal vaulted onto Arundel, but Alan stood still.

"Better to go westward, into the Forest," he argued. "The lordsmen will be hot after us, and we'll be easy game on the open Waste."

Hal leaned on his saddle, staring at his comrade. "You are right," he said softly, "but nevertheless I must go after my sword."

"How do you know that Corin has it?" Alan cried, furious because he suspected the boy himself. "Anyway, you have a weapon. You cannot go poking around, hunting that boy, when half the castle will be out after us! Are you mad?"

"Perhaps." Hal smiled a crooked smile. "I have some-

times wondered. Even so, I must go north." He turned
away. "Are you coming?"

"Why not?" snapped Alan. With this new challenge,
his mood had swung like a pendulum from frightened to
reckless. Still, he spoke bitterly. "I have already courted
death a dozen times since I last slept, for your sake.
Once more is of small importance."

Hal keenly felt the justice of the reproach, and bit his
lip to stop the stinging of his eyes. He stiffened his back
and sent Arundel down the twisting path to the Ford of
Romany. Alan and Alfie followed close behind. The
horses edged their way across the treacherous ford, snorting, then plunged wide-eyed up the opposite bank.

Within a few furlongs, the Forest dwindled into patches
of stunted trees, and then into true Waste, where only
sparse grass and occasional bushes grew. There was poor
tracking on this stony turf, and no sign of Corin and his
father. Also, Alan had not overestimated the danger of
pursuit. He and Hal had not been riding an hour before
they were seen. With a shout, six patrollers were after
them. But Arundel and Alfie were swift. They sped off
toward the west, and by midday not a lordsman was in
sight behind them.

Still, Hal and Alan did not dare to stop until they had
reached the sheltering Forest. All day they galloped over
the high, rocky plain and said no word. Alan, though not
easily angered, was stubborn in his wrath. His face had
gone as stony as the Waste, and Hal glanced at him and
kept silence. Even when the blue-green mass of the Forest welcomed them in the distance, they gave no sign.

Chapter Four

They entered the Forest at last in the gray dusk, and camped near a rocky upland stream. Supper was cooked and eaten without a word. Evidently Hal was distressed, for he ate lightly, dropped things and poked at the fire. But Alan was not yet ready to break his punitive silence. Finally, Hal threw a stone into the fire and abruptly asked a peculiar question.

"Alan. Is your birthday on the first of May?"

Alan's jaw dropped, and he was startled into response. "Ay! But how in the world—"

Hal interrupted him. "So is mine. And I think we are the same age. Seventeen?"

Alan nodded. Hal spoke rapidly, with lowered eyes: "There are many things I should have told you when we first rode together, if you were to follow me. . . . I feared to cause you pain, but now you have followed me blindly, and it has made you angry. I had better show you something of myself, Alan."

As he finished he slipped off his tunic, and Alan cried out in shock. Hal's entire torso was covered with scars, mutilated into a texture like a tapestry of suffering. The marks of whips scored him, and brands from hot irons, and the white, unhealing lines of canes. If Alan had ever been vexed with him, he had forgotten it now. Without realizing he had moved, he was around the fire and kneeling before him, grasping those wounded shoulders. "Who did this to you?" he choked, in a tone between rage and despair. "Tell me, and I will kill him, I swear it!"

"Softly," whispered Hal, much moved. "Softly, good friend. He is far beyond your reach, or mine."

Alan sat down, breathing hard. As his boiling blood cooled somewhat, he realized how he had assailed the wall of secrecy that had always surrounded Hal. He attempted to withdraw.

"I spoke hastily," he began. But Hal stopped him with a smile.

"Of all men that walk the land, I love you best," Hal stated, with dignity that allowed for no embarrassment. "I have known so since we met, and I do not wish to have any secrets from you. . . . But bear with me, for this is painful to me."

Hal slowly put on his tunic, lacing it tight before he continued. "I had better get the worst over with first. Those wounds you saw were given to me by order of my father."

"Your father!"

Hal nodded. "There is no great love between us," he said wryly. "The man is a fiend." He forced the words out, straining. "His name is Iscovar. And he sits on the throne of the Kingdom of Isle."

For Alan, it was as if the night sky had fallen in. Everything went black, pierced by flashes like falling stars. Involuntarily his whole body stiffened, and he drew back as if he had seen a serpent. His jaw clenched as he stared in horror at this gray-eyed youth whom he had thought to be his friend.

Hal cried out as if he were in physical pain. "Alan, do not look at me so! By my wounds, I would rather be the most pitiful beggar in all of Isle than the son of that man!" He covered his face with his hands and bowed his head, moaning like a child who has lost the only warmth he has ever known.

Alan went to him at once. No force of will or of men's bidding could have kept him away. Putting his arms around Hal, he spoke to him brokenly.

"I am all amazement and confusion. You should be my bitterest enemy. Yet I know you, what you are: the best man I have ever known, and the best friend. I do not know how it can be that such crop sprang from such seed. But it is so."

Gratefully, shakily, Hal touched his hand. They sat in silence, collecting their thoughts.

Alan had good cause to hate the name of Iscovar, King of Isle. In former times, folk said, Isle had been like a paradise. Every man served his own gods and tilled his own land, and the deer grazed up to the cottage doors. There were kings and chieftains, to be sure, but their warriors were their comrades, and their people were their kin. When they fought, it was the high, free strife of which the bards used to sing. But for the most part they kept the peace of the High King, who rode the land with his magical sword.

Then the invaders had sailed in from the east, and not even the mighty sword had been proof against them. It was undone by sorcery, folk said, or thrown into the sea. With ruthless force the Easterners raped Isle by way of the Black River, slaying the chieftains and herding the folk like so many cattle. So the people became slaves to the manor lords, seldom free to tend their own poor plots. And though great tracts were cleared, and the ground as fertile as it had ever been, hunger and disease stalked the land.

The Easterners came in the name of their god, the Sacred Son, and many were the warlocks and priests in their ranks. The leader was named Herne; he called himself the Sacred King. He divided the conquered land among his captains, and with every new lord went a priest. To people who had suffered, these spoke of the sanctity of torment, and many believed them, for their magic was strong. Only in the west and north Herne could not take hold. In these mountainous parts lived a proud, fierce people, scions of tribal Kings and the ancient Mothers. They could defend their rocky land forever against the invaders. So, since no great wealth seemed hidden in these barren parts, Herne left them to their denizens.

The Sacred King built his castle by the Black River, and in it a tower that came to be the terror of all the land. There Herne imprisoned those who had displeased him, so that their agonies might ease the torments of the Sacred Son. Folk called it the Dark Tower, or the Tower of Despair; everyone knew the place that was meant.

Seven generations passed. Herne gave way to Hervyn, to Heinin, Hent, Iuchar, Idno and Iscovar. The invaders had abandoned their harsh, guttural language, by and large, for the gentler speech of Isle. Some wed Islandais women, and here and there a lord ruled who was just, even kind, to his folk. Such lords were likely to be quickly overthrown by their more ruthless neighbors. Like their despotic Kings, most lords remained cruel.

But in the southwest of Isle, in meadow-ringed Laueroc, one such line of kindly lords had grown very powerful indeed. Perhaps Laueroc's people were akin to the war-like folk of Welas, the West Land that lay just beyond the Gleaming River, where the Blessed Kings still ruled in Welden. The folk of Laueroc looked often that way, and they loved their lords. Their armies were always victors, but never aggressors.

King Iscovar, however, had turned his attention to the west. He had captured the gentle lord of Laueroc, spirited him to the Dark Tower and placed one of his henchmen in his stead. And years earlier, by treachery, he had conquered proud Welas. That kingdom also now must bend the knee before Iscovar and his heirs.

"Your given name is Hervoyel, then," Alan mused, still grappling with disbelief.

"Don't call me that. My mother always called me Hal."

Alan knew well, as did everyone in Isle, the story of Hal's mother. She was Gwynllian, daughter of the royal house of Welas, a tall maiden with hair the color of autumn forests and eyes the stormy gray-green of the autumn sea. Through many lands she was famed for her beauty. When Iscovar came with his vast armies and laid siege to Welden, he offered peace on one condition: that she should be his bride. He knew that her son would be heir to the throne of Welas, for the West Land reckoned lineage in the old way, through the woman.

Torre, the Blessed King, Gwynllian's father, saw no hope for victory, but left the choice to her. Though bitter at her fate, she was proud to be the means of peace for her people. She was wed within the week. No sooner did Iscovar have her well away than his troops turned to take Welden and the whole of Welas. Torre, with his sons, fled to hiding in the mountains. The commanders of the army became the manor lords of Welas, and a noble named Ulger became known as the Wolf of Welden. Iscovar went on with his bride to his castle at Nemeton.

"What did he—what did Iscovar call you, Hal?"

"Nothing. Not once in my life has he ever spoken to me by any name."

"Was there not a time," asked Alan gently, "when you were very young, perhaps, that he—favored you in some way. . . ."

"Never."

Hal went on to explain, as best he could, how he had lived in the court of Iscovar, King of Isle. It was a jungle of intrigue, theft, bribery, extortion and petty cruelty. He had no friends. The boys with whom he took his schooling, sons of his father's henchmen, liked to torment him with their various forms of senseless hostility. He learned early that he must take care of himself. He was strong, and he soon became a skillful, quick-witted fighter, with or without weapons. Yet, though he taught the school bullies to let him alone, he never fought except in defense.

This was his mother's influence; she had taught him to love peace and singing. Hal and his mother were very close, and kept much to themselves. They avoided the King. They had two faithful servants who had come from Welas with Gwynllian: an old nursemaid, Nana, and her husband, Rhys. The rest of the hundreds of servants in the castle they could not trust. Many of them were spies bribed by the various lords, or by the King himself, to spy on the lords' spies.

"When we could, we fed the widows and orphans that the King had created," said Hal bitterly, "and provided for the care of the poor, maimed wretches that emerged from his Dark Tower. Certainly he knew what we were doing, but he said nothing. It is not his way to speak—only to torment.

"So, on my sixteenth birthday, my mother died. I was out practicing in the yard when Rhys shouted for me, and I ran in to find her in writhing torment. She grasped for me, and tried desperately to speak, but could not. She died in my arms. Obviously she had been poisoned, but no one could say by whom. The next day, with little ceremony, she was buried. The King did not come.

"The following day, Rhys was seized in order to be flogged, then killed by the bowmen for target practice. I swallowed my pride and went to the King, begging for his life. He flew into a rage at what he called my insolence, and I was taken to the Tower. I am sure now that poor Rhys's death was only for this purpose, to torment me. The condition of my release was that I should sign a writ of obedience to the King. Even he knew that I would not break my word. When I refused to sign, I was hung in chains by my wrists and flogged. There was no daylight in that hole, but I think this went on for two days and nights. From time to time they varied the treatment with canes, or clubs, or burning irons, but the effect was the same."

Alan looked sick, and Hal reached out to him. "Indeed, it was not as bad as it could have been. I was the heir to the throne, and the King had need of me if his vassals were to serve him. So he could not have me blinded, or castrated, or maimed. . . . They simply flogged me. After a while it became apparent that I was growing indifferent to the flogging and that they would have to try something else, so they took me down."

Hal paused to steady himself before he continued. "What they did next could only have come from the mind of the fiend himself. They brought before me a goodly man, handsome, near middle age but powerful and trim of body. They told me that he was to be tortured, slowly, to the death, unless I put a stop to it by signing the King's writ. At this he cried out, "Do not heed them, my Prince!" They hit him across the face to silence him, and the blood ran down from the corner of his mouth. I stared, for to my knowledge I had never seen him before.

"They started the tortures. After a while it seemed that he was senseless, and they left the room. He spoke to me at once, urging me never to give in to the King, but to escape him and fight him if I could. For, as he said, I was the only hope of the people of Isle. In wonder, then, I asked him his name, and he told me: Leuin, seventh lord of Laueroc."

Alan gasped sharply, and Hal faced him with pity in his eyes. "Your father, Alan?"

"Ay," Alan managed to say. "Is he—is he—" He could not say the word.

"Ay," replied Hal softly. "He is dead."

Alan groaned and lay back in the grass, breathing hard. After a few minutes he spoke. "In my mind, I knew he was dead. But in my heart, I always hoped that by some chance he was yet alive."

He sat up. "Tell me what they did to him," he demanded, fists clenched.

"Oh, by any god, Alan, nay!" Hal pleaded. "Remember him as he was! This much I will tell you: never once did his courage fail him. For five days and nights, as nearly as I can tell, they tortured him with every fiendish machine in that dark place of horrors, but always he was steadfast in his endurance." Hal spoke like one who, in spite of himself, must yet relive a bad dream. "If I cried out with him in his agony, or turned away my head, I was flogged. But the worst of it was that they tortured him even more cruelly then, thinking I would weaken. So I learned, for his sake more than for mine, to sit, and watch, and make no sign, though my blood ran cold. They let him keep his tongue, hoping that he would plead with me for his life, and they sometimes left us alone together for this purpose. But instead he always encouraged me. He told me that he was ready to die, that any life the King granted him would not be worth the living. He urged me, as before, never to yield to the King. And he spoke often of you, Alan. 'I have a son,' he would say, 'just your age, born on the day of your birth. His name is Alan, and you and he are much alike in many ways, I think. I have sent him to safety with kinsfolk in the north, and I hope he may strike a blow for my people someday. He is a bold lad, and great of heart. I do not mind dying, so long as I know he is alive.' "

"He spoke of me thus?" said Alan shakily.

"He spoke of you thus, more than once." Hal was silent a moment before he went on. "When they saw he would soon be dead, they put him to death in a way that they hoped would break my spirit. They tore him limb from limb on the rack. His last words were to me, and they were these: 'All good go with you, Hal. Be brave. And if ever you see my son, tell him that I love him.' "

Alan choked and turned away, hiding his face with his hands. Hal put his arms around him, and at last Alan gave in to his grief, weeping long and hard, as he had not wept since he was a child. When he could speak, his words were as bitter as his tears. "We parted in wrath on my side, sorrow on his," he said. "He would not tell me why he was sending me north, and I did not want to go. It was not until I had arrived that I learned he had been taken by the King. I never had a chance to tell him. . . ." His voice broke, and he could not go on.

"He knew your love," comforted Hal softly. "He needed no telling. Always he spoke of you with great joy and pride."

Alan got up and went to wash his face in the stream. Hal put more sticks on the fire. When Alan returned, he looked as pale as if he had himself been through torture. "How did you get out?" he asked in a low voice.

"When they killed him on the rack, I fainted—not for the first time. This time, when I awoke, I was alone, curled up on some filthy straw in a little cell. I suppose they had not yet decided what to do with me next. In the cell wall was a small, barred window. Looking out, I saw the full moon rising, shining on the ivy that covered the tower walls. In that instant I knew what I must do.

"I was very weak, but my worst weakness was not of the body. I felt that my spirit was almost gone, that I could not hold out much longer. And so, although I could scarcely stand, I somehow managed by strength of desperation—perhaps by some good sorcery, from where I do not know—to force apart the bars enough to let my body through. I climbed down the Tower wall by grasping the ivy. Once down, I stumbled to the stables; Arundel broke his halter to come to me. I somehow got on his back, and we were off. I think we traveled for three days, but most of the time I knew nothing. I had no idea where we were until we came to the Forest, and to Trigg, one of the outlaws with Craig the Grim."

Hal smiled, remembering that lucky meeting. "Trigg is a slow country fellow, but he has a heart as big as the sky. He was nearly in tears with coaxing Arundel when I came to myself. After I spoke to Arun, he got me to camp at last, and the outlaws cared for me well. . . . But it was a month before I could stand, and late autumn before I had regained my full strength. So I stayed through the winter with them, and finally left them early this past spring."

Hal and Alan were walking up and down the banks of the stream, talking softly, arms around each other's shoulders. Though they had not rested since Hal's capture, neither had any thought of sleep.

"I had been traveling about a month when I met you,"

Hal finished. "But how did you come to be wandering?"

"Some of my father's retainers took me to my mother's kinsfolk, near Rodsen," replied Alan. "Then they went their ways, to find service where they might. But my mother's people feared the King's wrath. They shunted me from one household to another throughout the winter, until I was glad enough to relieve them of my presence, with the coming of spring. I had some notion of going back to Laueroc for revenge, though I did not feel really ready to get myself killed. . . . But the robbers interrupted my journey before I was much farther south than Gaunt.

"Tell me, Hal, when did you suspect who I was?"

"When you told me your name," Hal smiled. "For I knew before then that you were brave, steadfast in suffering like only one man I had ever met—and you look like him, Alan. And Leon Aleron, whose sword you wear, was your cousin, was he not? And Alfie, Alf Longshanks, was your great-great-grandfather, who won himself a willful bride—"

"Ay, the lady Deona, fair as gold and stubborn as steel. Lauerocs since then have all looked like her, folk say."

"So I could have asked you your birthday weeks ago," Hal went on, "and discharged my duty to your father. I told myself I would not, for you were not yet well. But in truth, Alan, I did not speak because—because I was afraid."

"How so?"

"Afraid that you would hate me," admitted Hal, with lowered eyes.

"And why would I hate you?" asked Alan dryly.

"For two reasons. First, because the blood runs in my veins of the vilest man, the greatest ill-doer, in all of Isle. Second, because I could have saved your father's life, and did not."

Alan snorted. "Even supposing that the King kept his word, what sort of life would he have given my father? The width of a cell for pacing? He would have pined like a caged eagle. He felt pent even in Laueroc, roaming oftener than he was home. . . . And as for your tainted blood," Alan continued warmly, "I tell you what I have often wished in the past weeks, and still do: I wish that Ket and the others were right, and that you were my brother in truth. For I tell you, I love you well, and I would be proud if your blood, of which you speak so poorly, ran in my veins."

Hal ducked his head, unable to speak for emotion. Finally, softly, he asked, "Is this truly your wish, or but a manner of speaking?"

"This is my wish."

"Then," Hal said slowly, "there is a way."

"How?" Alan demanded.

"My mother, as you know, was Welandais. She taught me the language and customs of the west land. Indeed, Welas is the home of my heart, though I have never been there. It is the law there that, if two men wish to become brothers, they settle this between themselves through a ceremony they perform. They are then forever afterward considered to be brothers, in law and in love."

"What is this ceremony?" asked Alan eagerly.

Hal took a deep breath. "Each man takes a sharp knife, and nicks the vein of his comrade's left wrist, here, where the heart's blood flows nearest the surface. It must be skillfully done, or one might die; therefore great trust is required of those who undertake this ceremony. Then the wrists are pressed tightly together, so that the two bloods mingle and are one, and oaths are taken, such as are seen fit. Thus the two men are made brothers. The word for it in Welandais is *belledas,* meaning 'blood brother,' whereas the word for 'natural brother' is *mollendas.* Blood brothers are held not only in equality to natural brothers, but in an honor of their own."

Alan read the longing in Hal's eyes, and he knew that the same desire brightened his own. "Let us do it, Hal," he said.

In a few minutes they knelt on the bank of the stream, with bandages and hunting knives at hand. They bared their left arms to the elbow and laid the wrists side by side as Hal directed. Each grasped his knife with his right hand, and faced the other in the moonlight.

"I am loath to hurt you," whispered Alan.

"Of all my wounds, I shall have one that I cherish," answered Hal. "Fear not for me. Are you ready?"

Alan nodded. In one moment each tapped the stream of the other's life, and at once they pressed their two wrists tightly together, so that their blood ran down and dripped from their elbows.

Hal spoke huskily, reciting words dimly remembered

from his study of Welandais lore. "As our blood mingles in our veins and becomes as one, so let our thoughts and our lives mingle and become as one."

"Let us be brothers," responded Alan quietly, "in blood and in love and in law."

"So let it be written," Hal said as if speaking to himself, "in *Dol Solden*. Even unto the closing of the Age."

"So let it be written," said Alan firmly, "in our hearts. Is there any more need of words between us, brother?"

Hal looked into those brave blue eyes which gazed at him in joyous affection, and suddenly he knew that seventeen years of loneliness were at last over. He wept, and as Alan held him in a one-armed hug, his tears moistened the drying blood on their clasped arms.

Later, they bandaged each other in matching white wristlets, smiling, aware of their absurdity but not embarrassed between themselves. They talked for hours, lazily, of Alan's loss and Hal's burden. It no longer hurt to speak of these things.

Dawn was breaking before they unrolled their blankets and lay down. Hal fell asleep at once, like an exhausted and happy child, but Alan lay for a while looking at him. Much of the mystery of Hal was unfolding to him. So his comrade was a Prince! Hal's moodiness, his air of command, his self-possession and sense of purpose were all understandable in light of that fact. Moreover, he was of the royal Welandais blood! Even to Alan, pragmatist that he was, the name of Welas rang with a mystic summons. The Blessed Kings of Welas spoke with elves, folk said. Alan smiled, as he always did, at the ignorant superstitions of the peasantry. Still, he knew that the rulers of Welas were credited with a kind of second sight, an almost eerie wisdom. And their folk were something of a marvel. The Welandais were peaceloving, tuneful people; yet when war was forced upon them there were no fiercer fighters. Only by treachery, and by the use of armies ten times their force, did Iscovar at last succeed in subduing them.

Alan felt sure that something of the peculiar Welandais temperament was involved in a portion of his conversation with Hal—a tiny detail, yet it was often on his mind. He had asked Hal the meaning of that strange phrase, *Dol Solden,* that he had used in his oath of blood brotherhood.

"The Book of Suns," Hal had explained. "It is a con-

cept, like that of fate. In it are supposed to be written the events of men's days, their lifetimes, the ages of their history. One could call it the book of life."

Alan had always been impatient with the esoteric, and this bordered on the nonsensical. "Well, if it is the book of life," he had retorted scornfully, "then why is it called *The Book of Suns?*" A slightly pained look had washed across Hal's face, and Alan had said at once, "Never mind; forget it." But Hal had stared with knit brows, eyes puzzled and distant, like someone trying to recall a dream lost with morning's rising. "I don't know," he had muttered at last, more to himself than Alan. "I don't know." It had taken minutes to bring him out of his trance. Remembering the incident, Alan sighed, thinking of the strangeness that flickered behind the misty veil of Hal's eyes.

Indeed, he should have guessed before now that the blood of Welas ran in Hal's veins. And now in his own, Alan reflected with sober joy. He, like Hal, was an only child, and though his youth had been filled with family and companions there had been something missing. Now he had a friend and a brother such as come to few men in a lifetime, and he was glad. He knew that he loved Hal even more than he had loved his father. Still, even now he did not entirely know who it was that he loved. Was it a warlock, whose spells froze enemies and bent prison bars? If it was, Hal himself did not know his own power, Alan believed. But he felt that Hal was something more than sorcerer, something more than Prince, comrade or brother, and that something made him sigh. Something in those cloudy gray eyes saddened him. Hal had said that he would hold no secrets from his brother; but there was a secret in him, nevertheless.

Chapter Five

It was early afternoon when they awoke and eyed each other with half-humorous smiles. "I have not yet thanked you for saving my life," Hal remarked.

"Forget that." Alan was surprised to find himself reddening. "There is no need of such words between us, brother."

"There never was, even before yesterday." Hal knelt, fussing with the fire. "But nevertheless, Alan, I am ashamed. You freed me from a stronghold at great risk to yourself, and all I could find to say was, where is my sword."

Alan had to laugh, hearing his own sentiments so neatly mirrored. "Well, you have need of a noble weapon," he conceded. "How were you taken, Hal?"

"Dreaming," Hal admitted with a grimace. "Or thinking more of Corin than of the road. . . . Arundel tried to warn me, but I blundered right into the lordsmen. They knocked me down before I had a chance to draw a weapon. Then they tied me up and knelt to cast lots for my horse and gear. I had told Arundel not to fight; the odds were too great. But one of them held him slackly, like a palfrey, and I shouted at him to go. He broke away easily. And that," Hal added, grinning, "is when they started beating me."

"I thought as much," Alan said. "I thought you could not be taken knowingly. Well, I suppose we shall have to be off after your sword."

"Not today. I am exhausted, and the day is half spent."

Alan felt the same, utterly fatigued, though more from emotion than from exertion. So they tended their horses and hung their blankets up to air, and ate the meat that Corin had left them.

"What is the lineage of the sword?" Alan asked. He was still trying to understand Hal's recklessness in taking them onto the Waste.

"I don't know. Trigg gave it to me." Hal smiled sheepishly. "I am loath to lose his gift."

"And also," Alan ventured, "you had some plan in coming north?"

"At first I rode north to put more distance between myself and Nemeton. . . . Now I am worried about Corin. And I need to explore, to find friends and learn to know my land. . . . But my plans are more like dreams, Alan."

"Tell me."

"I thought to circle Isle from east to west . . . and of course I must go to Welas," Hal added with a faraway look in his eyes. "I have kinsfolk there, whom I have never known."

"And Iscovar?"

Hal sighed. "Well, I shall not have to be a father-slayer, Alan. The One be praised, that nightmare at least is kept from me. Within four years, the King should be dead of the disease that feeds upon lust. When I was not yet sixteen I knew this from my mother, who knew it from the royal physician. He told her then, five years, and one of those has gone by while I lived with Craig the Grim. So if I am to be King—and make my people some amends for the horrors of my forebears—I must have my bid ready in time.

"I have two great advantages over my enemies. One, that they do not know of this illness of the King. The secret is well kept, as you can imagine, or already the great lords would be worrying at Iscovar's throat instead of fawning at his feet. The second advantage is that they do not know I am out of the Tower. If they realized how far I am from the throne and the royal armies, they would have already moved to the kill and commenced quarreling over the spoils. So the King keeps that secret as well, though you may be sure he searches for me diligently.

"You saved me from a more horrible fate than you knew, Alan, when you spirited me out of that smelly tower of Gar's. Like all the great lords, he came to court often; Iscovar insists on such attentions. So he knows me, and if he had once seen me I would have become his pawn and prisoner, eternally dishonored."

Alan listened intently. "Then it is not the King you must fight, but the host of quarreling lords who will try to seize the throne upon his death."

"Ay. They who are now his liegemen will turn against him in his sickness, like the wolf who rends his wounded brother. Just as he would do to them. . . . Most of the ambitious lords are clustered in the fertile south, as you know. Daronwy of Bridgewater, Mordri of the Havens, Kai Oakmaster, and of course Iscovar's puppet at Laueroc. But more are scattered all over Isle. Nabon of Lee, Guy of Gaunt—and we have had a taste of Whitewater's power."

"Far too much power for my taste," Alan complained. "How can you ever fight them all, Hal?"

"With help," answered Hal earnestly. "I have said I am a dreamer, Alan. . . . But all over Isle are people who ache to be rid of the oppressors, if only they can be brought together, and given hope." He gazed into the treetops. "I see a signal in the night. And at that signal, folk rising up silently, taking their lord's horses, his cattle and sheep, the grain in his storehouse, the gold in his treasure room, the weapons in his armory. Any of these things, if done with stealth, would greatly cripple his garrison when he awoke to hear the brazen trumpets roaring the news of the King's death. And the peasants safely away, and the lords far too busy to retaliate." He sighed and turned his eyes back to Alan. "If only I needed no more force than that."

"Proud lords are not likely to yield without bloodshed," Alan stated wryly.

"I know it. Craig the Grim has great store of weapons, and the influence to muster over a thousand men, all skilled archers. I spoke with him before I left him, and surprised him little, for he, too, has his spies, and had long since guessed. Ket the Red is another one who will fight for me, I think. And if I am not mistaken, Margerie

can be a powerful friend to us in Whitewater. The time
has not yet come to tell them my need—so far, only you
and Craig know of me—but they will be there when I
have need of them. And others, Alan; I have heard that
there are strange folk in the north. Perhaps the roving
warlords of the Barrens will see fit to aid me, or I may
find even better friends, fearsome friends to bring a swift
peace, if my dreams lead me truly. . . ." His eyes glittered as he spoke, and Alan was reminded once again of
his Welandais blood.

They did not turn at once to the north, however.
First they backtracked to look for Corin and the sword.
After their day of rest they left the Forest toward Whitewater and cast about on the Waste, searching the occasional small thickets they had been forced to speed
past before. They found an old campsite, perhaps Corin's,
but they found no other traces. Several times they sighted
lordsmen in the far distance and fled northward, still on
the open Waste. They spent two nervous nights on the
bare, stony ground, sleeping restlessly in spite of the
watchfulness of their horses. Finally, Hal admitted tem-
porary defeat.

"Those two are farther to the north now, even at a
footpace," he grumbled. "And the only reason the lordsmen haven't come after us is because they can't believe
we would be such fools."

They returned to the Forest for a sound night's sleep,
then traveled northward for a few days within its shelter.
Oak and beech trees began to give way to pine and fir.
Hal felt more secure from lordsmen now, and ready to
search for Corin once more. It was reaping time at the
isolated cottages of the Waste. Hal and Alan found that
their help was welcomed at the hot, dusty work, and they
were paid as generously as the struggling landholders
could afford. But no one had any word of a blond boy or
his bald, blacksmith father.

For days they traveled northward on the Waste, returning to the Forest only to sleep or hunt. As they went on,
the holdings of cottagers grew fewer and farther between,
and the land grew wilder and more lonely, until at length
there came a day when they saw no living creatures except rabbits and sparrows. It was a strange land they traveled now, not much changed by the passing of time, for
everywhere were signs of ancient dwellers—cairns, strange

mounds and earthworks, and standing stones raised like monstrous fangs toward the sky. Hal's gray eyes gleamed as he regarded the great gray stones, but Alan shivered in their shadows. He was a native of the gentle green southlands, and he felt naked and exposed in this high, windy place.

"Ages ago, this was Forest," Hal said. "All of Isle was Forest, the soul and dwelling of the Lady Mother. Small dark people roamed from grassy glade to glade and fed their animals on acorn mast. But iron-armed men came, who wanted to make themselves a great nation, so they felled the trees with their iron axes and turned the ground with their iron tools, and raised great stones to their dead and their gods, and piled mounds of dirt for their timber towers, and circles of dirt for their timber battle walls. . . . Season after season they made war, and played at love and valor. And season after season the sea winds blew, and the sea rains fell, until all the rich earth was blown and washed from the land, and only rocky waste remained. This was long ago, long before the invaders came from the east, long before any Kings ruled in Laueroc or Eburacon or the north. Those iron-sworded newcomers moved on to become the Kings we remember in legend, and the small dark folk came out of the Forest to reclaim their wasted land."

"How in the world can you know?" Alan exclaimed.

Hal could not answer. "Dreams," he said at last. "And there come some now." He pointed. "The ancient tribes of Romany."

The Gypsies flowed darkly toward them over the Waste, ragged folk and shaggy beasts all in one rippling mass. Hal and Alan sat quietly on their horses as the band surrounded them. A ring of sober, dark-eyed faces looked up: solemn black-braided children in stammel frocks; stocky ponies; old crones with tame ravens on their shoulders; short, frowning men with shepherd's staffs and small stone-tipped darts in hand. No one made a sound; even the sheep were silent. Alan felt his flesh crawl at the thought of a dart in his back.

"Laifrita thae, mirdas arle," Hal greeted them with curbed excitement in his voice. ["Greetings to you, people of the earth."]

The staring circle gasped, then stirred into movement and welcoming smiles. A chieftain stepped forward, his rank marked by the broad metal collar that arced around his neck, shining like a crescent moon.

"Welcome, Mireldeyn," he said. "Welcome, Elwyndas."

They ate with the Gypsies, and shared the warmth of their campfire against the chill sea breeze. Hal spoke their strange language, and talked late into the night with the oldest men and women. Alan, who could converse with the others only in their broken dialect, was nevertheless much attended to. He was surprised to find that the Gypsies, horse experts that they were, had a high opinion of Alfie. "He is not handsome, nay," they agreed with him, "but he has much heart." As for Arundel, their dialect failed them, and they could only say, gesturing, that he was *elwedeyn*. When Alan signaled his noncomprehension, they shook their heads hopelessly, and sank back into the shelter of their dark faces around the fire.

"What are those names they called us?" Alan asked Hal in a whisper when everyone had settled for the night.

"Man-spirit, friend of the wind, some such. . . ." Hal stirred irritably. "I'm not sure."

"Never mind. What did you talk about all night?"

"They have seen a pair that I think are Corin and the smith." Hal cut short Alan's delighted response. "But we must be more careful. The talk of the Rough Road is that Lord Gar has set a fine price in gold on our heads."

After that, they kept to the Forest when they could. But the going was hard. This rocky northern land was scarred with shelving jumbles of rock, and sometimes thick with brambles. Often they were obliged to use the Rough Road that traversed the Waste from Whitewater to Rodsen. A few times they met travelers, and inquired about Corin to no avail. Some nights they shared the fires of Gypsy bands. But the dark tribesmen had no further news of the smith and his boy.

The day after a night with the Gypsies, just after noon, Hal and Alan were startled to hear hoofbeats approaching them from behind. They took cover in a copse atop a small rise until the rider came into view. It was one of their hosts of the night before, galloping hard on his sturdy pony.

With faces full of foreboding, they rode out to meet him. He spoke rapidly to Hal in his own language. Hal touched his hand in gesture of thanks, and the man sent his pony quickly back the way he had come. Hal spun

Arundel and set off at full speed toward the rise, with Alfie clattering after. Once over the crest, he changed direction, then pulled up behind a ridge of rock.

"Some time after we left this morning," he explained, "strangers came to the Gypsy camp, describing us and offering gold for news of us. Ten rough-looking men, mounted, with bows. Likely they are close by us, right now. The Gypsies told them nothing, of course, but if they are not fools they will have followed our friend. I hope he comes to no harm."

"Bounty hunters," muttered Alan. He felt suddenly quite uncomfortable. He was used to thinking of sword-fighting as an unavoidable part of life in these hard times, but he did not relish the thought of ducking arrows.

"We must get to more open ground," continued Hal, "where they cannot stalk us."

They moved gently off, glancing over their shoulders. "I fled before," Hal added, "to draw the chase on us. But it's no use running now; we could blunder straight into them. We must make them show themselves and then outrun them, if we like."

Threading their way cautiously among the rocks and thickets, they proceeded in what they hoped was the direction of a clearing. At last they came to a windswept space, which they carefully surveyed. Then they touched heels to the horses' sides and sped across the barren expanse, heading for a lonely clump of trees near the center. To their relief, they reached it without incident.

"There!" Hal exclaimed. "We might as well spend the afternoon here as anywhere else. Only to the south can they come near being within bowshot. They will set an ambush to the north, but they will see that we do not intend to move, and they will be forced to rush us from the south."

"They could split up," grumbled Alan. He was not nearly as well pleased as Hal with their situation.

"I think they will not. They fear our swords, and probably they do not trust each other. We might as well sit down."

Arundel lifted his head and snorted at the distant thickets to the north.

"*Allo*," Hal told him. "Very well, Arundel. I know they are there."

Letting the horses graze, Hal and Alan sat in the shade,

leaning against the tree trunks, facing away from each other so as to watch the largest portion of ground. The afternoon crept slowly by, and the sun grew low.

Alan broke the long silence. "What will they do when dark comes?"

Hal shook his head. "They cannot afford to wait. They might surprise us, but we might also slip away from them. They will make their move soon."

Even as he spoke the distant brush stirred. The two vaulted to their saddles. But instead of rushing away as Alan expected him to, Hal tarried, dancing Arundel slowly northward, until the last of the hunters had broken cover. Then he grunted in satisfaction. "All ten of them," he said. "Let's go."

They sprang into a gallop. But the foremost men were now within bowshot, and stopped to take aim. Alan whistled and cursed Hal's boldness as an arrow grazed his ear with its honed metal head; warm blood trickled down his neck. They were almost out of range when Hal gave a moan. A lucky shot had hit Arundel in the foreleg. The arrow passed neatly between the bones, then stuck.

Even though wounded, Arundel still ran faster than the ponylike beasts behind them. But Hal knew that every step added to his injury. They burst into the wall of thickets at the edge of the clearing, and plunged through a labyrinth of rocks, copses and undergrowth. Hal sighed with relief when they came to another clearing. A gentle rise faced them. Halfway up was a long outcropping of rock screened with bushes and stunted trees. At the crown of the rise was one of the ancient barrows or cairns, a large one, ringed by upright stones.

"This will do," called Hal as they pulled up behind the natural stone barrier. "Keep the horses behind the tallest cover, Alan, and see what you can do for Arun."

He grabbed his bow and arrows from his blanketroll, and ran to a position behind the stone ledge just as their pursuers broke into the open and sent a shower of arrows into their cover. Hal aimed his first arrow at the apparent leader, and the man yelped as his arm was pinned to his side. Hal's next shot tumbled a man from his horse, shot through the heart, and his next arrow parted one's hair.

The hunters stopped abruptly and looked at each other. They had not known that their quarry possessed a bow, and especially not such a powerful and accurate one. Though they were nine bows against one, he had shelter and they had none, and they were being picked off in the open like birds on a branch. Even as they paused, another of their number fell from his mount with a scream. They retreated hastily to the thickets from which they had come.

"Two down," sighed Hal. "How is Arundel, Alan?"

Alan had not enjoyed working while arrows whistled overhead, landed underfoot and rattled in the branches of the copse that sheltered him. Nevertheless, he had removed the arrow from Arundel's leg and dressed the wound. He brought Hal a bunch of arrows he had gathered from the outlaw assault.

"The wound is not bad," he reported. "The shaft passed between muscle and bone, hurting little but the skin. Still, he should not run on it, or carry weight."

Hal nodded, frowning. "Have I ever so many arrows," he muttered, "I can only shoot them one at a time. It will soon be dark. They must rush us, and we have nothing to set our backs against. They are four against one. We need some help."

Alan snorted at the understatement. "There is nothing to help us on this Waste except the crying birds and the little rabbits. I fear we must trust in our own luck, which has been a bit overstrained, lately."

The bounty hunters left their cover and ranged themselves in the open, just out of bowshot. Each one carried a freshly cut staff, long and stout, usable either as a blunt-headed lance or as a cudgel. The leader's arm was bandaged, and his face did not look friendly.

Hal looked at them and swallowed, as if he were swallowing his pride. Then he raised his head at an angle and called out in a clear, carrying voice: *"O lian dos elys liedendes, on dalyn Veran de rangrin priende than shalder."* ["Oh spirits of those who once lived, a son of Veran from peril prays your aid."]

As if from very far away, as if from the heart of the earth, a low voice replied: *"Al holme, Mireldeyn."* ["We come, Mireldeyn."] As if from the dome of the sky, and very far away, a gray voice called, *"Al holme, Mireldeyn."*

"What is it, Hal?" Alan whispered, frozen. His hair prickled.

"Friends," Hal replied.

"Holmé a eln!" ["Come to us!"] spoke the low voice. Alan could not tell from what direction it came. It seemed to fill the world. But Hal started walking up the gentle slope, toward the barrow and the ring of standing stones. Alan and the horses followed him. From behind them came terrified screams. Alan stopped in spite of himself.

"They are not being harmed," Hal said. "Look."

Alan forced himself to turn. In the failing light he could see the men running, stumbling, falling in blind terror, getting up to run again. From what they ran he could not tell, unless it was the same nameless fear which he felt choking his own mind, so that his eyes saw black and his legs felt numb. The cries of the bounty hunters faded into the distance.

Hal turned and continued up the rise. Arundel and Alfie followed him. As he was calmly passed by his own horse, Alan's pride was stung, and somehow he willed his reluctant legs to move. He drew abreast of Hal and felt the focus of the fear, ahead of them, at the barrow. They walked closer; Alan moved like a blind man, step by slow step. Then his legs stopped. They wanted to turn and run. He kept them still, but he could not force them to go on. He could not see. His tongue seemed stuck to the roof of his mouth. With great difficulty, he moved it.

"Hal," he whispered, "help me."

He felt Hal take his hand, and with that touch warmth moved through the frozen blood in his veins. Come on, brother," Hal said gently, and Alan walked on. He met the fear; he walked through it; and it melted away before him. Then a feeling of comfort and friendliness filled his heart, and the darkness left his eyes, and he found that he was within the circle of standing stones. That which had been a forbidding fear was now a protecting embrace which welcomed him in. Hal hugged him.

"I doubt if there is another man in all of Isle who could have done that!" he exclaimed proudly.

"Except present company," Alan retorted wryly. "You walked in here as if you were going to market. What was it that frightened me so?"

A low chuckle sounded close by Alan's ear; he jumped. A gentle voice spoke rapidly in a language he did not understand. Hal nodded and turned to Alan. "He says he is sorry he startled you. He did not mean to."

"Tell him no harm," Alan gasped politely. "But who, or what, is he?"

Hal sat down and leaned against the stone wall of the barrow. "They," he corrected. "They are the spirits of the men buried here."

"Ghosts?" Alan asked weakly, sitting also.

"I dare say you could call them ghosts," Hal answered doubtfully. "But most of what is said of ghosts is false. They do not clank chains, or rattle bones, or wander in the night, or in any way interfere with human affairs. Indeed, they are powerless to speak or move from their barrow unless someone calls on them for help, as I did."

Alan felt faint. "Are they all around us?" he asked uneasily.

"Ay. This ring of standing stones is their fortress. No mortal can enter it without withstanding the fear. The amount of fear depends in part on the amount of evil in his heart. I do not think the bounty hunters will disturb us again."

"You must be perfect in goodness, then, for you did not fear."

"Nay! I said 'in part,' " Hal protested. "Fear also arises from that which is unknown. I understood, and you did not."

"In very truth," Alan muttered, holding his head in bewilderment, "I never believed such things existed, and I always laughed at the tales the countryfolk told of them."

"You may continue to do so," Hal smiled, "for they are mostly nonsense. Yet they remind us that there are great mysteries in earth and sky, dwellers far beyond our comprehension. But always, in the peasants' tales, the denizens of Otherness come to work men woe. It is not so. Remember this, Alan, and you will walk beneath the dark of the moon like the Gypsies, without fear: no creature, neither flesh nor spirit, mortal nor immortal, will do you any reasonless harm, except one—and that is your fellow man."

They spent the night within the barrow ring, nestled against the lee side of the central mound. Alan felt warm and comfortable in spite of the cold, damp stone. He was full of wonder and questions. He learned that not all the dead became shades like those he had met; these spirits must have died in rage or hatred, Hal thought. Perhaps they had been warriors. But whether in life they had been good men or evil was of no concern. Their passing had

purged them; good and evil had gone from them with
their mortality, and they were now only bodiless reflec-
tions of the fears and loves of those who encountered
them.

And they could be summoned, Alan knew. "What is
the language that you speak to the spirits, Hal?" he asked.
"Is it the same that you speak to the Gypsies?"

"Ay."

"And to Arundel?"

"Ay."

"Is it Welandais?"

"Nay—"

"What language is it, then? Where did you learn it?"
Hal frowned helplessly. Even in the flickering light of their
campfire, his discomfort was evident. Alan retracted the
question. "Never mind."

"I would tell you if I could," Hal said plaintively.

It was late before Alan finally settled into sleep, still
marveling. He awoke to a foggy morning, and found Hal
already speaking with their invisible hosts in his mysterious language.

"You know they see everything, and they travel with
the speed of the wind," he explained to Alan. "Though or-
dinarily they may not move from their resting place. . . .
But last night I sent some of them scouting. Our friends
the bounty hunters have quarreled among themselves, it
seems, and are either dead or fleeing. And Corin and his
father Col are camped a day or two farther to the east,
near the sea."

"But Arundel cannot travel far or fast, with his
wounded leg," Alan grumbled.

"I know it. I shall be walking, for a while."

They ate some breakfast, rabbit and a few stunted
sorb-apples. Then they loaded all the gear on Alfie. But
as they prepared to leave, the low voice spoke. Hal stared
somberly, but made no reply. He motioned Alan to help
him remove some stones from the wall of the barrow.

When they had made an entrance, they crawled
through, being very careful where they placed their hands
and feet. The interior of the barrow was high enough to
stand in. By the light which filtered through the open
stonework, they could dimly see faded ruins of cloth,
dusty bones and dull gleams of once bright metal: helms,

swords and breastplates in odd, antique shapes. These were indeed warriors who lay here.

The low voice spoke again, beckoning, and they advanced to the center of the domed barrow, where there lay a still figure on a raised slab. By its ashy skull lay a crown, blackened with age. By its right hand lay a naked sword. Even through the grime of ages, they could see that it was a glorious weapon, the hilt intricately set with jewels, the whole of it golden, large and heavy so that it would deal a mighty blow. The voice of the dead king spoke again, at length, and Hal went to the sword. He raised it and reverently kissed the massive hilt. He set it down, and spoke quietly to the disembodied listener. Then he and Alan turned and left. As they led their horses down the hill, the warmth of the barrow followed them, slowly fading away with the morning fog.

Hal waited until they were well away before he spoke. "That king wanted me to take his sword," he said in a low voice.

"The golden sword!" Alan almost shouted. "But Hal, it is a marvelous weapon! Why did you not take it?"

"I have need of my own sword," Hal muttered.

Alan groaned in disbelief. "Hal, you are incredibly difficult. The jewel-studded brand of a former monarch—was it not enough for you?"

"More than enough," Hal retorted wryly. "He said that it was filled with the power of the Beginnings, that with it I would be invincible."

Alan stared. "The magical sword of the High Kings!" he breathed.

"Ay, it throbbed through my arms as I lifted it, and it throbs in me yet; I can scarcely walk for the ache of it. Alan, may I tell you a tale?"

They sat on the ground and let the horses graze. Hal did not seem to look at anything, not even at Alan, as he spoke.

"The king's name was Claryon, High King at Laueroc, and the mighty sword Hau Ferddas hung above his throne to enforce his will, and the writings of Cuin the Ancestor lay open in the council-chamber, and the weeping stone stood in the courtyard as a reminder that the Kings of Laueroc were honored vassals of the Very King who had gone beyond the sea. The water trickled down from the cracked stone and dripped from its golden pedestal to form a pool on the cobbles. The princes were Culean, Culadon and Cuert. When they were little, they would make boats from sticks and sail them in the tears of the Sorrowing Stone.

"Cuert grew to be a scholar, and Culadon to be a statesman, but the eldest, Culean, had no talent for bookish learning so he trained to be a warrior. He was not much honored as a warrior; there had been peace for half an Age, and it was thought that Hau Ferddas could keep peace forever.

"When the princes were grown, or nearly grown, Veran sailed into the Bay of the Blessed out of the west. Cuert, the youngest prince, knew him to be Very King as soon as he heard report of him, for Veran had brought with him a rayed silver crown. Culadon knew only that Veran had taken power in Welas, where the Kings of Isle held no sway. But Culean saw only a rival. And Claryon, the old king, found any change a threat.

"The real threat came from the east. Within the year Herne landed his warships, and old King Claryon took horse to meet him, proud in the invincibility of his legendary sword. A few hundred men followed him on the long forced marches across Isle. They met Herne in the midlands near the Black River. Hau Ferddas slew mightily, but Claryon's aging arms lost strength to hold the weapon. He staggered back before his foes, and only the coming of darkness saved him and the sword from capture. His remaining men carried him back toward Laueroc, and in a few days he died, though he had suffered no wound. His people met the invaders in confusion and despair, and yielded before them like grass.

"Herne's close companion was a sorcerer named Marrok, that is to say, the Werewolf. He had seen the battle, and had seen the sword Hau Ferddas, and coveted the blade for his master's sake, or his own, perhaps. With his secret arts he contrived a spell which would rob it of its mystic strength, for a time. The price was high; men lost their lives to the making of that spell. But Herne was well content.

"Veran had marched with five hundred men to Laueroc, for the danger which threatened Isle threatened Welas also. He bowed his elf-crowned head at old Claryon's funeral pyre. But Culean, the new High King, scorned his help, and set off hotly to rally his own people against the invaders. Culadon threw in his lot with Veran, and Cuert, barely fifteen years of age, stayed behind to steward Laueroc.

"Many brave men found their place at Culean's side, and for a time Herne was halted in his advance. Veran pressed him from the south and west, and Culean battered him from the north, and if only those two could have taken cause together, Herne might have been forced to yield. But they each fought separately from the other, not to best advantage. Then Marrok's spell took effect, and Culean fought with only manly might. And, as evil chance would have it, Culadon was slain by Veran's side. Then many followers fell away from the defenders of Isle, and Herne's armies moved again.

"Veran made his stand between the mountains of Welas and the Gleaming River, where the border runs to this day. All of Welas rallied to him, and he was able to bring Herne to terms for his own land's sake." Hal turned to Alan, seeming conscious of his listener for the first time. "Cuert went with him, and through him you are of that line, Alan; Deona wife of Alf was his granddaughter."

"I?" Alan murmured.

"You are of that royal blood. The king, High King Culean, was hounded through the north of Isle as the power of his sword waxed and waned with the power of Marrok's spell, until he could plainly see that Herne held all of Isle and wished only to hold Hau Ferddas as well. Then Culean and his few loyal liegemen devised a plan to keep the sword from Herne's hand, and I dare say to preserve their own pride—for they could have thrown the weapon into the sea. Instead they stood on a rise of the stony Waste, and they cursed fate with their deepest curses, and they died by their own hands. Their companions who had chosen not to follow them built the barrow over them, then departed. And there the sword has stayed to this day, for their sleepless shades protect it, as they knew they would."

The two sat silently for a while as the grim tale echoed down the passages of their minds. "Did—Culean—tell you this?" Alan asked finally.

"Nay."

"Who, then, Hal? The Gypsies?"

"No one, Alan." Hal spoke with a kind of desperation. "It is the—vision—I have seen, of how the sword is a shadowed thing."

So he is a seer, as well as a warlock, Alan thought. He accepted the fact almost casually; the recent events and Hal's revelations had shaken him beyond astonishment.

"If I could," Hal said softly, "I would take that bright blade and hurl it into the sea. But once it was in my hand, I think I would not have the strength to give it up. It is a seducer, Alan. But it is yours by right of lineage, more than it is mine."

"It was not offered to me," Alan shrugged. "Come, let us find your own sword, that Trigg gave you."

"He was like a father to me, for a little while. . . ." Hal looked away, remembering the love in the eyes of the good-hearted fellow as he presented the gift. "Ay, let us be going."

They rose, and Hal took a few weary, painful steps. Suddenly he dropped to the earth again, striking the stones with his fist. "Confound it, Alan! Why was this offered to me? Was it a trap which I rightly spurned? Or was it a key which I have thrown away? If a test, then why? If not, then I have made the wrong choice!"

Alan smiled wryly. "Trust yourself, Hal, even as I must. Do not things always seem to come to rights for you?"

"You think I should have taken it," Hal muttered.

"I would have taken it, ay, and probably got myself killed because of it. But you are not I, praise be. Perhaps you do not need such a sword."

"Do not mock me, Alan," said Hal tiredly.

"After all I have seen?" Alan faced him squarely. "Do I mock you, brother?"

Hal met his eyes with growing wonder. "I wish I thought as well of myself," he said at last.

Chapter Six

They went afoot for several days because of Arundel's wound. Hal was moody, and fatigued from something more than walking. When he regained his energy, he grew irritable because of their slow pace. They were making their way north and east, toward the sea. The Forest curved eastward with them, but indeed it was hardly to be called Forest any longer, mostly bramble thickets and stunted conifers. For days the two had only birds and rabbits and pine kernels to eat; Alan grew as touchy as Hal. They saw almost no one in this desolate land. There was no news of Corin.

It was fifteen days of walking and gentle riding before they came to the coast. The sea cliffs dropped straight from a weedy, windswept plain, and the surf crashed far below. When Hal heard the sea and felt the salt breeze, he straightened in the saddle, and his gray eyes gleamed with a silvery sheen. But to Alan, the roaring of the sea was a sound of doom, and the sad cries of the gulls were like weeping. It took the warmth of evening's campfire to drive the cold weight from his heart.

Autumn was fast approaching. The nights were chill, the mornings damp. The leaves of the twisted trees hung limp in the heat of the days. Thundershowers came and

went. Hal and Alan zigzagged northward along the coast,
looking for Corin; and one evening, when the ground was
still wet from the afternoon's rain, they found a trail. Two
pairs of feet had made it, one large and one smaller.

"Finally!" Hal exclaimed.

They followed the smudgy traces until it was too dark
to see; then they pressed on, afoot and feeling their way
through the brush, watching for a campfire. Before long
they spied a flicker in the distance.

"What luck!" Hal whispered. "But softly now; we can't
be certain it is only the smith and the boy."

To Alan it seemed like an eternity that they stalked
through the troublesome thickets. His heart pounded with
the suspense of slow movement, and he winced at every
clumsy noise he made. Hal went like a silent shadow
before him. But as they neared the fire at last, Hal drifted
back beside him and touched his arm.

"Kingsmen!" he breathed. Alan could feel the tremor
of his fingers and hear the catch in his voice. He had
named the name of terror; yet he moved forward again,
toward the firelight.

In a moment, Alan could see why. Corin sat there, tied
to a scrubby tree. Even in the ruddy glow of the flames,
the boy's face looked as pale as death. Col lay stretched
on the ground, near the fire. The kingsmen stooped around
him. King Iscovar bragged that his retainers wore helmets
of gold, but the metal was cheapened with copper until it
glowed orange, the cruelest color; their cloaks were dyed
black in imitation of the King's sable, and they were
obliged to wear them even in the summer heat. They
circled around the fire and Col like black priests of the
horned god around a ritual victim. Alan could see that
Col was staked to the stony ground. The man had stained
the earth with his blood. Alan shuddered and struggled
for breath.

"If we fight them," Hal warned in the lowest of whispers, "we must slay them all, for our lives' sake."

There were six kingsmen. The leader raised a sword,
Hal's sword, above Col's straining face.

"There is still time to tell me where you found this,"
he crooned, "before you die by it."

The smith turned away his head. "No matter," another
kingsman remarked. "We will have it out of the pup,
then."

"I tell you, I stole it!" Corin cried, but the man whipped around and clouted him with a heavy fist. The boy's head thudded into the tree, and Col screamed though his son did not, a roaring cry of despair. While the sound still echoed Hal and Alan drew their swords, and in voiceless unison they sprang.

They were not inclined to be sporting, at the odds. Hal lopped the head off Corin's assailant before the man could rise; the body lurched onto the boy, splattering him with blood. Alan sent a kingsman stumbling into the fire. The fellow shrieked as his heavy cloak burst into flame, and ran madly through the melee. Alan and Hal each stood battling desperately against two swords. Alan was backed up against Col's inert form, sick at the thought of stepping on the man. Shieldless, he had already taken half a dozen cuts. Hal found himself pitting a thick, hacking sword against the grace of his own lighter blade. He whistled a long, shrilling blast, then blinked; one of his foes had fallen, crippled. Someone had struck the man in the leg. The boy Corin, still reeling from the blow to his head, staggered toward the fire to help Alan, lifting a captured weapon.

But Arundel got there first, and Alfie. They bowled over the enemies with the force of their charge. After that it was soon over. Six kingsmen lay dead; Hal made sure of each of them. Alan sank down beside the body of the smith. Corin knelt there, quivering and pressing his father's hand, but Col was dead. It did not take much looking to tell that.

Hal came up with the flask, and a kingsman's shirt for bandaging. He glanced at Col and the boy, then silently handed the flask to Alan. Like Alan, he was bleeding from cuts on his arms and shoulders, though not as many. Alan gulped some liquor and got up, shakily.

"We had better be off quickly," he muttered, "in case there are more such vermin about."

"Arundel will tell us if anyone comes near," Hal replied. "We can take time to lay the smith to rest." He hastily wrapped Alan's worst cuts, and his own, then knelt by Corin. He bandaged the boy's raw wrists as he spoke. "Lad, my sword brought you the worst of luck. I am sorry."

"May it bring you better, for your goodliness," the

boy whispered. "My father said it was a princely weapon; and you have won it worthily."

Already Hal had buckled it on again; a strong blade, but lightweight, a weapon of skill more than of force. The hilt and scabbard were of silver-gray metal, sparingly decorated with black enamel scrollwork. The lights which played on the glossy metal were the same as those which appeared in Hal's eyes, sometimes, when he thought of his enemies and his task. Alan had seen the weapon before, but now he looked at it anew. Without doubt, it was Hal's connate sword.

"My father was angry at me for taking it," Corin added, "and now he has paid the price of my folly. . . ." The boy's voice broke, and he silently wept. Alan put his good arm around him and led him away; then he went to help Hal.

They cut Col's body loose, wrapped it in Hal's cloak and laid it in a shallow depression of the hard ground. They covered it against harm with loose rocks, piling them into a cairn. The bodies of the kingsmen they dragged into the brush. Horses were tethered nearby, as foul-tempered as their masters; Hal searched the saddlebags for food and then let the beasts go loose. He and Alan wanted no part of the kingsmen's gear. They stamped out the fire. It was the mid of a cloudy, moonless night, but they were eager to be gone from this place in spite of the dark.

"Come on, Corin," Alan murmured, and seated the boy before him on Alfie.

They rode through the night and the next day, heading north between the Forest and the sea cliffs. Bit by bit, through the day, Corin's story came out.

"Smiths have magic, you know, when it comes to metals," he explained. "When your broth had given him strength, my father was able to cure himself by the touch of your sword. Later, we were hungry, and he used it to conjure food. A gray goshawk came, and dropped a coney by our feet."

"It seems," Alan remarked to Hal, "that there is more than one magical sword."

"A sorcerer can work wonders with a stick," Hal snapped. "And those warlocks who den with Iscovar can smell such sorcery even from Nemeton."

"The magic in that sword is magic of perfect craftsmanship," Corin told them haltingly. "That fine smithcraft went into it at its making, and there is no evil in such power. . . . But Father did not like to use it often, just the same. There is more honor in catching your own fish than in drawing on another man's magical net."

"There is no fishing off these cliffs," Alan grumbled. The salt breeze was cold. Even the last stunted remnants of the Forest were behind them now, and only a ragged, treeless expanse faced them. They were riding the Marches now.

"We kept on walking north, to get well away from Whitewater," Corin said, much later. "And also Father was afraid of your anger, though I told him. . . . Well, and also the land grew harsher and harsher. There was no tilling it. Father thought we might walk as far as the Barrens, and wander with the warlords. He had grown fond of walking, I think. But those black and orange ghouls came up behind us." Corin stopped.

"So they followed the smell of sorcery from Nemeton," Alan said. "But how could they have known it was your sword, Hal? Or if they did not know, why would they care?"

"I can't say, either way," muttered Hal. "I know nothing of my own sword."

It was nearly dusk when they found a hollow sheltered by four standing stones. Here they decided to spend the night, protected from the never-ending sea breeze and from prying eyes as well. The mention of sorcery had put Alan on edge; he was imagining invisible trackers, relentless pursuit. What Hal was feeling, he could not tell.

They had Corin help with the camp chores, hoping that the work might ease his sorrow. Hal served up his best rabbit stew, with precious bread plundered from the enemy saddlebags; but the lad scarcely ate. Afterward Alan offered him his blanket. The boy politely refused.

"I cannot sleep," he said. "Do not let me hinder your rest; I shall sit by the fire."

They had to respect his wish to be alone. But Alan slept fitfully in spite of his fatigue, and it was not long before he rose to find the lad huddled over the coals of the fire, sound asleep, with tears still wet on his eyelashes. Gently Alan wrapped him in his blanket and laid him down. Then he himself hunched over the dying coals,

warming himself in his cloak. Hal awoke from a doze and
silently joined him.

"I'm glad he's asleep," he murmured, studying their
new companion. "What a plucky young nuisance he is,
Alan! To rip himself out of those bonds—his wrists are
mangled nearly to the bone—and heave himself out from
under that headless body, and come to our aid with a
dead man's sword. . . . And he can't be more than thir-
teen."

"Twelve, he told me. But he's likely to have the girls
after him in a year or two. He's a handsome rascal, and
well grown."

"Poor fellow," Hal whispered. "What are we to do with
him, Alan? This is no life for him."

Alan shook his head helplessly. He supposed they
would have to worry about that later.

But they had to worry about Corin sooner than they
expected. At daybreak, when they arose, Corin did not
wake, and his forehead was hot to the touch. Hal frowned.
"He needs his sleep worse than he does his breakfast,
but he shall have both. Let us ride till he awakes."

So Alan gathered him up, blanket and all, and took
him onto Alfie with himself. The lad moved and muttered
restlessly, but did not wake. It was midmorning when he
suddenly started from his doze and looked around him,
bewildered. Arundel moved up alongside Alfie as Hal
reached over to Corin's forehead, asking him how he felt.

"Things keep going around," he answered. "Sometimes
I can see your face, but then it fades into a fog."

Corin did not want to eat, but they persuaded him to
drink some meat broth strengthened with Hal's herbs. As
soon as they took to the saddle again, he lapsed into a
sleep that was half faintness.

They rode all day, turning inland in search of some
nameless succor, and not stopping until after dark. Corin
awoke at intervals, but his eyes were glazed and he said
little. He drank water and broth, but could eat nothing.
They took turns sitting up with him that night. By dawn
he was delirious with fever, moaning and calling for his
father. Hal was dismayed. "My brews have no effect," he
said. "He needs shelter, and the help of a wiser healer
than I."

They rode on, desperately looking for some sign of human habitation. In late afternoon they found a camp of

Gypsies. The dark folk gave them as much assistance as they could. They had blankets, food, shelter from the wind and a little medicine. They got some bread into Corin, and some more broth. They all took turns sitting by him, giving him water and swabbing his burning forehead. But he was no better.

"He is not fighting it!" Hal exclaimed.

Corin indeed seemed to be sinking into despair. He cried out for his father, and from time to time he shouted in desperate anger, "Murderers! Murderers!" Hal spoke with the Gypsy chieftain.

"Is there any holding nearby, or manor, or town, where the folk would be willing to help us, and where a healer might make his home?"

The Gypsy shook his head. "As you value your lives, do not go west, for Arrok's raiders scour the Marches even as far as the Forest, though his holding is in Rodsen. If you continue north, you will come to the trade town of Firth, on the Great North Cove. The lord there, Roran, is a good man, just but merciful, and kind to those in need. Surely he has a healer. But it is a seven-day journey. I doubt the lad will last."

"We will make it in three," Hal said grimly. "Tell me the way."

They left the Gypsy camp before day had quite broken, with Corin blanket-wrapped and with water, food and medicine in their saddlebags. They rode at a steady, loping run through that day, stopping only to give Corin drink. The miles melted away and the land swept past them faster than it ever had before, although to them the pace seemed slow. They went on until they could no longer see to ride, then stopped to boil some meat for broth. When the moon rose they went on again, and did not stop until the next nightfall. They gnawed bread in the saddle. Arundel and Alfie cantered tirelessly. Alan's heart bled for the steeds, but Hal spoke to them in his strange language, and they raised their heads and surged on like colts fresh out of pasture. Though the land they rode was still flat or rolling, jagged peaks now rose between them and the sea. They were moving into the Northern Barrens.

By the end of the second day Corin had ceased to cry out for his father. He lay as still as death in their arms, scarcely breathing, and they could feel the heat coming off his face as off a fire.

"We must make it by tomorrow," Hal said.

They pushed on through the night. The horses were stumbling with fatigue, but kept up the best pace they could without urging. By dawn they were toiling up a long, steep rise. Corin was on Arundel. Several times Alfie faltered and almost fell, but he never balked. Alan patted his neck constantly, and Hal talked to both horses. Arundel's head hung low, but he ran steadily on.

By midmorning they had topped the rise, and saw Firth far below. Within the hour they swept through the town gates. Scarcely pausing for the folk in the streets, they made their way straight to the lord's keep.

"Open up! It is a matter of life or death!" cried Hal.

The timber doors creaked open. A groom ran to take their horses. A servant appeared to lead them to the lord.

"Let no one except you touch the gray," Hal cautioned the groom. He set off after the servant, carrying Corin. Arundel's knees trembled, and his fine head hung almost to the cobblestones. But Alfie sank to the ground, where he lay flat on his side. Alan groaned, torn between Alfie and Corin; then he ran after Hal.

A doorkeeper gave them entry into a stone chamber. The inner walls were completely hung with rich tapestries. In the center of the room, in an intricately carved chair, sat a dark, fierce-looking man dressed in thick velvets. He glanced at them as they entered, saw the limp bundle in Hal's arms and at once strode across the room to them, leaving the man with whom he was talking. He laid his hand on Corin's burning forehead, looked at their haggard faces and clapped his hands loudly. Several servants came running.

"Call Bleys at once," he ordered. "Prepare rooms and food for these gentlemen, and whatever they need. Hurry!" As the servants disappeared, he turned to Hal and Alan. "Bleys is as fine a physician as can be found north of Nemeton. If he cannot help the lad, then he is beyond mortal aid. I am anxious to know your story, but I shall wait until your needs are seen to. I shall speak with you later."

"A thousand thanks, my lord," said Hal quietly.

"Here is Bleys now. May all good come to the lad."

Lord Roran went back to his seat as they followed the healer out of the room.

Bleys was an old man, gray-bearded but still hale of body and clear of eye. He took them to a large chamber where servants were busy building a fire and piling linens on a large bed. A tub was brought and filled with warm water, and Corin was tenderly bathed, then laid in the bed and dosed with warm milk and medicine. After that there was nothing to do but moisten his burning face with a cool cloth, give drink from time to time and wait. As soon as he saw Corin cared for, Alan slipped away to the stables.

He found Alfie lying on a thick bed of straw in a roomy stall. He had been rubbed dry and warmly covered. Arundel was in the next stall, also lying down, and he whinnied at Alan cheerfully enough. But Alfie lay without raising his head, and his whole body was tense with pain. Alan sank into the straw and took the horse's head on his lap, and Alfie nuzzled his hand.

Without warning, tears began rolling down Alan's cheeks, as he clutched the horse's neck and begged him, "Don't die! I need you. . . ." He knew that if Alfie died he would never forgive himself, even though it was for Corin's sake. For a long time he hugged and patted his horse, stroking the lean neck, telling him what a very good horse he was, who galloped so bravely night and day, and who hadn't needed a tether in over a month now, and who never ran away anymore. "Alfie the Great-Hearted," he said. "That's what we'll call you."

After a while he left the stables and headed back toward Corin's room. The tears still lay wet on his face, and many people stared at him, but he was beyond embarrassment. As he strode through the keep, Lord Roran of Firth entered the corridor and stopped in concern when he saw him.

"Is the news bad?"

"Nay, my lord. The boy was still the same when I left him. I have been to see my horse. . . ." For a moment Alan could not go on. "Pardon, my lord," he said finally. "For three days and nights I have not slept, and I begin to act foolishly. The horse is nearly dead from galloping, and it grieves me."

"How far have you ridden?" asked Lord Roran gently.

Alan told him. "Four days ago we were at the place where the Forest meets the sea."

Lord Roran whistled. "He must be no ordinary horse."

"Nay, my lord," answered Alan, then had to cover his face with his hands. Hal looked out of Corin's doorway, came and put his arms around him.

"Is Alfie dead?"

Alan shook his head. "Nay," he managed to say, "but likely to be." He stood breathing deeply, trying to calm himself.

"He will not die," said Hal with conviction. "He is far too stubborn. If only I could say the same for the lad."

"How is the boy?" asked Lord Roran.

"The same. There is nothing to do now but wait."

"Then come with me," said Lord Roran firmly. "You both need rest and nourishment. Your dinner awaits you."

"With your leave," Hal said, "I shall go to the stables first."

His Lordship nodded, and he and Alan went on. "I do not yet know your name," he said.

Alan told him.

"And your brother?"

"His name is Hal." Alan paused. "You called him my brother, and indeed in a manner of speaking he is, but not by birth."

"By the tides, I felt sure he was your brother. And Corin, is he no relationship to either of you?"

"None. We found him just four days ago."

"You found him? How is that?"

They came to a warm room with two beds, where a variety of food was set out on a small table. As they sat, Alan told briefly of Corin's rescue.

"The filth!" Lord Roran muttered as Alan told of the kingsmen. "The black-cloaked, dirty-handed, mother-hating filth!" He pounded the table with his fist, and his face flushed an angry red. As Alan continued, his expression turned from rage to astonishment.

"The two of you killed six kingsmen?" he exclaimed.

"Even so." Alan was too tired to think of taking offense.

"But how?"

"We surprised them, and two of them we took off at once. . . . Then Corin got loose somehow, and got ahold of a sword, and stabbed a villain in the knee even before he was able to get up. Hal whistled for the horses, and they helped us dispatch the rest."

"Remarkable horses," Lord Roran murmured in bewilderment. Obviously Alan was too wrung out to be bragging or lying. Roran listened in stunned silence to Alan's account of their four-day ride.

"Then Corin's sickness is as much one of the heart as of the body," he said at last.

"Ay. He thinks his father died on his account."

Hal joined them, and in answer to Alan's worried glance he only shrugged: Alfie was still the same. The lord of Firth dished out the meal. There were excellent soups, wheat bread, jellies and cold meats. In politeness Hal and Alan tasted everything, but they ate little.

"Will you sleep now?" asked Lord Roran when they were finished. "This is your room, but I shall have cots set up for you near Corin if you would prefer."

That was done, but they could not sleep. Restlessly they divided their time between Corin's bedside and the stable, pacing through the long afternoon. Alfie remained on his side in the straw, scarcely moving, cramped with exhaustion. Corin grew weaker and more wasted, his tongue parched and his face burning to the touch. He seemed scracely to breathe, and a dozen times they feared that he was already dead.

At dusk Lord Roran came in, and with him a lad about Corin's size, but as dark and hawklike as himself. It was Roran's son, Robin. They looked at Corin with pity in their eyes, and Bleys flung wide his hands in a gesture of despair.

"He need not die," the healer said. "He came to me soon enough, and took the medicine well. But he is sunk in his grief, and remembers no joy in his life."

In the reaches of Hal's mind a spark of hope flickered. He spoke, knowing quite well that what he asked was preposterous. "At the beginning of this Age, there was a small flowering plant in the south and west of Isle, called by some folk Elfin Gold, by others Veran's Crown. It is said that since Herne first sailed up the Black River it is no longer to be found. Have you ever heard of it?"

Lord Roran's face was blank, but Bleys showed interest. "I have heard of it. We have a room here full of quaint things collected by the third lord, Rob Roy. It seems to me that I have seen a small jar in there, full of dried plants. 'Bloome of Veran's Crowyn,' it said."

Hal leaped to his feet. "A single plant will save Corin's life. I swear it!"

In a moment they were all in the crowded, dusty room, frantically searching every corner, shelf and case for the little jar which said "Bloome of Veran's Crowyn." It was Robin who found it at last, triumphantly emerging from under a cobwebby table. They hurried with it back to Corin's room. The servants had followed Hal's directions; a brazier burned by Corin's bed, and on it a small pot of water boiled. Hal carefully removed from the jar a single brittle plant—root, stem, leaf and flower. Whispering what might have been a prayer, he crushed the little thing and dropped it into the boiling water.

Slowly a faint, clear aroma filled the room, essence of springtime, youth, birdsong and May sunshine. Without knowing it, everyone relaxed, their minds wandering back to the time when they were happy and young. Roran straightened in his seat, and spoke in wonder. "What magic is this? I thought I was a lad again, and my father still alive."

Alan thought of riding the green hills of his native Laueroc on his first pony. Hal remembered his mother's eyes. And Corin stirred in the sickbed and spoke.

"Father," he said dreamily, "hear the larks, how they sing." He sighed and smiled, turning his face to the imagined sunlight.

Bleys tiptoed to his side, and spoke in a hushed whisper. "His forehead is cool. He sleeps peacefully."

"The gods be thanked," Alan breathed, and started to weep again. But he was not ashamed. Except Corin's, not an eye in the room was dry.

Before they went to bed, Hal and Alan took one more walk to the stables. Alfie still lay in his straw, but fast asleep, breathing deeply and contentedly.

"Hal," Alan asked gratefully, "what manner of wizard are you?" But Hal shook his head.

"There is no magic here," he said, "except that which you yourself have wrought."

Chapter Seven

Though Hal and Alan slept soundly, they awoke early and ran at once to Corin's room. The sun was just rising, and all was calm and still. Corin lay sleeping, very pale, but with a peaceful face. By his side sat Lord Roran. He smiled at the two as they entered.

"I sent Bleys to bed," he whispered. "He is an old man, and needs his rest."

The keep faced to the south and east. Hal and Alan sat in a deep niche in the stone walls and looked out the window, now and then speaking to each other in whispers. Below them spread the shops and houses of the town. They could see the streets they had ridden so hastily the day before, and the town gates they had entered. To the east was the waterfront, where stood the masts of tall ships, for the Firthola were a seafaring folk; they worshiped brother and sister gods, Dunn of the islands and Dana of the tides. They had small interest in crops or herds, so they had built their stronghold on the Great North Cove, an arm of the sea which penetrated far into the barren northland.

The landscape was bleak enough, and the few small trees in view were dropping their brown leaves. But the rising sun which was finding its way through the haze turned everything to a golden shine, and gleamed on the gray sea water. Even these barren northern lands could be lovely. Hal and Alan felt a sense of peace and belonging which had not been theirs for many days.

As the last of the morning mist vanished and the sun shone clear and strong, Corin stirred and woke. They went to him. He looked into their still-tired faces, first puzzled, then dismayed.

"Ay," said Alan gently, "it is true; your father is dead." He sat on the bed and took the boy into his arms.

Corin lay very still, but he did not weep. At last he said, "Is your father alive, Alan?"

"Nay, Cory," said Alan softly. "He died a year ago."

"How?"

"He was killed, even as yours was."

"And your mother?"

"She died of fever when I was ten years old."

Corin thought for a moment, then turned to Hal. His face was firm. "And you, Hal? Is your father dead, too?"

"Nay, Corin, I have no father."

The boy was perplexed. "Then he is dead."

"Nay, he is alive. But he hates me, and would kill me if he could."

Corin was astonished, but then pity came into his eyes, as he realized that the only thing worse than the death of a loving father was to have no loving father at all. He searched for comfort for Hal.

"But your mother, does she not love you?"

Hal smiled, and his eyes focused on the past. "Ay, Cory, she loved me well."

"She is dead, then." The boy was discouraged.

"Ay, she is dead." Hal's eyes darkened, then glimmered with a brighter sheen as he looked away into the deeps of time. "But much that is sad can also be lovely, Corin. Let me tell you a tale." He settled himself at the boy's feet.

"Very long ago, when the enchantment of the Beginnings was still strong, the silver-crowned star-son Bevan fought the mantled god Pel Blagden and vanquished him into the dark reaches of inner earth. But the golden cauldron of eternal youth was shattered by that contest of wills, so that those who had called themselves immortal faced their long-delayed death. Bevan, who was still young, would not accept his doom, and took ship to seek

life across the western sea in Elwestrand. And his
mother, Celonwy of the Argent Moon, died when her time
came at the Blessed Bay, the estuary of the Gleaming
River, where he had left.

"Then her brethren came out of the hollow hills where
they had lived since the Mothers of Men took charge of
Isle. In all their ancient glory they came, and in daylight,
as men had not seen them for ten hundreds of years, and
they took a last long ride to the Bay to join their sister.
They went in cloaks of green samite with golden fringes
that touched the ground; jewels dropped like dew from the
foreheads of the maidens. From every rath there rode a
gold-torqued king and a golden-girdled queen with all
their court, and sleek spotted hounds paced at their sides.
The men wore tunics of pearly white and wine-red, and
some carried silver harps; columbine twined their heads.
They were named Follen the Stag-son, and Geryon the
Western King, and Fearn of the Seven Stones, and many,
many more. Among the maidens was one who went in
midnight hue, Menwy of the Sable Moon; her black
horse was all trapped in tiny silver bells. And all of those
riders were fair and young at the start of that processional,
and old and yet fair at the end.

"They rode on steeds of white and wheat-color and
barley-red and musteline and gray. The horses' hooves
were tipped in gold, and wherever one stepped there
sprang up a flower in the form of the crown that Bevan
had renounced. For the gods loved Bevan, though he had
cost them their immortality, because he had avenged the
dishonor done when Pel turned his power to evil. So as
they rode they left Bevan this legacy, and it bloomed
and remained long after they had gone to dust around the
Blessed Bay.

"Five hundred turnings later, Veran sailed back to Isle
with the crown of Bevan his ancestor, and found the
lowlands of Welas growing golden with the flower that
folk now call by his name. But not long after, Herne and
his henchmen struck Isle like a blight. Wherever they
came the fair flower sickened and died, for that was the
end of that age of peace. But some were gathered by wise
folk, and kept and dried; and even after all the years its
virtue is what gives you life today, Corin." With an effort, Hal brought his gaze back to the boy. "Those mighty
ones of old made shift to leave the veriest spring and surge

of their lives in their legacy, and because they cheated death of it, their shades still wander the dark fir woods near the Blessed Bay, unable entirely to rest. Your life was bought ages past, Cory."

For a moment the room rang with awed silence. "Never have I heard that tale," Roran exclaimed, "even from the bards of Romany. Are there no gods left in Isle, then?" His voice was yearning.

"Those gods were only mortals who were rich in the power of the Beginnings," Hal said quietly. "It may be that there are true immortals somewhere. . . . But what are gods, my lord? The fragments we worship?"

Roran did not have to answer, for a serving maid entered with a steaming dish on a tray. His lordship helped her place it by the bed, and Corin looked with surprise at the richly clothed, handsome man who spread a napkin like a servant. Alan made the introduction. "Cory, this is Roran, Lord of Firth, in whose home you lie. My lord, may I present Corin, son of Col the Smith." Corin attempted a recumbent bow, and Lord Roran shook his hand.

"You are a brave lad," he said, "and I hope you will soon be better. Now try a cup of soup and some bread. It is very light, baked especially for you by Hulde in the kitchen, and if you don't eat it she'll cut off your head and use it in the meat pie."

After Corin had eaten, they left him under Bleys's care, for he was still very weak. Hal and Alan bathed in hot water, a rare luxury, and breakfasted, and went out to the stables, where they found Alfie on his feet again and devouring incredible amounts of hay and oats. The groom shook his head in disbelief. "Never have I seen such an appetite," he said. "I fear he will make himself sick."

"No fear," Alan said, grinning. "He has a stomach of iron. I only hope that Lord Roran can afford his keep."

For the day they left Alfie and Arundel in the stable to rest, and they themselves spent their time lazily, napping almost as much as Corin did. On the following days they took the horses into the exercise yard, and themselves joined the young men of his lordship's garrison in the practice yard. There they played at mock swordfighting, quarterstaff bouts and many other sports. Though

they were younger than most, they found that they could
more than hold their own.

The days passed smoothly and quickly. Corin ate well,
and rapidly regained his strength. Hal and Alan spent
most of their spare time with him. When they were not
there, often Robin was, and the boys talked readily of
favorite pastimes. Sometimes Alan tried to teach Cory
chess and Hal talked with Robin. He was interested in
the dark, lively boy, so much like his father—fierce and
hawklike, passionate, yet kind and just. Though they did
not realize it, Hal and Robin were somewhat alike. Both
were sometimes moody and temperamental. Alan, with
his more even disposition, preferred Cory, who was a
courteous boy, intelligent but not quick. Two boys more
unlike than Cory and Robin would be hard to find: one
the lightest of blonds, sturdy, thoughtful and methodical;
the other dark, slender, talkative, emotional and sponta-
neous. Yet they took to each other, for they were both of
good heart.

By the end of the week Corin was up and walking
around a bit, and in a few more days he was almost back
to normal, spending most of his time with Robin. Hal and
Alan began to look anxious, wanting to be on their way
toward Welas, but not knowing how to leave.

One day in the middle of the second week, Hal was
riding Arundel in the exercise yard. He did not use saddle or bridle. Horse and master thought and moved as
one, and as they cantered and circled, spun and leaped
against imaginary enemies, both enjoyed themselves.

Lord Roran came and leaned on the fence. His was a
heart too great for envy, so he looked on in pure wonder
as Hal trotted over to him and dismounted. "If that stallion were trimmed and groomed," he said, "he would outshine any horse in my stable."

Hal thanked him for the compliment. "I keep him
rough not only against the weather, but so that folk may
desire him the less." Then, simply because it hung heavy
on his mind, he said what he did not know how to say.
"We must be leaving soon." He spoke miserably.

"Where will you go, Hal?"

Hal shrugged evasively. "Where the road leads me."

Lord Roran frowned. "I do not mean to pry, Hal, but
from what you told Corin, I understand you do not have
a home."

"There is no door open to me."

"And Alan; does he ride with you because he, too, is homeless, or for friendship?"

"Both."

Roran knew instinctively that his offer would not be accepted, but he made it nevertheless. "Then why do you not stay here? I would be proud to shelter two such valiant youths as you."

"I could be happy here," Hal said quietly, "but I cannot stay. I—we—have a. . . ." He searched for a less formal word, but could not find one to suit. "We have a quest."

"But what of Corin?" asked his lordship, growing excited. "He is too young to go wandering around Isle. Already his young heart has had as much peril and sorrow as it can well bear at this time. He needs rest, and warmth, companions of his own age and the guidance of older folk. Let him stay here," said Lord Roran eagerly, taking Hal by the arm. "We are all fond of him, especially Robin. And I believe they are good for each other, and learn from each other. The lad will be treated as my second son. . . ."

Hal regarded the fiery man with great relief and wondering affection. "You have read my mind," he replied. "It has been a great worry to me, the care of the boy. The choice, of course, must be his, but I will be surprised if he does not choose to stay."

They talked it over with Alan, and he, too, was relieved and pleased, though he knew he would miss the boy. That evening, when they were all gathered together, Lord Roran put the case to Corin, inviting and indeed beseeching him to become a member of his household. Corin turned to his first friend.

"Alan?" he questioned him. "Must you go, indeed?"

"Ay, we must go," Alan answered. "I shall miss you, Cory, but it will gladden me to know you are well cared for by good and loving folk, not out in cold and danger."

"Pray abide with us, Cory," Robin begged softly.

"It would hurt my heart to leave you, Robin," Cory said, "yet I long to be with Alan as well. But if I must choose between you, I will stay, for that is what you all wish."

"I would like you to stay," Alan agreed firmly.

So it was settled. And since there was no sense in torturing Corin with preparations, they left early the next morning. Roran and his lady presented each of them with new clothing, new fur-lined leather boots, and handsome chain-link supporters for their swords. They wore warm new cloaks, and they found their horses packed with extra blankets and a plentiful supply of food, almost more than they could carry.

Hal and Alan mounted quickly. Though it was still autumn, it was bitterly cold in these northern reaches of Isle. Their farewells were short. "The love of the gods go with you," said Corin.

"Farewell, you rascals," said Lord Roran. "Remember, this is one door that is always open to you, no matter why or when."

"Be careful!" called Robin.

As they rode away, they looked back. Their friends stood in a row, waving, and as they turned to go they saw Lord Roran take Cory's hand.

They headed south and west, back across the rocky ridge of the Cove, toward the Marches. For two weeks they angled across a sere, almost uninhabited expanse. This was Arrok's domain, and his mounted men roamed it constantly. Hal and Alan rode watchfully, ate their food cold and slept by turns, shivering through the chill nights, for to light a fire would have been to invite unwelcome guests. Arrok was a warlord by blood, from the metal-worshiping tribes of the Northern Barrens, and he was still more raider than overlord. His own people were his enemies, for he had betrayed them by extortion and conquest. So he turned his warriors both against them and against the gentler folk of Isle.

Twice Hal and Alan sighted his patrollers in the distance and were able to speed away from them, out of sight beyond the horizon of the flat land. But presently the land turned rolling, with thickets and groves of stunted trees. Alan glanced at Hal with a tired smile, for soon they would be out of the Marches and into the heartland of Isle. But, beyond a rise, five of Arrok's men rode quite close to them before they saw them.

The warriors came at them, whooping, out of a brush-screened dimple of the stony land. Hal and Alan did not turn or come to bay, but shot away southward, almost upsetting the startled riders. The patrollers thundered after them, jabbering excitedly at the thought of a chase. But after a while they were silent, finding they could not gain.

They galloped for hours, into the afternoon, with Hal and Alan holding their horses to a steady, rhythmic pace and the pursuers straining behind them. By midafternoon, even at the lope, they had left Arrok's men half a mile behind them. At dusk, they would speed the pace to lose them.

But as the sun dripped, Alan called tensely, "Alfie's taken a stone in his hoof, I think. He's lame."

The horse was hobbling, though still galloping as fast as he could. Hal frowned and loosened his sword in the scabbard. Arrok's warriors drew closer behind them.

"Look!" Alan exclaimed. "How can that be Forest?"

A solid-looking mass of varicolored trees rose invitingly in the distance. Hal whistled softly.

"We must have come farther east than I thought," he called. "Courage, Alfie!" He spoke to the horse in his strange language, and Alfie lowered his lean head to plunge painfully on.

The pursuit was almost upon them when they reached the trees at last. Hal spun Arundel and drew his sword, thankful for the protection at his flanks. Alan guided Alfie to a sheltering trunk and did the same. But Arrok's men turned away at the fringes of the Forest and galloped back toward Rodsen. Hal blinked into the setting sun.

"Huh!" he grunted, puzzled.

Alan was already off of Alfie, checking his hooves and legs. He removed a sharp stone and led the limping horse deeper into the Forest, patting him. Hal followed on Arundel. In a moment they found themselves descending a steep wooded slope to a hidden valley.

"Is it a haunt, Hal?" Alan murmured.

There was a change in the air, hardly definite enough to be called a fragrance, but something clear and fresh. They straightened and smiled at each other in wonder. When they reached the floor of the valley, they found an ordinary scene: a clearing with a bubbling brook, some sheep and a milk cow, a small cottage, a garden plot. Yet something was very special about this serene dell. The velvety grass fairly shone in the lee of the forested slopes, as if lit from within. Tiny golden flowers in the grass sparkled like jewels. The water in the brook shimmered silkily, and the very wood of the cottage glowed like finest ivory.

"Hal," whispered Alan, "is this valley enchanted?"

Hal was about to reply when out of the cottage came a woman, very old, yet straight and strong. She carried a pan of bread for her flock of chickens, but stopped and smiled when she saw them. At her smile, Alan's suspicions vanished.

"Mireldeyn, Elwyndas, come in!" she called. "It has been a long time since I had company."

"Think of nothing, ask nothing, but only enjoy," Hal told him as they forded the brook and dismounted near the cottage.

The woman fed them eggs, and porridge with honey; the simple meal seemed to them the ambrosia of the gods. They spoke of birds, perhaps, that come and go in their seasons, and of trees, the royal apple and the noble rowan, and of the Lady, the Rowan Lady on her Forest island of many trees, and of the Very King. All knowledge was theirs, and yet they could never remember exactly of what they spoke. That night they slept under a crescent moon, and their dreams were the color of springtime, though autumn burned all around them. The next day the old woman sat at her loom. Her web was green and golden, silver and black, but Hal and Alan could scarcely bear to look at it; afterward they knew only that it was lovely. They worked outdoors, tending the garden and gathering wood for the fire. Evening fell scarcely looked for, and the passage from day to darkness seemed a rhythm smooth as breathing.

They could easily have stayed there forever. In the valley, all of Hal's plans and cares were forgotten, for time did not nudge at him; time was like a still pool into which he looked, sitting apart. He could almost have forgotten that other world just beyond the trees, where thin streams of moments forever rushed and circled past. But the old woman knew of that world, perhaps better than her guests. The next morning she packed their saddlebags with fresh bread, eggs and cheese. Without ceremony they went on their way, and they still did not understand the meaning of their names. They slowly climbed the steep slopes, picking their way through the trees. There was no beaten path.

When they left the valley, the world seemed brown and dreary beyond bearing. They rode slowly southward along the western side of the leaf-littered Forest, quite silent. It was not until afternoon that they began, haltingly, to talk.

"We never asked her name," sighed Alan. "Or else I cannot remember. . . . And what were the names she called us?"

"I don't know. How long were we there, I wonder? I could almost believe the year to have come and gone, full circle. But surely the snow would have fallen there as elsewhere, and I remember nothing but sunshine."

"We were there two nights; I remember the moons," Alan said. "How drab everything looks! I could almost wish we had never found that valley, for it makes our lot in this world seem the harder. . . . Yet a happiness lingers, like a dream after waking. Is it enchantment, Hal?"

"Nay, only very great good fortune. That is a place, Alan, that has not been touched by the blight of the Dark Kings, but has been overlooked since the beginning of the Age or before. Do you remember the little yellow flowers in the grass?"

"Ay."

"They were Veran's Crown—gone from Isle seven generations now. Perhaps that woman is as ageless and timeless as the place itself."

The next ten days were the most miserable they had yet spent together. The east wind had brought the autumn rain, and it poured steadily almost every day and night. Their clothing and blankets were soaked through, and the cold, damp wind chilled them to the bone. The Forest turned to a stark, sodden nightmare of slippery, rotting leaves. It was impossible to start a fire from the dripping wood. Alan and Hal rode all day in the rain, slept in it at night, and lived on cold, wet food. Their tempers flared or were sullen, and even the horses drooped as they plodded along.

When the rain finally stopped, the cold wind continued. Soon their noses were clogged, their ears ringing and their heads aching with cold and wind. It took several days for their blankets and clothing to get really dry, and even a campfire was small comfort in the squelching Forest. So sometimes Hal and Alan went to one of the village alehouses to share the warmth of the evening fire. Their appearance usually caused a silence at first, but Alan had a friendly knack for inspiring trust, and folk talked to him freely, mostly of their crops or their lords.

One lord that was often mentioned was Pelys of Celydon. He was always named with respect, and his tenants were envied. The two travelers did not like to inquire too closely, but it seemed that Pelys was one of the more powerful lords of the Broken Lands, this hilly, central portion of Isle. Celydon, his manor, was situated on the Rushing River, and its fields were surrounded by the Forest—an odd chance, since most lords drove the Forest back from their lands.

It did not take Hal and Alan long to give up thoughts of pushing on to Welas through the winter. They agreed that Celydon should be their destination. Riders and horses alike were in need of shelter. And if fortune were with them, Lord Pelys might prove to be an important friend both now and in years to come.

It was dusk, several days later, when they finally looked down on the manor of Celydon from the fringes of the Forest that ringed its meadows and tilled land. They both felt a pang of longing, almost of recognition, as if they had known the place before, as if they were coming home. Celydon was not a walled town with a walled castle, like Whitewater, or even a walled town with a keep, like Firth. Instead, the Rushing River was dammed into a gentle meander through the folds of the bottomland, and on an island amid its curves stood Pelys's stronghold.

"It is sturdily built," Hal declared.

The fortress was of stone, as solid as if sculpted from the earth itself. Yet there was something peaceful about the quiet look of the place. The water shimmered, and Hal thought he glimpsed treetops within the walls. The manor village was ranged along the riverbank and along a dirt track which crossed a drawbridge to the island castle's tower-flanked gates.

"Tall and serene," Alan agreed.

They turned their attention to the village, which was likely to tell them more than the castle. The cottages seemed snug, and the yards were neatly kept. Apparently the lord of Celydon gave his folk the time they needed to look after their own affairs.

Suddenly Alan whistled. "Am I blind, Hal, or do I miss seeing a gallows?"

It was so. Never before had they seen a manor village where the gallows was not prominently placed. There were no whipping posts, either, no branding pit, stocks or pillory. Even in Alan's beloved Laueroc a gallows had stood, though only once in his memory had it been used, to hang a murderer. But here was a manor that threatened no harm to any soul.

It was a risk, riding into a strange manor. No one would know or care if they never came back out of those iron-sheathed gates. But warmth and food, and perhaps a sense of fate, drew them. With a wondering glance, Hal and Alan rode down the hill toward Celydon.

book two
CELYDON

Chapter One

The two travelers were surprised to be greeted by the empty street and dark cottages of Celydon. And they were startled anew when a blaze of fire shot up on a hilltop beyond the castle. One by one, wherever the land was open, the summits bloomed into flame. The newcomers had been living in isolation so long that it was a moment before they understood the fires.

"Hal," Alan exclaimed, "it must be the eve of November!"

It was indeed the time of the ancient festival of the dead, one of the four quarter-days of the turning year, when in the perilous transition of time all things of Other pass freely to the world of men and must be held off by fire. On the eve of May, the half-day, cattle were driven between the fires to charm them against harm or disease; and on the eve of November the slaughtered cattle were offered to placate the dead into repose during the dark winter months. There would be a feast while the fires raged.

Hal and Alan rode across the drawbridge to find the gates of Celydon fortress open, and folk thronging in the courtyard, awaiting the circling dance. They noted at once how healthy the people looked, how they were well

84

though plainly dressed, and no maimed victims among them, as were to be found at many manors. All eyes were turned with curiosity upon the young riders, and a few smiled a welcome. The old gatekeeper met them and courteously asked them their business.

"We come to request a boon of your lord," answered Hal, "but it seems he must be engaged."

The man shook his head. "He will turn no stranger from his door unanswered. Go see him now, and I shall hold your horses."

"Let no one touch the gray, or come too near," Hal cautioned, "for he is trained to know no hand but mine."

In the keep a page showed them the way to Lord Pelys's chamber. He sat in a comfortably furnished room overlooking the crowded courtyard, reading a book near the window. He was a small, shrunken man, with wispy gray hair and beard; yet his face was hardly lined, and his eyes were sharp and piercing, like those of a bird of prey.

"My lord," Hal began as they entered, but the lord interrupted him at once, impatiently.

"Now, now, come over here and let me look at you in the light, and I warrant I'll answer your question faster than you can ask it. So," Pelys said as they drew near the window, "tanned with a year's sun and wind, and worn with travel and weather. A bit pale under the tan; have you not been well, hah?"

"Nay, my lord," Hal began, but he was cut off again.

"You're a handsome pair of rogues. Brothers, hah?"

"In a manner of speaking, my lord," Hal answered, smiling.

"In a manner of speaking! Tell me plainly, are you brothers or not?"

"Only by pledge, my lord."

"Tush! I would have sworn you were brothers! Ay, but of course you are nearly the same age—about twenty?"

"Younger, my lord. We are both seventeen."

The little man's bushy eyebrows raised until they nearly touched his hair. "Never have I been so mistaken! Well, well, then give me the hands, and we'll see if I can do better."

They extended their right hands. "Nay, nay, both of them, it tells more so," he exclaimed, and, examining their callused palms, he looked up with respect in his eyes. He spoke more slowly. "These have known the hoe, the scythe, the ax and other tools. They have also known the sword and the quarterstaff. Yours," he went on, laying a finger on Hal's brown thumb, "have known the bow also. But one thing here puzzles me greatly. What is this?" He pointed at the small scar on each left wrist.

Hal and Alan glanced at each other and smiled, but Hal spoke a little sadly. "My lord, I cannot tell you."

"Cannot or will not, hah?" he snorted, then suddenly pierced Alan with his gaze. "What of you, hah? Cat got your tongue?"

"Nay, my lord," Alan answered, startled, but had no need to say more. The little man leaned back, regarding them with sudden mellowness. "So, so, what you came to ask. You look a bit washed out, you two, by the rain, and knocked about by the wind, and pinched by the cold. You are welcome to stay here as long as you like. Join us for the feast tonight, but you must sleep where you can; all the beds are filled. In a few days, when my guests have gone home, I shall speak with you again. Is that what you wanted, hah? Food, warmth and rest?"

They told him that indeed it was, and were trying to express their gratitude when the air was rent by the sound Hal most dreaded—Arundel's angry scream. He turned and fled headlong down the stairs, with Alan on his heels. As they fought their way across the crowded and tumultuous courtyard, they could see Arundel searching for escape from a young man who followed close after him. He was soon cornered in the buttress of a wall, and turned at bay against the stranger who hounded him. He reared as far back as he could, avoiding the outstretched hand, and as the youth took yet another step toward doom, Arundel struck him in the chest with his forefeet, sending him sprawling. He reared again, but Hal faced him, commanding *"Nelte,* Arun, nay!" Alan dragged the youth to safety, and the horse stood sweating and trembling as Hal petted him gently. *"Alle,"* he murmured, *"alle,* Arundel." ["Softly, softly, Arundel."]

"Is he hurt, Alan?" Hal asked, but even as he spoke the youth roughly threw off Alan's anxious hands and sprang to his feet. "That horse attacked me!" he cried. "I demand—"

"He seems all right, Hal," Alan remarked, straight-faced.

"I will have satisfaction!" the young man blustered.

"Silence, Rafe," commanded a voice which, though not loud, at once drew the attention of all. Everyone looked up at Lord Pelys in his window. The old gatekeeper spoke.

"My lord, the young gentleman instructed me to let no one touch the horse, but Rafe would not listen. Nor did the horse strike him until he gave it no other choice."

"Thank you, Bonar," said Lord Pelys. "I give this order: no one in my household is to touch this horse without the permission of its master. Rafe, report to your duties, and in future keep your hands off things that do not concern you."

Hal sighed, and glanced at Alan, then said what he felt he must. "My lord, we bring trouble to your abode. We had better leave."

"Nonsense," snapped Pelys. "Take your horses to the stable, and see them cared for. I think you will have time to wash before dinner."

Friendly hands picked up the baggage that Arundel had scattered in his frenzy, and the gatekeeper directed them to the stable. There they introduced Arundel to the head groom and some of his staff. Flann was a quick man, neither old nor young, who could only be described as having "horse sense." He soon had Arundel rubbed dry, fed and bedded in the stall next to Alfie, though this required some rearranging. He chattered cheerfully and insultingly to both horses while he worked. Hal and Alan could not keep from helping, so the horses were quickly cared for.

"Never fear, they will be well kept here," Flann said, smiling into their anxious eyes. "Nor will your mettlesome gray be troubled. When my Lord Pelys chooses to command, he is obeyed. He uses no tortures to enforce his will, but all his folk love him so well that if Rafe were to defy him no one would speak to him for weeks. So be easy about your horse. And as for this slab-sided hay chomper here," he added, slapping Alfie affectionately, "he shall be well fed."

Alan laughed. "How did you know he loves to eat?"

"He winked at me," said Flann, winking at Alan.

Hal and Alan put their things in the hayloft of the stable, where Flann said they could sleep. They changed into their best clothes for the feast, fastening their swords around their waists with the chain-link belts Roran had given them.

"I hope we don't cross Rafe again," Hal said ruefully. "What did I do wrong, Alan? We saved his life, yet he was angry."

"I think," Alan mused, "that perhaps he was frightened—and being frightened can make a person very angry."

"But if he was afraid of Arundel, why did he approach him?"

"I did not say he was afraid of Arundel," Alan retorted gently.

When they arrived in the great hall, most of the benches were already filled. They found some space with a group of young men, perhaps a little older than themselves. Rafe was with the group; he glared at Hal and Alan, but said nothing. The others were cordial enough, though puzzled by the strangers with their sky-blue tunics and their bright swords and their air of self-possession usually found only in leaders of men.

The feast could not begin until Lord Pelys arrived. A signal was finally given, and everyone stood. Hal and Alan nearly gasped in their astonishment; Lord Pelys could not walk. He entered the great hall in the arms of a remarkably large and muscular retainer. Though he was placed in his seat like a babe in its high chair, such was the dignity accorded the man, and the love his people bore him, that no one so much as smiled. With him entered a maiden, a slender girl with long, dark auburn hair flowing down her back, who took the seat to his right. Food was offered to the dead, and then the living were served.

The feast took hours. There were a variety of soups, baked meats and capons, jellies and preserves, pastries, bread and cakes. There were baked apples and apple tarts, dried fruit, relishes, sauces and gravies. Villagers kept going in and out, eating by turns and tending the hilltop fires. Hal and Alan kept their seats, though they could not taste more than a quarter of the dishes that passed them. By the time the puddings and custards appeared, they were almost ready to trade their overfull stomachs for the growling bellies they had brought with them from the Forest.

During the meal they talked with the young men at

their table, who they found were volunteer novices in his lordship's guards and garrison. They spoke mostly of their training, but during a lull in the meal Hal asked one of the questions that had been teasing his mind.

"If it is a thing to be spoken of at this time, could someone tell me how Lord Pelys lost the use of his legs? If it is not well to be spoken of, then forget I asked."

"It was done in battle," answered a tall, lanky fellow by the name of Will. "He took a spear through both legs above the knee, and though he lay abed, they never healed."

Others spoke further of Pelys, and piecemeal his history became known to the two who listened. His father, the late Lord Pelynger, was remembered by the older villagers as a typically overbearing, selfish manor lord. His wife was a good woman, but browbeaten by her husband. The boy, Pelys, was their only child, and from the first he was a dreamer, drawn to strange talk and old books but not to the sword and the practice yard. The father tried hard to mold him in a more manly frame, but the boy was stubborn in his own way, and insisted on leading his life as he saw fit. On the day Pelys came of age, he left his father's manor for a wandering life. He was not seen again for many years. He returned at last to Celydon as a middle-aged man, tough and weathered, a few days before the old lord died. The first thing he did—even before the funeral—was to tear down, with his own hands, the gallows which had stood for so long. Then he distributed among the villagers most of the food and gold his father had been hoarding for years. Many thought him mad, but everyone loved him for it.

A week later, the peaceable village was invaded by Lord Nabon of Lee, who anticipated an easy victory over this daydreaming son of Pelynger. But he and the people of Celydon soon found out that somewhere Pelys had finally learned how to fight. His folk rallied behind him and sent Lord Nabon home to Lee with broken armies. But Pelys was carried home with shattered, wounded legs.

Such was the magnetism of the man that all loved and obeyed him, even though he was crippled. He married a beautiful young woman half his age, the Lady Rowana. Their love, folk said, was touching to see. She died in the birth of their first and only child—a girl.

"Then the maiden by his side is his daughter," Hal said.

"Ay, the Lady Rosemary, fifteen years old."

Alan had noticed that often Hal's eyes had been turned her way, though from the distance it was hard to discern if her features were fair or not. But their attention was soon drawn by the ceremonies of soot-maiden and yew-king, willow-queen and the long, shuffling circle dance. The dancers went in crowns of elder with tapers set in, and the dance lasted until the tapers had burned to the base, almost until dawn.

At last the dancers filed out to the hilltop fires, and everyone else trooped up to pay their respects to Lord Pelys and the Lady Rosemary before leaving for home and bed. As they drew near the dais, Hal and Alan were able to get a better look at Lady Rosemary. Alan acknowledged her to be fair. But Hal noted her lovely clear skin, the color of palest fawn, and her richly dark eyes, fine, regular features and lips which hinted at fullness without being sensual, just as her brows suggested character without being willful. Everything about her breathed of the womanhood which slumbered just beneath the surface of this girl child of fifteen. Something in her had been whispering to Hal all evening, and his blood was racing as he came before her.

Alan sensed his excitement, and glanced at him as they made their bows. He saw Hal fasten a curiously intense gaze on the maiden—a stare, indeed, but full of such soft courtesy that Rosemary returned it without alarm. For a fleeting moment she felt—what she could not tell. But the moment passed quickly, broken by Pelys's warm greeting.

"So, my hearties," he was saying, "you are looking better already. Have you found a place to sleep?"

Alan answered, for Hal seemed not to have heard. "We are sleeping in the hayloft, my lord, with great thankfulness."

"So you are sleeping with the gray beauty, hah? I hope he is not upset by his adventure of this afternoon."

"Oh!" Rosemary broke in involuntarily. "You are the ones with that horrible horse that tried to kill Rafe!"

"He is well, my lord," Hal answered, then spoke to the lady with a slow smile. "My horse would not hurt anyone, my lady, unless someone tried to take him from me."

"Have no fear of me," she laughed. "I plan to stay well away from him."

"Pray forgive my daughter," Pelys smiled. "She has been frightened of horses since a very early age, and nothing can cure her of it. Sleep well, now."

They walked back to the stables in silence. Alan at once wrapped himself in his blanket and relaxed gratefully in the sweet-smelling hay. But Hal paced restlessly, finally stopping and standing interminably before the tiny window which aired the loft. The moon was at the full, and a bright beam shot past his head and lighted a square of hay, much as it had lighted the filthy straw of his dark Tower cell a year and a half before.

Alan could stand it no longer. The candles of the dancers were still wheeling before his inward eye like circling stars or the blurred turnings of fate. And though he thought he knew the answer, he felt compelled to ask the question. "Hal, whatever is the matter?"

Hal sighed. "You will say that I am out of my mind," he answered, without moving.

"I already know that," Alan rebutted lightly. "Tell me. It can be no worse than hearing you talk with the spirits of the night."

Hal smiled slightly at that, and turned toward him, speaking hesitantly. "That girl . . . Lady Rosemary . . . she is my . . . my *mendor*."

"Your *what?*"

"My destiny," Hal tried to explain. "But more than destiny. For every man there is one woman who is his *mendor*. Rosemary is mine. She is the woman with whom my thread of life is entangled. It was so before time began. It is written in *Dol Solden*. Whether it is for good or ill, I do not know. Whether for happiness or sorrow, I do not know. But it is so."

"How can you be so sure?" asked Alan, astonished.

Hal did not answer.

"What are you, Hal?" Alan wondered more slowly. "Warlock, or seer, or something more? How did this vision come to you?"

"I do not know, Alan, before all the gods, and my own as well, I do not know!" Hal appealed to his brother with an intensity of pain that startled even Alan, who was used to his moods by now. "By mine eyes, I have been no friend of sorcerers or charlatans. . . . Sometimes it seems to me that I can see clearly into the mysteries of all lives —except my own."

For her part, Rosemary was puzzled as well.

"Father," she asked, "who are they?"

She was visiting in his chamber, as she always did before going to her own. He knew at once who she meant.

"By the Lady, I do not know," he answered. "They told me nothing, but I surmise that they have been traveling. They seem to be fine young men, though much is strange about them. I think I shall enjoy having them here."

He did not say that his curiosity was piqued by these young men as it had seldom been before. Nor did he mention that he, too, had noticed the exchange of glances between Rosemary and Hal. He had long been an inquisitive man, but age and his afflictions had turned his knowledge to wisdom. He had learned to wait in patience for his answers.

Chapter Two

The next few days went by quickly. They saw Rosemary often as she walked or rested amidst the fruit trees and flowers of the castle garden. To Alan's surprise, Hal did not make any excuse to speak to the lady. Instead, he busied himself away from her. There was much work to be done in the aftermath of the feast, and the newcomers made themselves useful wherever they could, whether in the kitchens, the stable or the workshops. The servants soon learned to know and like these strange youths, who wore the swords of nobility and worked like peasants.

But Rafe, the elected captain of the novice guards, did not like them at all. He missed no opportunity to make life unpleasant for them, especially for Hal. His men held no grudge against the strangers, but they were loyal to their captain, and were careful to do Hal and Alan no favors. When the two entered the practice yard, they were surrounded by a wall of silence broken only by occasional taunts from Rafe. Sometimes he challenged them to bouts at swords or quarterstaffs. Rafe fought hard and impatiently, and always lost, which did not serve to improve his temper. With his men he was quite different; skillful, controlled, a fine fighter. Rafe was a good captain, fiercely proud of his men, and Hal and Alan could see why he commanded loyalty.

On their fourth day at Celydon, as they were exercising the horses, Lord Pelys was carried toward them in a chair between two retainers. Lady Rosemary walked by his side. Hal and Alan rode over to give them greeting; Rosemary stiffened at the approach of the horses, but held her ground. As the two reached the fence, Hal gave a soft command Alan had never heard before, and Arundel dropped to one foreknee in a graceful bow, arching his lovely neck and touching his nose to his extended hoof. Lord Pelys laughed delightedly, and even Rosemary could not help smiling. Arun straightened, and Hal slid to the ground.

"What a beautiful creature," Pelys said admiringly. "But alas, your horse is not nearly so handsome, Alan."

"Speak truth and say he is downright homely," Alan replied. Alfie shook his bony head menacingly, and rolled his eyes. "But for all his rough looks, and his mischief, and his monstrous appetite, I would not trade him for any horse in Isle." Gratified, Alfie stood still and arched his skinny neck proudly. Lord Pelys laughed again.

"By my poor old body, I believe he understood every word you said," he chuckled. "But tell me, Hal, how did your steed come to be so wary of strangers? Was it born in him, or was it a part of his training?"

"Both," said Hal, stroking the handsome gray. "When I first met Arun, he was only a colt, but no one could come near him. The horse dealer had him tied head and feet in order to control him, though he was nearly dead of starvation, fright and abuse. I bought him and nursed him back to health. He gave me his love, and by his own consent I trained him. At first he would never willingly let any hand touch him except mine, but if I commanded it, he suffered it. Since then he has learned to know other friends, such as Alan. The hand of a stranger he avoids, by his own instincts and my training, so that he cannot be stolen from me. But he is not vicious, and he never has hurt anyone except Rafe, who cornered him."

"I do not intend to come near him, nevertheless," Rosemary said firmly, betrayed by the fear in her eyes. Hal frowned in pity and spoke to her gently.

"How did you come to be so frightened of horses, my lady?"

"I do not remember. But my father tells me that when I was very young, I was knocked down by one. And to me they still look about twenty feet tall."

"Ay," said Pelys, "she was only a little thing, playing in the courtyard, when a skittish horse broke its halter and tumbled her over. She was not hurt," he went on, glancing at her affectionately, "but the fright did not go away. It is a shame, for there are few things you are likely to find so necessary in this world, my dear, as a horse."

Alan had kept an eye on Hal, but he saw no hint of Hal's interest in Rosemary. If anything, he seemed a trifle too courteously aloof.

"Come to see us later this afternoon," Pelys said as he prepared to go, "and share supper with us."

So Hal and Alan headed toward the keep near suppertime, wearing their good clothes. A servant ushered them into a dim little study where Pelys sat with Rosemary. A compass lay on the table before them, and they were examining several yellowed charts.

"So, so, there you are," cried the little man. "This is my haven of learning, where the lass and I do our lessons. You like it, hah?"

Hal's eyes were darting about excitedly. The walls were lined with books to the ceiling, and all sorts of odd things. Suddenly his eyes fixed on one object, and he strode across the room.

"A plinset!" he cried.

His lordship raised his eyebrows at the strange word, but, turning in his chair, he saw that Hal was reverently touching a stringed instrument hanging from the wall, almost hidden by the bookshelves.

"Ah, is that what it is called?"

"Ay," answered Hal. "But you are not of Welandais blood, my lord?"

"Nay, nay. That is an instrument of Welas, then?"

"Ay. How did you ever come by it?"

"A minstrel brought it here last winter, and played it marvelously well. He took a fever, and died within a few days, though we nursed him tenderly. That was a hard winter." Pelys leaned back meditatively.

"I wonder who he was," murmured Hal.

"He was near middle age, fair of skin and hair, very

handsome and gallant, though he did not wear a sword. . . . I wonder, too."

"Did he not tell you his name?"

"Nay, he smiled when I asked him, and said I was to call him what I liked. So I called him Bard. I believe I could have called him Lord." Pelys eyed Hal whimsically. "Can you play that instrument, lad?"

"Ay," answered Hal, dazed.

"Then take it. It is yours. And play us a tune!"

Hal took it down and cradled it in his hands, almost fearfully. "I thank you greatly," he said, "but you can hardly know the value of the gift. This was fashioned by Llewys Lay-Maker, in the time of Veran, first of the Blessed Kings. It is centuries old, and none better has been made since. A generation ago it would have been kept in the treasure room of the Old Castle at Welden, along with the crowns of kings." He gently dusted it as he spoke, and as he turned it to the light they could see its graceful carving.

"Then is not now," said Pelys sadly, yet with keen interest in his eyes. "And no one deserves it better than you, who value it highly. It does no good there on the wall. So take it, lad, and play us a tune."

Hal swallowed, and tuned its eight strings as carefully as if they were made of gossamer. Then he sat down and strummed thoughtfully. The strings sounded in a bittersweet mode as Hal began to sing.

> All my days have passed in vision
> Of a place beneath western skies
> Where peace flows like golden honey
> From the comb.
> But the east shows forth my burden
> With the rays of bright sunrise.
> In this land of strife my fate is
> Long to roam.
>
> All my nights have passed in dreaming
> Of the haunts of the sinking stars,
> Where the people of the reaches
> Make their home.
> But the east blots out night's gleaming
> Of fair Elwestrand afar,

Where the elf-ships cleave the silver
Salt-sea foam.

Elwestrand! Elwestrand!
Be you realm but of my mind,
Yet you've lived ten thousand lines
Of soaring song,
Elwestrand. Is the soul more sooth
Than that for which it pines?
Are there ties that closer bind
Than call so strong?

All my journey's passed in faring
Through a bitter glare of gore.
But the gloaming in the west
Imparts its calm.
When the burden seems past bearing,
Sunset speaks of ancient lore,
Of immortal sadness healed
With mortal balm.

Elwestrand! Elwestrand!
Where untamed the white steed runs!
When my life's last light is gone
Will you be mine?
Or, my weary battle won,
When I reach the setting sun,
Must I farther journey on
Some rest to find,
Elwestrand?

The notes of the song died away, and the four sat in silence for a moment. Pelys stirred, shaking himself from a reverie. "Wherever did you learn to play?" he asked admiringly.

"My mother taught me. She was Welandais."

Although his curiosity was aroused to its highest pitch, Pelys knew instinctively that further questions would be unwelcome. With the courtesy of a true gentleman, he changed the subject. "It has long been my wish that my daughter might have some musical instruction, but there is no one here to teach her. Can you?"

"*What?*"

"Tut, tut, teach her, lad, of course!"

Hal looked across at Lady Rosemary. "I shall do my best," he pledged, stupefied.

"Good," snapped Pelys cheerfully. "Come in the afternoons, whenever you have time. Now let us go in to dinner."

He clapped for his retainer. The meal was waiting in a towertop chamber that caught the light of the setting sun. Hal sat at the table with the plinset in his lap.

"I understand you have been working around the castle," Lord Pelys remarked as he passed the sweetbreads. "It is not necessary, you know. You are my guests."

Hal was still spellbound, whether from the plinset or the lady Alan could not tell. "We do not like to be idle while others work," Alan replied. "And we have learned much that is of good use."

"Well, well, since you have chosen to make yourselves useful, you must let me give you some pay." Hal was stirred back from his trance to protest, but Pelys insisted. "Only a few pence, forsooth! I will not have you destitute. And I will not have you overworking, either," he added, shaking a menacing finger at the two. "You are not to neglect your exercise, your horsemanship, or your education. I have a library of fine books here, and I would take it kindly if you would use them."

"Thank you, my lord," they murmured, stunned by this peculiar manner of bestowing favors.

"And I expect you to eat with me now and then," growled his lordship. "You can't always be eating in the kitchen or the barracks. Moreover, I expect you to start sleeping in beds. I shall have rooms prepared for you."

To Alan's surprise, Hal seemed disconcerted. "With your permission, my lord, might we stay on in the stables? I mean, if Alan will. . . . It is handy to be near the horses."

Wondering what the real reason was, Alan quickly agreed. Lord Pelys looked pained, but graciously acquiesced.

"Won't you freeze?" asked Rosemary, astonished.

"Perhaps," Hal answered wryly.

They walked back to the stable that night in silence. Hal stopped at a carpentry shop for a soft rag and a little flask of oil. In the loft he set their lantern well away from the hay and started carefully rubbing the dust and grime from his ancient, precious instrument.

"We could move into the keep if you would rather, Alan," he said without looking up. "It is a lot to ask, that you should spend your winter in a drafty stable."

"It is not drafty," Alan lied. "We can be very comfortable here."

"With no fire?"

Alan shrugged wearily. "So we will be cold. I dare say you had your reasons."

"I don't know my reasons!" Hal shouted, flinging down his rag. "I don't know my own mind anymore!"

"Well, if you must shout," Alan soothed crossly, "that is reason enough."

Hal sighed and went back to his plinset, cleaning and polishing, bringing the rich lights out of the dark golden wood. His frowning face softened, and he whistled tunelessly, lost in some happy dream, Alan thought, of the lady perhaps? It was seldom that Alan saw him so content.

Late that night Alan started awake at the sound of a muffled, inarticulate cry. Hal was sitting up, staring at nothingness, with teeth clenched and sweat beading his forehead, trembling and straining against invisible bonds. Alan reached for him in alarm, and felt all the muscles tensed like steel bands beneath his skin. "Hal!" he cried, shaking him. "What is it?"

The spell broke, and Hal went limp as a snapped string, though quivering worse than ever. "Oh, Alan!" he gasped, covering his face, torn between relief and anguish. Alan held his shoulders, and in a moment his trembling stopped. He lay back, breathing heavily.

"What happened?" Alan asked gently.

"Nothing. A bad dream."

"Hal, you are impossible," Alan sighed. "Did you know this was coming, then?"

Hal was silent so long that Alan thought he was asleep. "I know nothing," he said hollowly at last. "Not even the names of my fears."

The next day, Hal took his plinset and walked to the keep to see his lady.

The weeks passed quickly. Hal and Alan almost forgot there was a world beyond the castle island. Late fruit was still being gathered from the sheltered trees within the walls: sorb, pear, quince, apricot and apple. While Alan helped with the work, Hal and Rosemary would settle themselves with the plinset at the sunny roots of a red-tipped tree. Hal's greatest pleasure was the daily music lesson. Rosemary, daughter of Rowana, was a beautiful girl, bright, blooming and sunloving as the plants around her. She was very fond of both Hal and Alan; they were like brothers for her, and perhaps Hal was her best friend.

Hal was content to leave it that way, or so he told himself. It would hardly be worthy of him to make the lady love him, only to leave her on a harebrained quest after a distant throne! But his heart and his loins would not listen to this reasoning, and Hal ached for her every waking hour, so that sometimes he thought he would go mad if he did not speak. And at these times the thought whispered in the back of his mind: why struggle? Why not throw off his burden, settle in this peaceful forest clearing, marry, and be happy? He knew well enough that such happiness was only a dream; but the dream gnawed at him.

Sometimes when he was away from her, Hal could forget the struggle within him. But at night it harrowed him with worse dreams. Leuin of Laueroc's tortured face would call to him through the smoke and glare of burning towers, through screams of men and horses, through dripping veils of blood. Sometimes Hal thought that the lord of Laueroc was still dying in torment, never to rest. The nightmares were almost unbearable, and to avoid them he would pace the courtyard until late at night, like a feral creature courting the moon. Even there Leuin's gentle voice reached him: "Hal, be brave!"

Another thing troubled Hal's rest: the continuing problem with Rafe. To Alan, the situation seemed more ludicrous than painful. Throughout his youth he had known the love of family and friends, and the animosity of one person did not trouble him. But to Hal, who had known only the hostility of the King's court, Rafe's dislike was a painful reminder of the past. Often he wondered how he inspired such hatred.

One fine sunny day in the middle of November, Hal and Alan paired off in the practice yard. Others worked out at a distance. Rafe joined the group and greeted Hal with a sardonic comment; suddenly the day turned tense and bleak. When Rafe challenged Hal to a bout at the quarterstaff, Hal glanced at Alan with a wry half-smile as he accepted. The others, instead of continuing their exercise, clustered around the combatants. From whispered conversations, Alan realized that bets had been placed on the outcome.

The fight, however, went much as usual. Rafe attacked Hal furiously, and Hal calmly parried his blows, giving not even an inch of ground, biding his time. As the bout progressed and Rafe's frenzied thrusts continued unavailing, Alan could see that he was beginning to weep with fury. The group of spectators, which earlier had been in merry spirit, now stood silent and abashed.

Hal felt Rafe's discomfiture, though he was hardly to blame for it. To bring the bout to an end, he shifted his feet and raised his staff for the attack. At that moment Rafe, with all the force in his body, swung his booted foot into Hal's midsection. Hal doubled over and fell. But as Rafe, beside himself with passion, was aiming a second kick at Hal's head, he was hauled off bodily by those who had once been his friends and followers. Such foul play as they had just seen was unforgivable. They said nothing, but held him against the wall while tall, quiet Will stripped him of his captain's badge. Then without a word they left him and turned to Hal.

Alan's had gone white with anger. He wanted to kill Rafe, but first he had to care for his friend. Still, as Hal started to breathe easier, the blood-red fury gradually cleared from Alan's mind. The volunteers gathered around anxiously, and Alan realized that no physical punishment he could inflict on Rafe would be as severe as the mental anguish he now felt, knowing he had lost the respect of his men.

"How are you, Hal?" asked Will.

"I'll live," Hal managed to reply.

Will hesitated. The others seemed to be looking to him to voice their thoughts. "Hal, Alan," he said, "I think we are much to blame for this."

But Hal silenced him lightly. The young men crowded around him while, leaning on Alan, he hobbled inside. Rafe was left alone in the corner of the practice yard.

From that time on, Hal and Alan were welcomed by the volunteers, and Rafe was shunned. The night of the incident, the young men elected Will as their new captain.

None of them would speak to Rafe, even if spoken to, for he had disgraced the unit. Hal and Alan were lionized, and found their new, false popularity almost as unpleasant as their former state. After a few days, however, things settled down. But Rafe no longer came to the practice yard.

Chapter Three

It was near the end of November when the first snow fell. Hal and Alan were helping with the evening cleanup and rubdown at the stables when the news came. Everybody turned out into the courtyard to watch the big, downy flakes dropping through the dusk. The bit of a child in each of them stirred with excitement, and a festive mood prevailed.

Then came a new cause for stir, as the gates opened for a stranger, a trader of horses with his string of nags in tow. One look, and Flann's happy face twisted into a scowl. The trader was an unwashed, rough-looking rascal, and his horses were listless and half starved. But as he drew his wares toward the stable to see if he could drum up some trade, there was one pair of bright eyes to be seen, one lifted head. Third from the end of the line was a pretty little filly—or at least she could be pretty, once the dirt was cleaned off her and some flesh put back on her bones. Something in the intelligent eyes, the flaring nostrils and the small, beautifully shaped head reminded Alan of Arundel. He heard Hal catch his breath sharply between his teeth, and glanced at him. Hal's face was fearsome.

"An *elwedeyn* horse," Hal breathed, "here, and in such

a state! I must help her. If I cannot buy her, I will steal her."

With a hard hand, the horse trader showed off his nags one by one, but got no offers. As he came to the little filly, he seized her roughly by the forelock. Her eyes blazed as she bared her teeth and snapped at him, and he struck her with his fist on her tender nose. "Stop that!" Hal cried, starting forward.

The filly plunged and reared, breaking her leather harness. It seemed impossible that such power could be in her emaciated body, but somehow she fought her way clear. As the horse trader backed away in fright, she darted and circled about, searching for a way out of the crowded courtyard. Folk fled from before her, but Hal stepped into the clear. He spoke to her softly in his strange tongue, and she froze in her tracks, trembling, staring at him with astonished hope beginning to replace her fright and despair.

Hal spoke to her again: *"Mir holme, Asfala, nilon tha riste."* ["Come to me, Asfala, no one will hurt you."] She ran to him like a beaten child, hiding her head under his arm as he whispered to her and gently stroked her heaving flanks.

The stable hands slowly ventured from their retreat against the courtyard walls, staring in wonder. The horse trader once again began to bluster. Alan bit his lip and began to unbuckle his sword; it was the only thing he had to bargain with. But Flann saw the gesture and stopped him with a touch and a jaunty wink. Then he strode toward the horse dealer with a swagger quite unlike his usual gait.

"Saucy little piece of horseflesh ye have there," he remarked.

The fellow boasted of the trouble he had had with her. He had traded for her because of her looks, sure he could tame her. He had tried force and starvation, but to no avail.

"I might take her off yer hands," said Flann casually. "I wouldn't mind having a crack at her." His hand twitched in midair, seeming to flick an invisible whip.

The horse dealer's eyes gleamed. He and Flann dickered eagerly, but Flann shook his head and turned away at the trader's asking price. He flung a taunt at Hal, who fell in with the farce and glared at him in reply. The horse trader liked Flann, who appeared to be just such a bully as himself, and he was anxious to be rid of the troublesome filly. He soon offered to sell her for a reasonable price, and Flann counted the coins into his hand. Then he hit the man, hard, in the face, knocking him to the ground.

"Now get you hence," Flann grated, showing all his disgust, "you and your nags. And if you ever visit these parts again, I'll have you locked up until you rot. Now go!"

The fellow did not stay to argue the point. He scurried to his nags and rode out, glad of the coins in his pocket. Flann let out a grunt of fury, shook himself, and turned toward Hal. The filly had stopped trembling, and was watching with interest the departure of her former companions. The stable hands returned inside. Hal, Alan, Flann and the filly were left alone in the gently falling snow.

"She is yours, Hal," the groom said, "by her own choice."

"Flann," Hal answered huskily, "I can never thank you enough. I would have given anything for her." And before Flann could protest Hal added, "I will repay you when I can."

Flann gestured impatiently. "The value of the work you have done here is already more than the amount I paid for the horse. Let us have no more nonsense."

The next few days were busy ones for Hal. Early the next morning the filly got a bath and a grooming. As caked dirt and dead hair were brushed away, her coat began to shine a beautiful sorrel color with dapplings of a darker russet. She was painfully thin, but her bone was sound and her mouth good. Hal talked to her constantly, even when he was with Arun in the next stall, and she became much calmer and more cheerful. Alan came over when he was done with Alfie, and at Hal's bidding she let him pat her.

"We shall just let her rest for the next few days," Hal said. "Then we shall start taking her out."

"What do you intend to do with her?" Alan asked.

Hal was silent for a moment. "She has fine spirit," he said, "but she is sensitive, and gentle as a kitten. She cannot be broken by force; she would die first. But once she has given her heart, she will do anything." Hal paused and looked at Alan, seeking and finding reassurance that he would understand. "When she is feeling better, I shall tell her about my lady. Perhaps she would like to be her horse."

So he truly does speak to the animals in a language they understand, Alan thought. He was not entirely surprised. In the half a year he had known Hal he had come to believe, and hope, things he would never before have considered possible.

"You call her Asfala," he said. "What does it mean?"

"It means 'Daughter of the Wind.' "

For several days it continued to snow hard, and the exercise yard was covered to a depth of nearly three feet. The wind blew snow about, and it was bitterly cold. Alan and Hal burrowed deep into the hay in their loft at night, warmed also by the body heat of the horses below. They spent long hours working in the stable, feeling indebted to Flann for the price of the filly and the cost of her feed. But he continued to make light of their obligation.

Flann marveled constantly at the progress Asfala was making. She was gaining flesh rapidly, and was much more content than before. Flann and Alan were now her trusted friends, and she had learned to tolerate the stable hands, for none of them were allowed to be careless or rough. Now that her fear was gone, she was beginning to exhibit coy, playful tricks, and was likely to become the pet of the stable.

"How ever did you do it, Hal?" Flann asked one day as Asfala nibbled his sleeve. "She came here a shivering, frightened wretch, and within a week she has become a happy-go-lucky little lassie."

"How not?" replied Hal evasively. "There is nothing to frighten her here." But Flann looked at him askance and grunted his disbelief.

When Hal and Alan took their own horses to exercise, Asfala went along, looking like a pony beside the larger horses. She followed close by Arun's side and listened carefully to everything Hal said. Alan had the uncanny feeling that the filly was learning how to behave under a rider without ever having been mounted.

"Do you plan to ride her, Hal?" he asked.

"Nay, I'll let my lady have the training of her. It will make a bond between them."

Though they made no effort to keep the filly a secret,

there was little risk of Rosemary's seeing her before it was time, for she never came near the stable if she could help it. And the occasion was not too far off. The Festival of the Winter Solstice was only seven generations old in Isle, having come with the Easterners and their stargazing sorcerers. But it was embraced by the countryfolk, for it was a gift-giving time and followed conveniently on the slaughtering of the pigs. In Nemeton, the court people called it the Natal Day of the Sacred Son, and they gifted and feasted and sacrificed victims in his honor. But through most of Isle folk called it only Winterfest, a welcome break at that bleak time of year.

The festival day came at last, and Hal was up before dawn, brushing and shining Asfala until any ordinary horse would have kicked in protest. She, however, seemed to enjoy the proceedings. After her dappled coat was shining, her mane and tail were brushed until they were smooth as silk and her hooves were rubbed with oil. Alan and Flann watched in amusement as she arched her neck and minced about, tapping her shiny hooves. For a finishing touch, Hal brought out yards of green ribbon and plaited it into her mane and tail, ending with a love knot just over her left ear. Asfala looked as if she would burst with vanity, and cocked her head under her pretty bow, drawing applause from a circle of grinning stable hands. Then at last they were ready to go to the keep.

Pelys and Rosemary were sitting in the study when Alan came to them with an air of suppressed excitement, requesting that they follow him to the audience hall on the ground floor. Pelys clapped for his retainer, and they went downstairs. When they were seated, Alan rapped on a window. In a moment there were odd shuffling noises outside the door.

"What in the world!' Rosemary began, but her breath was taken away as Hal led Asfala in. The gentle beast wore neither bridle nor halter, but followed Hal freely. He led her to the foot of the dais where Rosemary sat, dumbfounded.

"Here is my gift to you, my lady," he said. "Her name is Asfala, which means 'Daughter of the Wind.' There is not a better-mannered horse in all of Isle. I know there are other things you would rather have, but pray accept her with my heart's regard, for she is all I have to give you."

"She is lovely," said Rosemary in a tight voice. She would sooner have jumped in the river than touch that beast. Yet she knew that if she did not pet her, Hal's feelings would be gravely hurt. So she clenched her teeth and walked toward Asfala, a nervous smile on her face. But as she approached, a marvelous thing happened. Asfala backed away from her and whisked behind Hal, looking out over his shoulder with big brown eyes, like a child peeping from the shelter of its mother's skirts.

"Why, she's afraid of me!" exclaimed Rosemary, astonished.

Behind her back, Alan and Pelys were grinning broadly, but Hal's face was perfectly sober.

"She's a bit shy at first," Hal admitted, "and she is very sensitive. You must be very gentle with her." Then he coaxed the filly, "Come out, Asfala. The lady will not hurt you."

As the filly daintly, hesitantly emerged from behind Hal's back, Rosemary saw her as if seeing a horse for the first time. She noticed the shining hooves dancing on the floor, and the beautifully colored, soft and glossy coat. She noticed the mane and tail, smooth and clean as her own hair, plaited with green ribbons. She saw the delicate, finely shaped face, the pretty, pricked ears, the soft nose, the intelligent eyes. The filly's head stood little higher than her own. Amazed at herself, Rosemary realized that she longed to comfort this beautiful creature, so gentle and timid. She held out her hand to Asfala, wheedling. "Come here, Asfala. Poor little thing, I wouldn't hurt you."

"Here," said Hal, handing her a lump of bread. "Give her this."

The horse's touch on her hand thrilled her. Asfala took the bread courteously. Delighted, Rosemary patted the smooth cheekbones and the arched neck. Pelys looked on in astonished joy. Hal allowed himself to smile now, and he took the lady's hands and placed them on either side of the filly's head.

"Now, Asfala," he said seriously, "this is your mistress, and you are to follow her and obey her. Be a good horse." Then he stepped back. "Walk away from me, my lady, and see if she does not follow you."

Rosemary walked toward her father, and Asfala trotted

after her like a big dog. "Father!" she cried happily. "Look! She likes me!"

Pelys nodded, his sharp eyes glowing like hers. "Well, well, lass, let us take her to the saddlery."

This was across the courtyard, near the stables. Pelys rode in his chair, and opened the door with a large key. In the dim light, generations of saddles and trappings shone with mellow splendor. There were war saddles and hunting saddles, ornate pleasure saddles, large and small, each richly tooled and ornamented with metal and jewels. With his quick eye, Pelys picked out a few that might do.

"She will need one neither too large nor too heavy," he mused. "That was your mother's, with the rowan design, but she rode a larger horse. I believe that one yonder might be the very thing." He pointed to a smaller saddle made of soft, plain russet leather. Hal fetched it down. The matching bridle had a light snaffle bit and reins trapped in green cloth, in the old fashion.

"If I mistake not, it belonged to the second daughter of the fifth lord," said Pelys pensively. "It was meant for a pony, but it seems broad enough, for ponies are often as broad as horses. But we shall see."

Alan had found a green saddle blanket. Hal put the things on, and Asfala looked lovely in her green and russet finery. She flirted her head as if to exclaim, "See me!" and Rosemary laughed out loud.

"Fally the filly!" she quipped. "I should call you Folly rather, for you are as foolish as any woman in a new dress!"

"Would you like to get on her?" Hal asked. "She has never been ridden, so she will not know exactly what to do, but then, neither will you."

"Never been ridden!" cried Rosemary. "Won't she fight?"

"Well, she had never been saddled, either," smiled Hal. "If you like, I will try her first, but I may be a bit heavy for her."

"Nay," protested Rosemary, "I will try."

Hal took her by the waist and set her in the saddle sideways, for her skirt was not divided. Then he laid his hand on Asfala's neck and slowly walked her off. Asfala paced sedately, and after a few strides Rosemary's frown of concentration changed to a pleased smile. She waved to her father, who was sitting at the saddlery door with Alan. The auburn sheen of her hair was almost identical to her filly's russet dapplings.

"Alan," asked Lord Pelys, "why did Asfala shy away from Rosemary?"

"Because Hal told her to."

"By the mighty moon, he has the wisdom of the Gypsies," murmured Pelys. "But what marvel is this, Alan? Never have I seen a horse so spirited, yet so gentle and trusting."

Alan did not know how to reply. What, indeed, was an *elwedeyn* horse? And what was Hal, that he could capture one's heart with a few words?

By afternoon Asfala was back in the stable, resting contentedly, and everyone else was on tenterhooks, waiting for the feast. In the kitchen and great hall grand preparations were in progress, but no one was allowed to look. Hal and Alan were shooed away like the village children. Pelys and Rosemary had given them gifts, shirts of fine white linen with gold embroidery at collar and cuffs, and they had nothing to do but put them on and wait. In the early winter dusk, they joined the rest of the folk gathered outside the keep.

At last the big wooden doors swung open, and they all poured in, each person individually stopping to gape at the sight. The big oil lamps which hung from the rafters were not lit, and no smoky torches burned. Instead, the hall was lighted by hundreds of fragrant wax candles ranged along the tables and in sconces on the walls; more of the rare, expensive tapers than anyone had ever seen. In each of the several huge fireplaces a roast pig lazily turned. Instead of the usual rushes, the floor was strewn with sweet-smelling evergreen boughs.

As they had at that other feast two months before, Hal and Alan sat with the volunteers. But this time Rafe was not there. Since the incident at the practice yard, he had become almost a recluse. If he was at the feast, he was sitting elsewhere.

The food was sumptuous, but not quite as overwhelming as before, since no one planned to appease either the gods or the dead; this gathering was purely for pleasure. After the soups and breads, the roast pork and roast apples, the fruits and tarts and nuts were all consumed, the tables were cleared and everyone sat back to wait for entertainment. There were some jugglers and gymnasts, and a mime. And of course there had to be speeches by the steward, captain and other castle officials. Pelys spoke last, and drew roars of approval by stating his intention to say nothing, since it had all been amply said before. From behind a curtain he called a troupe of musicians, and with great enthusiasm the tables and benches were pushed to one side for dancing. Couples lined up for the "carrole."

Rosemary's eyes sparkled, and her foot tapped impatiently. She dearly loved to dance, but there were no guests of noble rank present, or at least no one who claimed noble rank. . . . It was not always easy, being the lord's daughter. So she caught her breath as Hal approached her, faced him with shining eyes as they took their places on the floor. What a marvelous day it had been; first Asfala, and then music and Hal.

Without need of much thought, Rosemary had long known that Hal was special. He was unfailingly gentle and considerate, yet beyond his courtesy she had sensed great courage. He was purposeful, yet at times she thought she discerned loneliness and doubt. He was mysterious, and masterful if need be. He was the only one who had dared to ask her to dance. And even in his dancing he could not be faulted. He was looking at her, and a strange, soft fire burned in his gray eyes. The smile faded from her face to be replaced by a gaze of rapt attention. For a moment, time stood still.

Three people noticed that long, intense meeting of eyes as the slow dance drew to an end. One was Alan. One was Pelys. And one was Rafe, who stood by himself near the door. Something snapped inside him as he watched this upstart who danced with the lord's daughter. Pushing his way through the happy crowd, he strode up behind Hal and seized him roughly by the shoulder.

"Take off your fancy shirt, whoreson churl, and fight!" he grated. "Steel against steel, and to the death, you—"

"Hold your tongue!" Hal commanded. "Have you no thought of the lady?" Alan had reached his side now, and he turned to him. "Alan, would you escort the Lady Rosemary back to her seat?"

"Take off your shirt and fight, bastard lordling!" Rafe hissed. It was the custom to strip for hand-to-hand knife fighting, so that the blade might more easily slip between the ribs. Rafe already was naked to the waist, muscles sliding under smooth, glistening skin. Knowing from many defeats in mock battle that he was no match for Hal with a sword, he carried instead a steel dagger with a ten-inch blade.

Except for a few women's cries of protest, the crowd was deathly silent as Alan led Rosemary back to her seat on the dais. Though Hal spoke softly, his voice sounded throughout the hall.

"Are you mad, Rafe? It is a festival day! Do not mar this happy gathering with bloodshed."

"Coward," crooned Rafe.

Will came forward, followed by other volunteers. "Rafe," he said gently, "you are not yourself. Pursue your quarrel if you must, but to do so at this time does you dishonor."

"Even you are on his side!" howled Rafe. "Look at him! Can't you see that he is a changeling; some heartless, evil spirit in human form!"

So that is what preys on him, Alan thought. *The strangeness. The eyes.*

No one else understood what Rafe meant, but many thought him mad. Will scowled with pity. "Come away, Rafe, or we must take you by force."

"You cannot deny me my blood-right!" Rafe cried. "He must answer the challenge!"

Will looked at Pelys, who nodded sadly. According to the custom of the times, Rafe's demand had to be met. Will and his men reluctantly joined the ring of spectators.

"Very well," said Hal. "Then let us go outside, where the women and children need not watch."

"We will fight here where all can see, lady's man. Are you afraid of dying a coward's death?"

Hal sighed, then turned and spoke to Rosemary, his words traversing the hall. "My lady," he requested, "pray leave."

Her face was pale, but her eyes flashed. "I am staying," she answered, lifting her head proudly.

"Fight, coward!" taunted Rafe.

There was nothing else to do. Hal laid aside his sword and began to unlace his shirt. Will brought him a dagger.

Alan remained near Rosemary. He was not overly concerned about the outcome of the fight, for he knew Hal's ability. He also knew why Hal was so reluctant to fight, especially in front of Rosemary, and as the shirt came off he placed a steadying hand on her shoulder.

Her cry of shock was lost in the gasp that went up from all around. Pelys bit his lip, and even Rafe's jaw dropped. Back, front and sides, neck and upper arms, Hal's skin was etched and crisscrossed with the scars of a thousand wounds. But even in contrast with Rafe's smooth form, his tortured body had a grace all its own. Broad shoulders, well-developed muscles and self-possessed movement gave the onlookers an impression of power and beauty, like the well-weathered granite of a seaside cliff. Rafe felt a vague unease, a stirring of second thought. Then Hal dropped to a crouching, catlike posture, and the fight was on.

It hardly lasted long enough for Rafe to know what had happened. This was not one of those practice bouts in which he attacked and Hal waited while he wore himself out. Instead, Hal came at him in a blur of motion. Rafe struck at him hastily, but Hal eluded the knife with fluid grace, moving under Rafe's arm and grasping his wrist. The room spun around, and Rafe found himself on his back. A grip of great power crushed his hand; he cried out in pain, his fingers loosened and the dagger dropped. Then the blade touched his throat. He closed his eyes and waited for certain death.

But, unbelievably, no blow was struck. Rafe opened his eyes and saw two daggers, nearly point to point, stuck like a V in the rafter far above. The crowd was in an uproar. As he scrambled to his feet, he came face to face with his gray-eyed adversary. "Why did you not slay me?" he demanded. "From the day you first came here I have offered you nothing but enmity."

The crowd fell silent again as Hal spoke slowly, with lowered eyes. "You are a brave man, Rafe of Celydon. Even with the knife at your throat, you did not flinch or beg for mercy. It seems to me that my Lord Pelys may one day have need of you."

"So I shall," growled Pelys tartly, "if he ever regains the sense he was born with."

"If you really want me dead, or worse than dead,"

added Hal bitterly, "there is no need to fight me. Just carry news of me to the Dark Tower. You might soon see me in such torments as should satisfy even your hatred."

As he spoke, their eyes met and locked. Rafe probed those gray eyes with his own, and all his confused feelings came to one focus: he had been wrong. Hal was not a cold-blooded, calculating being in human form. He bore a gentle heart; he was no stranger to human emotions. In those eyes Rafe saw loneliness, longing and hurt. Suddenly Rafe realized that Hal rather liked him. Shaking, he passed a hand across his forehead, as if waking from a bad dream.

"I have been acting like a fool," he said brokenly. "These past three months I must have taken leave of my senses. Can you forgive me, Hal?"

Hal took his proffered hand with joyful relief. "If you will forgive my childish words. You are indeed a brave man, Rafe, and honest to your core. I want no better gift than your friendship."

They gripped hands before all present. Rafe turned next to Alan and took his hand in friendship also. Then he apologized to Pelys and Rosemary. "My lord, my lady, I beg pardon for my unseemly conduct."

"Put your shirt on, boy," snapped Pelys happily, "and let us have some merriment. Musicians, ho!"

As the fiddlers struck up a lively tune, and as the volunteers surrounded Rafe to welcome him back to their fellowship, Hal walked slowly toward Rosemary. He was grieved to see the pallor of her face. She had been pierced by the sight of his scars and the thought of the torment he must have withstood. She had been faint with terror when he flicked his knife into the rafters and moved empty-handed against Rafe. When the dagger was at Rafe's throat, many had turned their faces away, but she had watched stonily; a moment later she chided herself for her fear. Now that the fight was over, Rosemary felt weak. And still, ringing in the back of her mind, pushed there by the pressure of recent events, was the echo of that timeless moment with Hal.

He did not know what to say to her. He came to her with saddened heart, met her eyes, and suddenly the memory of that moment came back to both of them. Its warmth glowed in their faces and lifted their heads. Nothing needed to be said; they clasped hands to dance once more.

Thus it was that Hal did what he had vowed he would not do. The seed of love was planted in the young heart of the lady of Celydon.

Chapter Four

The next day Rafe came back to the barracks and the practice yard, for Pelys had let him know quite certainly that he was to do so. But he was hanging his head, though not sullenly, and all the volunteers tried so hard to welcome him that he grew more abashed by the moment. Will even offered to return his captain's badge, but he shook his head in red-faced shame. He could not face Alan or Hal.

After a few days of this, Alan grew anxious to talk to him. Many other people had the same thought, and Alan was finally forced to follow Rafe through the courtyard in order to speak to him alone. He cornered him against a buttress.

"First you were tireless in rage," he scolded, "and now you are as persistent in sorrow. When will I know your smile, Rafe?"

But Rafe looked more likely to cry. Alan gesticulated helplessly.

"Rafe, whatever is the matter? Can you not see that everyone likes you, even when you are being bullheaded?"

"Bullheaded!" Rafe burst out. "I must have been insane, Alan! I was like a rabid dog. And what if it happens again? I—I could have killed him, and I am not worthy to clean his boots."

"He cleans his own boots, and you are as worthy of that task as he." Alan settled back against the wall, seeing he had a long talk ahead of him. "Rafe, everything that happened is quite understandable."

"Understandable!" Rafe shouted.

Alan waved him into silence and plunged on. "Rafe, do you believe in goblins and nixies and that sort of thing?"

"Believe?" Rafe stared, not comprehending that there was an alternative. "I have lived with the unseen folk since I was born. What of it?"

"Well, think, Rafe! What was the day that Hal and I came?"

"The eve of November, when the denizens of the dark. . . . Ay, I thought that of him then, Alan, but no more! I—"

"Believe your senses, Rafe!" Alan interrupted. "What happened, that day?"

"You saved my life," Rafe said miserably.

"And you were angry, frightened perhaps. Why? What happened as I dragged you away from Arundel?"

Rafe covered his face with his hands.

"Rafe!" Alan urged him.

"Hal's eyes," he whispered. "They flashed like cold fire, like spook lights. I thought I was mad then, but perhaps I am mad now."

Alan nodded in satisfaction. "He spoke to the steed in the language of power, and you saw. No one else saw, or perhaps no one else had eyes to see, Rafe. Now let me tell you a tale."

They sat down on the cobblestones; Rafe was limp with unbelieving relief. Alan told him about his first meeting with Hal. "The horses ran away," he explained, "and perhaps I would have run too, if I had the strength—I can't say; it is hard to know what we might do when we are put to the test. But I held no credence in any things of Other then, whether gods, demons, warlocks or whatever. So I told myself that I had seen nothing, I was faint and confused. Hal took me into the Forest, to safety, and nursed me."

"To the Forest?" Rafe asked weakly. The Forest was a dark haunt of terror to him.

"Ay, the Forest. The touch of the Lady lies on it, Rafe." Alan told him more, something of the Gypsies, and the spirits, and Veran's flower. Rafe listened in awe. Hal himself came and sat down quietly with them as Alan finished.

"So, having seen what you saw, and believing what you believed—do you still think you were mad, Rafe?"

"But I was wrong," Rafe protested. "He is—he is good."

"I dare say I am not entirely evil," Hal acknowledged softly, "but I do not know all of myself, Rafe. Often I am afraid." He was thinking, Alan knew, of his sire, King Iscovar.

"And you had been taught, Rafe, that things of Other are evil," Alan pointed out.

"Things of Other!" Hal exclaimed wryly. "Is that what I have become now? Truly, I want only to be a man."

"You are all of that, and more!" Rafe defended him hotly.

"And I am your friend?" Hal inquired.

"And my friend." Rafe smiled sheepishly.

"Then do me a favor, Rafe, as a friend," Hal requested equably, "and forget pain awhile. No more gloom."

Rafe squared his shoulders and met Hal's eyes. "No more gloom," he promised, and they touched hands on it.

They talked again in days that followed, and became better friends than they would have previously believed possible. One day Rafe showed Hal something he had kept secret from almost everyone else, hidden among the tall thickets of his grandfather's overgrown pasturage.

"What a splendid horse!" Hal exclaimed. "And big! He will make you a charger, Rafe. What do you call him?"

"Night Storm. I have had him since he was a tiny foal. The mare dropped him and died, out in the dark and the thunder and pouring rain, up yonder, near the Forest. I carried him here and nursed him on goats' milk, day and night, all but diapered him. His mother was not one of Pelys's mares, of course; he cares for his animals better than that. I'm not sure where she came from, and I didn't try too hard to find out." Rafe smiled guiltily. "I hid the carcass."

The colt raised his sleek head and regarded them with

a kingly, appraising glance. He was more stallion than colt by now, coal black in color, long-legged, with a thick, highcrested neck and a strong spring to his haunches. "He's a runner," Hal murmured. "What are you going to do with him, Rafe? You can't keep him here forever."

"I know it. He's over three years old now, and never been ridden, because I don't know how to start. I love horses, Hal, always have; it was the child in me that longed to touch Arundel, that first day. And how I envy you your ease with him! But there's been little riding for me since my father died. One by one, his steeds were sold to keep us in food." Rafe looked away from Hal; his cheeks were flushed. "Now I am afraid someone will try to take this one from me, say I stole him. All because— because he is beautiful."

"No one will say that who knows you well." Hal glanced at him fondly. "And your rearing of him has given you the labor-right, Rafe. Take your horse to the castle, and let Flann help you with him. He is bored here, restless; can you not see it in him? He is thinking of kicking his way out of that tumbledown shed."

"Really?" Rafe stared at Hal with half-superstitious alarm. Though Alan had not told him so, he sensed that Hal could communicate with animals in some way he could not understand. He chewed his lip a moment, then made his decision. "Well, my name is black enough already, I suppose it can stand a little more scandal. . . . Come on then, Stormy." He reached for a rope, and the horse came gently to his hand.

"Will you help me with him, too?" Rafe asked politely as they led the jet-black steed back to Celydon.

"If you like." Hal eyed him humorously. "But you will do well enough without me, and then you will know you have trained him yourself, with only ordinary help. No wizardry."

"I never said that," Rafe murmured, ashamed to admit his relief.

"Small blame if you did. And anyway," Hal added lightly, "I have enough to keep me busy." An undertone of warmth crept into his voice, for he spent most of his time with Rosemary and Asfala, these days.

Rosemary was thrilled by the new turn in her life, and spent hours in the stables. She had everything to learn about horses, and Hal was very glad to teach her. He was touched to watch the communion that grew between the lady and the filly. Rosemary found her horse to be willful but loving, spirited and free but dependent on her for sustenance and comfort, a creature of moods and emotions like herself. In time, she grew fond of Alfie and Arundel also, and better understood the loving bonds between the beasts and their masters.

As Rosemary became a proficient rider, all three of them took long jaunts across the snow-covered meadows around Celydon, as far as the Forest rim. That encircling barrier embraced the manor as if the Lady of the Forest had given it her love; Hal and Alan felt safe from any harm in Celydon. They taught Rosemary how to jump her filly over low bushes. The icy winter air brightened her eyes and put blooms of color in her cheeks; Hal looked at her as if he could not look away. Sometimes Alan made excuses to stay behind, thinking to take himself out of the way of wooing, but Hal always insisted that he come along.

"Don't tempt me, Alan!" he would say earnestly. "You'll have Pelys after me with a mace."

Pelys looked on his daughter with pleasure. He had never seen her so glowing and happy. He reflected that this was not entirely due to the bracing outdoor exercise, for her eyes rested most often on Hal. But he also knew that Rosemary was hardly aware of her own happiness, and he trusted Hal with her innocence.

Hal also was as happy as he could find it in his moody nature to be, and he had regained his ability to sleep. Seeing so much of Rosemary, he had found contentment in learning to know her better every day. He liked her matter-of-fact approach to life, her warmth and fun-loving spirit, her patience and cheerfulness, her impulsive tenderness and even her occasional outbursts of temper. He loved the grace of her hair and face, her dress and movements. And he loved the poetry of her mind and soul. Yet, as sensitive and intelligent as she was, Rosemary was only dimly aware of what was happening to her, like a sleeper just drifting out of dreaminess.

The vernal Feast of Fires, the quarter-day, went by, and February drew to a close. Hal and Alan became aware that their stay at Celydon must soon end. Once more Hal woke shaking in the night, and once more he prowled the dark courtyard, torn between his desire to stay and the knowledge that he must go. His days passed in a trance of waiting. It no longer snowed, and the earth lay frozen, breathless for the spring thaw. Everyone caught cold, and longed for warmer weather. Hal paced restlessly through the shortening nights, sniffing the air like a creature of the wilds.

"The wind is warm, and out of the west," he told Alan one morning. "It will not be long now."

The next day the spring rains came and washed the snow away. For the next week the earth was a gurgling morass, and anyone who ventured beyond the courtyard was wet to the skin and muddy to the knees. But the rain was warm, and the softened earth smelled like spring. Slender green blades of grass started to appear.

One night the rain stopped, and the morning dawned clear and fine. It was traveling weather, and still Hal could not bring himself to leave. He vaulted onto Arundel and cantered out of the gates, fleeing toward the solitude of the upper meadows. Alan looked after him with anxious eyes, unable to help him.

As it chanced, however, Hal was not alone for long. As he neared the Forest, he heard a birdlike whistle, and a wondering smile spread across his face. It was not yet the season for birdsong. He answered the whistle and rode into the woods. There, standing in his path and smiling, was Ket, red hair blazing under his leather cap.

"Ye look sad, Hal," he greeted him cheerfully.

"No more," answered Hal as he sprang down from Arun. "Well met, Ket, you fox!" They gripped hands, laughing.

"Aren't you a bit far from home?" asked Hal.

"No home for the outcast," mourned Ket. He explained that he and his men had left their old haunts; they found game more plentiful on this side of the Forest, and life more peaceful. Pelys's folk were kind. But Ket had a warning for Hal.

"Ye would do well not to ride alone, lad," he said soberly. "There are kingsmen about."

Hal was stunned. It was as if a bloody corpse had been thrown into the peaceful pool that was Celydon. "What?" he stammered. "I—I have heard nothing about them."

"Oh, they leave off their pumpkin hats before they ride," Ket growled. "They have been spying about at the alehouses, looking for a fellow with a sword much like yers, Hal." Ket eyed the black and silver blade meditatively. "But they say he is a fair-haired man of middle years, perhaps carrying a kind of lute. . . . Still, they may have heard talk, as my men have, of a young blood with more scars than anyone deserves. Ye must be wary, Hal."

"Ay, well," Hal sighed, "I will be gone by the morrow, Ket."

"I have seen ye often, riding with Alan and the lady Rosemary," Ket remarked obliquely. "Ye wished to stay?"

"I must go." Hal sat a moment in silence. "I am not loath to tell you what you have already guessed, that I love the lady well, and my Lord Pelys also. If you had not by good fortune come to me, I would have come to you, for I have been troubled, and I have a great favor to ask."

"I will do whatever I can," Ket vowed.

Hal scratched at the dirt with a stick, trying to name his fears. "There is Nabon of Lee, for one," he said slowly. "From what I hear, he is making ready his armies to have his revenge on Pelys. To the north, Guy of Gaunt waits to pounce on whatever remains of both of them, which may stay Nabon's hand yet awhile. . . . But danger is more common than such warmongering lords. All I can say is, pray look after my lady and my lord while I am gone."

" 'Tis a small enough request from one friend to another," Ket smiled. "I will do my best. Where will ye go?"

"Where the road takes me. I shall see you from time to time, I dare say."

They chatted for a while longer. Then Hal returned to Celydon Castle and greeted Alan with a wry smile. "Let us pack our things."

"It's already done," Alan retorted.

They loaded their horses. Flann was shocked and sorry to find that they were going. But he could tell that they wanted no fuss, and bid them a quiet farewell. They went next to the barracks, and spoke to Rafe and Will. Rafe faltered, trying to tell them what knowing them had meant to him.

"I believe you understand me more completely than

anyone except Alan," Hal told him quietly. "I hope we shall meet again."

Rafe set his jumbled thoughts aside and voiced his feelings as best he could. "All the gods defend you, Hal. And if ever I can aid you in any way, pray call on me . . . my friend."

They asked Will to give their regards to their other friends in the barracks, the kitchen and the workshops. Then they reluctantly went to take their leave of Pelys and Rosemary. Hal cradled his plinset in his arms.

The lord and lady were at breakfast in Pelys's chamber. "The sun shines, and the wind blows warm, my lord," Hal said. "It is time for us to go."

Rosemary gave a cry of sorrow. "But where, Hal? And when shall we see you again?"

"Where the road leads me, my lady," Hal replied softly. "When we shall meet again, I do not know, but surely I will come to you if I am alive." He held out to her the precious instrument in his arms. "This is too old and valuable to suffer the weather and the chances of travel. Will you keep it for me, till I return?"

"But what will you have then, to comfort and cheer you?" Rosemary knew how Hal depended on his plinset when he fell into one of his desperate moods. "Wait but a moment," she said, and ran from the room.

Pelys regarded them quietly with his eyes that always searched for truth. "So you are leaving us," he said thoughtfully. "I am sorry to see you go, you two. You have brightened my winter greatly. I thank you from my heart, both of you, for a great many reasons." Hal and Alan were embarrassed, and glanced at each other sidelong. Pelys changed his tone abruptly. "Now, now, don't just stand there, you two! Give me the hands, quickly!"

Grinning, they extended their hands to him as they had when first they met him. "Ay, so you have taken up woodcarving, Alan, and smithying. What were the results?"

Alan brought from his pocket a hunting knife he had made for Corin, complete with its tooled leather scabbard. The polished handle in the shape of a horse's head shone darkly. Pelys admired it, and looked appraisingly at Alan.

"I believe you can do anything to which you turn your hand," he remarked. "Hal's works are of a different sort. . . . But am I never to know the meaning of this?" He pointed to the small scar on each left wrist.

Rosemary entered quietly and stopped near the door. Hal and Alan looked at each other. Then Hal spoke.

"It happened, my lord, that this summer past there was a terrible and wonderful night when I was greatly in need of Alan's comfort and love. Yet I felt that he had good reason to hate me. But he told me a marvelous thing, that he wished I were his brother and my blood ran in his veins.

"In the country of Welas, the West Land, where my ancestry lies, it is the custom that two men who wish to be brothers may make themselves so by a ritual that requires their trust and confidence in each other. Each must put a knife to the other's left wrist, where the heart's blood flows, and cut. And the wounds shall then be pressed together, thus."

He and Alan joined left hands somewhat as wrestlers do, so that their fists pointed skyward and their wrists pressed together. Each attempted, playfully, to pull the other over. This gesture, at once a contest of strength and a demonstration of affection, had become their habit of greeting each other.

"And so we did," said Hal.

"And so," finished Alan, "we are indeed brothers, as you say, my lord, though some may not see it so."

For once in his life Pelys was at a loss for words. Rosemary moved from her place at the door and came to his rescue. She held an intricately seamed leather sack with a long carrying strap. It was provided with tight fastenings, and it was so sturdily sewn and so well waxed as to be practically waterproof. Into this the plinset would fit as snugly as a turtle in its shell.

"Take this case, Hal," she said, holding it out to him. "It will keep your instrument from harm. But you must bring it back to me when you can, for it is not yet finished."

Wonderstruck, Hal accepted the finely wrought case. On the front, over the place where the strings would lie, shone a sunburst, delicately picked out in metallic thread, but only half done. He had never dreamed that she was making a gift for him. His eyes, full of emotion, met hers for a long moment. No words were exchanged between them.

"Tush, tush," Pelys broke the silence. "The day is grow-

ing older by the moment. Go on if you are going, you
two!"

They needed no further urging to move toward the
door. "All blessing be with you, my lord, my lady," said
Hal.

"Thank you both for everything," added Alan.

Then they were gone. As their footsteps faded down the
stairs, Rosemary bolted for the door, weeping. "Come
here!" Pelys snapped at her, as sternly as he had ever
spoken to her. Surprised, but still weeping, she came
slowly to stand before him. He reached up and took her
by the shoulders, shaking her.

"Are you a woman or a child?" he scolded her.
"Would you have him face his journey with a heavy
heart? Dry your eyes, quickly! We go to the battlements,
to wave them on their way." He clapped for his retainer.

Hal and Alan rode out of Celydon as soon as they
could, bidding only a quick farewell to the old gatekeeper.
They turned north, toward Rodsen, back the same way
they had come the fall before. As they topped the rise
near the Forest, Hal drew Arundel to a stop. He could not
bear to look back, but neither could he bear not to.
Slowly he wheeled Arundel, and on the topmost platform
of the keep he saw two tiny figures, one standing, the
other seated. Even at that distance Hal could not mistake
them, and as he smiled his relief, they waved. Hal and
Alan waved back, then sent their horses cantering over
the rise.

"Now, daughter," said Pelys, in a voice that was once
again gentle, "you may weep as much as you like." And
with his arms around her she did just that.

That night, miles to the north, Hal and Alan lay down
under the light of a young moon and a spring sky crisply
studded with stars. Hal slept well; better than he had in
months. He was on his way again, and he was relieved
that Rosemary had not taken the parting as hard as he
feared. The winter of inaction and inner struggle was behind him; the future was all that concerned him now.

But in Celydon, sleep came hard to Rosemary after a
day spent first in weeping and then in trancelike misery.
Though she was outwardly calm, her thoughts were whirl-
ing. The young moon which peeped in her window
mocked her with its serenity. Finally, like a pot suddenly

boiling over, she threw off her covers, stamped her bare
feet and padded off to her father's chamber.

He was sitting up reading, and he smiled as she entered
almost as if he had been expecting her. He patted the
bed, and she sat, sighing. "I can't get to sleep," she mumbled.

"Tut, tut, Rosie," he said, touching her hair. "Out with
it. What ails you?"

"Oh, Father," she burst out, "why did he not speak?
Why did he go? Was I mistaken, and does he not love me
at all?" She buried her face in her hands.

"Whoa, lass," said the old man, gently placing his hand
on her trembling shoulder. "One thing at a time. First of
all, do you love him or not?"

She glared at him in astonished annoyance. "Of course
I love him!" she shouted.

"Good!" smiled Pelys. "Fine spirit!" He grew more serious. "Never be ashamed to say it, Rosemary, and never
regret it, no matter what may chance. But does he love
you? What do you think?"

She was almost ready to burst with irritation, but sensing that he was testing her, she replied quietly, "I have
thought so."

"Then think so still," Pelys said. "Trust your feelings,
daughter. And, for what my opinion is worth," he added,
"I think so too."

A wave of relief swept over her. "Father, do you really?"

"By my beard, girl, would I say it if I did not? I thought
so before Winterfest. Indeed, I will even declare that if
he is not very much in love with you, then I am a suckling
babe, for I am as sure of it as I was of your mother's
love for me."

Some color came back into Rosemary's pale cheeks at
her father's tender words. She no longer spoke in desperation, but only in weary puzzlement. "Then why did he
go? Or, if go he must, why did he not speak?"

"Well, well, is it not obvious, Rosie, that there is something he must do? And that being so, would he speak to
you before he had done it? He is above all a man of
honor. And what has he to offer you? Only a wandering
life full of danger and heartbreak. Nay, nay, do not mistake me," he continued as she started to protest. "There

is not a better man in Isle, and I warrant you he will make his mark before long."

"But why did he not trust us?" Rosemary insisted. "Why did he not tell us where he must go, and why?"

"I dare say he has his reasons." Pelys fixed his daughter with a faintly humorous gaze. "Do you not have faith in him, Rosie?"

"Oh, Father!" she exclaimed in exasperation.

"So, I take it that you do. Then do you not think he will keep his promise, and return?"

She smiled slowly. "I dare say he will." Then she sighed. "But it is likely to be a long time."

"Well, then I shall say one more thing. Even if he had home and fortune waiting for you, and no barrier between you two except his own honor and wisdom, I think still he would not yet have spoken, for one reason: you are not yet ready. You are only newly awakened to love, daughter. Savor it, and let it season. Your life is yet very young, and though you are but two years younger than him in fact, you are many years younger in wisdom. He has known many a sorrow, if I mistake not, and this is your first. Do not pout at me, miss, for I speak simple truth, and it is hardly your fault. Indeed, you have made me proud of you, these months past."

"Proud of me!"

"Ay." He put his arm around her once again. "You have become a woman and a lady. He will think of you with pleasure while he is absent."

"Indeed, Father, it is a marvel that he thinks of me at all." She was dreamy-eyed. "My heart knows that he loves me; yet it is hard for my mind to believe. He is such a man as I have never known. . . . A warrior, yet gentle, wise and passionate, full of mystery and poetry and strange knowledge. Whatever does he see in me?"

Pelys smiled. "Always lovers wonder this. I remember how I marveled at the love of your mother, for she was a young beauty who had her choice of many, and I was a crippled thing more than twice her age." Rosemary patted him in affectionate protest.

"For the most part," Pelys mused, "we wonder thus because lovers are blind to the loved one's faults. But in your case, I believe you hit not far from the mark. I have seen many fine young men in my time, Rosie, but never

one as rare as he. There is a mystery in his eyes. . . .
I confess, I do not understand him, yet I know very well,
lassie, that you could not have chosen a better man. If
the gods let him live, perhaps someday we shall know
him better. Till then, we can only wait for him to fulfill
his quest."

book three
THE WEST LAND

Chapter One

The next day Hal and Alan turned westward, hoping that the kingsmen had been thrown off their track. They would cross the Broken Lands at the narrowest point to the Westwood, the other great Forest of Isle. Once within that shelter, they would turn southward toward Welas.

Their road to the Westwood lay across the lands of Guy of Gaunt. They were not in great danger, however, for the cover was good. The Broken Lands were criss-crossed by many streams which wound through wooded ravines, and the hills between bore crowns of trees. A hint of coming leaves cloaked their branches like a green mist, and a whisper of bloom clung to the hedgerows. This was the heartland of Isle at the dawning of the year; the spell of its beauty was strong. Hal and Alan traveled in quiet happiness. They were well provisioned, and reached the Westwood before they felt much need of fresh supplies.

By then the beeches had put out achingly bright green buds, and deer were everywhere. Hal and Alan rode steadily southward, trading meat for bread when they felt the need. Spring had become summer before they turned the corner of Isle. Gradually the land grew steep and precipitous, until one day the Westwood ended. They found themselves on the bare, rocky shoulder of the first mountain, looking down into Welas.

Hal's eyes sparkled as he pointed out the places that had been the food and drink of his mind since he was a little boy, but which he had never seen. Below them spread the lowlands of Welas, and in the distance shone the curves of the Gleaming River. To the westward was the dark mass of Welden, ancient home of the Blessed Kings of Welas, now defiled by the presence of Ulger, Iscovar's henchman. Mountains surrounded the lowlands on three sides, and in the distance one of them rose above the rest. Hal pointed to it reverently. "That is where we are going," he stated.

"Why?" Alan asked. "Do you expect to find your grandfather there?"

Hal hesitated. "It is hard to say what I expect to find there. That is Veran's Mountain." He stopped, as if that alone said all.

"Veran's Mountain?"

"Veran did what no one else has done: he ventured upon that mountain and returned unharmed."

"Indeed, is that so?" Alan gave him a wry glance, wondering what sort of strange peril Prince Gray Eyes was planning to lead them into now. He phrased his next question delicately. "What is so special about that mountain?"

"Folk of that time said it was the home of the gods, and worshiped it. Those who ventured upon its slopes came back witless. Some never returned at all. But Veran returned, and brought with him a bride so beautiful that folk called her the daughter of the gods, though she died a mortal death."

A year earlier, Alan might have laughed at this talk of gods. But now he looked at Hal sharply. "And you, Hal? Do you believe that yonder mountain is the home of the gods, who gave Veran their daughter and their blessing?"

"I believe in the One. But I have seen. . . ." Hal fumbled for words to explain his dreams. "I have seen other folk, fairer than sun or moon or circling stars. That mountain calls me, Alan."

To get there or indeed to get anywhere in Welas, they had to travel the lowlands, which were held by the captains of Iscovar's conquest of twenty years before. These were harshly oppressive lords, struggling to rule a rebellious people. Their men patrolled the county constantly, alert and heavily armed. Hal and Alan decided to ride by night. But even so, it was not long before Alan found himself caught up in an anguished search.

One evening at dusk, as they were making ready to travel, Hal vaulted onto Arundel and trotted half a mile to a spring for water. Only a tiny village stood near the trickle of water, and Alan did not think any harm of the venture. But Hal failed to return. Uneasily, Alan rode after him, and found the torn earth where Hal had spun away from an ambush, and the straight trail where he had led his pursuers across the countryside, away from his friend. There might have been tracks of half a dozen horses, Alan thought. He felt sick. But darkness was falling, and he could not follow the track.

He spent a restless night at their campsite, hoping against reason that Hal would return. The next day, scorning fear, he followed Hal's tracks until he lost them in the rocky uplands of some lord's sheep pasturage. He circled in ever wider spirals through that day without finding a sign of his brother. Perhaps Hal had managed to shake the lordsmen from his track, but he had most assuredly lost Alan as well.

Alan scoured the countryside through days of rising panic, scarcely troubling himself to avoid the lordsmen. The few words of Welandais Hal had taught him were painfully useless to gain him any information. Finally, quite desperate, he turned Alfie toward Veran's Mountain. If Hal was alive and at liberty, perhaps he had resumed his interrupted quest.

For the weeks of the journey Alan rode mercilessly hard, ate little and slept only from exhaustion. Alfie grew thin, and his eyes rolled constantly, showing the frightened whites. But Alan fixed his bloodshot eyes on Veran's Mountain, cursing feverishly as it scarcely seemed to grow larger at all. He set his course straight toward it, impatiently outriding the lordsmen who pursued him.

At long last the peak grew, and changed, and filled the sky. Alan left the lowland habitations behind him and traversed the wild, steep shoulders of his goal. Then utter despair stabbed his heart, for he could not find a sign of Hal. He rode at random in the shadows of the crags for three days, until a certain afternoon. Then he heard harsh voices raised in shouts of cruel triumph. Fearfully he drew his sword, wrapped his left arm in his cloak by way of a shield and cantered toward the ominous sound. But it was not Hal that he found.

In a hollow of the mountainside grew a graceful ash tree. Around the tree circled five mounted warriors, chanting an ugly taunt. Tied to the trunk of the tree, with dry branches and kindling piled about her, was a slender maiden. She stood motionless and silent, her head bowed so that her long golden hair flowed down to hide her face. One of the warriors struck flint to steel. But before he could set the kindling aflame, Alan sent Alfie leaping into the dingle.

His sword and the force of his charge left two men dead, but three strong fighters remained. They rallied swiftly, attacking Alan from all sides. Alfie whirled and darted like an iron-shod bird of prey. He rose on his hind legs and struck out with his deadly forehooves, lending his force to Alan's sword. The enemy fell back momentarily, and Alfie managed to set his hindquarters against a giant stone. But the warriors advanced once again in renewed strength. Alan took several cuts on the head and shield arm, and then a thrust through his left shoulder. He went white with shock, nearly losing his seat.

Silent and unmoving as a stone, the maiden watched with smoky gray-green eyes while Alan fought for his life and hers. But as she gazed, the cloudy sheen of her eyes grew darker and more intense, until all at once tears flooded down her cheeks. She strained against her bonds, crying out words which Alan could not understand: *"O Aene so loften, ir shalden, el prien, trist a mirdas frec engriste!"* ["Oh One so high, help me, I pray, lest the brave man die!"] Even through the roaring in his ears Alan heard the maiden's cry. But little did he guess that tears had never moistened her face before, and that her strange words were a plea not for herself but for him.

Somehow she broke loose, whether by sorcery or merest luck Alan did not care. "Run!" he shouted to her. "Run quickly and hide! I cannot last much longer!" But she had no thought of running, even if she had understood. She picked up a dead man's sword, and with strange words she called a horse. With frightful, blazing eyes she mounted and spurred toward the fray. She aimed a clumsy blow at the back of the nearest warrior. But as he turned to face her, he froze in unreasoning terror, and she struck him full in the throat. The other two foes swung around quickly, and Alan, fearing for the maiden, summoned all his strength to strike one in the sword arm. But the two were unnerved, and fled headlong out of the hollow and down the mountainside, leaving Alan in amazed relief.

He leaned heavily on his saddle and gazed at the strange maiden who had just saved his life as he fought to save hers. She was lovely beyond belief, with a perfect beauty that defied his reason. *If the bride Veran brought back from this mountain was anything like her,* Alan thought hazily, *it is no wonder folk took her for a goddess.* She was looking at the sword in her hand with a peculiar expression, and then she dropped it abruptly to the ground, traces of tears were still wet on her cheeks as she turned toward him.

He vaguely knew that he should be afraid. He knew that armed men had fled before this maiden. But he was tired beyond fear. He met her eyes without hesitation, knowing that all of his despair, weariness, longing and love were in his gaze. For what might have been an hour or an instant her eyes engulfed him. He saw a white-haired patriarch with a face as young as the new day and as old as time. He saw a great horse running in a green valley where golden birds flew, and his heart leaped with hope that it was Arundel. He saw argent ships on tourmaline seas. Then weakness overtook him. The vision turned to blackness. He felt arms around him, and with what strength he could muster he lowered himself from Alfie's back and sank to the ground.

When he opened his eyes, he found himself propped against the ash tree. The maiden had unlaced his tunic and was stanching the flow of blood from his shoulder wound, weeping silently as she tended him. Alan reached out with his good hand and wiped away her tears. "Hush," he said gently, "it is not so bad." Then he caught his breath, dumbfounded. The words he had spoken were not in the language of Isle. Different sounds had left his mouth, musical emanations of the concern and comfort he meant to convey. The maiden still wept, but joy shone in her eyes.

"Tell me what to do," she said in that harmonious language that Alan had not understood before. "I have never healed a man."

Alan reached across his body and took the fold of cloth she pressed against his wound. His fingers tingled as they touched hers. "Get the flask out of the saddle-bags," he told her. "It will give me strength."

A gulp of the burning liquid sent his memory back to the first time he had tasted it, when Hal had befriended him. The maiden's steady gaze reminded him of the gray eyes he had seen for the first time that day. Perhaps she was a relative of Hal's; it was not impossible. He watched her as she fetched water from a mountain tarn. She wore a simple garment of soft fiber, spring green in color. Her only ornament was a dark green stone which hung from a golden chain around her neck. She was lovelier than any bejeweled noblewoman Alan had ever seen. She was slender but stately, like the ash tree in the hollow. She moved as gracefully as its branches in the summer breeze, and her dress floated about her body like soft new leaves.

"What is your name?" Alan asked when she came to him. "If you wish to tell me," he added quickly. In this strange tongue, he instinctively knew, a name revealed the essence of the bearer.

She smiled, not with her mouth so much as with her shining eyes. "Certainly I will tell you," she replied. She bathed the cuts on his head with cold, pure water. "It is Lysse."

Alan knew at once that her name meant "the graceful one." Even as she applied thick black ointment to the cuts on his head, her every movement flowed with the grace of perfection, quick and precise. When she had bandaged his head, she bared his left forearm and bathed off the caked blood. He lay still, his eyes intent on her. The touch of her hands thrilled him.

"What is your name?" she inquired.

He told her, then asked, "Does it mean something to you, as yours does to me?"

Again she smiled with that strange glow in the eyes. "Ay, surely. It means 'handsome.' It also means that you are a gentle man, one who would live in harmony, not in strife." He reddened at her praise, but she went on, not seeming to notice. "What are you doing here, Alan? Do you have some quest here? I know that your heart is sorely troubled."

"I am searching for my *belledas*, my blood brother. We

were separated in the lands of the evil lords, and I—I fear he might be dead. He had planned to come to Veran's Mountain, and so I came hoping to find him here."

"But why did he wish to come here?"

"By my troth," replied Alan slowly, "I believe he himself hardly knew. He seeks his grandfather, but I do not think he expects to find him here."

"And who is his grandfather?"

"I am sorry." answered Alan. "It is not my secret."

She seemed surprised and puzzled, but not angry. She bandaged his arm in silence. When she had finished, she looked into his eyes, studying his strength.

"If you can ride," she said, "we shall go to my people. Perhaps my father can help you find your *belledas*."

"But who are your people?"

"That," she said, with her hint of a smile, "is not my secret."

They padded Alan's shoulder wound and put the arm in a sling so that it would not be moved. Then Alan bandaged Lysse's wrists where they were cut and burned from the thongs which had bound her. She did not consider it necessary, but he insisted. He offered her some dried meat, but she refused, saying she ate no flesh. Weak as he was, his own stomach turned at the sight of the stuff, but he nibbled at some anyway, for strength. Lysse did not eat; she had shown no sign of such faintness as he felt.

Her home, she told him, was no more than three days away, less if they traveled quickly. As soon as he was ready, they started. Lysse rode her captured horse. "He is a good steed at heart," she explained, "and did not willingly serve such a master."

They conversed very little, for Alan needed all his strength for riding. Every jolt and jounce sent pain through his hurt limbs, and his head was throbbing from the blows he had taken. Their course was steep and rough, over boulders and around crags. There was no beaten path to soften the way. After a while Alan's shoulder began to throb like his head, and he could scarcely keep from crying out in his misery.

They stopped just before dark, when Lysse found a grassy place for them to stay. Alan was beyond pride. He staggered off Alfie, sank to the ground and fell at once into a stupor. Lysse carefully covered him with his blanket, then unsaddled the horses and sat watching over him late into the night.

The next morning, Alan was awakened by the touch of cold water as Lysse bathed his face. His shoulder was red and swollen, and his whole body was pulsing with pain. Lysse put cold cloths on the wound while Alan ate some dried venison. Before the sun was well up, they were on their way once again.

For Alan, the day soon faded into a haze of wretchedness. If anyone had asked him to retrace his path, he could not have done so, for he saw nothing except the rump of Lysse's horse moving in front of him. He followed it blindly, trusting Alfie to avoid the pitfalls of the trail. Lysse was pushing the pace. She knew she could not have mercy on Alan and let him rest, for infection was setting in. If she did not soon get him to shelter and proper doctoring, he might die. She had seen the utter weariness and despair in his eyes, his empty saddlebags, his haggard face. And she knew what Alan himself hardly realized, that he had worn himself to the thin edge of exhaustion, that his wound was more dangerous to him than it seemed.

Only three times that whole long day they rested. On those occasions Lysse brought Alan cold water to drink, and bathed his face and wound. Then, while he lay on the grass, she foraged for berries and wild fruits to sustain herself. But by the end of the day they had seen the last of the plants and shrubs tucked away in the crevices of the slopes. Far above them the mountain rose in barren cliffs. The air was thin, wrenching Alan's breath. He panted at even the slightest exertion, and the pain in his chest made him feel so weak that he leaned over and clung to his saddle as his tears moistened Alfie's mane.

Alan never remembered stopping and dismounting to sleep that night. The next morning he thought he could not move. "Elwyndas!" Lysse called to him sternly, and with a groan he sat up; the name was a summons of power to him. He could not eat, but Lysse made him drink what remained in his flask. "We should be there by early afternoon," she said, "but the hardest part is yet to come. You must have your strength about you." She spoke bravely, and turned her face away so he would not see the pity in her eyes.

That day they scaled the cliff. The horses walked along

a ledge cut into the face of Veran's Mountain, spiraling
around it like the staircase of a tower. Alan was hardly
aware of the steep ascent, but when he finally noticed
hawks circling far below, he pulled Alfie to a halt, waiting
for his faintness to pass. Lysse paused anxiously, but they
soon pressed on. Alan did not look down again, but followed her closely, and did not find it strange that he
trusted her with his life and his love.

At the top of the mountain curved a valley, a giant circle protected on all sides by ramparts of rock, filled with
dells and streams, green trees and sunny meadows. Alan
did not notice when they arrived. Only gradually he realized that Alfie's hooves fell on grass instead of rock, and
that they were moving down, not up, a slope. With great
effort he raised his head and focused his eyes. Lysse was
leading him toward some brightly colored cloth shelters
scattered amidst a grove of trees. People were coming out
of them, calling to each other. Perhaps the fever was af-
fecting his mind, Alan thought, or perhaps he had died
and reached some realm of the blessed. He had thought
no living creature could be as lovely as Lysse, but these
folk were beautiful beyond description. There was a light
all about them, an unworldly glow like the shimmer of
Lysse's eyes. In spite of his pain and sorrow Alan felt his
heart smiling, though he could barely see their faces.
    Then one of them rushed through the group, running
to meet him. One of them and yet not one of them! Alan
reeled in his saddle as relief and happiness struck him
with all the force of unbearable sorrow. "Hal!" he tried
to shout; his voice came out a husky whisper. Then strong
arms helped him down from the saddle, and he wept un-
ashamedly in Hal's tearful embrace.

Chapter Two

Alan awoke to the feel of soft blankets on his bare skin, and found himself lying on a thick bed of down comforters. He found it hard to believe that he had ever been exhausted and burning with feverish pain. Overhead shimmered a canopy of finely woven gold cloth; the glow of the sunlight that filtered through was like the glow of health he now felt. Luxuriously he stretched himself beneath his covers, but stopped as a stabbing pain in his shoulder reminded him that his troubles were not a dream. More cautiously, he raised himself on his good elbow and looked around. Hal lay sleeping a few feet away, one muscular arm thrown across his blanketed chest with childlike abandon. Alan thought that Hal looked rather pale and worn. He did not realize that he himself looked considerably worse than he felt.

He vaguely recalled his illness, the many people that ran to meet him and Lysse, and Hal's arms supporting him. He remembered Hal's broken words of comfort, the horrible pain as his wound was lanced and drained, the cool water and fresh bandages, and a springtime fragrance which made him forget he had ever known sorrow. But it all seemed so long ago.

There was a slight sound outside, and Lysse peeked

in at the tent flap. When she saw he was awake, she entered, carrying a tray with a pitcher and two goblets. Her eyes were shining.

"Lysse," Alan whispered, and reached out to her with his good hand. She put down her tray and settled herself on the grass beside him, taking his hand in both of hers. Her touch was warm, like the glow in her eyes.

"You are feeling better," she said softly.

"Much better. How long have I slept?"

"Only a night. It is the morning of the day after we arrived. Veran's flower works quickly. They gave it to me also, for I was overwrought, and now I feel as rested as if I had never left the valley."

"And they cared for your wrists," Alan said, touching the fresh white bandages. "It is well."

"Not so much talk," she smiled, "till you are stronger. Drink this." She poured him a goblet full of sparkling amber liquid and helped him raise it to his lips. It was delicious, cool and tangy. Alan lowered his drained glass in wonder.

"What a marvelous draught," he said. "It makes me think of nectar and honey and the juices of bright-colored fruits I have never known. What is it?"

"All of those things and more," she replied, but her eyes glanced past him.

Alan turned and saw Hal staring at him with a startled look. "What is wrong, Hal?" he asked.

"Nothing," answered Hal, his expression changing to one of joy and wonder. "I am taken aback, that is all. How did you learn to speak the Old Language?"

Alan had not even realized that he and Lysse were conversing in this tongue which had once been strange to him, so natural had it now become. And Hal was speaking to him in the same tongue. This, then, was Hal's mysterious language that had puzzled him for so long! He was staggered, and hard put to reply to Hal's query.

"I hardly know," he murmured. "From her eyes, I think."

"In very truth, your brother is a marvel among men, Mireldeyn," Lysse replied gravely to Hal. "His soul touched mine fearlessly. His name shall be Elwyndas among my people, for he is a brave man, and great of heart. It is no wonder you love him so."

She poured Hal a drink of her nectar, and as he took

it Alan saw that he made no effort to conceal his scars from her. "You call him Mireldeyn?" he blurted.

"Ay. What do you call him?"

"Hal. Does it mean something to you?"

"Ay, indeed; it suits him well." She took a deep breath. "It means 'he who rules.' "

Lysse took her goblets and rose. "My father will come to you soon," she said. "Pray make your needs known to us." She gracefully took her leave.

Alan's eyes followed her, and his confused thoughts formed themselves into one compelling question. "Who are these folk, Hal?" he demanded, this time speaking in the language of Isle. "Are they of mankind, as we are, or not?"

Hal came and sat close beside him. His scarred body glowed golden in the diffused morning light. "Ah, Alan," he replied in a voice low with wonder, "by my troth, my dreams come alive and walk in the light of day. They are elves."

"Elves!" exclaimed Alan. A hundred childhood tales flickered through his mind, stories of cold-blooded, heartless creatures who stole babies from cradles and ensnared the soul with their eyes. Hal saw the alarm in his face, and glanced at him keenly.

"Ay," he stated, "elves. Remember your friends of the barrow, and take care how you heed the tales of ignorant folk. These elves are not much like the pixies which old women use to frighten children."

Alan smiled, shamefaced. "Tell me about them."

"They are the true immortals," Hal said with a sort of awe. "They will never sicken or grow old, though they can be killed. They face death bravely if need be. But the death of one of their number is a terrible tragedy, a cause of deeper mourning than we can well imagine, for it is not the necessary end of their lives. All of them are deeply grateful to you for saving Lysse from such a fate."

"She could have saved herself," Alan protested, recalling how the men had fled before her. "She could have killed them all with a thought!"

"If she has that power, she could not, or would not use it; not for her own sake." Hal sighed. "There is much I do not understand about the People of Peace, Alan; until yesterday I did not dare to hope that they existed except in my dreams. But this much I know: like the spirits of

the dead, they may not, or will not, intervene in the affairs
of men or the coming of fate."

"But she did intervene. She saved my life!"

"You must be a very special person, Elwyndas."

Alan understood now that his *elwedeyn* name meant
"elf-friend, elf-spirit," like Veran before him. But if he
was an elf-friend, was not Hal the same?

"What is the language that you and the elves speak,
Hal?"

"It is the Old Language, the language of the Beginnings. It is the language of power, which the One used to
sing the creation, when the mountains rose out of the
deeps. Those who use it know all creatures and are like-
wise known; it is the language of the inner self. But
pride fears it, for it hides nothing. So mortal men have
long since fallen away from it, to quarrel across the bar-
riers of their many tongues. Only the Gypsies, who know
no boundaries, no nations and no wars, use it still."

"How did you come to know it? Did you learn it from
the Gypsies?"

Hal looked hesitant, almost fearful. "Nay," he answered, "it cannot be learned or taught; only those who
conquer pride and fear can speak it. The Gypsies raise
their children to be selfless and brave, but many fall
away, and some of the Mysteries are lost. As for me, I
suppose it was somehow born in me. I do not remember
a time when I did not know the Old Language, though it
was known to no one around me."

Alan studied his brother. The mystery in Hal's gray
eyes, he sensed, might find its answer in this mountaintop
valley. "Hal," he questioned abruptly, "are you one of
the People of Peace?"

"Do you think so?" asked Hal slowly, and Alan realized that he was frightened, with no answer to offer. He
seemed to shrink into himself for a moment, bent with
thought. Then, with an effort of will, he squared his
shoulders and faced Alan, speaking the Ancient Tongue.

"Today you know me, I believe, as well as I know myself," he said. "Help me find myself, Elwyndas. You who
love me, discover my soul."

Alan felt the same peculiar abeyance of fear as he had
with Lysse. Knowing that he should be terrified, he
looked deeply into Hal's eyes; clouds of misty gray melted
from before him. For a moment he was surrounded by

profound darkness, deep and warm as a womb. Then a speck of light formed, growing larger and more brilliant, so that Alan's vision was filled with wheeling circles of shining light, warm and marvelous. He stared without blinking, until he realized that in the center of the swirling light was a crowned figure in mail of burnished silver. He thought he had never seen a more noble form, though the head was bowed and the face turned away. Then the figure looked up and strode toward him, till the face filled his sight, and Alan felt fearless and consummate joy such as he had never known. He went down on his knees and reached out, still gazing into those marvelous gray eyes. "Mireldeyn!" Alan whispered, as the meaning of the name was manifest to him.

The vision disappeared suddenly; Alan was engulfed in a darkness of panicky pain. A voice cried to him from a great distance, "Alan! Don't! I beg you—" Then he found himself once again in the light of day, on his knees before Hal, who tugged at him with both hands while tears streamed down his white face. Alan rose quickly and put his arm around him.

"Hush," Alan said gently in the Old Language. "Do you not know that I love you? In Lysse's eyes I saw the past of the Blessed People, but in your eyes I see the future. Some day I shall kneel to you and you will understand. You are Mireldeyn. There has been no one like you, nor ever is likely to be again."

"I don't want to be different!" choked Hal, weeping like a child. "I don't want people kneeling to me! All I have ever wanted is peace and friendship and a little love!"

"Don't you see," Alan explained softly, "how special that makes you? All men, to some degree, lust for power and fame—except one. All men are greedy for wealth and comfort—except one. Only you, of all men, can heal this land which is scarred even as you are, for only you cannot be corrupted by these things you do not desire."

"What of you? cried Hal desperately. "I saw no such lust in your soul!"

"It is there, nevertheless," Alan replied wistfully. "Even now I feel the stirrings of envy over that marvelous crown I saw you wear. I am not Mireldeyn. The blood of the elves does not run in my veins, except that bit I received from you."

"Your brother speaks words of great wisdom," said a quiet voice. Adaoun stood before them; Adaoun, the elf-father, the patriarch. Alan stood fixed in wonder at the age in his youthful eyes, but Hal stumbled toward him with outstretched hands.

"Adaoun," he appealed, "what is this Alan tells me? Am I not a man, like other men?"

"You know you are not, Mireldeyn," Adaoun replied, placing a hand on Hal's head in calming benediction. "You have felt it from your earliest days. Now that the truth is finally within your grasp, do not seek to flee from it!"

Hal hurled himself onto his bed. He pummeled his pillow in anguished fury, then sank back, clenching his shaking hands. Finally he took a deep breath, set his jaw and sat up.

"Very well," he stated, "I am not just a man; I am something different, something called—Mireldeyn. What does it mean?"

"We must eat before we talk," Adaoun told him. "Elwyndas has had little for days, now, and is weak from fever. Put on your shirts, and we shall eat outside."

Alan was indeed white and trembling from just the slight exertion of standing. "I'm sorry," Hal murmured to him. "I have been thinking only of myself."

"Never mind that," Alan grumbled. "Just help me with this sling."

They put on the garments that were laid out for them. Alan was surprised to find that they were of a very soft, fine, lightweight wool, not at all like the coarse woolen garb he had known, brilliantly dyed in shades of sunshine, leaves, sky and water. Though innocent of any ornament, the clothing was so delicately stitched and brightly colored that they felt they were arrayed like kings; and indeed Adaoun himself wore no better. They pulled on their boots, but left their swords behind, wearing only their chain-link belts for girding.

They found Adaoun on a grassy hill which sloped down to a lake set like a jewel in the center of the valley. Lysse was there with one of her brothers, a golden-haired elf who seemed like a young man in his twenties except for the centuries of wisdom in his eyes. His name was Anwyl—"beloved one." They sat on the ground to eat. On wooden plates were eggs and cheeses, honey, fine breads and a variety of fruits, some of them unknown to Hal in spite of all his lore. They drank milk from wooden noggins. It took Alan a while to realize that there was no meat. Remembering that Lysse would taste none of his, he suddenly understood why the elves' feet were bare, and why their belts were of cord, not leather. "Of course," he thought. "They do not kill animals, creatures who speak to them heart to heart."

From the talk, Alan gathered that Hal had arrived at this place not long before himself. "I scarcely know how I found the spiral path," Hal explained. "I was drawn to it somehow, and though I could hardly hope to find you on it, Alan, yet I knew I must ascend. As I neared the top, I felt the presence of Anwyl, and I spoke to him, though I could not see him: '*Ir holme, wilndas elwedeyn, ir selte, to nessa ilder daelen frith.*' ['Come to me, friend of the old blood, talk to me, for the sake of the former days of peace.'] He leaped down from above. I was terrified that he would fall, but he landed squarely on the path. He seemed much moved."

"Indeed, I was as much disturbed in my mind as an elf is ever likely to be," remarked Anwyl. "I asked him who he was, that spoke to me in the Old Language, and he answered me: 'Hal, son of Gwynllian, heir of Torre, Taran, and the line of the Blessed Kings of Welas.' Then I longed to kneel and swear fealty to him, for I knew he was Mireldeyn. But great weariness and distress weighted him, so I refrained, and led him hither."

"Greatly was my heart torn, Alan," Hal said quietly, "between my joy and wonder at this place and my fear for you. I poured out my anguish to Adaoun, but scarcely had I finished when you arrived."

"I believe I was sent to bring him," said Lysee. "There was no reason for me to go to the lower slopes, where those cowardly men fell upon me, except that I felt I must."

"What does it mean, Adaoun?" asked Hal. "I feel the threads of destiny all around me."

"Before I can tell you," Adaoun replied, "I must know how much you understand."

"Where must I start?"

"At the Beginning."

They cleared away the breakfast and settled back against trees. Lysse brought pillows for Alan, and he lay

at her side. The air was not hot, though it was almost
midsummer, but mild as springtime.

"Before there was time," Hal began, "there was the
One."

"And what is the One?" Adaoun asked.

Alan understood, as he seemed to understand everything now, that the One was an essence and emanation
neither good nor evil, neither female nor male nor yet a
sexless spirit, but all of each of these. There was a word
for such essence in the Old Language; it was called Aene.
But he could not have explained it in the language of Isle.

"The One is sun and moon, dawn and dusk, hawk and
hunted," Hal averred.

"Ay," Adaoun agreed softly, "Star Son and Moon
Mother, Fatherking and Sacred Son, Black Virgin and
snowy Babe and russet rowan Lady of All Trees; they are
all in Aene. Even the crescent-horned god is in Aene.
But man has made his worship a divided thing, to his
sorrow."

"At the Beginning of Time," Hal went on, "the One
sang out earth and sky, days and seasons, and all the
plants and beasts. And Aene loved that song. You were
in it, Adaoun, and your mate Elveyn. You loved peace
and beauty, and lived alongside the beasts. Progeny came
to you."

"Anwyl here was among the first."

"What was it like, Adaoun, in those Beginning days?"

"Ah, Mireldeyn, it was beautiful, so beautiful," Adaoun
sighed. "Great birds flew in the air, and little ones made
music in every tree. Life was abundant; nowhere was
there desolation, for even the deserts bloomed. Many
wonderful creatures have since vanished from the earth;
shining dragons and playful sea-beasts. . . . But of all
creatures that walked upon earth, the noblest were the
horses, and their kin, the unicorns. And of all creatures
that soared the sky, the noblest were the eagles."

Adaoun rose to his feet and, putting fingers to his
teeth, blew a piercing whistle. From the distance came a
musical cry like that of a great bird. Then around the
curve of a hill swept a herd of great horses, clean-limbed
stallions and long-legged mares, such lovely horses as
Alan had seen only two of before. . . . One of these,
Arundel, ran at the fore, his silver-gray flanks flashing in
the sun. But ahead of him, and the leader of all, sped a

blazing white steed who stood shoulders above the rest, and from his sides rose a shimmering pair of golden wings. His fetlocks also shone golden, and as he and his herd reached the shore of the lake, a white and golden image sparkled below him in the midnight blue of the water. The steed raised his head; Alan was stunned by the flash of his deep eyes. The winged stallion shrilled an eerie whistling scream, and from the skies overhead came reply. Great golden birds appeared, led by one whose aureate wings were almost as broad as those of the stallion below. For a moment they formed a brilliant tableau, the white and the gold mirrored in the blue of the unfathomable lake. Then, like the last flashing beams from a westward sun, they were gone, and the thunder of hooves faded in the distance.

"Dweller in the Eagle Valley," breathed Alan. "Did Arundel come from here?"

Hal seemed unable to answer, but Adaoun was quick to reply. "While he was still a colt, Arundel was called away from here, as Asfala was a few years later. But, Mireldeyn, how did you know?"

"Many times I have seen this place, Adaoun, in dreams and waking visions. But I hardly dared hope I could ever find it."

"Have you also seen the past, Mireldeyn?"

"I have seen one who may be Elveyn. She has rippling hair of dark gold and wears a garment of deep, stormy purple. I see her on rocky sea cliffs, facing the gray water."

"Ay," said Adaoun, "she always loved the sea. When men overran the earth and forgot the Ancient Tongue, it was she who showed us how to sail away from them in ships."

"Why was man put on earth?" Hal asked bitterly. "He has turned it into a desolation of strife and bloodshed. Was it not better, the way it was?"

"Too good! Nothing ever chanced; and Time, which had just begun, was likely to pool itself into eternity. Moreover, the One was lonely still. We elves could not satisfy Aene's craving: we know only mindfelt love. We choose our mates with judgment; we are quiet, patient and reasoned. We do not shout or laugh for joy, nor do we weep."

Alan glanced up at Lysse, startled. Her smoky green

eyes were as deep as the mountain lake, as intense as the brilliant gem that hung about her neck. She smiled down at him, and Alan wondered at that smile.

"So the One made man," Adaoun went on, "a being could feel the strength and passion of Aene's love. . . . But the wisdom which counters passion could not be man's. Only in Aene are wisdom and love complete, together, and this is one of the great Mysteries."

"I can imagine what happened, though I was not there," Hal muttered. "First we began to kill the animals—"

"That is your nature," Adaoun interrupted. "The fox kills the pheasant and the marten slays the mouse and men hunt the fleet red deer; they are all in Aene. But alas, I believe that is why man fell away from the Old Language; it would be a hard thing to kill a creature which speaks with you soul to soul."

"I know," said Hal wryly, "for I have done so, many a time. And then, I suppose, we began to kill each other. Is that also in Aene?"

Adaoun sighed. "As the wolf is in the Forest, Mireldeyn, or as the old sow slays her farrows—but not often. It seems to me that the great wheel is wobbling off of balance. There is need of more love in your world." Adaoun paused significantly. "Say also, Mireldeyn, that man began to kill the elves."

"I had hoped not to say so," Hal faltered, stricken.

"A few of us. My son Freca was the first. . . . Because we do not know the love that burns in the heart, men called us cold and evil, and ran from us, or stoned us and laughed, or hunted us ruthlessly, according to their whim; for men are above all creatures of passion. The One had made them mortal so that they might know to the fullest every passion of living, joy and sorrow and the begetting of progeny. This was forbidden to my children, lest they in their immortality overrun the earth. But in spite of death, men grew more and more numerous, so that even in the wilderness we could not avoid them. At last, at Elveyn's advice, we built ships and started across the sea in search of a new place.

"Six times since then have we sailed, and we call this our Seventh Age. Sometimes we have found peace, but always it has collapsed in war as a blight of man's greed has spread across the earth. Five hundred turnings ago we came to this Welas and withdrew to this mountaintop, as we had learned to do, for we knew war would not be long in following us. As indeed it was not. But first Veran came.

"He sailed up the Gleaming River, out of the west, a dark man, but with a glow about him like ancient gold. The tribal chieftains bickered and brawled across the marches between their wooden towers, as they had always done, but Veran cowed them with a glance and the power of his grip. Within a season all of Welas hailed him as King. Then he came straightway to this mountain, and no fear of us was in his heart. That was marvel enough, but something chanced which we had never known before. One of my daughters, she whom we named Claefe, the dove, clave to Veran and chose to go with him as his wife, committing herself to a mortal death. We rejoiced in their love, though we mourned her going from us. Lysse was begot to replace her in our number. But Veran had to lead Welas against the invaders from the East. While he was gone, Claefe died in childbirth, as a mortal woman will. Then overweening grief seized my Elveyn, so that she went to the sea cliffs and hurled herself into the gray salt waters she loved so well.

"It was then, Mireldeyn, that I first heard of you. For with the death of my mate and the coming of war's blight yet once again, I cried out to the One in great pain and despair of mind. And Aene came to me here, in this valley, walking on earth in a cloak of flesh, as often is Aene's wont, whether seer, sage, youth or prophet, mother, maiden or ancient hag. But I knew the Songmaker at once, for we have met before.

"Elwestrand awaited us, Aene said, the western land from which Veran had come, where there were folk with whom we could live in harmony and whom my children could take to mate—they who have been celibate these thousands of years. And in the fulfillment of this prophecy, the One said, elves and men would join and a new creature arise, the best of each. But first the Age must be fulfilled in this Isle, the farthest outpost of the Middle World. For if the blight of war which has followed us so long is not stopped here it will follow us yet, to the unicorn fields of the west. The Wheel teeters in its rounds, Mireldeyn. Not even the One can foresee how it will go.

"But Aene foretold that at this time, when the blight of

the Easterners had reached even to Welas, a youth from the world of men would come to us, a descendant of the line of Veran, heir to the throne of Isle by a right far greater than that of birth. The blood of the elves would run strong in his veins. He would find us and speak to us in the Language of Eld, which no one learns unblessed. He would arm himself only with friendship and unensorcelled steel, for the Easterners have made magic an accursed thing. He would know all mortal joy and sorrow, but not mortal greed and pride; an elf's vision, an elf's thirst for knowledge, and an elf's keenness of mind would all be his. And we would call him Mireldeyn, the elf-man, for he would be neither fully elf nor fully man, but the best of each. You are he, Hal, son of Gwynllian, heir of Torre and of Taran and of the Blessed Kings of Welas, for you have fulfilled all that was said, and more."

Hal saw his destiny as a doom. "Brand, the son of Veran and Claefe," he protested. "Was he not an elf-man, more so than I?"

Adaoun gently shook his head. "When Claefe went with Veran, she became woman, though perhaps the most golden and gifted of women. She bequeathed her heirs insight, a quickness of perception rare in the world of men, and also the love of lore and wisdom. Nothing more."

Adaoun had been speaking steadily, but now he hesitated before he slowly continued.

"You are the one person, Mireldeyn, who can stop the plague of war which has followed us for seven ages. You are the one person who can end the age of bloodshed and terror in Isle. You are also he who must help us, the People of Peace, to Elwestrand across the Western Sea. Only if you vanquish the evil lords of the lowlands can we ever reach the Bay of the Blessed to set sail.

"I do not know whether you will succeed. Not even the One knows that, I believe. It depends not only on you, but on every person in Isle, on every man, woman and child. Only if the balance can prevail—the stakes are so high—the future of the race of men as well as the entire race of elves—" Adaoun struggled to voice what he had to say. "The People of Peace can no longer withdraw from the bloodshed of life. At whatever sacrifice, we will do what we must do, Mireldeyn, to survive. We will fight for you, He Who Rules."

The magnitude of the gift fell on Hal like a burden of fire. To be fated the deliverer not only of Isle but of the elves as well—it was an obligation that smote him nearly to the ground. Hot rebellion swept him up, and blindly he strode away from the anxious elves. But Alan walked beside him, weak with fever though he was; and in his steadfast mortal friendship Hal found the strength he needed to win his struggle with himself.

Chapter Three

Ay, it was a hard knowledge to accept, thought Hal. *And yet, I am amply blessed.*

He lay at ease on a comfortable rock, the late summer sun pleasantly warm on his bare shoulders. Near him sat Alan and Lysse. She was trimming Alan's hair and smiling, almost giggling, at the woebegone faces he made as his long, sun-streaked locks fell to the ground.

It was nearly a month since the two had first entered the mountaintop valley of the elves. Alan's wound had fully healed and his health was restored. Yet neither he nor Hal thought of leaving. They were hardly aware of the passing of time, for eternity hung like a fragrance in the air, as it had in that hidden valley they had chanced upon nearly a year before. The elves also lived in a place untouched by the blight of the invaders. Adaoun had discovered it while riding Wynnda, the great gold-winged horse for whom he had begged immortality from the One. With great labor the elves had cut the spiral path to the top of Veran's Mountain, but the years passed like moments in their immortal lives. When at last they reached the valley, they had found a paradise like the one they remembered from seven ages past. Here the elves had released their special joy, the horses of Wynnda's blood,

and these flourished in the mountain air. Indeed, this was
a place that worked its weal on all creatures. Alfie ran
with the *elwedeyn* horses now, and his eyes sparkled
with the wonder of it. But Alan's eyes glowed as warm,
and, looking at him, Hal knew that it was not only the
valley that filled him with love.

Dear Alan, Hal thought. *The One grant him his heart's
desire. I owe him so much, but I cannot help him in this.*

Since their first full day in the Eagle Valley, Hal had
known that Alan was in love with Lysse. And he could
see that Lysse knew herself to be Alan's *mendor.* Yet
Alan labored to conceal his love, though it crept into his
every word and glance when Lysse was nearby. He held
back from openly wooing her, for to win her would be to
bereave her of her immortality. Hal knew she would sacrifice it willingly, in her wisdom as a woman and as an elf.
But even with this knowledge, he was not sure he could
act differently in Alan's place. For Alan, his dilemma
was a honeyed torment. Every time he saw Lysse, his
heart bounded with the sweetest of pain. They were together nearly all their waking hours, riding through the
meadows, singing in the moonlight, working together and
exploring the peaceful valley. Already she had given
Alan more of her immortal wisdom than he realized, and
his head rose high with the strength that welled in him.
But whether he would find strength to accept her as his
destiny, Hal did not know.

Only in one way can I help them, he mused, *and that
is to give them time together.*

He left them where they laughed in the sunshine, and
wandered away up the mountainside.

Adaoun had been greatly relieved when Hal had given
over brooding about the burden Aene had placed on him.
The destiny of the elves was not secure, Adaoun knew,
but a fate which trembled on the Wheel. Mireldeyn's
choice must be made firm; indecision at the wrong time
could cause eternal disaster. So when the Elf-father found
Hal sitting alone and troubled, he moved quickly to his
side.

"What ails you, son of the mortals?" he asked lightly.
"You look as if the sky has fallen on your head."

Hal's solemn face broke into a smile at the elf's cheerfulness, but he was not fooled. "Never fear, Adaoun," he

answered dryly. "I am not thinking of myself. We have
never spoken of Elwyndas and Lysse. Are you pleased
with their love, Adaoun?"

The elf sat beside him to answer.

"Neither happy nor saddened, Mireldeyn; not yet.
Elves seldom feel such things. Indeed, what is there to
say? They are coupled in *Dol Solden,* like you and the
Lady of Celydon."

Hal looked at him in surprise; he had never mentioned
Rosemary to Adaoun. "Then do all things written in *Dol
Solden* come to pass?"

"Nay, indeed," Adaoun replied slowly. "Written there-
in are things that should be; but Aene cannot, or will not,
make them come to pass. Elves and men must carry on
the affairs of the world to the End, whatever that may
be. Each of us has a destiny to help direct the force and
flow of life. If we heed it, then all is well. If we choose
to ignore it, then our lives run counter to the current of
the world's weal—"

Adaoun's voice faded away as Hal envisioned thousands upon thousands of slowly spinning years, cycle upon
cycle, millions upon millions of lives like shimmering
droplets converging into a circling stream of gold. The
years resolved themselves into ages, and the ages into the
Whole, the golden flood of countless lives swirling slowly
but remorselessly toward the vortex of some unseen End.
Time spun before him like a great golden wheel, hum-
ming in a minor key.

The vision faded, and Hal became aware once more of
Adaoun sitting beside him.

"Do they know?" he murmured.

"Lysse knows," Adaoun answered at once. "Now tell
me, Mireldeyn, for the mind of your brother is hidden
from me: Does he love her, and will he fulfill her in the
course her heart has chosen?"

"He loves her well," Hal declared. "But his course is
not yet clear to him, and he is troubled. It is hard to con-
ceive of a better man, Adaoun, but his pride and reason
battle against the direction his heart would take." Hal's
lips tightened in frustration. "My heart aches to help him,
but I dare not speak to him, lest the choice be mine and
not his."

"What strange creatures you mortals are," Adaoun
sighed. "Well, I see that I can only hope and wait."

"So must we both," Hal replied.

Three days later Hal and Anwyl, his first friend among the elves, were climbing among the rocks of the outer ramparts, searching out deadwood for the cooking fires. They moved silently, for the elves never disturbed the forest creatures without cause. Many marvelous things had they seen, but they scarcely expected to see what next met their eyes. As they rounded a corner of rock, in a wooded hollow below them stood Alan and Lysse. He was giving her a little bunch of violets; purple, blue, gold, lavender and white. He looked not at her, but at the flowers, as he spoke.

"Each is different from the others, Lysse," he said. "Yet all are lovely. None is more perfect than another."

"Ay," Lysse answered softly, puzzled.

"So also with the bright elf maidens of this valley. All are different, yet all are perfect in loveliness. No sane man could choose one over another."

With an effort he faced her, meeting her eyes. "Yet I have made that choice, Lysse!" he told her earnestly. "To me no maiden, mortal or immortal, can begin to match you in loveliness. Your eyes and your hair outshine those of your sisters as the sun outshines the stars. I desire no woman in my life except you, and without you I will have none." He took her by the shoulders, for her face revealed her consternation. "Do you understand me, Lysse? I love you, so help me, with the love of a mortal for a mortal. I must make you understand or I shall go mad!" He kissed her, tenderly but strongly, full on the lips. Her eyes closed and her face went deathly white. Then with what seemed to be the last of her strength she wrenched herself away from him and wordlessly fled down the mountainside. "Lysse!" Alan called once after her, but the mountain returned only the echo of his cry. He struck a young ash tree furiously with his fist. As he stared down the way she had disappeared, his face grew hard as rock, and the blood dripped unnoticed from his bruised hand.

Anwyl and Hal looked at each other with pain in their eyes. To move away would have been to risk interrupting Alan's wooing. So they had remained, involuntary witnesses of his anguish. Hal clenched his fists, his face white and taut with misery. But when Anwyl signaled, "Go to him," Hal's eyes flashed back, "Nay!" Alan must never know that his courtship had been observed.

Alan stood like a statue until shadows began to deepen in the hollow and darkness gathered in the dome of the sky. Then, with a gesture of decision, he set off rapidly toward the pavilions in the valley. The instant he disappeared, Hal and Anwyl ran in another direction. They must arrive at the camp before he did.

"Why?" Hal panted. "Why did she flee from him?"

"I believe I would have done the same," gasped Anwyl haltingly. "Mireldeyn, try to understand. She is standing on the brink of the unknown. What is to you mortals the very stuff of life is to us elves the greatest of mysteries."

They paused to catch their breath outside of camp. Then, pledging each other to secrecy, they parted. The cooking fires gave off delicious aromas, and all around rose the hum of contented talk. Hal walked through it like a stranger and went to the tent to wait. Alan was not long in coming. Hal looked up in carefully arranged surprise as he entered.

"Alan! Your hand! It's all blood!"

Alan did not even glance at the hand. "Hal," he said hoarsely, "we must leave this place at once."

Hal was too busy fetching water and bandaging to reply. Anxiously he tended the injured hand. When he was done, Alan spoke again, calmly but with a dogged persistence that Hal knew from long experience would take no denial. "Hal, we must go. I am well now, and strong, and our business is finished here. There is much yet to do, and time outside this valley does not stand still. We should have left before now."

"Very well," Hal said quietly. "I shall speak to Adaoun tonight, and we shall leave tomorrow morning. Come to supper."

"I am not hungry," replied Alan, throwing himself down on his bed. Hal knew better than to argue, and went without him.

Neither of them slept much that night, though Alan might have thought Hal did. Toward morning Alan fell into a doze and Hal slipped out in search of Anwyl. When he found him, the news was brief. "Not a sign of her," Anwyl said. "She has not been back to camp at all."

Morning dawned bright and sunny, but the elves seemed oddly quiet. Farewells were brief, for in spite of Alan's courtesy his restlessness was apparent. For the first time in a month, he and Hal wore swords. Their saddlebags were packed tightly with provisions and new clothing of soft wool.

"I have no gift for you," Adaoun said, "except memories and hope. Cherish them well, for my sake."

"Farewell," said Anwyl. "May we meet again in more peaceful times. The One be with you both."

Within a few moments they were trotting up the trail that led to the mountain's rim. When they reached the edge of the woodland, they looked back for a moment. Lysse was nowhere to be seen. Whether Alan was relieved or disappointed, not even Hal could tell.

They entered the leafy shade and moved rapidly and silently up the slope. But as they came to the upper reaches of the elves' domain, a slim form in green emerged from the shadow of an ash tree like a sprite materializing from the living trunk. Lysse stood before them.

Hal flashed her a delighted grin. "I'll wait for you at the top, Alan," he called as casually as he could, and sent Arundel onward at a gallop. Alan tried to shout after him, but his voice would not respond. He who had traveled over half a kingdom, slept with the spirits of the dead, braved the perils of the White Tower and fought unshielded against mailed foes was now very close to panic at the sight of a slender, golden-haired maiden.

The realization made his face burn. He set his jaw, took a deep breath, and looked at her. He gazed into her smoky green eyes, and before he knew what he was doing, he had dismounted and taken her hand. Only then did he realize that she was trembling. All the speeches he had prepared vanished from his mind.

"Lysse!" he exclaimed. "Are you afraid?"

"Afraid?" She tested the word, savoring it in her mind, and a tiny smile started at the corners of her mouth. "So that is the name of what I feel! Ay, then, I dare say I am afraid."

"But how—why—oh, Lysse, frightened of me!"

"I have heard my father say that men fear that for which they do not know the name." Her smile broadened. "I have now found that it is not only men who fear the unknown. When you did this thing yesterday—"

"It is called a kiss, Lysse. Something a mortal man does with the woman he loves."

"A kiss." Her eyes widened in the pleasure of discovery. "So that is a kiss! It is not fearsome at all, now that it bears a name. When you made this kiss, Elwyndas, my head spun; my body grew hot, then cold, my heart pounded and my breath came fast and shallow, so that I did not understand what was happening. I thought perhaps I was dying, and I was afraid, as an elf ought not to be afraid. I walked all night on the mountainside, thinking, and now I am sorry and ashamed, Elwyndas, for I see that I was concerned only for myself, and I caused you great pain." Alan was startled to see tears growing in her eyes, so that they became unfathomably deep, dark pools, like the lake at the heart of the mountain. He sensed the meaning of those tears, and he ached for her; all his wrath was lost in his love and his desire to comfort her. He put his arms around her shoulders, stroking her hair and gently kissing her face. Suddenly her trembling stopped. She looked up to him with eyes that were still bright with tears, but bright with joy as well.

"Alan," she said, using his mortal name for the first time since he had entered the valley, "that which you told me yesterday. . . ."

"Ay." He kissed her eyes. "I love you well, Lysse."

"That is the name of what I also feel." The tears at last overflowed her eyes and began to wet her cheek. "I love you, Alan of Laueroc."

Agonized, as if obeying something greater than himself, Alan leaned to kiss her. But before their lips could meet, he paused and asked her a yearning question with his glance.

"I will never flee from you again," she answered him aloud.

On the rim of the mountain Hal waited patiently, the rising sun warm on the back of his neck. Finally, from around the bend of the trail came the sound of hoofbeats. Hal stiffened, then relaxed and sighed with relief. Alan carried Lysse in the saddle before him, cradled close to his chest.

But when they reached the top of the rampart, Alan wordlessly set her down. "Wait," she said, and from around her neck she lifted the pendant she always wore. Alan lowered his head, and she slipped it onto him, centering the darkly glowing green stone on his chest. "The past and future of your people and mine glimmer in that stone," she said. "Wear it in hope of a better dawn."

Alan shook his head with a gesture of pain. "Oh, my

love, my future is dark to me. My hopes are dreams, without substance."

"Dream them still," she answered, "and let your deeds shape the substance. Remember me in your dreams, Alan! Farewell!"

Alan bent in his saddle to kiss her for what he felt sure was to be the last time.

He and Hal lifted arms in final salute to the People of Peace assembled below. Then they rode over the rim, and a wall of rock hid from their sight the secret valley which they knew they might never see again. Alan blinked hard as he faced the rising sun, but he did not look back.

Chapter Four

Summer's green was just tipped with the pale gold of early autumn when they left the mountaintop valley of the elves. The sun shone brightly, and the air was fresh and crisp. But the trees were all to be bare, the skies dark and windy, the earth sodden and cold with autumn's rains before they again found welcome.

They traveled south and east, along the curve of the mountains which rose between Welas and the sea. Their progress was slow, for they followed no beaten track. They wound their way as best they could along ridges and into ravines, picking their path between great rocky crags and ancient ruins. Somewhere in these deserted reaches of Welas Hal hoped to find his grandfather. His bright eyes probed the landscape eagerly at every new vista, though for days on end they would not see a living thing.

They traveled openly, by daylight. The henchmen of the lowland lords seldom ventured into these parts, for many outlaws lurked among these peaks. Hal, confident that he and Alan would not be attacked, rode fearlessly. Alan followed sullenly, caring little for the danger. He had fallen into a black moodiness, seldom saying a word. Lysse was a constant torment at the back of his mind. He

160

did not plan ever to see her again, for he was sure he could not deny her the immortality of an elf. His declaration of love had been a cry wrung from his tortured heart. He bitterly berated himself for his weakness, and he cursed this stark and soaring land from which Lysse's voice seemed continually to echo, "Remember me."

As the weeks wore on, the journey began to jangle Hal's nerves as well. They were frequently soaked by rain or chilled by bitter winds. Even the fires which warmed them at night seemed cold without the cheer of conversation. But finally, after two months of travel, a shout pierced the mountain wall. Suddenly, as if dropped from the dismal sky, a group of swarthy, fur-clad men blocked their path. Overhead, more rough-looking men lined the jagged cliffs. Resistance was impossible, but Hal had no such intention. He looked on them undaunted, waiting for the question he knew would come.

"Who are you to roam the mountain ways without fear?" asked the leader harshly. "What is your business here?"

"My business is with your liege, the Blessed King," Hal boldly declared. "To him I will tell my name, and no other."

The man muttered and moved toward him threateningly, but an outlaw called down from the rocks above, "Hold! Do you not see the sign upon his back? 'Tis Veran's token, the Setting Sun!" A chorus of voices called affirmation.

"Is this true?" the leader asked him.

Bewildered, Hal brought the plinset case around so that the man could see. Rosemary's half-completed sunburst shone brightly even under the cloudy sky. The man stared at it for a long moment, then faced Hal with a searching gaze from which all hostility was gone.

"Are you indeed of Veran's blood?"

"Good outlaw," answered Hal quietly, "I can tell you nothing until the King has given leave."

"Any spy could wear Veran's emblem," growled one rough man.

"By the Mothers, it is a risk we must take," replied the leader. "My Lord Galin is at the outer defenses; he cannot advise us. We must take them to the fortress."

He turned back to Hal and Alan. "We shall take you

to him whom you seek. But you must surrender your weapons, my lords."

Hal unbuckled his sword and handed it over. Alan followed more slowly with his. The man gazed at the finely wrought blades.

"If those be lost, or come to harm," Hal warned him in a low voice, "no mountain in Welas will be big enough to hide you."

"I am a King's liegeman, not a robber," the fellow replied with dignity. "And I have seen this sword before." He held up Hal's gray-glinting brand.

"Where?" Hal asked swiftly.

"I can tell you nothing until the King has given leave," the man parried grimly. "Now come with us, my lords."

They spent the night in a deep cave hidden in the flanks of the mountain. There were many such hollows and tunnels within the crags, protected by cleverly concealed fortifications. Central to the earthworks, nestled into the bosom of the forbidding mountain, was an ancient stronghold known as Cair Indel, the Deepest Haven. There the old King had taken refuge. And on the morrow, Hal and Alan were led to his shelter.

Torre was an old man, and life had not been kind to him. Kingdom, daughter, sons—all were gone. And with them went the light of day, or so it seemed to Torre, for he spent the long hours brooding in his dark cavern at the navel of the mountain. He often dreamed of the bright days of his past along the Gleaming River, when his beautiful wife Megolyn was still alive, when his sons Galin, Glondil and Gildur were strong, bold youths, and his daughter Gwynllian was his cherished pet. But he could never quite fool himself; he knew that those days and those faces were gone forever. He could dream, but the grim, cheerless Now returned inexorably each time.

Out of the shadows of his gloomy chamber came a figure from the past. Smiling a welcome, he looked to envision one of his dead sons. But this was not Glondil or Gildur; this young man had Gwynllian's eyes.

Torre sat bolt upright, scarcely daring to believe his eyes saw truly. Yet he knew in his heart that this figure was alive. The young man moved with the powerful grace of a warrior, and his weathered clothing could not obscure the breadth of his shoulders and the strength of his chest. He held his head high, and the straight lines of his jaw and brows reminded Torre of the sons who had once been his pride. But those eyes! Their gray depths held him spellbound. Here was a man of great power and strong will. Here he saw also a dream, and the torment of time. But above all, Torre recognized Gwynllian in the gray eyes. This youth was of his blood. He was sure of it.

"Who are you?" he whispered. He reached out, and his uncertain fingers met firm muscle and solid bone. The vision was real.

The young man knelt before him, and the leather bundle which had ridden on his back slipped down to rest on the floor. In the dull light an embroidered sunburst glowed eerily brilliant. The aged King became aware that in the far corners of the room his people were gathered, listening.

"Torre, son of. Tamar, of the ancient line of the Blessed Kings of Welas, I crave your blessing," the young man said. His voice was melodious, and though he spoke softly, the great hall vibrated with his words. "I love best to be called Hal, the name my mother gave me. She loved you well, and often spoke of you." Hal broke off, hardly knowing what to say to the fierce-looking old man who sat glaring like a blinded eagle in a darkened aerie. "Grandfather," he whispered, "don't you know me?"

"My grandson," the old man faltered, "my grandson!" His fumbling hands touched Hal's hair in the gesture of blessing. Then tears began falling from Torre's bright black eyes, and Hal found himself awkwardly kissing the King on both his parched cheeks, encircling Torre's thin shoulders with his strong and comforting arms.

Outside of Torre's chamber, Cair Indel was all in an uproar. Excited servants had brought out word of the Prince's coming, and the news ran like spring torrents among the soldiers and servingfolk of the keep. Some, who had noted the half-sun emblem on Hal's leather case, eagerly hailed him as an heir of Veran. But others called him impostor, and many thought of him as a hated Easterner. The fortress buzzed with ardent and wrathful talk.

When Hal and Alan emerged from the keep, a sudden silence came over the crowded courtyard, and all eyes were fixed upon them. Hal, deep in thought, seemed not to notice it until suddenly a voice boomed out: "Donkey prince! Filthy son of the fiendish Iscovar of Isle! Can a jackass beget anything else, be the mother the finest blooded mare?" From the crowd came a muttering of approval.

Hal's head snapped up as if he had been stung by a whip. Under the gaze of those steely gray eyes, the crowd grew silent and seemed to shrink back.

"Hear me, men of Welas." Hal's gaze skewered the listeners. "If I am weak or craven, then judge me. If I am bloodthirsty, cruel, or savage, judge me. If I am treacherous, foolhardy, stupid or arrogant, then judge me sternly." He had spoken softly; now he shouted. "But judge me not that I am the son of that blood-black King!" The echoes died away as he stood panting with emotion. "I do not deserve it. As the One is my witness, I do not. I cannot explain how it came to be. The greatest fear of my life is that I might somehow, someday, come to be something like him." Hal spoke passionately, but with dignity. "He is vile, villainous, sick and evil beyond belief and beneath contempt. I tell you this, I who know him well. See the proof!" In one wrenching movement Hal ripped off his patched tunic, leaving the tattered remnants swinging from his muscular arms. The crowd gasped in shock; no one spoke.

Hal went on more calmly. "This is but a paltry thing. Thousands of broken men would have been thankful to escape with my light punishment. But if there is anyone here who thinks that I bear love or likeness to the Islandais King, then let him think again." Spent, he turned to go, but there was a stir in the shadows of the doorway where he stood. The onlookers gasped and fell to their knees. "Sire!" Hal exclaimed. The old King was coming forth from the darkness of his refuge.

All clad in black, but with his thick hair blazing white against the lowering sky, Torre tottered with outstretched hands and stricken face toward Hal. "My child, my child," he whispered as Hal reached out to help him, "what has the brute done to you?" His withered hands touched the scarred shoulders tenderly.

"It is a small matter, Grandfather, and long healed." Hal cursed himself for having distressed the old man. Alan, who had knelt to the King along with the rest, now rose and came forward, unfastening his cloak. Hal took it gratefully and set it around his shoulders as Alan bowed before Torre. The King scanned him with keen black eyes. "So! This is your brother?"

Hal looked at him in surprise. "My blood brother, ay. This is Alan of Laueroc. But how did you know?"

"Perhaps later I will tell you. But where is your great gray steed? I have not seen him yet."

Hal exchanged a puzzled glance with Alan. "In the stable. I will get him, sire."

"Nay, let us go together. I have not been out of doors, Hal, since I received the news of your mother's death. I had forgotten how bright and pleasant the sun can be."

Alan cocked a wry glance at the gloomy sky, then watched as Torre and Hal disappeared in the direction of the stable, the old man leaning on the young one's arm. He would leave them alone to share a score of lost years.

He did not see Hal again until they dressed for the evening meal. When they went downstairs, they found Torre with one who had not had the advantage of such leisure, a dark man who looked tired and travel-soiled. Though his body was youthfully trim, his face was lined, and he regarded the newcomers with weary skepticism as Torre introduced them. "Hal, Alan, this is Galin, my eldest and, I fear, my only living child. I had no sister-sons to honor the Mothers, so Galin is my heir, and through Gwynllian you are his, Hal, as Iscovar knows well enough. Galin, this is Alan, heir of Laueroc, and his blood brother Hal, Prince of Welas, he who is King to be."

"With much help, perhaps," Hal acknowledged.

Galin did not smile. "You should not have called me in for this, Father," he said. "It is dangerous to leave the outer defenses without my leadership. The lads could have ridden out to see me."

"I see no lads," retorted the old King stiffly, "but two seasoned travelers and warriors. The men will do very well without you, Galin. You are becoming as set in your ways as I. You must be growing old."

"Ay, old and fussy," muttered Galin.

"And on my account," added Torre half-humorously. "Out in all weathers to protect my royal person. I am indeed grateful, my son." He cast Galin a soft glance from under his shaggy eyebrows. "But I grow lonesome for your company."

"You had two other sons," Hal interposed quietly.

"Ay." Torre's eyes focused on the past. "Glondil was killed in the attack on Welden. We buried him in an unmarked grave along the road of our flight. But Gildur, my youngest son, I never saw after that terrible night. The assault, you know, was very sudden and treacherous. Gildur ran to the treasure room to save a few precious things, the heritage of our people. He should never have tried. We who escaped did so with nothing except the clothing on our backs. For months I hoped he would walk into this room. . . . But in the course of time I came to believe he must have been captured and killed."

Galin stirred restively. "Perhaps, Welandais Prince, you will tell me how you came to be wearing my brother's sword?" Almost contemptuously he returned their weapons to Hal and Alan, pulling them from a pouch at his feet.

Dazedly, Hal accepted the black and silver sword from his hand. "Gildur's sword? I cannot say! An outlaw gave it to me."

"Then why do you say, Gildur's sword?" Galin snapped. "I had another brother."

"And he was killed. But somehow these things came to Isle, and to my hands." He drew the antique plinset from its leather case. "Was this not one of the precious objects from the treasure room of the Elde Castle?"

"Ay," Torre whispered, "ay." He took it into his ancient hands tenderly. "This is the first plinset, crafted by Llewys Lay-Maker for Claefe, Veran's queen, she whom he brought from the Mountain of the Gods. But wherever did you get it?"

"I found it in the study of the Lord of Celydon, in the Broken Lands; a good man. He had it from a minstrel who had died of fever under his care." Hal phrased his next question carefully. "What sort of man was my uncle Gildur?"

Torre only swallowed, and Galin answered for him. "Glondil and I were dark, like our father, and his uncle the Thunderer, and Veran, and the others. But Gildur was golden, like Ban, and Claefe, and your mother. He was a musician, and a dreamer."

"He loved the ancient legends and lore," spoke Torre reprovingly. "In the days of our kingdom's glory, he would have been revered as a great bard. It is hard when a man of peace cannot be respected for his own talents."

"The minstrel was a fair man, not yet past middle age," mused Hal. "It could have been Gildur." He took back the plinset, idly striking a few chords.

"Do you play it!" Torre exclaimed.

"Ay, Sire."

"Who taught you?"

"My mother." Hal raised his eyebrows at the shocked stares he received from both Torre and Galin. "Why?"

Galin answered in bewilderment. "Gwynllian did not know how to play."

They ate their dinner in puzzled silence. After they had pushed their plates aside, Hal spoke as if replying to an audible query.

"If Gildur lived, and for some reason could not come to you, perhaps he went to my mother."

"Probably we shall never know," sighed Torre. "But it is good to think that he might have lived—that he might not have been tortured to a slow death."

"The minstrel of whom I spoke died abed, among good and loving folk." Hal traced on the table with his fingertip, studying some invisible design. "Besides the plinset, what was my uncle Gildur likely to take?"

"There were the crowns, of course. The silver one Veran brought with him from the land of the Setting Sun. It was never worn; legend reserves it for the Very King who comes at the close of the age. But Veran wore the crown of the Rising Sun, made for him of the yellow gold of the mountain which bears his name, whence he brought the green Elfstone, and his bride."

Hal and Alan exchanged a surprised glance. Galin drummed his fingers impatiently, but the old King went on serenely with his thoughts. "Indeed, the most precious thing in the room, especially to Gildur, would have been the Book."

"The Book?"

"Ay. A thick tome, written in Veran's own hand, in a strange language. Only the Blessed Kings could read it. Then Ban died while Taran was still in Branwyn's womb, and the secret of the strange language died with him. But much of what was in the Book has come down to us by word of mouth."

"*Dol Solden!*" breathed Hal. "*The Book of Suns!* It is written down here on earth!"

"Ay, we have many strange prophecies. The fall of the House of Veran was foretold, though little did I fear, when I was a youth, that it would happen in my time. But

it was said that a leader would come, a young man of
Veran's line, who would possess wisdom, vision, and the
knowledge of the lost language. He would come on a silver steed of elfin blood and bear with him the emblem of
his destiny. The marks of suffering would be on his body
and the sheen of moonlight in his eyes. He would be
called Elf-Man, Healer, Ruler, and Sunset King. With the
aid of his people he would turn back the Eastern blight,
and bring peace at last for the closing of the Age."

"Father," protested Galin, "you cannot be serious!"

"And with him," continued King Torre, unperturbed,
"would come his brother, a man great beyond the borders
of blood or nation, a man of heart, like Veran before
him. He would come on a steed of golden bay, and he
would be called Elf-Friend, the Golden One, and Sunrise
King. The emblem of his destiny would reside in the green
Elfstone, gift of the ash maiden."

Alan sprang up, overturning his seat, and strode to the
door, where he stood breathing deeply. Hal picked up the
bench without comment.

"Why, what is this?" inquired Torre blankly.

"Your pardon, sire, for my churlishness," said Alan,
returning, his face still dark with emotion. "Something that
you said is painful to me. Here is the stone of which you
spoke." He pulled it from under his tunic, and slipped
the chain over his head to hand it to the old King. But
Torre stopped him.

"Hold it up to the light."

Alan obeyed, and gasped at what he saw. In the depths
of the gem, glowing golden and growing like a living light,
blazed a half circle of radiant beams, brilliantly symmet-
rical. Brighter and brighter it burned, till it far outshone
the torchlight, and even Galin gaped in wonder. Trembling, Alan lowered his hand, and the vision faded.

"What manner of sign is that?" he whispered.

"According to legend," explained Torre, "this is the
stone given by Claefe to Veran, brought by her from the
land of the Rising Sun. It shows the sun emblem at
the center, after which the crown of Veran was fashioned.
Would you tell me how you come to wear it?"

"You seem to know as much about it as we do," Alan
muttered.

"More," remarked Hal. "It seems that Adaoun did not
tell us all that he might."

"Adaoun!" exclaimed the old King. "Then it is true!"

"What is true?" growled Galin. "Am I sitting in the company of madmen?"

"Elves," replied Hal quietly. "Veran's memory is still young atop the tallest mountain."

He tried to give them some feeling of the glow of timelessness that hung in the air of the elfin valley, of the bright glimmer of wonder which clung to the very grass of the place. He did not mention Lysse, and Alan sat silently, with lowered head. When Hal was done, Galin and Torre gazed for a moment with strangely intent but peaceful faces, as if a whiff of that mountaintop air had drifted their way.

Then they had many questions, and in the course of the evening Hal and Alan related most of the events in the two and a half years since Hal had escaped from the Dark Tower. Hal described plans for claiming the throne, and the talk turned to troops and strategy. Charts and maps were brought out. Hal sensed Galin's wariness changing to hope, if not to belief.

It was late when they finally left Torre. On their way up the spiral steps to their tower rooms, Galin addressed Hal with respect, even hesitation.

"Hal," he asked, "do you believe all these—ah—prophecies?"

"Not that they will necessarily come to pass, nay. Things are not often as they ought to be. But I must fight to bring them about, not for my own glory, but for the sake of my people. It is the burden of my birth to prevent another such fiend as my—father—from ever sitting on the throne of Isle again. The course of my life was plain to me long before I had heard of *The Book of Suns*." Hal paused on the landing. "Will you lend me assistance, Uncle?"

"Ay, I'll lead my men on your behalf," answered Galin gruffly.

Hal glanced at him again. "With your heart, my lord, or only to please your father?"

Galin stood a moment marveling at the perception in those gray eyes. Then he stretched out his weathered hand. "With all my heart, Welandais Prince," he vowed. "If ever a brighter dawn is to come our way, it will be through you."

In his chamber at last, Hal flopped gratefully on his narrow cot. It had been a long, heartspoken day, and he felt drained by it. But Alan paced the floor restlessly, involved in some sort of inner struggle. Hal watched him askance. Were the months of silence at last to be broken?

"It is harder than I had imagined, Hal," Alan remarked haltingly, "all this destiny. I feel that a great weight of expectation is put on me. And yours is far heavier. Small wonder that you found it so difficult to bear."

"You were a greater help to me than I can say." Hal rose to pace beside him. "You are a very special, wonderful person, Elwyndas. Is that so hard to accept?" Then, as Alan gestured impatiently, he plunged on. "Listen to me only a moment, Alan. Why should prophecy trouble us, indeed? Does it change anything? We never intended to do less than our best."

But Alan was not to be put off. With courage born of his misery, he spoke a name they had not mentioned in months. "But the prophecy concerns me and—and Lysse, does it not?"

"Ay," replied Hal quietly.

"What does it say?"

"Only that she is your *mendor,* as Rosemary is mine."

"But—" Alan nearly choked, but once started he was far too stubborn to stop. "I do not intend to have her. I must never see her again."

"Do you not love her, Alan?"

"Ay!" Alan banged his fist so hard against the stone wall that the blood ran freely down his wrist. "Mother of mercy, Hal!"

"You have told her so, have you not?"

"Ay." Spent, he spoke dully. "It was an act of great weakness. I should never have spoken to her."

"Nay, Alan, nay!" Hal seized him by the shoulders, almost shaking him. "Never regret it! Your love is your talisman. It was your brave love which taught you the Elder Speech and took you to the place where only Veran had gone before—and he a god-man, from out of the west. Never have I envisioned a man with a greater gift of love than you, Alan. Yet, all things won, would you let it go down to defeat from pride?"

Stung, Alan threw off his hands. "Would you have me deliver her over to death?"

"You are her *mendor,* too!" Hal cried. "Do you not

think the choice should be hers? There are many fates worse than death, even to an elf!"

Alan threw him a black glare and stamped across the room to stand by the narrow window. As he looked into the midnight sky, he remembered the elves' lake: serene, dark, unfathomably deep. Tumult swirled through him, and he grew short of breath.

From behind him Hal spoke wearily. "Alan, must we quarrel? This thing that turns you from me—I've been miserable these months past—I beg pardon if I've meddled where I have no say."

"Say what you will," Alan muttered perversely, and like a string that has been tuned too tightly, he broke. For the first time in his months of anguish, he wept. As Hal's arms steadied him, he could feel the tears dissolving the hard knot of bitter pride that filled his chest and replacing it with hope. Dimly he realized that even the impossible might happen, that Lysse's hand might yet rest once again in his. Faintly, he heard her reassuring voice: "Wear this in hope of a better dawn. Remember me!"

Hal rubbed the hardness of Alan's shoulders, feeling tight muscles slowly relax and tortured gasps turn to deep, quiet breathing. But the gray-eyed Prince did not think of the ash maiden. Instead, Torre's words, already forgotten by Alan, echoed joyously in Hal's mind: ". . . and he would be called Elf-friend, the Golden One, and Sunrise King. . . ."

Chapter Five

Three days after the comrades came to Cair Indel, the eve of November was celebrated, the ancient Feast of Fires. Galin rode in for the occasion, and Hal took his plinset and sang the lays his mother had taught him. For the old King, it was the merriest holiday in many years. But to Hal and Alan it seemed a gloomy affair compared to the previous year's feast at Celydon. Food was scarce at Cair Indel, for these mountains were not farmed. The meal was acorn cakes and dried apples. Torre's chamber was dimly illuminated by torches and rushlights. Like all of the rooms at the fortress, it was bare of hangings or decoration. The stone was cold, and the rude furnishings few.

In the weeks that followed, Hal spent many hours with Torre. The old King was a deep well of history and all kinds of lore, but it was not only his learning that drew Hal to him. It was father love such as he had never known. Torre cherished his grandson, and Hal looked to him like a boy. Alan watched the two of them with a smile. All the bad humor had gone out of his system, and he marveled at the change in Torre. Years had dropped away from the old King since Hal's coming. He walked strongly, without support; his hands were steady, his voice clear and true. Torre, who did not bestow friendship lightly, treated Alan with a friendly distinction that was more than the politeness of a host. Alan justly felt honored, and he was glad of Hal's happiness. But even Alan did not know how often Hal's thoughts turned toward Celydon.

Winter came. The mountains put on thick cloaks of snow, and the air developed teeth. Torre came out often, even in the biting cold, to help Hal and Alan with the horses; he loved to look at Arundel. But one freezing day, Hal did not come to the exercise yard. Alan met Torre, frowning. Hal was on the battlements, he explained, staring eastward in a kind of a trance, and not at all reasonable. Torre did not seem put out. "Mothers, then let us go to him," he remarked.

They climbed up the icy steps. Hal was gazing into the gray distances of winterbound Welas.

"What is it, Hal?" Torre asked. His voice caressed the name.

Hal did not answer, and Torre and Alan settled themselves to wait. Hal hardly seemed aware of their presence. After a few minutes, words burst from him, but not, they sensed, in answer to their query.

"Rosemary!" Hal cried. "She's in danger!"

"Where? How?" Alan demanded, but once again Hal seemed not to notice. His face was straining.

"The wolves!" he blurted a little later. "Why doesn't she see the wolves! Asfala sees them. . . . What can Pelys be thinking of, to let her ride out alone!"

"Thinking of you," Alan murmured.

"She flees," Hal said with immense relief. "But why into the Forest, into the trees? A horse cannot outdistance wolves among trees!" He grew tense again, biting his lip in consternation. "Asfala is small, she twists among the trees, but her legs are short, the snow is deep. Why did she go that way?" Hal panted; he was Asfala, and the wolves, and Rosemary, bent low over the filly's neck. To Torre and Alan, it seemed that the chase lasted an hour. They stood rigidly, waiting.

"A haven!" Hal shouted. "A refuge, a—a sacred grove. . . ." His voice trailed away in sheer wonder, and his shoulders sagged as he went limp with ecstasy. "Of course, she went there," he murmured. "It is her natal home, which she has never seen. Did the wolves drive

her there, or was it she who led them?" His voice sank to
a whisper; the listeners could hardly hear him.

"The lady has ridden her steed into the circle of rowan
trees. The wolves cannot follow, for there she is mistress;
more, she is essence. The wolves circle in the sacred
dance. Now Ket and his men come, with bows and clubs,
to drive them off. The wolves scud away, and the outlaws
stand agape; they also cannot enter the Rowan circle.
But, in time, the lady leaves it to join them." Hal spoke
in a dreamy chant, an onlooker aside from self. "Ket
asks her name, though he knows it well enough, and she
tells him: Rosemary, daughter of Rowana of Celydon.
She senses that she is a daughter of her mother, in this
place. Ket kneels at her feet. He loves her. He nearly
weeps with love; he will love her until he dies. But she is
mine; he knows she is mine. She is the Lady, and I am
the Very King."

"Ay," breathed Alan, remembering a dream he had
forgotten, once seen on an ancient woman's loom. "Ay.
The Lady of All Trees dwells on the Forest island of
Celydon."

Hal turned to him, shocked out of his trance, shaking
at his own words, terrified. "Name of Aene, Alan, what
did I say?"

"Truth." Alan put an arm around him.

"I called myself Very King!" Hal whispered, ashen.

"Merest truth, Mireldeyn," Alan told him whimsically.
"Think no more of it."

"Will the lass be all right?" Torre asked, bemused.

"Ay, Ket will see her home." Hal turned to the old
King remorsefully. "Grandfather, how long have you
stood here while I babbled nonsense?"

"I heard no nonsense," Torre retorted, "and I am not
yet too old to stand for a while. Moreover, it has been
said before now that the Lady of the Forest must wed
the Very King, as the Forest is the soul of Isle and the
Very King its heart. But what are the rites of this Lady?
What must she do?"

"She does not do; she is." Hal seemed to know the
answer in spite of himself. "She lives, as the Forest lives."

"Why did she not tell us, or show us?" Alan murmured.
"How blind we were then, Hal!"

"She does not know it herself, Alan! She is more being
than knowing. She is the fruit tree and the dappled deer."

Hal shook his head, blinking back tears. "Aene's power go with her! Knowing is only pain."

"Come in to the fire," said Torre gruffly.

It took Hal a few days to shake off the lethargy of his trance, and for a few nights he paced the corridors, afraid to sleep because of what his dreams might be. He hated the thought that Ket might someday kneel to him. . . . But the warmth of Torre's love drew him away from his fears more quickly than he would have believed possible. In the evenings he sat by the hearth and sang for the old man.

The quiet winter months passed slowly for Hal and Alan, in spite of their contentment. There was much to be done in the year ahead, and they longed to be on the road once again. If Iscovar's physician reckoned rightly, this would be their last year of preparation for the war to come. Hal paced for nearly a month at the thought of it, until one day he smelled spring even in the icy mountain air. "The snow is melting and the grass is green in the lowlands," he said, "though the crags here are still white. It is time for us to go."

Torre came to watch them pack. "You roam about the land," he chided, "without shields, helms or mail? Your fighting skills are great, but it is a wonder you have not both been killed."

"We have tried to avoid fighting," Hal explained. "We could appear to be only wastrels, or farm lads, when we chose. Though truly it was not often a matter of choice."

Torre shook his head. "Two years ago, perhaps, you could do that; but no one would mistake you now for farm lads." He studied their powerful shoulders and chests, noting their purposeful movements and steady bearing. "You are warriors, and leaders of warriors. There is no disguising it."

"Just as you say," Hal acceded cheerfully. "But what are we to do about it?"

"We have gifts," came a voice from the doorway. They turned in surprise to see Galin, but the King smiled. Galin's voice, as always, was somber. But Alan thought he saw a flicker of emotion in his black eyes.

From the corridor came a procession of servants, bringing Hal and Alan the accouterments of combat. Galin and Torre first presented tunics of fine chain mail, lightweight but very strong, crafted of the mountains' best metal. Then they brought half-helms with a noseguard attached; these were much less hot and heavy than full helms, and could be stored in the saddlebags until needed. The mail could be worn under an outer garment, if Hal and Alan wished to hide it.

Last, Torre and Galin gifted the comrades with shields. These also were lightweight yet strong, and rather small, so as not to hamper freedom of movement. They were of a graceful shape, the point not too long but somewhat rounded. In the center of each was embossed a half-circle sunburst, like that on the plinset case, or like the emblem of Veran's crown in the heart of the green Elfstone. Hal's shield and helm shone silvery gray, like his sword and his steed. Alan's were of the same metal, but treated with an overlay which made them glow a brilliant gold, like sunlight.

The two soon gave up trying to express their thanks. They knew that Torre understood, and beneath Galin's toughened exterior they felt his love as well as his reluctance to show it. So in mutual silence and regard they saddled their steeds, slung on their bedrolls, and prepared to leave.

"I shall miss you both," said King Torre. He stood tall, and in his eyes glowed the hope of a new dawn. As they rode down the gorge they looked back at him. With his dark eyes sparkling, his thin lips pressed tight, his snow-white hair bristling in the crisp air, he seemed a roused bird of prey, poised to strike his enemies, swift and deadly. In farewell he raised the clenched fist of war.

Galin rode with the brothers as far as the lower defenses. From the foothills they could see the lowlands in the hazy distance. Hal was right; green patches were beginning to appear.

"Farewell," Galin said simply as they turned to leave. Then suddenly he added, "Hal, Alan, I never told you—"

"We know," Hal assured him, smiling at the love in his thunder-dark eyes.

"Go with all blessing," he said.

They left the mountains behind them and rode toward the lowlands, Iscovar's demesne. Galin watched them go. He was troubled by the emblem on their shields—was it the rising sun of a new dawn for his land and his people, or was it the setting of their sun forever? There was a mystery in Hal's eyes which he did not understand, but which caused him both hope and fear. Something in Hal, he knew, was more than man, even more than legend— but even an elf-man could be killed. With the difficulty that comes of pride, Galin bowed his head and begged the Mothers to keep his kinsman from harm.

book four
THE DARK TOWER

Chapter One

Hal and Alan set their course straight toward Nemeton, for they needed to establish communication with the castle before they could lay their final plans. Hal hoped his old nurse was still alive. "She was always clever, and tough even in tenderness," he grumbled, to temper his concern. "Still, I wish I knew what happened to her, after Rhys was killed."

Since they had to travel through the heart of the lowlands, they put the bold face to it, riding abreast of each other with jingling mail, helms on and shields at the ready. In this land of petty lords, they believed, few folk would pay them any mind. But they were mistaken. Peasants gaped at them from the fields, and once an ancient woman scuttled into their path and seized their hands. "The Mothers be praised that I have lived to see this day!" she cried, and kissed their hands, and wept. Hal and Alan did not know what to think. Another time, to their surprise and discomfiture, a group of peasants knelt by their road. "Why are you kneeling?" Hal demanded.

"Because you are the Very King," a fellow answered huskily, "who comes to rid us of the oppressors, all gods be thanked!"

"But how can you know that?" Hal exclaimed.

"Why, the old song, my lords," the man blurted, and recited:

"Silver sunset, golden dawn
Bid the fiend from Isle begone.

Silver steed and golden bay
Bring to Welas brighter day.

Two that from Cair Indel ride
Very Kings of both shall bide."

Hal smiled crookedly at Alan. "I should think Torre might have warned us."

"He knew just what he was doing!" Alan averred.

The lowland lordsmen also took note of their passing. Several times they outran groups of armed men, and twice they had to cut their way to freedom. Their new equipment stood them in good stead, for neither took any wounds. So they wore the gear when they forded the Gleaming River, wore it while they fought and fled and dared their way across Isle, and wore it still when, in early summer, they entered the southern Forest.

Deep within its green belly, they rode down a leafy corridor just wide enough for the horses to go abreast. For no reason Alan could discern, Hal stopped, signaling Alan to halt as well. Hal listened intently, and a slow smile spread on his face. He gave a chirping call.

A little way ahead of them, a man dropped from a tree to the center of the path, facing them with nocked arrow. At once other outlaws dropped to both sides of the path, until an even dozen stood poised for combat. The first man, a tanned, country fellow of middle age, knitted his brows in consternation. Hal's grin broadened even as his eyes grew damp.

"Trigg," he chided, "don't you know me?"

The man's jaw dropped and his bow clattered to the ground. In an instant Hal was off of Arun, and the two friends were hugging and pommeling each other's backs. Trigg's cheeks were wet.

"Dear Hal!" he gasped. "Who would ha' thought it!"

"If you could not recognize me," Hal teased, "I should think at least you might have known Arundel!"

"Ye've both grown," Trigg marveled, "but ye the most.

A warrior knight, in mail and all, with the muscles of one of them whatchacallums—dragon slayers! Y'know, ye were scarce more'n a lad when I last saw ye, though mighty enough e'en then—"

"Spare my blushes, Trigg!" Hal protested, laughing. "This is Alan, my brother in blood."

Trigg gripped Alan's hand and scanned his face under the helm with an intensity strange in one so slow seeming. "I'd scarce ha' thought there could be more'n one," he murmured.

"There is not," Alan answered. "Are you not the friend who gave Hal his sword? Where did you get it?"

"No credit t'me," Trigg shrugged. "A minstrel fellow traded it f'r food, said he'd no use f'r it—but I thought 'twas a pretty thing."

"It is, indeed." Hal raised the shining weapon.

"He would not give it up even for a king's brand," Alan said, and Trigg's eyes sparkled with pleasure.

He directed them to the outlaws' base camp, where they found Craig the Grim sitting at the entrance of his hut, apparently watching the trees grow. He was a hatchet-faced man, worn and honed by weather and enemies. His eyes were sharp as flint, but subtle nevertheless. Craig greeted Hal with composure, but Alan could see his pleasure, warm like a hidden fire behind the mask of his face.

Hal and Alan stayed three days, spending most of the time in close talk with Craig, catching up on the events of two years, laying plans, setting up signals. Alan soon found that, unless he had reason to be otherwise, Craig was as shelly and inscrutable as an oyster. When he chose to command, his men obeyed him implicitly. Alan was glad he was on their side.

"I have heard news of you now and then, Hal, since you left us," he remarked on the third day. A hint of a smile showed at the corners of his straight mouth as he watched their surprise.

"News came to us from Ket's camp by the woodland ways, so that I knew you had found a friend in Alan here. Then rumor came of a handsome reward offered by Gar of Whitewater for a couple of rogues so bold I knew they could only be you two. Again, the Forest ways brought me news from the Gypsy camps. But after that, all is confused. From all quarters, vague rumors came of two noble youths, poorly clad, but mounted, and armed with swords and skill, who fought the armed henchmen of the rich oppressors for the sake of common folk. There were tales of kindness, of healing herbs and strength-giving meat. And lately there are whispers that the Very King had returned, a King that the Speaking Stone would have proclaimed, before it cracked, ages gone by, and was destroyed by the invaders."

"Then how has it been proclaimed, now?" Alan asked. Hal looked too thunderstruck to speak.

"Why, your shields, to be sure! All parts of you, indeed. . . ." Craig showed scarcely a hint of a smile. "There are many old jingles, and stories, and all of them have to do with rising sun and setting sun, silver and gold, and many other omens besides. The peasants hum old singsongs that a year ago were thought fit only for children, and every time you're seen the word runs like fire. All over Isle you are said to have traveled, fearlessly, like living legends, and wherever you went the oppressors were foiled and the poor folk blessed. So you see," Craig concluded, "I was not entirely surprised when you came here."

"It is all nonsense!" Hal sputtered. "We left Welas only two months ago, and we have traveled no farther than here. We helped a lass with her cow, once, and once we saved a fellow from a scourging by happening past. . . . And there was that sick child near the Western Way, and that burning cottage at Lee; we had to fight a few lordsmen there. But that is all. We are not legends; only men trying to do what we must."

"It is of such men that legends are made," replied Craig gravely. "And I think it is not *all* nonsense." He ran his appraising eyes over them both.

"I do not wear this shield in policy, Craig," Hal told him sharply. "It was given to me."

"I did not think otherwise," Craig declared.

An old woman stumbled along a Forest track, her eyes dull and vacant, her mouth hanging slack. Fearful of outlaws, she hastened her plodding feet. But when a golden steed stepped from the underbrush to block her path, she could only gasp. Her eyes traveled upward from the horse's hooves to a shield with a sunburst design, and then to blue eyes beneath a golden helm. The eyes were kind, and reminded her of some she had once known. Speechlessly she allowed Alan to place her in the saddle, and he took her through the leafy Forest wall. In a cool space under a giant silver beech, a silver-gray horse grazed by a still figure with eyes of gray. Hal waited to welcome the dear nurse of his childhood.

"Oh, Halsey! Oh, my poor little princeling!" she wept as she flung her arms around this broad-shouldered warrior; her head scarcely reached his chest. Alan had to grin. Still, he swallowed hard as Hal bent to kiss her.

"Strange chance, Nana," Hal marveled, "that sent you our way. It was merest luck that we saw you."

"Strange chance, indeed," she faltered, wiping her face, "for I have not been out of Nemeton in many years. I have been to see my cousin. . . . But you do not need that news."

"You speak wisely, as ever." Hal helped her to a seat on the ground. "Rest awhile, Nana. Eat with us and tell me what I must know. How is the health of the King?"

"He is a sick man, though he manages to present an appearance of health. I believe he will not last longer than a year."

She went on, acquainting Hal with circumstances at court. Alan was startled by the change in her manner. Her eyes were now bright and clear, her words rapid and to the point, her movements sure and purposeful. He began to realize that her doddering stupidity was only a protective device. How else could she, formerly the Queen's favorite, have survived so long in the hostile court? Her repulsive senility placed her beyond suspicion. She went everywhere and saw everything, but none of the great ones noticed or cared.

"I have nosed about these three long years," she explained, "trying to find out what had become of you, my poppet. But nary a sign of you could I spy, and I did not know what to think."

"I knew you would be hunting and grieving, Nana," Hal said regretfully. "And now I must ask you to labor for me."

"Willingly! Since I have seen you, my heart is as light as if I were a girl again."

"You must make shift, then, to let me know every month how the King fares. When he takes to his bed, I must come to Nemeton. But how is this to be done?"

She thought awhile. "I cannot do it myself," she said at last. "To leave the castle often is to invite suspicion. But there are others who remember you. I believe Tod, the master of hounds, will serve. Once every fortnight, or month at the longest, he takes the dogs out to the wealds, to romp and roll and stretch their muscles."

"That will do admirably," Hal agreed. "Tell him not to expect me, but a messenger. He must wear a quail's feather in his hat, and the messenger will carry a bow and bird-tipped arrows feathered with quail."

When they had finished their meal, Hal finally asked the question that haunted him. "The Dark Tower, Nana, is it as full as ever?"

"Many poor wretches have met the misfortune of attracting Iscovar's notice," Nana replied. "Why, the very day I left, a bold lord came from the north to pay his tribute, and begged the King to curb that robber, Arrok of Rodsen. By my poor old eyes, the King's answer was to clap him and his son and all their retainers into the Tower, and there they'll stay until he takes it into his head to either free them, torture them, or kill them. There's no reason for it, no reason at all, just cruel whim and the excuse of the Sacred Son—"

"Who was that lord?" demanded Hal. Alan's face was pale.

"Some strange northlandish name. . . . Ror—Roran—of the town of Firth."

They bid the old nurse farewell and set her far enough upon her way to make up for the time she had lost. "Put on your sulky look, Nana," Hal reminded her as he kissed her. When Alan looked back, she was once again a sullen, shambling old woman.

They set off at a gallop into the Forest. By dark they had found Craig the Grim, and Hal informed him that he intended, at whatever risk, to free Roran and his men from the Tower.

"You're mad, Hal, mad!" entreated Craig more earnestly than Alan had thought he could speak. "You can in no way succeed. Even if you escape with your life, the kingsmen will be after you like hornets out of a hive. Think well; it is not only yourself that you risk. You are the only hope of all the poor folk in this land. Would you plunge them into another long age of misery, for the sake of some who are already as good as lost? Think of the stakes!"

"If I thought of the stakes on my life," Hal replied quietly, "I would not stir from bed. So I pay no heed, but do what I must do to be a man. I shall succeed, Craig, and the kingsmen will not know where to look for me. You fear too much for me! I know secrets unknown even to you, and have powers you have not seen."

Craig shook his head distractedly and took breath to argue, but Hal silenced him with a flash of his gray eyes. "There is no time to talk! Just keep your men on the watch to help any poor wretches that may wander this way."

Craig stood frozen by the icy intensity of that glance. His vision went black for a moment, and he rubbed his sleeve across his eyes. When he looked up, Hal was off his horse, grasping him anxiously by the shoulders. For the first time, Craig noticed that Hal had to stoop slightly to meet his eyes.

"Are you all right, Craig?" Hal asked. "I am sorry, but perhaps now you understand."

Craig reached out and touched Hal's arm, as if to make sure he was real. "So that is the power of a Very King," he whispered with a tinge of awe.

Trigg had stood silently by during this strange scene, understanding little except that Hal was going into great danger. "Master," he broke in now, "let me go with 'em."

"You have no horse," Craig said.

"We shall get him one," Hal put in. "Craig, if you can spare him for a few days, I would be glad of his help."

"Hal," asked Craig slowly, "can you possibly have a plan?"

"Of course I have a plan! Do you think I would take Trigg to his death? He will be back within the week."

" 'Twill comfort me that he goes along to keep an eye on this harebrained venture. Go, then, all of you, with my blessing." He turned and stumped off into the Forest.

Chapter Two

They borrowed a few things from Craig's stores: a lantern, bandages, extra blankets. Then, with Trigg on Arundel behind Hal, they rode through the night. By dawn they had reached the southern end of the Forest and forded the Black River. Before them stretched the wealds, the empty, grassy uplands that Iscovar reserved for the cavortings of the royal hounds and hunters. Though no one stirred for as far as they could see, they camped on the fringes of the Forest for the day, taking watch by turns.

In late afternoon they broke camp and left the shelter of the Forest. By the time they reached the little villages beyond the wealds, dark had fallen, and they breathed easier. They traveled quickly but quietly, following the furrows of the country roads by the faint light of stars and crescent moon. At the first light of dawn they started searching for cover, and daybreak found them hidden in a copse of trees. On the road not far away passed the King's patrols. Hal and Alan had to force themselves to rest.

With dark, they took up their journey once more, pressing silently through the murky night. Time passed with grudging slowness, like a sullen stream. The three travelers had lost hope for dawn's dim coming when Trigg gave a startled gasp, and Hal signaled the horses to a sudden stop. Not too far ahead, black shapes of walls and towers loomed against a graying sky.

"Nemeton!" Hal muttered.

They stared at the lowering walls with mingled apprehension and relief. Nemeton squatted toadlike, a dark hulk upon the plain. Bats circled ominously above it, flitting toward a patch of woods that surrounded a jutting crag of rock.

"There is our journey's end." Hal pointed out the shelter and led them quickly toward it.

They worked their way deep into the woods and made camp at the bottom of the bluff. Directly across from them, beyond the trees and the city wall, rose the Dark Tower. Bright day had dawned by now, but they all felt shadowed by the Tower's presence. Trigg offered to take the first watch. Hal had different plans.

"Today we all should sleep," he said. "We are well hidden, and Arundel is as good a guard as any man." He spoke to the steed in the Old Language, and Trigg marveled to see the answer which sprang up in Arundel's eyes. Hal smiled and turned away.

"He can rest later," he remarked, "and for us it will be a long, arduous night. Sleep well."

But they did not sleep well at all, and arose with relief that the waiting would soon be over.

"Why does no one come here?" Trigg asked at supper.

"Folk say it is haunted," Hal replied. Trigg shuddered, but Hal seemed not to notice. "And so it is, in a manner of speaking. When I was young, some lads of the castle went on a dare to explore that cave from which the bats come. They returned soon after, running and shouting, half crazed with terror. Yet, when they were asked what had frightened them, they could not say."

Alan caught his drift. "Hal," he remonstrated, "how can you expect him to withstand it? Will he have you by him to help?"

"Nay. He must stay here with the horses. But I would put my hand in fire for Trigg," answered Hal. "He is great of heart, and faithful even where his understanding does not reach."

"Withstand what?" demanded Trigg shakily.

"There can only be one meaning to what I have told

you. The bats' cave must lead to the catacombs, the charnel pits under the Tower. Alan and I will go into it that way."

"I ha' often fought men," Trigg gasped in protest, "but never spirits!"

Hal placed a steadying hand on his shoulder and met his honestly frightened eyes. "Now hear me well," he charged him gently, "and forget all those false tales told to you by idle folk. If you do any fighting here tonight, it will indeed be with men, for only they would harm you. But your most difficult fight will be with your own fear."

"I hear ye," muttered Trigg.

"Once Alan and I have found our friends, we must summon up the spirits to rid us of the guards. You are likely to see armed men run, and hear them scream. If you stand your ground, you will learn that they run from nothing, and substance of nothing, except the evil in their hearts reflected back to them in the form of the unknown."

Trigg gazed for a long moment into Hal's gray eyes, and a seed of wisdom took root in the good soil of his honest soul. "I think I grasp ye," he murmured.

"Good. By the end of this night you shall be able to call yourself one of the dragon slayers, the true heroes of Isle."

Trigg laughed. "Pshaw!" he exclaimed, but stopped wide-eyed when he saw that Hal was not joking.

With the coming of dusk, the bats began to issue from their crevice in the rock. Alan and Hal equipped themselves with lantern, bread and bandages. "Have the horses in readiness, Trigg," Hal instructed. "If we succeed, we must be off quickly, before the panic subsides. If any kingsmen come this way, keep out of their path if you can; protect yourself and the steeds if you must. And remember, fear is only fear—of itself, it cannot hurt you. Farewell."

"Go with all blessing," Trigg whispered.

The cave of the bats was pitch dark, and the stench terrible. Hal whispered to the remaining bats as they entered: *"Este selle, bissel arledas, al donn tha ne riste."* ["Be calm, little brothers, we mean you no harm."] So the small creatures were silent except for their usual rustlings and chirpings. But Hal and Alan did not dare to risk a light, not where eyes from the Tower might see, and their fingers grew foul and slimy as they felt their way along. Their feet slipped and squished across the uneven floor covered with dung.

After what seemed an eternity, they cautiously lighted their lantern. They moved more freely now, but Alan became sickeningly aware that the floor was one great writhing mass of maggots and insects feeding on the dung of the bats. His stomach turned, and he tried not to look at his feet.

Abruptly the realm of the bats ended, and gratefully the comrades made their way along bare, damp stone. The cave narrowed, turning into a crevice which descended at a steep angle into the depths of the earth. The two found themselves sliding down a crooked chimney of stone. Presently Hal felt his feet dangling in air. He lowered himself and dropped lightly to the floor below. Alan followed more slowly. These strait underground regions choked his heart. Grimly he steeled himself against whatever treacherous cavern might await him.

He landed beside Hal. But the lantern cast its light on a large domed passageway, and Alan realized at once that they stood in a work of man, not nature. The fissure through which they had entered showed as a dark flaw overhead. Alan stood gazing in amazement.

"Ancient people dug these," Hal explained. "No one knows quite why. As mines, perhaps, or retreats in time of attack. My ancestor Herne, curse his name, very sensibly used one of them as the deepest dungeon of his despicable Tower. Let us go."

They padded along quietly but at a good pace until they came to a halt at a wall of rubble which blocked their way. Part of the tunnel had at some time fallen in.

"Confound it!" muttered Hal, poking about, then recklessly climbing up the huge crumbling mass. Near the top he stuck his head into a black hole and called down excitedly, "This goes through, Alan, I can feel it! Bring the light!"

Alan climbed gingerly up the sliding stones with the lantern. "Hal," he asked in a low voice, "are you never frightened?"

Hal wheeled and looked at him sharply, then remorsefully took his hand. It was icy cold. Hal chafed it as he spoke. "Seldom. But you're far braver than I."

As Alan sputtered in protest he went on, sadly but without self-pity. "I have always held loosely to life. But you, who have the heart to embrace life, must brave the fear of losing it. The old fears that strike deepest, fear of dark, and depths, and heights—these I scarcely know, and I can only imagine the courage you spend to overcome them."

"Can you not imagine what it would be like to get stuck in a hole like that?" Alan broke in.

"Imagining doom! Why, Alan, that's not like you at all!" Hal chided, smiling. Then he sobered. "Do you really want to turn back?"

"Nay," answered Alan ruefully, "go on, as ever. I will follow."

The next half hour might have been the worst in Alan's life if it were not for Hal's generous words. They wormed their way through the tiny tunnel, pushing their baggage before them. Sometimes they stuck fast, making their way through only by main force. Then rock fragments would shower them till, hearts frozen in terror, they were sure they would be buried alive. When they got through at last, it was tricky work not to go tumbling headfirst down the other side. But they reached the bottom and sat there for a few minutes, panting.

"How long have we been in here?" sighed Alan. "It seems like hours."

"Not so long, I hope," murmured Hal, "but long enough. We had better be moving."

They had not walked too far when Alan felt the presence of the spirits of the dead, though only as a bodiless weight in the air. Within a few paces the dim lantern light began to reflect on jumbled human bones, many of them broken, intermingled with bits of hair and clothing. Through the darkness they sensed that the pile grew into a mountain, reaching far above their heads. This was the work of seven generations of oppression, thousands upon thousands dead. The stench struck them to the core, for it was the stench of death, of rotting flesh and the creatures which feed upon it. Hal and Alan could not face each other's eyes.

"You who died in pain and hatred," Hal spoke to the waiting spirits, "we come not in idleness, but because we must."

The rustle like a breath of new air went through the

still place. A deep voice rumbled, as if from afar: "We know you, Mireldeyn and Elwyndas, and we have waited long for your coming."

"We must ask your help," Hal continued, "or we are not likely to live through the night."

"Wherever you move, you shall be the center of our circle of friendship and ringed with our Otherness." As the voice spoke, Alan felt the heavy chill in the air turn to warmth and comfort. He raised his head and breathed deeply; the stench of death no longer troubled him.

"Many thanks," said Hal. "But wait in this chamber until I call." Businesslike, he began to climb up the latticework of skeletons. Alan's eyes widened in distress.

"Hal! Must we?"

"It is the only way to reach the door." But Hal paused a moment, listening once again for the spirits. "Is it not, our friends?"

"The only way," echoed the deep, distant voice. "Go, Elwyndas, with our blessing. We are proud that our shattered bodies can yet be of such use."

"It will cause you no pain?"

"None."

"Then, many thanks."

They toiled silently up the macabre slope. The light of their lantern fell sometimes on the half-rotted flesh of a more recent victim, or on the retreating forms of squeaking rats and scurrying beetles. Hal struggled along, eyes fixed on his footing, trying not to wonder whether they might find Roran and the others atop this grisly hill. From behind he heard a half-strangled gasp, and spun around just in time to save Alan from falling. Trembling, Alan sank to his knees, white as the bleached bones beneath him. From the tangled heap of remains protruded a skeletal hand, and on its chalky finger was a silver ring set with a deep black stone. Hal stared silently as Alan's shaky hand reached out as if to living flesh.

"Father," Alan breathed, and he searched the darkness around him as if for a familiar face. Hal knelt beside him, gripped his shoulders.

"Alan," he whispered, "even if he is here, you do him no service to call him."

"The dead can have no place in the lives of those they leave behind," said the deep voice from its distance of Otherness. "Lover shall not speak to lover, nor father to son, but the Wheel shall spin out its seasons. So it is written in the Book." Alan thought he heard tears in the voice.

"Alan," urged Hal gently, "think of the living—if they are yet alive."

Alan raised his head and clenched his jaw a moment, and his trembling stopped. "May I take the ring?" he asked presently, in a voice he could not quite control.

"It belongs to the son of the one who wore it."

Alan removed the ring reverently and slipped it on his own finger. Then he rose, and they went on without looking back.

Streaks of dim light guided them to the door of the charnel chamber, over piles of fresh bodies which Hal examined hastily and turned from in relief. They extinguished their lantern and hid it among the gruesome contents of that cellar. On the threshold they listened a moment. The door was not barred; who would think to prevent the dead from escaping? So, hearing no voices or footsteps on the other side, they pushed it open.

Far above, Lord Roran lay in the darkness of his cell. The barred window overhead told him that it was night, but he did not sleep. He could not think. He had lost track of the days, for his head was light with hunger. Nothing but moldy bread and stale water had passed his lips. The first day he had been given a morsel of rotten meat, not fit for dogs, and he had scorned it. The guards had jeered at him. "By this time next week," they had laughed, "you will be ready to beg for such as that." They were right.

Since then they had paid him no unwelcome attention. His lump of bread and pannikin of water were wordlessly thrust at him each day. But now he heard the sound of harsh laughter approaching. The creaky door of his cell swung open and a body was thrown roughly on the stone floor just out of his reach. As the door crashed to and the men tramped noisily away, the still form on the stones stirred and moaned.

"Father?"

"Robin!" Roran sprang to the end of his fetters like a maddened dog on a chain, lunging and wrenching in his frenzy to reach his son. It was no use, and as he sank

back in the straw, exhausted, he heard Robin whispering,
"Father, don't . . ."

"Robbie," sobbed Roran, "what have they done to
you?"

"Father, pray stop. Your tears hurt me worse than the
blows."

Roran lay still, collecting himself. When he spoke
again, his voice was calmer. He could tell from Robin's
panting that his son struggled to suppress great pain.

"I am better now, Robin. Tell me the truth. What have
they done to you?"

"They have tied my hands behind my back, and forced
a spear through my legs behind the knees." Robin could
not quite steady his voice. "I cannot move without crippling myself. I cannot come closer to you." There was a
long silence. Finally Robin asked, "Have you seen Cory?"

"Nay." How like him to ask for Cory, Roran thought
with painful pride. Since that autumn day nearly two
years before, the boys had been inseparable. Boys! No
more. In that time they had grown to tall youths, skilled
in the arts of war and peace, bold in body and mind, and
as alike in their regard for each other as they were different in appearance. Trust each to think of the other before himself!

"I hope he has not been hurt," Robin whispered.
"Probably they do not realize how high he stands in our
affections, or that he knows anything. . . ."

Slowly the last phrase sank into Roran's mind. "Anything about what?"

"Hal. They kept asking me about him. I told them that
I knew nothing of him, but it seems they do not believe
me.",

"Hal!" breathed Roran. "So that is what this coil is
for!" Abruptly he shouted, "Guard!"

"Father! What are you doing?"

"If it will get that spear out of your legs, I will tell them
an earful about Hal! Ay. I would lead them to his front
door if he had one!"

"Father, nay! You must not betray him. Do you think
it would make any difference, even if you did? They
would kill us all the sooner, having had their purpose of
us."

"Better even that than this," grated Roran hoarsely.
"Guard!" His mind was numb and fixed in his despair.

"Father." There was a tone in Robin's voice that cut through the haze of Roran's wretchedness, a note of loving command that could not be ignored. "Let them slay me if they must, but do not let them torture my heart, Father! Do not let them change you."

Roran lay panting in his filthy straw. He was exhausted, too exhausted to feel or think, but suddenly the situation presented itself to him with a clarity that reached beyond hope or fear to the depths of his soul.

"So you want to fight them, Robbie." His voice was as calm as if he were discussing a day's plans, but full of proud affection.

"Ay. They can have my body and welcome, so long as I keep my soul, and you yours."

"You have saved it for me, my marvelous son. We will fight them together."

When the key turned in the lock and the door swung open, Roran looked up with fortitude, expecting the torturers. But it was Hal and Alan who entered his cell. Between them walked a pallid guard, and the Tower keys dangled in Hal's hand.

In the copse beyond the walls, Trigg struggled against sleep as the night wore on. He sat on the ground between the horses and nodded. But suddenly his head snapped up, and he jumped to his feet. The night rang with the horrible shrieks of men in mortal terror. The black windows of the Tower came ablaze with torchlight. Trigg blinked in disbelief. Panic-stricken guards were leaping from the windows to an ugly death on the hard ground below.

Others ran out through the courtyard or atop the walls. The shrieking continued, and the windows of the keep beyond the Tower began to glow bright. Then the postern gate in the Tower wall swung open, and in the torchlight Trigg could see people streaming to freedom. They did not run or scream. Some tottered on maimed legs, supported by others almost as weak. Some had unbandaged stumps of fingers or arms. Some had blind sockets for eyes, and were led by others almost as blind from long darkness. All of them moved off quietly, turning pale, smiling faces to the night sky.

In the midst of this strange procession came Hal, carrying someone wrapped in his cloak. At first sight of him,

Trigg crawled onto Arundel's back, gathered Alfie's reins in one hand, and sent the horses toward him.

He felt as if he were being pushed through a solid wall made of nothing but fear. He lay flat on Arundel's back and tried not to let the darkness crush his lungs. He thought that his head would burst with soundlessness, but he could not scream. He believed that he was slipping, falling to his death. With the last of his strength, he forced his arm around the warmth of Arundel's neck. Then, just as he felt his senses leaving him, he seemed to burst through.

He sat up, bewildered, smiling. The whole world was filled with friendship and praise. Just ahead was Hal, calling him proudly by name. Trigg slipped lightly to the ground and looked at the still form in Hal's arms. It was a dark-haired youth, his face deathly white, with ugly knots and cuts all over his head.

"Water," directed Hal rapidly. "And any food that we have, give to those who need it most. Then go help Alan at the stable."

Trigg hastily handed out bread and dried meat. The people took it quietly, with wondering thanks. When it was all gone, he ran to find Alan deeply enmeshed in a welter of saddles and bridles. The stable was empty of its staff, the doors ajar, horses streaming out into the countryside like the prisoners. Alan held a dozen or so steeds clustered around him by the power of the Elder Tongue, and even Trigg's unpracticed eye could see that they were some of the finest in Isle. They slung gear on them as quickly as possible and trotted them around to the postern gate.

Hal was still working over the injured boy while Roran and his retainers stood by. Hurriedly Trigg and Alan helped them onto their horses. Hal carried Robin on Arundel before him. Trigg had a steed to himself. This made him anxious, for he was no horseman, but he need not have worried. The spirited creatures stood like statues while Hal and Alan bid their farewells to the spirits. When the deep voices came out of the night air, Trigg was surprised; but he was no longer afraid.

They rode hard for the remainder of the night. Before many miles had passed, Lord Roran dropped his reins and slumped in the saddle. Alan slung him across the horse and secured him as best he could; then they pressed on. One by one the retainers also toppled from the weakness of their starvation. By dawn, only a few were still upright.

At first light, Hal found a spring of clear water with trees growing around, and there they stopped. Alan and Trigg got the men off their horses and rolled in blankets on the ground. Then Trigg went to see if he could help Hal, who had Robin beside the spring, changing the hasty dressings he had put on in the Tower. Trigg had not realized how badly the youth was injured. Neither, apparently, had Cory, for he fainted at the sight. Trigg caught him as he fell, and carried him off to a blanket on the other side of the spring.

"No wonder," muttered Hal as Trigg assisted him. "He's been starved for a week and a half. And he's one of the lucky ones, in the Tower. Did you see the others, Trigg? The tortured and maimed. . . . By blood, I'd forgotten how horrible . . ." Hal gulped and stopped, dabbing fiercely at Robin's wounds.

"But did ye see their faces?" Trigg exclaimed. "Full of peace 'n' wonder, despite their hurts. D'ye know what ye've done, Hal? Ye've breached the Tower! All of Isle will be abuzz with it."

"The Tower will be as full as ever in a week," Hal answered in a low voice, "and most of those poor, crippled wretches recaptured. I released them to confuse the kingsmen. . . . I might have been more merciful to leave them in their cells."

"No whit!" Trigg protested. "Ye're too tired to think aright, Hal. Their faces—they smiled 's if they'd looked for midnight and found dawn."

But Hal had scarcely heard. "Robin, here, had a spear in his legs," he panted in a kind of desperate monotone. "We took it out as gently as we could, but he shrieked and swooned. They all shrieked, when the spirits came. The prisoners would have run like the guards, except they were chained in their cells. The whole night has been full of screaming, and none of it mine. Alan took a ring from a dead and tortured hand. Horrible—"

"Ye're babbling," Trigg said, and took the cloth away from him like a mother taking a toy from a cranky child, stretched him on the ground and covered him. Within a few moments, Hal was deeply asleep. Alan returned from puttering with the horses, lurching from tree to tree in his weariness. Trigg looked at him and sighed.

"Go get yer rest," he told Alan. "I'll watch."

"You're a godsend, Trigg," Alan mumbled, and fell asleep as he met the ground.

Hal awoke in late afternoon, still exhausted, but calm. Alan sat up groggily beside him. Two cheerful campfires gave them welcome; over one bubbled a pot of gruel, and the other licked at spits of roasting birds. Trigg, looking tired but content, was dishing gruel for Robin, crooning to himself. Hungrily turning the spits was a stranger, a burly peasant with a homely, open face, who could almost have been Trigg's twin. Beside him, rendering the air poetic with its aroma, sat a bag of fresh, hot bread.

"'At's Drew," Trigg explained as Hal and Alan blinked. "Lives nearby, 'n' came for water. We got along fine; he's a cousin t'me that I ha' not seen these many years. Bread 'n' gruel from his wife, in trade for one of my grouse."

Anxiously, Hal went to kneel beside Robin. The boy opened his eyes, and the ghost of a smile played around his pale lips. "Hal," he whispered. "I thought it was a dream."

"No dream," he murmured, caressing Robin's forehead. "Are you in pain?"

"Nay. Trigg has comforted me marvelously well."

"He is a good nurse," Hal agreed softly. "I know."

"'N' he knows a need when he sees it," grumbled Trigg from behind their backs. He handed Hal a ladle full of whitish goo. "Go wash. Soap from Drew. No dinner till ye do."

Hal and Alan looked at each other, and their weary dismay suddenly gave way to shouts of laughter that woke the camp. From head to foot, they were covered with bat dung, dirt and dust, filth and cobwebs. Only Hal's fingers were clean from bandaging Robin. He whooped until tears wet his grimy cheeks. "A pretty pair of rescuers we are!" Alan choked.

"Like gods, you appeared to me," remarked Roran, going to his son. "Anyway, we're no sweet-smelling lot ourselves, after sitting for a week in our own dirt."

"'At's truth," Trigg said bluntly. "But ye I'll let eat before ye wash."

They all ate and washed by turns, gradually becoming

clean and full through the course of a lazy evening. When they finished at last, Trigg was asleep. The rest of them felt sociable for the first time in days, and clustered companionably around the campfires. Even Robin sat with them, resting against Cory. At his waist Cory wore the hunting knife Alan had given him, with its polished handle in the shape of a horse's head.

"You seem almost as done in as the rest of us, Hal," Roran remarked.

"It was hard, going back to the Tower," Hal acknowledged quietly. "I have been there before."

No one wanted to ask him when. "And Alan, what has come over you?" Cory inquired lightly. "You are so silent, and brooding—" Corin stopped abruptly. For a moment, Alan's glance pierced him with fear. But Alan's reply was calm.

"I have been watching the Wheel in motion, and I can't see the tilt of it. Look here." He reached under his tunic and drew out the glimmering Elfstone upon its golden chain. He held the green jewel aloft in the firelight, together with the black and silver ring on his hand. Corin gasped as brilliant light bathed him.

Glowing like a vision in the heart of each stone was a radiant half-circle sunburst in the form of a mighty crown. Corin squinted into the dazzling depths and vaguely perceived twin faces under crowns of silver and gold. But the vision faded before he could recognize the faces. Alan lowered his hands.

"Did the ring ever do that before?" asked Hal softly, as amazed as Corin.

"Never to my knowledge." Alan laughed harshly. "But then, I paid it little heed."

"Whence came the ring and the stone?" asked Roran, his face pale under his swarthy skin.

"The ring came from my father's hand, long dead in the King's charnel pit." Alan scarcely seemed able to go on, and Hal spoke up in his stead.

"It's a marvel that we found it. They always loot the bodies before they discard them, even of the gold in their teeth." He froze, and a peculiar pain washed across his face. "Corin," he said suddenly, "try to take the ring off Alan's finger—but be careful."

Puzzled, Cory obeyed. But as soon as he touched the ring he jerked his hand back with a yelp of pain. "Are you all right?" asked Hal anxiously. "What happened?" cried Roran.

"It stings like nettles!" gasped Corin, laughing even as tears of pain sprang from his eyes. "I dare say I'll live. But I should think, Hal, that if you were expecting something like that to happen, you might have taken it on yourself!"

Hal took the ring gently from Alan's finger and set it upon his own. Lord Roran touched it, then winced and put his finger to his mouth. Hal returned the ring to Alan, who sat in silent bewilderment.

"I knew nothing of this," he said at last. "How did you?"

"A buried memory. He wore it to his death, all through the torture, and none of the guards would touch it. But I touched it without harm. . . ."

Roran looked startled, and drew breath to speak, but kept silence.

"I had forced it out of my mind along with the rest of those black days," Hal concluded grimly.

No one had the heart to pursue the matter further. Corin tried to return the conversation to a former topic. "And the green stone? Whence did it come?"

But Alan sprang up and strode away from the fire. Cory looked after him in dismay, unable to follow; Robin had fallen asleep on his shoulder.

"Never mind," Hal said gently from beyond the fire. "He will be back shortly."

"He's so changed," Corin blurted.

"With reason," Hal replied. "The green stone is a gift of love from a certain maiden whose people remember back to the Beginnings. It was with her that he learned to watch the turnings of the Wheel. . . ." Hal looked into Corin's perplexed face and sighed. "It is difficult to understand."

"Impossible," grumbled Alan from behind Cory's back. "Pay no mind, Cory. . . . Here, let's get Robin back to his bed."

They all went to bed, and slept late into the following morning, and rested by the spring all that day, regaining strength, since Drew had no word of kingsmen being near. Then they chatted by another evening's fire and slept another night, and in the morning started gently northward. Robin was strong enough to sit on a horse, though he had to let his feet dangle below the stirrups. And still there had been no news of any pursuit. It seemed that Iscovar was having trouble in Nemeton.

Hal did not know that he had paralyzed the whole court city with a night of terror that would be made legend, and written into the lore books of the sorcerer scribes. No kingsmen would be able to ride from Nemeton for days to come. And Iscovar himself was roaring with rage to hide his own cold fear. No one knew how he had shrieked in the spirit-laden chill of that night, sensing an omen of his own approaching death.

Chapter Three

A few days later, in the shelter of the Forest, the fugitives paused to hold a council. Hal made his birth and his quest known, and Roran found hope in his words. It was decided that Roran and his retainers would speed northward to prepare Firth for siege, since surely Iscovar would be eager for revenge on him. Trigg would guide them to Craig, and Craig would help them on the way. Hal and Robin, riding more slowly because of Robin's wound, would travel to lay plans with Ket, Margerie and the Gypsies. Alan and Corin would journey to Alan's relatives in the north, though he did not expect to win much help from them. By midsummer, Hal and Alan hoped, they would be back together. Hal would warn Ket to keep an eye on Nabon of Lee in the meantime. If Nabon marched against Celydon, Ket must cut him off before he reached Pelys's domain, and send a messenger to warn the castle.

The company faced a sad leavetaking. Roran, knowing that he would soon face the King's armies, bade farewell to his only son. Cory felt the wrench of leaving Robin, though he was glad to ride at Alan's side. And Hal felt strangely reluctant to be parted from Alan, though he saw no other way to make his bid ready in time. He watched his brother ride away until Alan was only a flash of gold through the summer leaves, and he wondered at the heaviness of his heart. At last, he turned northward with a sigh. The young heir of Firth patiently awaited him.

Hal and Robin made their way through the Forest as fast as Robin's strength would allow, looking for Ket the Red. Craig already knew that the King's army marched toward Firth, and he would harry it to the top of his bent. But Hal needed to enlist Ket's support. Still, when they had located his camp, Hal would not approach him before his men. Robin wondered why, for Hal had said they were friends.

When Ket walked off at dusk into the shadowy Forest, a cloud-gray horse drifted through the thick-woven trees to meet him, soundlessly, like an apparition. Ket paled and swayed where he stood, the more so when he saw Hal's face beneath his silver helm.

"Liege!" Ket whispered, trembling.

Hal was off of Arundel in an instant, taking him by the shoulders, restraining him, for he had started to kneel. "None of that, I beg you," he told him. "Ket, why are you afraid?"

"My Prince. . . ." Quaking, Ket turned away his face; he could not go on.

"How does he know that?" Robin blurted.

"He just knows. He knows my Lady, he knows me. Ket, look at me!" Hal almost shook him.

The tall outlaw raised anguished eyes. "I had not thought to rival ye," he faltered.

"Of course not. I would know it if you had. How could you see her truly, and not love her? Ket, why are you so afraid?"

"Ye—ye're so changed." Still, his trembling had calmed, as Hal did not fail to note.

"I am the same man you knew before. Perhaps you see me better. I think it is you who have changed, more than I." Hal released Ket and settled himself on a twisted root, and as he had hoped, Ket sat by his side. They both kept silence a while, letting their words trickle through the mesh of their emotions, until Robin awkwardly turned and rode away. Hal put his head back against a thick old tree.

"How did ye know?" Ket murmured at last.

Hal shrugged. "What matter? I want no accounting

from you, Ket; I want help. But can you tell, now, what I want from you even more?"

"The greeting of a friend." Ket turned, his brown eyes dark with remorse. "But I have failed ye, Hal."

"Not entirely." Hal quirked a smile at him. "You have just called me by my name."

Ket gulped out a laugh that was half a sob, and they hugged each other, bursting into eager talk. Ket wanted to know where was Alan, who was Robin? And Hal asked plaintively about his lady; he would not see her yet awhile.

The next day he and Robin, with Ket and all his band, started east. For a month or more the two travelers spent their time helping the outlaws, and later the Gypsies, slow the advance of the King's army. It was a difficult time of hard riding and long waits in ambush, snatched sleep and nighttime raids. Hal did not dare to show his face near Whitewater town, so with many misgivings he sent Robin as his messenger to Margerie. The youth returned triumphant—cocky, indeed. Robin loved the excitement and danger of his new life. But the pace, and worry for his family, wore him more than he cared to admit. And, though he would not complain, his legs still pained him, making him feel weak and sick. Some days he thought he could not have kept on if it were not for Hal's unfailing kindness. He never guessed how lost and lonely Hal felt without Alan.

After they had seen Iscovar's army to the Marches, they turned southward again, hurrying toward Celydon, for Ket had said that Nabon's preparations were far advanced. It was late in July when they reached him at last.

"Alan?" Hal demanded.

"Not yet."

"And Nabon; when will he move?"

"Any day." Ket raised his eyebrows as a panting messenger ran into camp. "By my beard, I believe it is now!"

Rosemary was crossing Celydon courtyard when a warrior cantered in at the gate, and she stopped in her tracks. "Hal!" she breathed. Yet she felt as if she stared at someone she had never seen before, someone in shining helm and mail, with straight lines to his arms and back and a hard set to his jaw. He sped toward her like an arrow, and leaped down while Arundel was still in stride.

"Lady!" he exclaimed. "Rosemary. . . ." It was the first time he had called her by her given name, and she believed he had almost called her Love; his eyes on her had gone soft as evening mist, his face breathless and still. His hand had stopped in midair. She moved her own; fingertips just touched, but warmth sprang through them.

The other rider trotted up, and Hal tore himself away from her with a rending like the parting of flesh. They both felt that pang. "Lady," said Hal hurriedly, "I must go to your father at once; Lee is on the march. Will you keep this for me? I will be back for it, after the fighting." He slipped off his plinset and handed it to her. How odd it had looked, slung over his warlike mail.

She watched after him as he strode into the keep, and silently watched as he rode away, a few minutes later. He turned to her once, met her gaze mutely, then galloped toward the Forest. Within the hour, Pelys's garrison marched out to battle. Near their fore rode Rafe on a giant black charger. He was lieutenant of guards now, and Will was his captain, but this was their first fray.

Alan had found his mother's kinsfolk in the north to be of even less help than he had feared. Determined to bring some good news to Hal, he led Cory into the depths of the Westwood, where they encountered outlaws, as they hoped they would. After eavesdropping on some sentries, Alan allowed himself to be captured by a band under the leadership of a spearlike man called Blain the Lean. Within a few hours, Blain was feasting him like a longtime friend, and Alan was glad of it, for the word of the wilds was that Blain commanded nearly a thousand bows.

"I serve a certain Prince," Alan remarked obliquely over his meat.

"A Prince who is imprisoned, you mean?" Blain shot him a sharp glance. "He and the King do not agree, it seems, which is all to his favor."

"Nay, he roams, as I do," Alan answered cautiously. "The peasants call him Silver Sun."

Blain had seen Alan's own shield, of the golden sun

design, and Alan thought he might have heard of Hal's. But he was not expecting the force of Blain's reaction. The outlaw lurched toward him, almost leaning into the fire. "When?" he cried.

"What?" Alan nearly choked on his food.

"When will that vile Tower break? Already it cracks. Tell me when!" Blain's eyes stared wildly through the smoke.

"What do the songs say?" Alan softly threw the question back to him.

"Spring." Blain subsided to his seat. "When outlaws march in light of day, and fires burn bright at end of May. Spring. *This* spring?"

"You have said yourself, the dark den cracks," Alan murmured, mindful of listeners. "Will you march, Blain?"

"I and my men, till we drop!" the outlaw promised fiercely. He leaned back with a sigh of admiration. "How clever of you and the Prince to have planned your timing according to that song! And you have patterned your very shields after the old tales! You'll have every peasant in Isle ready to give his life for your cause."

Alan stared at him, frowning uneasily. "The time was not of our planning," he said at last.

"As you say." Blain smiled eagerly, avoiding a disagreement. "Where should we march, my men and I?"

"Laueroc."

"Ah." Blain nodded, his narrow eyes glinting. "But more, my lord, tell me more of this Prince, and of yourself! We have need of hope, here."

"Make yourself some." Alan rose. "I will return another time to tell you more. But now I must hasten back to his side. I have been away from him too long."

Blain gave him escort out of the Westwood. Alan and Cory left the keen-edged outlaw at the last fringe of trees and hurried eastward. Their search for support had taken more time than they had wished. Though they journeyed as quickly as they could, speeding back across Isle, July was nearly over when they entered the Forest once more.

They cantered toward Celydon, anxious to be reunited with their comrades, looking for Hal at every turn of the woodland trail. But as they neared their destination, they noted a cloud of dust above the trees, and heard the distant clang of weapons.

"Nabon must be attacking sooner than expected," Alan muttered as they hastily buckled on their helms. "Do your best, Cory!"

The road to Celydon ran through a valley beneath a knifelike ridge. It was here that Ket had chosen to set his ambush. Alan and Cory urged their horses to the top and looked down on a raging battle. Ket had arranged a rock-slide, first, to divide the invading army. Now his outlaws, together with the guards from Celydon, struggled against the remaining invaders. Many of Nabon's men lay dead beneath the rocks or with tufted arrows in their throats, and the rest were trapped against the rocks and the steep slope; but they still numbered more than the forces of Celydon. Ket's men had laid aside their bows, fighting with the quarterstaff, and could do little except defend themselves and contain their enemy. Pelys's men killed, but they were bloodlet and tiring.

Alan and Corin thundered down the slope. Nabon's men were taken off guard, but the defenders were expecting something of the sort, and pressed the attack. The momentum of the charge broke Lee's defenses, and several invaders were killed. Alan circled Alfie and sent him into the jumble of rock. The horse climbed with the agility of a goat, and Corin's steed hesitantly followed his lead. Though they were only two against many, Alan and Cory devastated the rear of the invaders' defenses, gaining great advantage from their height.

All was confusion now in the ranks of the enemy, for they did not know which way to turn. Celydon's forces cheered and attacked with renewed vigor, some of them joining Cory and Alan on the rocks. They wreaked havoc on the forces of Lee until, finding a gap where men had moved to climb the slope, Nabon's warriors fled as best they could, leaving their dead and wounded behind them.

Rafe was furious that they had escaped. "Forward!" he cried fiercely. "Track the rats of Lee to their burrow! Now is our chance to put down the menace to the South forever!"

"Softly!" retorted Will. "What would you do with Lee if you had it? Divide our lord's forces, peradventure, and leave him open to the attack of Gaunt? Or perhaps you expect Lord Pelys to leave Celydon and move to Lee?"

"Are we then to leave Nabon to attack us again in a year or two?" Rafe persisted hotly.

"Have better hope," drawled Ket, limping to his side.
"Have ye not heard the whispers that fill the land?" Rafe
stared, uncomprehending. But before he could speak,
Alan rode up with a troubled face.

"Have any of you seen Hal?"

"He should have been here hours ago!" exclaimed Ket.
"He and Robin rode this morning to warn Celydon. D'ye
think he would be dallying with the lady, at a time like
this?"

"Some ill must have chanced," muttered Alan. He and
Corin shot off before the others could express their concern.

They rode far apart, zigzagging in search, whistling to
each other now and then to stay abreast. They had not
gone a mile when Corin heard Alan's frightened cry. The
sound came from a tree-lined knoll, and Corin hastened
to the spot. He found Alan bending over Robin, listening to his chest. "He is not so badly hurt," Alan said,
trying to sound sure. Wrapping the still form in his cloak,
he gently lifted it to the saddle before Corin. "Take him
to the castle," he said. "I must find Hal." Cory left at the
fastest pace he dared with his precious burden.

The other two bodies were those of kingsmen. They
stirred and groaned. With averted eyes, Alan ran his
sword through each. Then he mounted Alfie and set off
at top speed on the plain trail that ran through the Forest,
following the prints of horses' hooves. How many sets?
Eight? Ten? Even a dozen? He could not tell. From time
to time the Forest mold was splashed with great clots and
dashes of blood. Fiercely Alan told himself that it was
not Hal's, but relentlessly the truth contradicted his
hopes. Why else would Hal not lose his pursuers in a
fox's maze of twisting tricks, as he had done so often before? Because the blood trail made all such devices
useless. The spoor led straight as an arrow toward Whitewater. What lay there? No friends outside the walls,
though the kingsmen did not know that. In his time of
need, Hal's concern had been only to lead the enemy
away from Robin, and Celydon, and from Ket's men, so
exposed in battle. Bad luck, or worse than bad luck, that
he had been attacked when there were none in the Forest to aid him! Alan cursed that luck bitterly as he sent
Alfie at merciless speed along the trail.

By dusk, Alan had regained some measure of calm. He

stopped Alfie at a stream and let him sparingly drink as he forced himself to consider. Now that night was falling, what would Hal do? Alan knew his tactics almost as well as he knew his face. Darkness would hide the blood trail. He could almost see Hal lifting Arundel out of the tantalizingly labored gallop to which he had held him all afternoon, letting the kingsmen know at last the speed of the dweller in the Eagle Valley. Like a gray ghost they would disappear into the darkness of the Forest; and then? Surely Hal would make a wide circle and ride back toward Celydon, hoping that his enemies would continue on the straight line he had laid out. To circle to the north would be to trap himself against the Rushing River. Surely he would circle to the south.

Unless he had already died, or been captured. Unless he no longer had strength to ride Arundel at his full speed. Alan pushed the thoughts from his mind. Though he felt he had gained on the kingsmen, they were still hours ahead. He could do nothing to hinder them. But if Hal still had the strength to play the fox . . . there was a chance.

When he rode on again his pace was easier, and he bore to the right, leaving the trail he could scarcely see. After he had ridden a couple of hours into the night, he began to pause from time to time. He would whistle a long, low tone, listen intently for a full minute, and then ride rapidly on.

It was not yet the mid of night when his whistle was answered by a distant neigh. He raced toward the sound, and tears of thankfulness and agony wet his face when he saw them. Arundel stood still, his silver flanks darkly blotted with blood. Under his nose lay the crumpled form that was Hal, fallen when his great strength had finally given out.

Alan fetched the flask, and soon Hal's head stirred in his lap. "Alan," he whispered, knowing even through the darkness who it was. "By the sweet Lady, I have missed you." Then his head fell limp again. "Hal!" Alan cried in panic, and felt frantically for his wrists. The flutter of life was still there. "Mireldeyn!" Alan called desperately, and felt Hal's body painfully respond. "Ay," Hal breathed through clenched teeth. Alan made him drink again from the flask before he spoke to him, and his voice shook.

"Mireldeyn, for the sake of the love I bear you, I beg you—don't leave me!"

"Elwyndas," Hal breathed from afar, like the spirits of the barrow, "I am wounded to the death, and my life is torment in me."

"Try to live!" urged Alan, as sobs tightened his chest. "If you love me—try!"

It was a long moment before Mireldeyn spoke. "As I love you, I will try my best. I give you my word."

With every pace of the long ride back, pain shot through Alan like that which filled the body he held before him. Arundel limped behind, for he had taken a deep cut in the shoulder. Alan had spoken to him, telling him to fall behind and make his way to Celydon at his own pace. Still he would not leave his master.

The long night hours stretched themselves out into a black tunnel of pain which, somehow, had to be traversed.

Chapter Four

Celydon castle was full of dead and wounded. Too many were friends, but most were from Lee. As Rosemary moved from bed to bed, wiping brows, giving water, she did not see the one she dreaded to find there; nor was he among the dead. Why, then, did he not come to her?

A gentle voice behind her shattered her troubled silence. "Are you the lady Rosemary?"

She spun around to face a towheaded stranger crouching beside a slim dark youth. Quickly he answered her puzzled glance. "I am Corin. I have been traveling with Alan. He has gone to find Hal, who has seen battle, it seems, along with Robin here."

Robin was unconscious with a deep cut on the head, and his shield arm was smashed at the shoulder. It took both of them to set it. Rosemary was as pale as Cory before they were done, for Robin writhed and moaned in his pain, though he did not wake. To distract both of them, she asked Corin how he had come to know such comrades. The story he told made her long more than ever to see her gentle warrior.

Far into the night she labored, and till the dawn she waited, walking quietly but restlessly from place to place. The servant girls rested, nodding, against the walls. Robin slipped into the deep sleep that comes after pain, and Corin slumbered, exhausted, beside him. Rafe dozed in the gatehouse, and the wise, sure-fingered old physician slept on a straw tick in the midst of the wounded, ready to rise at an instant's notice should there be need. Now and then a man stirred or moaned in his pain, but none woke. In all the world, it seemed to Rosemary, only she kept vigil. She had never felt so alone.

But then a clatter of hooves roused Rafe, and Rosemary shook the physician into wakefulness. In the hour before dawn Alan came, bearing his burden before him.

The physician's face grew grave as he peeled off blood-stiffened clothing and gently probed Hal's weakened body. The wounds were many, but one was deadly. In the break of the mail beneath the arm a sword had pierced deep, through muscles, ribs and vitals. Incredibly, Hal had wrenched himself away with such force that the sword had broken off in the hand of his foe. Yet he had kept his seat and fought and fled, with the point of the sword buried perilously near his heart.

Hal stirred at the first touch, and his eyes searched the many who stood around him, holding candles, holding his hands and feet. "Robin?" he whispered.

"He will be well," Corin hastened to assure him. "He is sleeping."

The healer's probe opened Hal's wound, and he stifled a cry by biting his lip so that the blood flowed in yet another place. His eyes went to Rosemary's. "Love," he panted when he could speak, "pray go from me."

She started to protest, but the healer stopped her with a sharp glance. She kissed Hal, and went, but only as far as the next room. She knew that Rafe held down his shoulders, that Alan placed the biting stick in his mouth. She knew that Hal panted and trembled as the knife cut into his side, and she could see in her mind's eye how he willed himself to keep still. Then she heard him struggle, shouting, "Fiends! Bloody, bloody fiends!"

"He thinks he is in the torture chamber!" choked Alan. "Hal! Hal—" With gentle words he brought him back to himself for a moment as the knife bit deeper yet. Then the castle rang with the terrible, racking scream of a strong man in unbearable agony. Rosemary rushed into the room. Corin leaned against the wall; Alan looked pale and shaky. Hal lay still. "By the gods, he is dead," Rosemary breathed, but the old physician shook his head. "Fainted, praise be. Hold the basin, my lady."

The knife moved delicately, warily; one slip could mean death. The healer pulled out the shard with cautious fingers, then wiped the sweat from his brow with a sigh that was more like a groan. They washed and dressed the wounds, and the still form did not move. But as Alan and Rafe laid him in the lord's own bed, Hal stirred and thickly spoke. "You can cage and torture the body," he grated, "but the soul flies free as the eagles."

Alan touched his forehead with cool fingers and called pleadingly, "Hal!" His distant eyes focused slowly and painfully on Alan's face.

"Brother," he whispered, "if I die, will you carry on what I have begun?"

Rosemary felt a chill like ice grip her heart, and she swayed on her feet. Alan's face went as white as the blood-drained one he faced. "Hal!" he exclaimed. "Do not say that!"

"My soul is weary within me, and longs for escape," murmured Hal. "As you love me, will you not do this thing for me?"

"But I am not you, Hal!"

"Alan!" Hal pleaded.

But Alan had risen to his feet, his face awesome. "Mireldeyn!" he commanded, and Rosemary wondered at the strange words she now heard. "I charge you, by the love we bear each other, to give over such thoughts!"

"Elwyndas," groaned Hal, "let me go!"

"For the sake of those who have suffered under seven generations of oppression, I will not! Only you can save them!" Alan's voice was as compelling as a trumpet call; then it gentled. "Let us see your innermost strength, Mireldeyn. Look at me."

Eyes met and embraced. Like dawn, or moonrise, Hal's flickered into tentative light.

"Say it," Alan commanded.

"I promise you, Elwyndas." The words were dragged out from under an immense weight of pain, but they came.

"Promise me what?"

"To carry on the fight."

"By what do you swear?"

"By the love between us."

"What more?" Alan was merciless.

Hal knew what Alan wanted. Under that adamant gaze he summoned the last shred of strength in his soul. "By the burden of my birth," he gasped, his face glistening in agony of spirit.

In deepest love and gratitude, Alan did what he had never done—he knelt and kissed Hal on the brow. Then he turned and spoke in a low voice to Rosemary, who stood stupefied by this strange scene.

"The shadows of black memories lie on his soul," he told her. "Sit by him and talk to him; remind him of every moment of love you have ever shared, every ray of light in his life, every reason to live. I have done all I can for him. Now I go on a fool's journey—to seek Veran's balm for his heir's ills."

Like the wind of war Alan swept across the land. He did not ride Alfie, spent in spite of his great heart, or the wounded Arundel. Instead he rode Rafe's giant black charger, Night Storm, and sat like blond lightning on his back. He bore neither shield nor helm, nor even blanket, but rode on the lightest of saddles and carried only water, sword and a little food. His cloak spread in the wind of his passing like the wings of an eagle. Folk who marked his going blessed themselves, as if they had seen an omen.

The little jar at Firth marked "Bloome of Veran's Crowyn" was as far beyond his reach as the moon. The elfin gold which flowered in the Eagle Valley was farther yet. For unspoken reasons, he and Hal had never carried with them any of the precious plant; it was not fitting, somehow, to pluck the lovely remnant of the legendary past and hoard it in concern for self. But now, in direst need, Alan fiercely prayed that Hal's strength would hold out as he urged the black steed toward a little valley he remembered, where an old woman worked at her loom, where time stood still and the blight of warlike greed had, some way, not yet entered.

He left Celydon in the early day. Two long days and two nights passed, and still he rode. He used no caution and sought no cover, but set his course like the bird who flies before the gale, as straight as the fields and roads could take him. Though he galloped through a lord's meadow or past a manor gate, men had scracely time to shout before he was gone from view.

Late in the second night he stopped. Stormy lay flat,

but Alan could not rest, though his eyes were bloodshot and his face twitching from lack of sleep. He paced impatiently through the dark hours. At the first faint light of dawn, he spoke to the steed in the Old Language, and Night Storm rose trembling to his feet. "By my troth, you are worthy of your master's love," Alan praised him.

He cast about the countryside, searching. As the first rays of the morning sun struck the tops of the trees, he found what he sought. But his lips parted with a groan of the deepest despair he had ever known. Some nameless battle of a petty war had raged across the little valley. The turf was torn and scarred, the stream muddied and stained with blood. Bodies of men and horses mingled with the bloated carcasses of sheep. The stench of death and war lay on the place. No trace of the indefinable fragrance of timelessness remained.

Eyes clouded by tears of helpless wrath, Alan turned to leave. Then he stopped. There was no need to hurry back and watch Hal die, he told himself, taking a perverse satisfaction in the agony of his failure. Stubbornly he went to the ruined cottage and found the charred body of the old woman lying near her loom. He wrapped her in his cloak and took her to a spot less defiled than most, by the stream and under an old willow tree. From the forrested slopes he carried stones and raised a cairn over her. Finished, he knelt and commended her to Aene, though he eerily felt that it was not her grave that he had made. But as he knelt, an inexplicable feeling of peace stole over him, and the mist cleared from his eyes. His left knee rested against a root of the great willow. Just beyond the ridge of the root, and almost hidden in its sheltering curve, shone a single tiny golden flower. . . .

Rosemary sat by Hal's bedside as Alan had told her to, and spoke of the good things in life, of flowers and green growing plants, furry creatures, warmth after winter, food after hunger, cool water in the heat. She spoke as best she could about dreams, deeds, friendship and fellowship. But most of all she spoke to him of love, her memories and dreams of their love.

She could only hope he heard her, for he gave no sign. He lay burning with fever both of body and spirit. His wounds did not heal, but remained raw and open, and he wasted away day by day, even minute by minute, until she could plainly see that no strength of body kept him alive. His eyes were open, bright and staring, but he saw only scenes of horror. He whispered his defiance, and sometimes cried out in agony. At such times the sweat stood out on his forehead and his every muscle strained, though she knew he had not bodily strength to raise his head.

Sometimes, at her father's bidding, she took a few hours' rest while Pelys or Rafe sat by the bedside in her stead. But her sleep was as troubled as Hal's waking nightmare, and when Pelys saw it did her no good he no longer insisted on it. From time to time, when her mind grew blank of things to say to Hal, she took the plinset and played the songs he loved the best; happy songs, songs of sweet sadness, love songs. As the haze of her tiredness and despair thickened, she said and sang whatever came to mind, scarcely realizing anymore what passed her lips.

She sang, without thinking whether it would help or harm, one of the old jingles that had lately become prophecies of hope for the people of Isle. She had heard it from one of Ket's men in the Forest.

> Bearing balm of Veran's flower,
> Man born blest with elfin dower.
> Eye to make the evil cower.
> Breaker of the darkest tower.
> Silver is the springtime shower,
> Rids the land of wintry power.
>
> Elfstone green on chain of gold.
> Bright dawn forged in Veran's mold.
> Sword in sunlight blazing bold
> Drives the wolves from out the fold.
> Each his own to have and hold.
> Rising sun has conquered cold.

Rosemary stopped, not sure what she had done. Hal spoke in the language that was strange to her. Though suffering still strained his face and the sinews of his body, his eyes no longer stared at present horror. Instead, they looked far away and inward, at a place where he longed to be.

Veran's balm. . . . Rosemary clung desperately to a

hope of which she scarcely knew the meaning, and she begged for Alan's swift return.

Alan had plucked the little plant tenderly, even in his frantic haste, and with a whispered apology he stowed it carefully in his pouch. But he rode Night Storm away at breakneck speed. It was midmorning, and precious hours could never be regained.

"The single hope of Isle depends on you," he told the steed in the Old Language.

Night Storm ran through the day on numb legs that moved under him by the force of a will scarcely his own. Alan's skillful hands guided him around the obstacles that the exhausted horse no longer noticed. The night was harder yet. Stormy plunged and stumbled, and Alan talked to him constantly, encouraging him through almost every stride. Not too far ahead, a normal three days' ride from Celydon, he knew that Corin was waiting with Alfie. Night Storm had to make it that far.

But the horse did not think he could. Never had he been so pushed to the limits of his strength. If it had been Rafe who lay on the sharp edge of death, perhaps he would have discovered by himself the strength that lies beyond the limits. But love of Hal or Alan was not in him, and there came a time when the authority of the Old Language no longer moved him. He stumbled, fell and lay still.

Alan jerked his leg out of the way in time. He said nothing. He loosened the girth and tugged the saddle clear. He poured his remaining water over Night Storm's head and down his throat. Of his own gear he threw aside water flask, food, boots—everything except his sword and his precious pouch. Then he went to the horse's head.

"Now," he ordered, "up!"

Stormy did not even twitch an ear.

Desperation had made Alan ruthless. He straddled the inert body, drew his sword and deliberately struck the horse on the flank with the flat of the blade.

With a scream of fury, Night Storm scrambled to his feet. Never, from the time he was a tiny foal, had he met with any treatment but deepest respect. Now his only thought was to crush, maim, kill the one who had done this indignity—but the man was not within his reach. A weight was on his back, and a coldly mocking voice said, "Now, you coward, run!" And, unbelievably, the sword struck again.

Night Storm whirled away like the wind of his name. He did not realize that day had dawned, that the blackness before his eyes was not the blackness of night. Blinded by exhaustion, hatred and shame, he ran until he felt his heart would burst. He ran for fear of the punishing sword. He ran in unreasoning hope of leaving the terrible man behind. He burned with mortification and the angry desire to prove his greatness, to win revenge with his own suffering and death. He ran until, incredibly, he was pulled to a stop. But his legs which could still carry him along would not support him, standing. Blackness engulfed him as he fell gently to the ground, conscious of nothing until Corin woke him.

Miles away, darkness had come before Alan's eyes also. He laid down his head and entrusted to Alfie the task of taking him with all speed to Celydon.

He came with the first sunlight of the new day. Rosemary heard the clatter of Alfie's swift hooves on the cobbles of the courtyard below, and in a few minutes Rafe had helped Alan to the bedside. Alan was a ghastly sight, with blackened, bloodshot, sunken eyes in a hollow face that twitched with sleeplessness. But Hal was like a spirit barely visible in daylight. So wasted was his body that he only seemed to live in the tortured soul that cried from his gray eyes. Fever burned him like torment, but it was not that which troubled him. He still cried out softly, in unintelligible words, and would have moved if he had had the strength.

Servants brought a brazier with boiling water, and Alan shakily placed the little flower in it, whispering words Rosemary did not understand. But she sensed it was a prayer, and bowed her head. In a moment a feeling of peace and comfort crept over her, and the anxious lines of strain fell from her face. She looked at Hal, no longer in desperate suspense, but in breathless hope; her mind's eye saw him sleeping sweetly. Alan knelt, leaning on the bed, and from under his tunic he pulled a green stone. "Lysse," he breathed, as if to a presence in the room, "you and your people, help him." Alan pressed the cool stone to his lips, and though his eyes showed unconsolable longing, Rosemary saw that the quivering nerves of his face had stilled.

Hal stirred and sighed, murmuring something she did not understand, something about Adaoun. Then his lids closed gently over eyes deep and calm as a mountain lake. Alan, scarcely breathing, reached out to stroke his peaceful face, and Rosemary also came close to touch. She smoothed the pillow and drew up the covers around Hal's neck, but Alan buried his face in the blankets and wept for sheer relief. Rosemary touched his shoulder, then left him there with Rafe.

"He is sleeping quietly," she told her father, where he sat keeping Robin company in Corin's absence. Then, feeling not at all strange, she went to the stable, to where Arundel and Alfie shared a large box stall. "He lives," she told them. "He lives. Do you understand me?"

Arundel arched his lovely neck, and over the serene waters of Celydon he sent a great, ringing neigh of triumphant joy.

Chapter Five

Alan never remembered going to sleep after his four-day ride. When he awoke, much later, he found Rafe sitting by him anxiously, as if he were the invalid. He ducked Rafe's offers of food and hurried to Hal's chamber. Hal was awake, with Rosemary in attendance, but too weak to do more than gaze with faintly wondering eyes. Alan could see that he scarcely knew where he was.

In the days that followed, Alan and Rosemary tended Hal constantly. Rosemary held the cup or the spoon while Alan raised the helpless head on the pillow. Alan lifted and bathed the frail body while Rosemary changed the sheets. Together they put on fresh bandages and dressing. Within a few days Hal started to mend. His wounds closed and dried, and he gained some flesh. He moved sometimes, trying to care for himself. Once in a while he whispered a few words in answer to some query of theirs. He slept most of the time. But when he woke, his eyes were puzzled, wondering how he had come from the horrors of the torture chamber to the care of these loving people.

On the third day, Corin came back with Night Storm. Alan met him at the gates. "Hal is much better," he told him gladly, and told it to the steed in the Elder Tongue, with fervent thanks. Stormy lifted his handsome head, and for a moment Corin's sober face glowed with happiness. Then he asked about Robin.

"He is mending well," answered Alan, wincing guiltily. He had only been to see Robin once. The youth had been seriously hurt, and deserved more attention from his friends, but even Corin had been torn from his side. Alan could only hope he understood. Snared in his thoughts, he burst out, "Cory, it had to be you. You had traveled that way with me, and knew the place I named."

"Of course," replied Corin in surprise, and peered at Alan. "Your troubles are not yet over, are they."

"I'll take the horses to the stable," said Alan gruffly. "You go to Robin."

"And Hal."

"Nay, not Hal. He is not yet ready."

Another person came to the castle that day, anxious about Hal, a daring and unaccustomed visitor: Ket. Rafe brought him to the lady, and he was glad enough to give her his news. The kingsmen, after searching near Whitewater for a few days, had backtracked into the Forest, and Ket's men had dispatched them. Rosemary thanked him for his good tidings, but explained that Hal was not yet strong enough to see him.

"Would it help if you spoke to him in that—that secret language of yours?" Rosemary asked Alan, privately.

"Perhaps. But it would be like pulling a flower into bloom. He will come to himself in his own time, and his own peculiar way."

Hal's way was to dream. He no longer slept quite so much, but spent hours staring into the distance with clouded eyes. Alan sat silently by, hours on end, as if his wordless presence could somehow be of help; he did not dare to offer any other help. Rosemary looked in on them from time to time, and then quietly went away. She sensed that she was not needed—not yet.

Sometimes, in his trance, Hal would whisper words in the Elder Tongue, snatches of song and legend. He spoke of Bevan of Eburacon, and later of Veran, and Brand, and Brent; all the Blessed Kings. He spoke of Adaoun and Claefe, even of Lysse. Alan watched and listened day by day, waiting for the name of Mireldeyn.

"*Elwyndas,*" Hal murmured. "*Elwyndas, mir belledas kellarth.*"

His trance broke like a thread, and he sat bolt upright

with a cry; tears rolled down his face. Hastily Alan caught
at him, afraid he would fall.

"My brother, my brother!" he choked. "How could I
have forgotten!" He stared wildly into Alan's eyes, and
Alan put his arms around him, trying to steady him with
his embrace. In a moment, Hal let his head fall to his
brother's shoulder.

"You gave me your blood," he sobbed.

"Some time ago," Alan acknowledged. "I would do it
again if I thought it would help. Softly, Hal."

"It all rolls on me now, like a tide," Hal groaned. "The
accursed Tower, and Roran, and you riding away. . . .
And Robin, wounded! And Arundel!" Hal stiffened in
anguish.

"They are nearly healed," Alan told him earnestly.
"Robin is longing to see you, but we thought it would
distress you. Softly, Hal!"

"Softly!" Hal pulled back to face him as if facing his
judge. "I had forgotten them; I had forgotten you and—
and Rosemary. . . ." His voice trembled with the magic of
the name.

"Hal," Alan charged him gently, "do not be so hard
upon yourself. You have been hurt to death; indeed you
have passed through death's dark realm with only your
innermost strength of will to sustain you. You have been
spent in body and spirit. It is not strange that your heart
heart has rested, these days past."

"Still. . . ." Hal faltered.

"Still, nothing!" Alan barked in exasperation. "Not another word, brother. Lie back; you are ailing."

Hal settled into his pillows with a tremulous smile. Alan
stood by his side.

"If you like, I will send her to you now," he added.

Hal nodded. Alan touched his hand, then strode off to
find Rosemary.

The next day he and Hal talked for hours, retracing
the events since they had taken different paths. Hal recalled little of his illness, but one thing he did remember: the pitiless majesty of Elwyndas. "You made me
swear. . . ." he murmured.

"By the burden of your birth." Alan said it for him.

"Why, Alan? Was not the pledge of our love enough?"

"My love would have let you leave me, or forgiven
you for breaking your word. You knew that," Alan ex-

plained grimly. "But the burden of your birth has no escape and no forgiveness to offer. I could bind you by nothing less." Alan's eyes were lowered. "Do you hate me for it, Hal?"

"You brought me Veran's balm," answered Hal, and that one sentence said all.

But in the week that followed Alan saw less of Hal, as Rosemary and the others saw more. When Hal and his love were together, Alan roamed the castle aimlessly, unable to set his mind to anything except the thoughts of Lysse that tormented him. He was glad of Hal's happiness, and of the healing comfort that Rosemary gave him, but Alan had no such solace. Sometimes Rosemary glimpsed the darkness in his face, quickly hidden, a sadness too noble to be called envy, and she wished she could bring him to his lover. She never guessed what distance of more than miles separated Alan and Lysse.

She was astonished daily at the change in Alan. There was a new knowledge in his eyes; wisdom, indeed. Rosemary had always thought of him as a straightforward, generous fellow, his greatness shining in his face and deeds. But now he had known some sorrow which was not easily defeated, and the bearing of it had given him stature that made him seem more Hal's brother than ever before. Rosemary wondered about the strange green stone she had seen, the pendant that hung, hidden, by his heart. Whence had it come, and what was the meaning of its glimmering light?

Somehow Alfie seemed to have changed along with his master. Next to Arun or Asfala, he had always seemed an awkward, ramshackle beast. Now he looked as sleek and finely molded as a greyhound or a deer. He moved with a powerful grace born of rightful pride. His muscles rippled in his long limbs; his flanks shimmered in the sunlight; his eyes sparkled with a golden glow. Gazing into their amber depths, Rosemary thought she saw something of the mystery that was in Hal, for Hal was always uppermost in her thoughts.

How he had reached out to her, once he had come back to himself. He had whispered her name, pressed her hand to his thin face; later he slept with the warmth of her lips still lingering on his. Even in his weakness he thrilled her, his words and his touch at once tender and bold. No question, now, that he loved her! He no longer kept a courtly distance between them, and every hour with him brought her new happiness.

One day, when Rosemary went to the walled garden to gather flowers for the sickroom, Alan stood there, waiting beneath the trees. She saw at once from the set of his jaw that something was afoot.

She had just come from Hal. "How is he?" Alan asked, and for a moment she forgot Alan's brooding face in her joy. "Much stronger," she replied. "Today he sat and ate without help. I think he will soon be able to walk."

"Then the burden will soon be on him again," Alan muttered. "As soon as he has taken a few steps, you will find him swinging a sword, preparing himself to take up his journey once again." Striking his thigh with a fist, he turned to her. "I am no good here, my lady. I am leaving."

"Leaving! But Alan, why?"

"As the best gift I can give to him and you. I give you both the precious days for your own. Let him have time for healing, and let him be yours alone, for the time. Let him not think of his task, or of leaving you, until I have returned."

She sensed the pain that underlay the gift, and her eyes brightened with unshed tears as she gave him the only comfort she could. "Oh, Alan," she whispered, "it is no wonder that I love you like the brother I never had."

For a moment his face softened as he reached out to her in mute thanks. Then he turned away, and she watched the hard set of his back as he strode off to see Hal.

"There is nothing for me to do here," Alan explained to Hal, a little later. "I will go to Laueroc, to see how time turns in the home of my fathers. I shall be back before the leaves fall."

"Will you take Cory with you?" asked Hal, after a long silence.

"Nay. He needs the rest." That was not true, and Alan groped for a better reason. "I would rather have him here with Robin. I feel that I must go alone."

Hal looked searchingly at him, seeing love and foolishness and perhaps a touch of shame. He found no words to give to Alan. "Go with the One at your side," he said at last, and held out his left hand. They passed their grip in silence; then Alan quickly left. Hal lay staring at a closed door.

There was a sort of timelessness in Celydon, Hal found, timelessness which Alan had given at some nameless sacrifice to himself, but it had its source in the lady. Rosemary sat at the bedside, sewing Hal shirts of soft linen, for hours, or days, he scarcely knew which; the time passed on tiptoe, unnoticed. As he grew stronger, they talked more, and sang to the plinset, old songs and new. Soon Hal was strong enough to spend part of each day in the garden. Rosemary could almost see the sun and air nourishing him, as if he were a blossoming plant. After a while they took walks, longer each day, until they were roaming far afield. When they rode the horses, they roamed farther yet. Hal was strong and healed by then, but he did not visit Ket in the Forest or go to the practice yard. Never had Rosemary seen the burden lie so lightly on him. For whole afternoons they would lie in the sun amidst the long meadow grasses, and he would make her flower garlands for her hair. They would talk of love, and kiss long kisses, deep and warm. Rosemary would gladly have given herself to him entirely, but he would not take her; not while the likelihood remained that he would be killed to leave her destitute and dishonored. Only in this way did he acknowledge his burden—except for one day.

It was three days after Alan left. Hal had asked Rosemary to fetch her father to his bedside, and when Pelys arrived Hal asked for her hand in marriage. But before Pelys gave his consent, he felt, he must reveal his birth to them both. Pelys would hear nothing of it.

"Tut, tut, lad, do you not think that I know you after all this time? You are wise, and brave, and well suited to be my daughter's husband. I do not need to know anything more."

"There is peril all around me. It may well reach out and touch her, and you."

"I always knew that you walked in peril! She knew it too. Do you not know that the gravest peril of her life is to be without you?"

"I must tell you!" Hal said desperately.

"Ay, ay, tell it then, if you must," Pelys acceded. "But understand that she is yours, not by your words or my consent, but by the choice of her own heart."

"I am Hervoyel," Hal burst out.

"I thought your other name was Mireldeyn," Pelys remarked.

Haltingly Hal told them his story, searching for words that would help them understand the pitfalls of his destiny. Pelys whistled and looked somber, but Rosemary, with the insight of love, saw beyond the danger and the awful responsibility to the deepest wound in Hal's soul. "Oh, poor Hal," she whispered, almost in tears. When he told about his mother's death, and his torment in the Tower, she cried outright. He put his good arm around her. "It is not a pleasant tale," he murmured. "I am sorry, love." But her tears were balm on his wounds.

As the narrative continued, he explained why he had not taken her more into his confidence. "I knew that Nabon of Lee would make his move soon, likely within the year. Ket and his men watched him while I was gone, and also guarded you, my lady, as well as they could. But even so, if you had been captured—perhaps taken for extortion—then a hint that you knew something of the Welandais Prince would have spelled your death in some foul torture chamber. I know your courage, but you cannot keep your thoughts from showing in your face; your eyes are like mirrors for truth. So, for your own sake, I judged it best that you should know little of me or my doings. But the danger is over, for the time, and before Nabon has gathered his strength again we can expect to put an end to him, in an unseasonal feast of fires."

The tale flowed long into the afternoon, and Hal grew tired and weak before he was finished. There was much that Pelys and Rosemary did not yet understand. Most of Rosemary's questions, if she had asked them, would have been about Alan, and the hidden ache in his eyes, and the green stone which hung from his neck. But she did not ask them, for Hal slept, and when he awoke he was purged of care. Throughout the lazy, happy days which followed, Rosemary kept her perplexities to herself.

So she was now betrothed. She and Hal would wed within the year, if he lived. She shivered when she remembered how closely death followed on his heels, but as much as she was able, she turned her thoughts to the present and its joy. Still, she was often puzzled. So much more she knew about Hal now, and yet she hardly knew him at all. He spoke to the horses sometimes in words she could not understand, and did not tell her what language he spoke. There was a mystery in his eyes that went beyond facts of birth or life, a knowledge and vision which she could not begin to name or explain. She wondered when he would tell her what it meant, if he ever would, or could. Her musings made her sad, sometimes, and wistful. Looking at her, Hal thought his heart would break for love of her, though he could not understand her moods; this maiden, of all things, was a mystery to him.

When the leaves began to turn and a chill came into the air, Hal's cares came back with a vengeance. Time ceased its slow, stealthy passing and began to rush by. Hal started spending his days in the practice yard with Cory and Robin. His time with Rosemary no longer passed in long, dreamy wanderings, their thoughts and their talk roaming like their feet. Instead, they sat in silence, clinging to each other like desperate children, their kisses made urgent by the pressure of the passing days.

When the leaves had turned golden and scarlet, but still clung to the trees, Alan returned. Hal and Rosemary met him as he rode from the Forest. Alan's glance was hard, his face set in grim lines. Hal seemed not to notice, for his eyes were moist as he gripped Alan's hand and thumped his shoulders. Wordlessly returning the rough greeting, Alan ducked his head—hiding what, Rosemary wondered? But when he turned to greet her, she saw that something of gentleness had come back to the tired lines of his face.

For two days he rested at Celydon. He sparred with Hal in the practice yard, and could not help smiling with pleasure to find him as well as ever. But smiles did not come easily to Alan these days, not even when he was in the boyish company of Robin and Cory and ardent Rafe. Once he lounged an hour with Hal and Rosemary in the sunshine of the meadow, and he slowly relaxed, as if something inside him had let go for a while. But he would say little about where he had been, except for a brief talk with Hal.

"We see it everywhere," he blurted then, as if the words rushed out of him almost against his will. "The petty cruelties and persecution, torture and crippling, broken men and broken spirits, the dead and the slowly dying. But when I saw it happening to those I knew and loved as a boy . . ." He paused, clenching his teeth. "You have heard me mention Tynan."

"Your father's old seneschal."

"Ay. He is still alive. Crippled with torture, and living only because he is too old to pose much threat. But he is fierce and loyal in spite of it all. I stayed at his cottage. The rest—either dead, or only half alive, surviving at the price of their souls."

"Do they have hope now?" Hal asked, but Alan looked away and answered only with a shrug. Hal was puzzled, for he felt that Alan had something more on his mind. But Alan stayed strangely silent. There was one visible sign of change: he no longer wore the ring he had got from his father's hand. When Hal asked him about it, he took the silver shining thing from a pouch slung under his tunic. But he offered no explanation, and he would not meet Hal's wondering eyes.

On the third day after Alan's return, they left Celydon. Parting from Rosemary was a painful wrench for Hal, but they hoped that perhaps in a year they need not be parted again. Another hope eased Hal's going, a hope that maybe, once they were on their way, the comradeship of the road would return and Alan would be more himself.

And indeed he did become more easy as the days went by. Robin and Cory seemed to notice nothing wrong, but Hal still sensed a barrier between them, a distance, which hurt and fretted him. What had caused it, he could not understand. Was he somehow to blame, or had Alan found something in Laueroc which made him so aloof? If Alan had a secret . . . Hal remembered years past, and sighed. He could not probe, when Alan had so patiently borne with his own unfolding mysteries. Sadly, reluctantly, Hal acknowledged that a door had shut between them when Alan went to Laueroc, and stood between them still.

Chapter Six

They spent the winter in danger, not so much from men as from freezing cold and ravenous beasts. So great was the pressure of their task that, in this season when all men kept within doors if they could, they sought no shelter, but moved across the empty surface of the land like ants braving a cottage floor. The horses grew thick coats of fur for protection, and spent their nights stamping and snorting, huddled nose to tail against the cold. The comrades wore layer upon layer of clothing, but in spite of it their fingers and faces were frozen and thawed and frozen again. They grew hardened to the weather, and found a fierce joy in their defiance of it. Only in the worst of storms, when blinding curtains of white would have frozen them entirely, did they take refuge in some cottager's hut or outlaw's cave. They watched the weather signs carefully, for to be caught by such a storm would have spelled certain death.

When they left Celydon they turned northward. They hastened across the Marches, wary of Arrok and avoiding Firth, for the King's army still besieged Roran's town. It would be to his advantage, Hal thought, that Iscovar's forces were divided, for the commander who had marched to Firth would almost surely have turned his army against the Prince.

Before winter struck, the company reached the harsh Northern Barrens, where Hal went to parley with the war lords, as Roran had arranged months before. These were mettlesome men, vain and quarrelsome as peacocks, chieftains of the barbaric tribes which roamed the far north in constant warfare. Tent dwellers even in bitterest winter, they were gaudy in their apparel, brawling in their ways. Robin and Cory found themselves fighting them from time to time, but Hal dominated them by force of his will and his flashing eyes. And Alan looked grim enough to give any man pause.

The warlords agreed to join forces against Arrok when the time came, and also to drive the besiegers from Firth. They hated Arrok and respected Roran, so these were tasks to their liking. Hal only hoped they could keep peace among themselves long enough to accomplish them. But winter would help enforce the truce he had ordered in preparation for the greatest war of all.

By the time the worst cold came, Hal and his comrades were on their way southward through the Westwood. There they spent several days with Blain the Lean, the outlaw whom Alan had met the summer past. Blain was a strange man for an outlaw, thin, dark and intense, not at all like the usually sturdy and stoical folk who are able to survive in the woods. He showed no skill in arms. Yet in his own way he seemed very clever, even worldly-wise. He discussed with authority the overthrow of power and the taking of power, describing in detail schemes of kings and nobles, sorcerers and priests, present as well as past. He even had some knowledge of military maneuvers. Hal wondered where he had got his education, since he was not of the nobility. From the sorcerers at Nemeton? It almost seemed that he must have been a novice, at least, in that coven of subtle and ambitious men. Yet Winterfest, that most sacred of Eastern yearly-days, came and went while they were with him, and no notice was taken.

Hal and Alan learned much from Blain, and listened more than they spoke. The keen edge of his intelligence, and its almost fanatical force, commanded their respect. His men, none of whom could read or write, almost worshiped their leader, as if he were a seer. But the visitors sometimes felt an indefinable lack in Blain, like an ingredient missing in a complicated dish. It was difficult to know how he felt toward them. Though he could not seem to restrain himself from showing strong feelings about all matters of the mind, concerning matters of the heart he revealed little. Still, he offered his allegiance readily and with conviction. He seemed to like Alan, for he spoke most often to him. This was all to the good, since he would be fighting beside Alan at Laueroc. Hal sat back contentedly, saying little.

When they left Blain, their ways once again parted. Alan and Cory traveled south toward Laueroc, while Hal and Robin headed back across Isle toward the Forest and Craig the Grim. Relentless winter was at its height, and their journey was a slow one. It was a weary month and a half before Hal and Robin came to shelter. They settled into outlaw caves gratefully, waiting out the stormy skies.

Once every fortnight or so, as for many months past, Tod, the King's master of hounds, took his charges out for a few days on the open weald. Each time, he chanced to meet a fellow of indeterminate occupation, going bird-shooting with quail-feathered arrows. And as planned, Trigg would return to the Forest and report news of the King to Craig. When Alan and Cory rode in from Laueroc, after Hal and Robin had already been with Craig three weeks, the report was still the same: no change in the King's health. But on a night when a hint of spring stirred in the breeze, on a night when Hal paced restlessly in his den and thought of sleeping outside, Trigg burst into camp on a lathered horse with the news that King Iscovar had taken to his chamber at last.

The four comrades were off before sunrise the next morning, and three nights later they made their camp in the same copse that had provided shelter the night of the Tower raid. The next morning, while Robin and Cory stayed in its concealment, Hal and Alan boldly galloped the main road into the place that Hal had once hatefully known as home.

They won their way into the castle by main force of arrogance. In shining helms and glittering mail, with shields at the ready, they pounded the gate with the hilts of their naked swords. When the gatekeeper asked their business, Hal shot him such a glance as froze his tongue to the roof of his mouth. Fiery golden flecks filled Alfie's eyes as they rode through the courtyard, and the proud steed arched his neck and struck out his hooves as fiercely as an eagle striking at his kill. Arundel's eyes glowed darkly dangerous; he moved with his own peculiar ghost-like grace. Hal and Alan held the horses to the slow trot past groups of kingsmen who gaped in floundering amazement. The news had spread quickly, and the groom who joyfully ran to take their horses was one who had known Arundel before.

Hal and Alan strode swiftly through the cold stone corridors of the keep. Servants, guards, even noble scions flattened themselves against the walls to make way for the two warriors. The lines and scars of four years of hardship were on their faces, and the memory of those years in their eyes. Their consummation was now at hand.

Only the guard at the King's chamber door attempted to stop them, for his was the ultimate responsibility, and his life the forfeit. Hal scarcely looked at him, but struck the sword from his hand in one blow, knocked him to the floor with the hilt and threw open the door without a backward glance. Alan followed him, though distaste for Iscovar repulsed him like an odor in the room. He stationed himself just inside the door. But Hal strode to the foot of the great canopied bed and looked down at the wasted form of the man he knew as his sire.

King Iscovar had been a grossly corpulent man when Hal had seen him last. Now his overlarge skin lay in puckered folds around him, toadlike, yellow and wrinkled. His body, once vigorous and overbearing, lay limp. But the passions which had dominated his life still glared from his eyes: cruelty, greed, pervasive ill will. His face was as expressionless as a mask, staring blankly at his heir. But he could not mask the malignancy of his soul; it lurked in his eyes.

He and Hal observed each other silently for some moments. The King seemed detached, but hot hatred smoldered in his gaze. Hal's face was hard and flat with his dislike. "I have come for my inheritance," he said at last, "little though I desire it from you. Will you help me or hinder me?"

Iscovar's eyes glittered as he moistened his lips to answer. But before he spoke, the guard entered, staggering, sword raised. Hal ignored him, but Alan blocked his path. "Hold!" he commanded. "Do you not know your Prince?"

King Iscovar's glance shot to the figure by the door, and his face paled beneath the yellow of his skin. "Laueroc!"

he hissed in the voice of a cornered serpent. He struggled to lift himself, words tumbling from him in a panic of guilty hatred. "Out! Get away from my presence!"

Alan stared with frank repugnance at the man who had sent his father to the torturers. In his disgust, he was quite willing to leave, but Hal stopped him with a glance. "He will stay with me," he told the King curtly. "What assurance do I have that you will not order him thrown into that loathsome Tower of yours?"

The King's face flared sickly purplish red. "Guards!" he shouted in a paroxysm of passion. "Guards!" Hal drew his sword as running footsteps sounded outside. But when the guards entered with a clatter of weapons, Iscovar summoned them impatiently to his bedside. "Command Chamberlain Waverly to come to me," he ordered them. "Also Kepp the Steward, and Derek, Captain of Guards, and Guy Gaptooth. At once!"

In a few moments the puzzled minions of the King hurried in, cheerful as ghouls at the thought of a crisis: jaundiced old Waverly, master intriguer and sorcerer; Kepp the Steward, a small, round man with a perpetually frightened look; Derek, lean and leering, harshest master of torture; and Guy Gaptooth, burly warrior, one-eyed, scarred and pitted with the marks of a thousand combats.

"Nay, I am not dead yet," sneered the King as the gleam faded from their eyes. "Nevertheless, you are to have a new master. This is your Prince, whom you may remember. From this moment, I give my authority over to him. Obey him in all things. Now," he continued, turning to Hal, "get that Laueroc out of here!"

Hal looked his officers over with cold gray eyes. Each in turn cowered and shrank, thinking there might be a price to pay for past deeds. Derek in particular felt the cold finger of fear, for he had known Hal under different circumstances, and he was certain that Hal had not forgotten those days in the Tower.

"This is Alan, Lord of Laueroc," Hal told them at last. "Think of him as my second self, and obey him in all things. Now go. He will give you your orders until I can come."

Hal glanced at Alan as he turned to leave, but the new lord of Laueroc would not meet his eyes. Sighing, Hal turned his attention to the prostrate monarch. Drawing a chair to Iscovar's bedside, he settled himself to hear whatever information his sire might care to impart.

Within just a few days, many changes took place inside the castle walls at Nemeton. On the evening of the first day, Laueroc and the Prince ordered the gates thrown open wide, and under their watchful eyes tall, grim-faced men came marching in by the hundreds, each carrying a fearsome bow as tall as himself and razor-tipped four-foot shafts. These men did not lodge in the King's stinking barracks, but settled in the open air of the courtyard, where they surveyed with hard eyes all who passed. Yet they did no dishonor to maid or man, and the castle folk soon learned to respect their new guards, captained by hatchet-faced Craig the Grim. Toward Laueroc and the Prince they scarcely knew how to name what they felt. There was something in their eyes which caused great fear, which made people think it would be death to displease them. Yet they showed none of the harshness that was usual in Nemeton; indeed, they showed unwonted generosity. All prisoners were released from the Tower, healed, fed, clothed and sent home. And orders were given that servitors and soldiers were to be better fed, and not to be beaten! Half suspicious and half unbelieving, the common folk who were the pulse of the castle watched and waited.

Chamberlain Waverly, head of the Nemeton sorcerers, was no longer to be reckoned with. Either braver or more craven than his fellow officials of the castle, he had left the King's chamber, walked through the gates and kept going. He had taken ship toward foreign ports, word had it, hoping to find a suitable patron for his sinister talents. In the absence of his leadership, his coven-mates had discreetly scattered, and the rites of the Sacred Son had come to an abrupt halt.

Derek of the Guards had made for the gates as well, but Alan had stopped him. Now, for the first time, he worked side by side with his men. Since there were no prisoners to guard and torture, they spent their days digging long trenches on a sunny hilltop outside of town. It was backbreaking work, but they scarcely raised their eyes from the earth they turned, so great was their awe of the gray-eyed Prince. Derek's leer had left him, and like his men he was half mad with wondering why he was yet alive. When would the order be given, as he was sure it would be, that would make them target meat for the grim-faced archers? For all they knew, they dug their own graves. But Derek clung tenaciously to life under any conditions, and did not complain.

Derek knew by now that there would be no more guarding of the Tower. Even Derek himself, when he had tried to bolt that first day, had not been put there. Even the kingsmen had not been put there, though Alan favored the idea. But Hal would have no one lodged in that Tower. "Not even the foulest fiend," he said grimly. So there was a problem of what to do with the kingsmen, the mounted elite of Iscovar's warriors. Many of them were out on patrol and never came back. Those in Nemeton gave their oath of allegiance to Hal, but they gave it glibly, obeyed him churlishly and disobeyed him when they could. One by one, he found it necessary to strip them of their gear and turn them out of the city. Their black cloaks went flapping into the Tower dungeons; Hal seemed to think the place fitting for such cloth. Their gaudy helmets went to the smithy, to be melted down and made into more comely things. Their horses Hal kept.

He would need mounted warriors to fight the southern lords. To find men to fill his empty saddles, he appealed to the troops. "I need riders," he told them bluntly. "Anyone may try." Once he had picked his candidates, he and Alan worked them mercilessly hard. They had only a few months at the most, and to send them against trained warriors as raw fighters would be slaughter. Yet Hal's discipline was not the brutal durance that these men had known before, but a kind of concentrated freedom. Without knowing quite how or why, the men thrived on it. Like the rest of the household, they began to experience obedience that casts off fear.

Guy Gaptooth continued training the foot soldiers under the Prince's watchful eye. A hateful tension grew in him, for he was no longer allowed to vent his spleen on the hapless youths under his command. He had not kept Hal's strange new order quite a week when he broke. During drills one morning he suddenly went berserk, rushing at a recruit in blind rage and attacking him with his sword. Hal interceded as the youth was laid low, and Alan dragged him out of the way. Then the gaping recruits witnessed an exhibition of swordfighting worth remembering. Guy was a behemoth of a man, a head taller and five stone heavier than Hal; he fought with the crushing force of a charging bull. But Hal led him in circles like a baited bear, reaching effortlessly through his frenzied strokes to prick him to greater fury, so that while Hal remained cool and untouched his opponent ran wet with sweat and blood, steaming like a pot on the fire.

From where he knelt by the injured youth, Alan called in disgust, "Have done, Hal!"

"When he is worn out," Hal called back, "we can tie him up."

"To what purpose!" Alan shouted. "Death is in his eyes! Be merciful and kill him, before he is forced to slay himself!"

Hal hesitated, regarding his opponent carefully as he continued to play his circling game. The man indeed showed only the look of a maddened beast in his eyes.

"Torment him no longer," grated Alan. "Kill him, or I will do it myself!"

With one swift thrust Hal buried his blade in Guy's heart, and almost in the same movement gave him the mercy stroke to the throat. Then he walked toward Alan, bemused, absently holding his dripping sword at his side.

"Now what sort of thing was that to say, in front of all who watched?" he asked, more puzzled than vexed.

"It got results, did it not?" Alan retorted coldly. "You, of all people, to be squeamish! If you are to win your throne, you cannot afford to be so chary of shedding blood."

"Ay, blood will be shed," muttered Hal, "in plenty. But I hope and pray I will never grow careless of it. This is not like you, Alan."

"Was I right," Alan shot back, "or not?"

"You were right," Hal assented wearily.

"Well, then." Alan's eyes were hard and dark as jewels, blank of all feeling. Hal could find no love in them, no understanding. He sighed and shifted his glance to the dazed, white-faced youth who sat at his feet.

"How is he?"

"Flesh wounds," Alan answered, his voice gentler. "He will be fine in a few days."

By the recruit knelt another, as pale as the first. "Your brother?" Hal asked. Gulping, the youth nodded.

"Well, get him to his bunk, and you stay with him."

Hal watched as they walked slowly across the practice yard, the one carefully supporting the other. He could not help thinking how another pair of "brothers" had once been, and he sternly held back the tears of misery burning in his eyes.

Six days later Robin rode into Celydon on a tired horse, and knelt with courtly formality to hand Lord Pelys a piece of vellum bearing the royal seal. Pelys read the missive, dismissed the youthful messenger with a smile and summoned Rafe.

When Rafe came before him, Pelys showed him the letter with the royal seal. "The Welandais Prince sends for you," he told him. "He has need of you."

Rafe's jaw dropped as he sputtered in astonished dudgeon. "I serve no son of the Black Kings!" he shouted hotly at last. "Most likely he has horns, like the god he serves, for the fiend himself is his sire!"

The twinkle broke into Pelys' eyes then. "Hal had no horns the last time I saw him," he chuckled.

"Hal?" whispered Rafe weakly.

"Even so," answered Pelys dryly, enjoying his joke.

"Hal," muttered Rafe, frowning. "Son of the torturing fiend of the Dark Tower! I always knew there was something strange about him!"

If Pelys had had the use of his feet to carry him the distance between them, perhaps Rafe would have felt the weight of his fist. As it was, Pelys became, for once in his life, quite speechless with wrath. "Rafe!" he thundered at last. "It would break his heart to hear you!"

"I know, I know," Rafe faltered, ashamed. "It is hard to believe, that is all."

"Then believe what you like! Believe that he is a changeling, as you once said, that the Otherfolk are playing tricks on the evil king! But know this for a certainty: he is the same Hal you always knew, and no finer man in Isle. Are you going to him, or not?"

Rafe met the eyes of the choleric old man, and mischief glowed in his own eyes. "Of course!" he replied in insulted surprise. "I must go to him at once!" He bowed and marched out of the room, leaving Pelys red-faced and seething.

Chapter Seven

Throughout the land of Isle there was a quickening of more than of new life and green leaves. The lords, of course, knew that the King was nearing his end, and eagerly planned their strategies to seize the throne. But the wars of scheming lords were commonplace in the lives of the countryfolk, and it made small difference to them whether the wars were for a wench, a plot of land or the kingdom itself. War was war whatever the reason, and their fields were likely to be trampled, their homes burned, their sons forced into the soldiery and their lives forfeited to the indiscriminate clashing of opposing armies. What, then, caused the peasants to whisper excitedly in the village streets at night, to do the foreman's bidding by day with a sparkle behind the dull-surfaced veil of their eyes? Most of them knew only that there was something in the air, a hopefulness born of half-forgotten legends that seemed to have come to life. All the countryfolk felt it and rejoiced.

In the town of Nemeton there was a quickening too, the quickening of love for a firm but gentle ruler. Just as hardy green shoots sprout from the stoniest of soils after a warm spring shower, so results of Hal's kindness were springing up in the strangest places. The round face of

Kepp the Steward lost its constant frightened look, and his cruelties disappeared with his fear. In the practice yard, Rafe drilled the troops in place of Guy Gaptooth, the burly warrior now dead. His men were a motley lot, but they came to love hotheaded Rafe, who forged them with the fire of his passions. On the sunny hilltop outside of town, the former guards still bent to their shovels. They no longer feared imminent death, but worked with a willingness hardly understood even among themselves.

On the day that the trenches were finished at last, Hal led the diggers to the Tower, where wagons were waiting outside the grim gates. "Today we lay your victims to rest at last," he told them. "But I will have no cowards in my legions. Anyone who panics and runs risks joining the company of the dead."

Strange how their hearts warmed to that word "my," though they did not understand what Hal had said; they thought he threatened them with execution. When Hal opened the doors of the charnel pit they froze in fear of the spirits before them and the Prince behind them, each as great as the other, and they squirmed as if in a vise. Then they moved, slowly and deliberately, willed forward by a strength not yet their own. A few screamed and ran to their death on hard flagstones or the bottom of the pit, as Hal had said they might. But still the Prince urged the others to the work at hand.

They loaded the wagons with disjointed bones and bits of human debris, the horror of the scene lost in the blackness that swam before their eyes. They followed the wagons to the communal graves they had dug, and the fear went with them. They unloaded the wagons and rode them back with fear clinging to them like an odor. They worked, though they did not know it, through the day, into the night and through the next day. Alan helped, though Hal had told him not to. When the last human remains were placed in the graves and covered with fresh earth, Hal led the men like sleepwalkers to their barracks, where they slept through half the next day. When they awoke, they remembered little and understood less. But they felt a change in themselves, and smiled in the spring sunshine as they had not since they were children.

Within a few days, and of their own volition, the guards had managed to find a great, pillarlike stone, which they dug out of its bed and laboriously drew to the site of the communal graves. They set it upright at the crest of the hill, where it could be seen for miles around, and chipped on it the runes for honor, and sorrow, and the repose of souls. Then they knew that the spirits slept, and they turned, unburdened, to the tasks Alan set them.

All except one. On the softest bed he had ever known, Derek of the Guards tossed and moaned in a sickness that was not of the body, and Hal sat by him, unable to help.

Rafe did not know about Derek. He had little comprehension of the events at the Tower, and little time to wonder about them, busy as he was with the training of his men. He took hardly any time for himself, but when he could, he rode Night Storm on his rounds.

A few days after the mass burial, Rafe went to check the sentries he had stationed at the gates, patting Stormy's neck and whistling under his breath. As he approached, his men hailed him. There was a stranger outside the gates, and they could get no sense out of him. He had showed no hostility, but even so they were reluctant to let him in. When Rafe asked them why, they fumbled with words. He looked like Death, one said at last. Rafe muttered impatiently to himself. "Let him in," he said finally, "and I'll take a look at him."

He continued to whistle softly as the unwieldy gates creaked open. But as the rider came through, his whistling ended in a sharp intake of breath. Rafe had not thought there could be another such horse in the world, a splendid creamy-gold creature, like a brother to Arundel. At first, Rafe was so taken up with the horse that he scarcely noticed the rider. Then he focused his attention on him, and an unreasoning chill tingled his spine. Head to foot, the fellow was covered by a long, dark cloak, and a hood concealed his face in its shadows. Moreover, he rode the incredible horse without a scrap of harness. Dark clouds scudded overhead, and the world was filled with the ominous rumblings of thunder, the eerie flickerings of lightning. In the chilly light, the silent rider seemed less flesh than a spirit of the approaching storm. The cream-colored horse shone pale as the lightning, the rider thundercloud-dark in his shroud.

The very air was tense with waiting, though only a few seconds had passed. Time seemed to have come to a standstill; between the mutterings of the thunder silence yawned like an abyss. Rafe heard every little creak of his saddle as he rode up to the stranger. "Who are you?" he asked, trying to keep the edge out of his voice. "What is your business here?" The stranger turned toward him as if to answer. Then time leaped from its crawling pace to a race out of control, as everything happened at once.

A malicious gust of wind caught the stranger's hood and lifted it back from his face. Rafe was dazzled by the sight of bright golden hair, a jaw chiseled to perfection by some unearthly sculptor, a face like that of a god. But it was the eyes that held him—eyes as fearful and as wonderful as eternity. He thought he would die, disintegrate with love. He wanted to flee in sheer terror, yet he longed for strength to stay. As if from another world, he heard the shouts and screams of his men. " 'Tis an evil spirit! A demon—a nixie—run! Its eyes will freeze your blood, turn you to stone!" Many ran, screaming in panic. Some stood with pale, staring faces that rather looked as if they had been carved from stone. And one, perhaps the bravest, perhaps the most bloodthirsty, drew his bow, shouting that he would make an end to the evil thing.

The stranger did not move, but Rafe reacted with desperate haste, leaning forward to strike the arrow with his hand. With blood dripping from a long, jagged gash in his palm, he turned on his men in fury. "What are you doing?" he screamed. "Would you kill someone who has offered you no harm, who does not even show a weapon? Get back to your posts, and wait till I return!" Though Rafe himself was white-faced and trembling, the force of his words made them ashamed of their fear. They returned silently to their places.

With the eyes of his men upon him, Rafe turned once more toward that terrible personage in the dark cloak. But the hood was up, the awful Otherness veiled. The stranger held a strip of clean, soft cloth, and with this he wordlessly offered to bandage Rafe's injured hand. Unreasoning fear still gripped Rafe, but his stubborn pride took precedence. He let the hand be bandaged, and then he led the rider across the courtyard. Death followed him on a pale horse; or was it essence of life, too much life?

Hal and Alan were drilling the horses. When they came in sight, the stranger guided his golden steed past Rafe's and sped toward them like the wind, his hood falling back

and his golden hair streaming. He called out to them, a
melodious greeting. Rafe had heard those haunting sounds
before. . . . Hal and Alan turned, shouting "Anwyl!" as
they rode eagerly to meet him. Rafe watched them embrace, talking excitedly. A dizziness of release came over
him, turning his vision black; he clung to his saddle. He
heard hoofbeats, and felt hands helping him to the ground.
Then, for the first time in his life, he fainted.

It was only a few moments later when he woke, with
Hal, Alan and Anwyl all bending anxiously over him.
"Rafe," Hal told him huskily before he could speak, "from
the bottom of my heart I thank you. If anything had
harmed Anwyl here, my crown would have scarcely been
worth the gaining."

"I have fought strong men in battle without faltering,"
whispered Rafe. "He threatens me no harm, and yet I
am weak with terror of him. Why, Hal? How does he un-
man me so?"

"Because he is not man, but elf." Hal helped Rafe sit up
against the wall. "You feared the unknown; you knew,
without knowing, that he was not like you. Yet you neither
fled him nor attacked him, but helped him in spite of your
fear. You are a marvel among men, Rafe."

"I have learned my lesson, that is all," Rafe muttered.
"When I remembered how I would have killed you once,
because of something strange I saw in your eyes, I thought
that someday this one might be as dear to me. But the
fear—I cannot live with this fear, Hal, even if I never see
him again. It clenches my heart. Is there no cure for it?"

"Only to go through it," Hal said slowly, "and come out
the other side."

Anwyl sat chatting with Alan, but rose gladly when Hal
called him over. Panic surged through Rafe as he watched
Anwyl approach; he clutched at the ground, and could not
keep from trembling. Hal spoke to Anwyl in the Old Language. He and Alan knelt by Rafe, one on either side,
holding him. "Look into his eyes," Hal instructed him,
"for as long as you can withstand it, and when you can
bear it no longer—keep looking."

He looked. Fear stabbed him to the heart, rent him,
scattered him to the winds. He struggled until his body
seemed lost to him, and his fear was a cowardice only
of soul. Rafe felt as if he were floating down a long, dark
corridor, hanging back at every turn. But at last, with a

glow of warm light and a great surge of relief, he came out into a beautiful place of abundant life. There Anwyl dwelt, and something called Aene, and in an instant Rafe understood what he had feared—the vast, awesome, paradoxical power of love. And he knew that the elves could destroy men with a thought and a glance, and he knew that they never would. The knowledge spun in his mind like a wheel of light, fading into blackness. He woke to find himself still leaning against the wall, with Anwyl holding his hands. Tears started down his cheeks, and he buried his face in the crook of Hal's arm.

"It is not the spirits of the night, or any spirits, or even the fiends of sorcery that cause the evil of this world," he faltered. "Nor is it the Ancient Ones, whom men have called heartless, cunning, cold of blood."

"Nay," replied Hal softly, "and if the folk of the First Song could destroy evil without destroying man, certainly they would do so. But evil is as much a part of man as heartfelt love; sometimes evil begins in love, or love is called evil. . . . It is a hard knowledge, but better than ignorant fear, I think."

"Far better." Rafe raised his head to face Anwyl. "I thank you. But my head is spinning with questions, Hal. Where do the elves live? How did you and Alan come to know them?"

Hal smiled. "Anwyl and I must go to Derek. I'll talk with you later."

"Alan?"

"I could tell you," he answered, "but I'd rather not." He turned his back and walked away, for when he looked at Anwyl the pain of remembering Lysse filled his heart.

Derek still moaned softly and tossed upon the soft sickbed, fighting a fever of the mind. For five days he had recognized no one, said no word, touched no food or drink.

Hal placed a brazier by the bed, and on it a pan of steaming water. Into this he put what Anwyl had brought him, and they both sat down to wait.

Anwyl carried two canvas bags full of Veran's golden flower. "Why, Anwyl?" Hal protested. "You must have stripped the valley clean of it, laid it waste."

"Because you will have need of it, Mireldeyn."

"There has always been need," Hal muttered.

"But now the close of the Age of Veran is at hand. Soon my people will leave the Eagle Valley, and whether we live or die, we can never return. This is no time to think of saving or holding back. In the new Age, whichever way the tide turns, there will be no place for Veran's Crown, or for elves either."

"Much that is wonderful will then be gone from our land."

"But much new and different wonder may yet come into it, that we cannot foresee. Hold fast to hope, Mireldeyn."

On the bed, Derek lay quiet, sleeping peacefully. Hal and Anwyl shut the door carefully as they left.

Hal came to Derek the next day, to find him wide awake and anguished.

"My Prince, my Prince," he cried in agony, "I have seen my soul and it is black—black!"

"Not one man in a thousand would have realized it, and not one man in a hundred thousand would have remembered it," Hal said, with admiration in his eyes. "Derek of the Guards, you will make a liegeman yet."

He looked back at him, and the sweat was running down his face. "My Prince, your forgiveness is the burden I must carry the rest of my life."

"Will you eat now," Hal asked him, "and grow strong again, and serve me?"

"Ay. I must serve you the rest of my life."

That day was the eve of May. At dusk, hilltop fires sprang up to mark the vernal half-day; the great stone that marked the graves loomed in the red glow like a tower of blood. All night, Hal and Alan wandered the grassy uplands between the fires, plucking the spring flowers and tossing them onto the raw earth of the mounds in memory of Leuin of Laueroc, wherever he might be.

In the morning, Alan and Cory left for Laueroc. There Alan would lead the battle to regain the home of his fathers. Anwyl rode with them, bound toward Welas and Veran's Mountain. Cory stood in awe of the elf, but his previous experience with the spirits spared him an ordeal such as Rafe's. Hal and Robin rode with the three as far as the crossroads.

"Happy birthday!" Hal remarked on the way. "Happy

birthday, yourself!" Alan retorted. They were both just twenty, but they had moved as men in the world of men for years past.

When they parted, Robin and Cory eyed each other in shy affection, saying little. Each knew that he might not see the other alive again. Hal gave Anwyl the embrace of a brother, though the elf hardly knew what to make of mortal caresses. Then, almost hesitantly, Hal offered Alan his left hand for their own distinctive grip. Alan returned the gesture, but his grasp was hasty, hard and rough, and he would not meet Hal's eyes. "Go with all blessing," Hal said at last. Cory waved to Robin, but Alan rode away with a stiff back, without another glance. Hal bit his lip, and Robin looked at him with sidelong sympathy, for neither of them knew that Alan turned away his face to hide the anguish in his eyes.

With the aid of old Nana, Hal had ferreted out most of the spies in the castle and sent them packing. Therefore, the great lords knew less than they would like of the doings of the Prince. The best-kept secret in Nemeton was the condition of the King. The healer was a man of peace, physician in the castle not entirely of his own will. He soon allied himself with Hal, and dropped cleverly erroneous hints. Thus, when Iscovar lay glaring at nothing but his own death, talk would have it that he might live a month or two yet. With this information the great lords had to be content.

One May evening, when Alan had been gone a little over three weeks, the physician came and spoke privately with Hal. Days before, Hal had ordered the filthy chambers of the Tower filled with straw and soaked with barrels of oil. Now he said no word to anyone but, taking a torch from a sconce on the wall, he strode to the main door of the prison that had been the nightmare of Isle for seven generations. He thrust the torch into each of several cells, then threw it down and made his way out to the courtyard, where he joined Craig the Grim and his men. Tongues of flame showed at the barred windows. The soldiery and the castle folk came out and silently filled the courtyard, watching and waiting. Suddenly the blaze streaked up the sides of the Tower and burst from its top like spray from a fountain. A pillar of fire reached hundreds of feet into the air; at its apex, flames spread like the petals of some giant, exotic flowers. There was no shouting in the courtyard, but an excitement that ran too deep for words. The fire lighted upturned faces set in lines of grim exultation. Their time had come at last.

To the south, in Bridgewater manor, the peasants stood watching the glow in the sky with blinking awe, hardly comprehending. But westward, along the Black River, the villagers looked to the sky, and within moments their own giant piles of straw and brushwood were lit, sending the news yet farther westward. Like bright pollen from the giant flower, sparks of light lit up across Isle, on some hilltop in the domain of every lord between the Forest and Laueroc, between Nemeton and Whitewater, and northward through the Broken Lands to Lee, to Celydon, Gaunt, and on to Rodsen.

Alan saw the fires from a cottage near Laueroc, and on a hilltop of his childhood home he lit the pyre that sent the news on to the faithful in the lowlands of Welas, and thus to Galin, Torre and Adaoun in their mountain fastnesses. Pelys saw flames in Lee, lit his own signal, kissed Rosemary and marched his troops toward Gaunt, riding in a litter between two horses. North of Whitewater, the Gypsies poured oil on the waste and set great patches of fire. Looking from his battlements in Firth, Roran knew the siege would soon be lifted. Outside of Rodsen and Firth, a smattering of bonfires carried the news on to the warlords of the far north, and they began to move.

In their strongholds of oppression, the great lords slept a sleep heavy with years of having their own way. On their watchtowers, the drowsy guards yawned and wondered wearily what crazy superstition the peasants were celebrating now. Little did they realize that the entire land was on the move. Armed men issued from the Forest and the Westwood as quietly and relentlessly as ink trickling from the bottle. Blain and his hundreds sped in forced march toward Laueroc. Ket and his men took position around Lee. Smaller bands, and even lone men, emerged to avenge themselves where they might.

There was no sleep for the countryfolk this night, but they did not mind. In Lee, Gaunt, and scores of petty domains all along the rim of the Westwood and the Eastern Forest, men, women, and children toiled through the dark hours until great piles of stolen food and goods arose in hidden Forest places. Then the women and children took a few belongings and went to the Forest to keep out of harm's way, with only a few graybeards to protect them. The men and youths kissed their loved ones and went forth with willingness to die.

Thus it was that Nabon of Lee awoke from his sound night's sleep to find his storehouses empty. His goods were in the Forest, his walls surrounded by outlaws, and many of his own men in their midst. Haughty Gar of Whitewater had to walk around his domain that morning, for his horse wandered on the waste with the Gypsy ponies. His town was nearly empty, and many were the gaps in his ranks where the youths he had forced into his service had slipped away in the night to rejoin fathers and brothers. Margerie laughed to herself in her close-shuttered house, for she knew that of all people she was the last he would suspect of having defied him.

In Weldon and all the petty realms of Welas, lords awoke to stolen supplies and missing men. In Laueroc, guard was strict and rule was harsh, but no one knew the ancient, secret passageways better than Alan. Iscovar's puppet could not march forth to war this day, for almost all of his great stores of food and weapons were gone.

Only in Nemeton, of all the places that knew Hal as friend, no movement took place. All night the courtyard and streets stood packed with ten thousand people, each of them as silent as the stars. The gray light of dawn grew, and still they stood: soldiers, outlaws, servants and townsfolk who had learned to love their strange Prince. But as the rays of the rising sun sprang from the sea at their backs, Craig the Grim appeared beside Hal where he stood on the platform of the keep.

"King Iscovar is dead!" he cried. "Long live good King Hal!"

A shout like a battle cry went up from the waiting multitude, and the courtyard bristled with uplifted fists. "The crown! The crown! The crown!" chanted Hal's people as Robin came forward with the ceremonial cushion. But they fell silent as Hal spoke, and though his voice was low, it was heard by all.

"I will wear no crown of the cursed Eastern Kings," he said.

"Alan thought as much," answered Craig, "and therefore made this one for you, and greatly regrets that he could not be here to place it on you. It is a plain thing, but will you not wear it for his sake?" Craig lifted the gold-bordered linen cloth to reveal a circlet of silver with the half-sun emblem graven on the front.

Hal's eyes shone like the crown. "By my troth," he breathed, "I will wear it gladly." He knelt. Craig placed the crown on his head, murmuring, "All the gods be with you, Hal." When Hal rose and faced his people, he gulped, for every knee was bent to him, and beside him Craig and Robin knelt as well. For a moment the silence was intense. Then Craig raised his fist in salute, and led the joyous shouts that followed: "Long live King Hal! Long may he reign!"

Hal flushed under the acclaim, and his lips tightened in discomfort. "King in name only," he said when at last he could make himself heard, "until the strong lords also bow to the crown. It is time we were moving, as I am certain they are."

book five
LAUEROC

Chapter One

Hal had no intention of being trapped in Nemeton like a fox taken in his hole. Caution would not avail him against far superior force. His only hope was to out-maneuver his foes in open battle.

He marched his men into the heart of the south, the fertile and oppressed Soft Lands, trusting his friends in the north and west to keep Nemeton from attack. On the sixth day, his army crossed the sinuous southern branch of the Dark River and entered on an ancient, eerily level plain. The long, brazen horns of the town trumpeters had bellowed news of the King's death before him, so Hal sent his scouts far ahead on the watch for enemies. Wherever they came, peasants bundled together their few belongings and fled for their lives, for they knew that war was more merciless than the winds of a tempest in sweeping over a land. Hal's men told them to go toward Nemeton, where they would be fed and sheltered. Some were unbelieving. Some scurried like mice toward this unexpected sanctuary. And a few who had heard a whisper of hope knew that the time had come of which the legends spoke—and turned to follow Hal.

News was that from the south Mordri of the Havens was marching, and from the west, Kai Oakmaster.

Daronwy, a powerful lord, gathered strength at Bridge-water, not far away. It was no use trying to besiege him, with the other lords hastening to his aid. Hal felt his way to the south and west, watchful for the enemy. Word came that Daronwy had left his stronghold to join his allies for an attack on the new-crowned King.

A few days later, at dusk, the opposing forces met, camping on open fields, facing each other across a space as flat as a chessboard, naked to each other's eyes. The combined armies of the lords made a force almost three times the size of Hal's. Looking over at the dark, fire-flecked mass of their numbers and the glint of their weapons in the twilight, Hal inwardly winced, feeling dread tighten around him.

"Prospects don't look good," he remarked to the young captain at his side.

Rafe pulled a face at the wry understatement. "Did you expect better?"

Hal sighed. "Not much better. This was a fool's venture from the first, Rafe. Yet, what else was I to do? Nemeton is not built to withstand siege; the Easterners were too proud for that. And a King . . ." He let the sentence trail away.

"A King must show his mettle." Rafe completed it for him.

"Especially a new King," added Hal bitterly, "and no matter whose blood might be shed. . . . Well, perhaps help will find us."

"If Alan takes Laueroc with dispatch," Rafe asked carefully, "when might he come to our aid?"

"In a few days, at the earliest. More likely a week." Rafe watched, without comment, the slight shadow that darkened Hal's face. There was some nameless trouble between Hal and Alan, he knew. And Alan seemed changed, lately. . . . Rafe wondered, briefly, guiltily, if they could expect help of Alan.

"Even longer, for Ket or Roran to get here," Hal added. "I don't know where else to look for aid. . . . But until some comes, we must survive."

They watched the men planting pieces of sharpened lumber in the ground, angling the pointed stakes outward into a sort of Forest of spiky trees to shelter Craig's arch-ers. There was no other shelter on this featureless plain, not even a swell in the ground. Behind this makeshift fence, Hal and his army would have to await the enemy charge, in the morning.

He did not sleep much that night, pacing through the hours as restlessly as his sentries. Though Rafe would not say it, he knew that even survival might be impossible. He flinched away from thoughts of Laueroc, not wanting to wonder whether Alan was wounded, even dead. . . . He envisioned Rosemary, safe in her tower at Celydon, and held that dream for as long as he could. Some comfort in that; nothing threatened her except his own death. . . . Hal gulped, and stood for a moment weak as water, longing for her embrace, and knowing he might never see her again.

Rosemary had long since left her home to ride to Hal's side. That they expected her to idle in empty Celydon, when all the land was on the move to aid her beloved! She had barely been able to restrain her impatience until the nightfall after Pelys left. Then she had bundled her hair into a helm, found herself a brown cloak and boyish boots, saddled Asfala and slipped out past the dozing old men who guarded her. Transformed into a cocky-looking lad, she traveled steadily southward. She met only harmless farm folk, for the Forest was nearly emptied of its usual inhabitants. Once she was accosted by a skulking pair of ruffians. But they quickly gave way before the bright sword she drew, never guessing that she did not know how to use it.

She rode with urgency. By the sixth day, she had made the southern reaches of the Forest. She drew rein as she came to the end of the trees and looked out over open weald. The Forest, once strange to her, had become her shelter and friend. Nemeton! All her instincts told her to stay far from that place of horrors. Yet she must go there, to find Hal. Setting her jaw, Rosemary urged Asfala onto the treeless expanse, toward the distant court city.

Six days into the campaign at Laueroc, in the fields just outside the walls, Alan lounged in his tent. His tent! He smiled with amusement at the thought. As commanding officer and declared Lord of Laueroc, he had come to merit the luxury of shelter. Cory was cleaning up after the evening meal; impressed with Alan's new status, he no longer let him help with camp chores. So Alan lay at ease, musing on the victory that was likely to be his on the morrow, when he heard footsteps outside and a voice asking, "May I come in?"

"Certainly, Blain, you may," called Alan happily. The lanky scholar-outlaw had showed a keen understanding of the intricacies of their situation. His advice had prevented more than one mishap, and his strategems had been of significant help. Other men, Alan knew, were warmer of heart, finer of instinct and sympathy. But a mind like Blain's was not likely to be soon found again.

"May I speak with you alone?" Blain asked.

"Go ahead," Alan replied. The outlaw glanced meaningfully at Corin, and Alan frowned with annoyance. "What ails you, Blain? You know you can speak before Corin as before myself."

"Not this time," Blain stated mysteriously.

Alan heaved himself up to protest. But Cory had a statesman's instinct for smoothing over differences. "I must go to the well," he remarked cheerfully, and left. Alan sat back, scowling, to hear what Blain had to say. But Blain's usual directness was given over to fumbling and hesitation.

"You are a man of great heart," he said at last. "A man of strong will and much wisdom, but chiefly a man of great heart."

"You are not in the habit of idly paying out compliments, Blain," replied Alan dryly. "What is on your mind?"

"The sacredness of the Sacred Kings is a tale told by conniving priests and sorcerers, to further their own ambitions and fatten their purses!" Blain spoke with sudden passion. "I have seen no gods, and I know you cleave to none, but put the poor, superstitious folk under the fear of such vengeance and they will never try to free themselves. No son of Iscovar has any better right to the throne than his manhood can win him. It should go to a man of heart, such as yourself."

An icy fist seemed to grip Alan, choking his power of speech. Blain went on, intensely: "Take it, my Lord Alan! You have the occasion and the power to grasp it, and are twice as worthy as he. For the good of the people who love you—"

Like the shock of a sudden blow, an inhuman noise

overpowered the camp, a roar loud and terrible as that of an enraged lion. Cory, like the others, was paralyzed for a moment where he loitered by the well; then he dashed back toward the tent. He was in time to see Blain come stumbling out in blind panic, followed by Alan, raising his naked sword and possessed by fury. He overtook Blain in two leaps, like an attacking beast, and Blain never drew a weapon, so helpless was he in his fear. Alan pinned him to the ground with the sword at his throat, gasping out words choked with passion: "Traitor! Filthy traitor! He is the finest man that ever lived. To think that I would strike down my own brother, he who trusts and loves me!"

"Mercy, my lord," Blain faltered.

Alan barked a short, hard laugh that sent chills down Corin's spine. "Ay, you shall have mercy—for a few moments. You do not deserve to die the clean death of the sword. You shall die a traitor's shameful death, hanging by a rope. Corin, fetch cord to tie his hands."

Cory was back in a moment, and Alan jerked the prisoner to his knees. Cory's hands shook so that he could scarcely manage the knots. Alan took Blain's blade and sheathed his own. The blood-red rage was gone from his face, replaced by a look of unswerving purpose. "Mercy," Blain started to plead again, but stopped at Alan's icy glance, for he saw that his death was doomed by a force greater than that of wrath.

"Waste no breath begging for mercy," Alan told him in a low, calm voice, "but try to go out like a man, Blain. You have no gods to aid you?" Blain lowered his head as the question bit into him.

The whole camp stood gathered around, silent as the prisoner. Alan spoke to them. "This man has traitorously urged me to seize the throne of Isle from the one to whom I owe my love and allegiance. Though my rage has calmed, I cannot let him live. I do not require you to be present. Those who would not see, go with all honor."

No one moved.

"I need a hangman," Alan went on. "I will not appoint any man to this task. Does anyone offer?"

No one moved or spoke. "Then I must do it myself," said Alan, reaching for the rope. Gray-bearded Tynan stayed his hand. "I will do it," he said quietly, but then several came forward, shamed by the old man. The rope was quickly knotted and fastened to the bough of a tree. A stump was set beneath it, and to this Blain walked unescorted, scarcely swaying as he was helped up and the noose placed over his head. He shook his head to the makeshift hood he was offered. With clear eyes he faced Alan in unspoken request.

"Speak," Alan granted.

"You men of mine, stay with my lord Alan and serve him," he told them earnestly. "Serve him well, I charge you, for my sake. I love him well, though I love myself more, and would have overthrown him when I could. . . . But if you serve him, perhaps my soul will gain some merit yet. And beware of pride, which has undone me." Taking a deep breath, he turned to Alan. "I am ready," he said.

Alan suddenly became aware that Corin stood silently by his side. "Cory," he whispered urgently, "go to the tent." He kept his eyes on Blain.

Few grown men would have dared to cross Alan that day, but Corin had his own notions of duty. "I am staying with you," he said firmly. Alan shot him a piercing glance and saw no youthful defiance, only unflinching love.

The hangman waited for his signal.

"Let it be done quickly," Alan ordered. The fellow nodded.

"Torture me no longer, my lord," said Blain in a low voice, and Alan bit his lip to see the sweat that beaded his face. Suddenly he strode forward and showed Blain the only mercy he could: struck him hard on the forehead with the pommel of his sword. Then he jerked the stump from under his feet.

Though Blain was unconscious from the moment of Alan's sudden blow, there was no escaping the choked breath, the contorted, purple face, the convulsed body, and the jerking heels which beat a frenzied rhythm against the trunk of the tree before they slowly stilled. Blain's body took a long time to die. Alan wanted to turn away, to sob, to run, to crumple on the ground like a rag doll and beat his fists against the dirt. Many eyes watched him for signs of weakness; he did not care about them. But beside him stood Corin, and for the lad's sake Alan stood like stone.

When at last it was over, Alan asked for volunteers to

tend to the burial. Only when that was done did he walk
deliberately to a copse of trees darkened by the approaching night. There he leaned against a tree and vomited,
and wept in shame, knowing that the strength of his rage
had been proportionate to the strength of his secret desire.

Chapter Two

By the time Rosemary reached Nemeton, Hal and his army had survived one day of war. Their shelter of pointed stakes lay splintered and buried in bodies. The troops were reeling with exhaustion. A full tithe of the foot soldiers lay dead, and more were terribly wounded. Hal and his warriors, Rafe, Craig and the outlaw-archers under his command, all stood dazed and stumbling, encrusted with drying sweat and drying blood. But they held their ground. Their enemy had engulfed them, broken on them like an ocean, and their flimsy line, formed along borrowed lumber, had withstood the tide.

Yet, the army they faced the next morning scarcely seemed diminished. With sinking heart, Hal called his men into line of battle behind their shattered defenses.

"Those posts are smashed to bits," Craig grumbled.

"I couldn't use the same ploy twice, anyway," Hal sighed. "Today, we attack, and hope they aren't expecting it. Ready, Rafe?"

The young captain only nodded. He looked strained and pale beneath his layer of grime. Hal himself was bleary-eyed after a sleepless night spent among the wounded. Now he would not be able to spare men to tend them.

"All right. I must go to the horses." Hal strode away, but turned back after only a few paces. "Luck, you two," he added quietly, and went to find Robin and Arundel.

He led his mounted warriors in charge after charge that day, and the next, and the next. Rafe hurtled along after them, shouting hoarsely, his soldiers close behind. And Craig's archers took a heavy toll of the lordsmen—but it seemed that the enemy ranks never thinned. Hal and his army were pushed back, back, through the grueling days, until he could have wept, until he was past weeping. He wouldn't have blamed the troops if they had broken ranks and fled, but their valor tore at his heart. They made the enemy pay dearly for every step gained, and they paid dearly in their turn. Wounded comrades had to be left at the mercy of those arrogant lords. . . . And Trigg, faithful Trigg, was among the missing.

On the fourth day, only the coming of darkness saved Hal's army from being trapped against the river. "Cross the water," he ordered when his dwindled forces regathered. "It's our only chance." So, half swimming, half fording, exhausted beyond fear of drowning, they put the river between them and their enemy. Then each man collapsed to the damp ground, unmindful of food, fire or blankets. A deathly silence spread over the camp.

"I'll take a spell at watch," said Craig gruffly. "A few of my men are still standing. . . . Hal, you look like a wraith. Go get some rest!"

"I'll try," he mumbled. "Where, where, is Alan!" But Craig had no comfort to offer him.

There was no fighting next day, for a blessing. Seeing Craig's hard-eyed archers stationed on the shore, the lordsmen chose not to risk themselves in crossing. The enemy soldiers set to knocking together covered rafts. Grateful for their caution, Hal wandered his camp, helping where he could, taking stock. He used the gift of the elves to bring relief to many of his men, curing weariness of body and spirit. His followers regarded him with wonder, and called him the Healer King. But he had no cure to offer for death, watching his men give into mortal wounds. And he had no cure, seemingly, for his own despair.

A messenger from the north came early in the day. He left soon after, and Hal offered the men no hint of his news. But he spoke privately to Rafe and Craig.

"Roran has failed. Gar of Whitewater marches on Nemeton." They stared at him, stunned as if by a blow.

"For my own part," Hal added, anguished, "I am not reluctant to die in such loyal company. Still, I wish you were in safety."

Rafe snorted. "This is unlucky talk, Hal. Help may yet come."

"Ay, it may," echoed Craig. But his face was bleak.

At sundown, Hal and Craig rode the perimeter of the camp to make sure all was secure. At the outpost farthest from the river a beardless boy stood holding a fine sorrel mare. Craig was certain that Hal had gone mad, for he spurred toward this lad and hurled himself from the saddle. Trembling, Hal reached out and delicately removed the helm. As Rosemary's auburn hair tumbled about her shoulders, Hal dropped the helm and kissed her, deep and unashamed, in front of all who watched. When he released her at last, she saw that his eyes were moist.

"Oh, Love," he choked, "you should not have come."

"Why not?" She stood smiling and breathless from his greeting. "I believe you are not entirely sorry to see me."

"I love you. The sight of you is like wine in my veins. But oh, Love—" The words were torn from him. "I would not have you see me die."

She caught her breath as the cold grip of fear closed in her heart, but her eyes remained steady. "Why?" she challenged him.

"The past two days we have fought against a force three times our size. We have done well." Hal spoke ironically. "They are now only twice our number. My men are weakened by wounds and exhaustion. If we fight tomorrow, that day will be our last. If we retreat, we shall be hounded like rats at the haying, for Gar of Whitewater marches on a handful of men at Nemeton. My fighters are great of spirit. They will follow me to the end, whatever that may be. For myself I do not grieve, but it grieves me that I can find no hope for them—" Hal stopped short, suddenly recognizing his grief for Rosemary.

"Have better hope, Liege." She tucked her hand into the crook of his arm. "Alan has taken Laueroc, and no doubt is speeding to your aid. Moreover, Gar of Whitewater is not marching on Nemeton. The siege of Firth was quickly overthrown, but Roran was very low on supplies; it took him a few days to stock his ships and set sail. Then he sped before the wind, and came to Whitewater only hours after Gar had left, after the Gypsies had harried that lord as much as they could. And news travels quickly these days. Ket heard of Gar's march, and since his business at Lee was done, he cut swiftly across the Forest to stop him. I have not heard the end of it, but I think there can be small doubt of the outcome. With Ket at his fore and Roran and the Gypsies on his heels, Gar is doomed."

"Craig!" Hal shouted. "Do you hear that? Gar ambushed, and Alan riding to our aid!"

"I hear." He rode over, struggling to conceal the doubt in his face. "Good news, if it is true. But what are we to do until Alan gets here, if indeed he is coming?"

Hal turned on him with blazing eyes, but Rosemary touched his arm and lightly mounted Asfala. "Follow me," she ordered. "I have something to show you."

Not a word more would she say. After a few minutes they topped a rise and found themselves facing a silent mass of men, at least a thousand in number. Hal recognized prisoners he had released, peasants he had offered shelter in Nemeton, townsfolk he had left behind. Indeed, they comprised a motley crowd, but with a uniform determination of mien which made their random ranks seem as formidable as the battle lines of trained armies. At their fore, scowling, stood Derek.

"He guessed my secret when I came to Nemeton," Rosemary explained. "He, too, was anxious to go to you, but he feared your wrath. He asked me to intercede for him."

"He needs no intercession," Hal muttered. "I could kiss the fellow!" Suddenly dismounting, he strode to Derek and hugged him like a bear, thumping him on the back. Derek's lean face broke into a smile, perhaps a smile of love such as he had never known.

Before dawn the next day, Hal's army was roused and ready. They eagerly took their positions behind the slight rise Hal had ridden the night before. The enemy could have no knowledge of the fresh men who had come with the previous twilight. When the lords' armies crossed the river after their apparently fleeing quarry, they would find themselves trapped between water and Hal's warriors.

Hal rode with Rosemary until the army was in place. Then he sent her well to the rear of the lines, with Robin and some others to guard her. "Now, as you love me," he charged her earnestly, "keep yourself far from the battle, for this day will come to no good for me if I must be worrying about you. Promise me."

She silently agreed, with a kiss for good luck.

"Robin, stay by her, and if I fare badly, take her toward the guards at Nemeton. But I do not doubt that I shall see you both later. Take care."

So it was that Robin was not with Hal when Hal needed him most.

Arundel was not with him either; he was also with Robin. The horse had been wounded several times, and was too stiff to defend himself properly. But Rafe would not see Hal mounted on anything less than the best steed available. So Rafe rode a hack, and Hal took the black charger, Night Storm.

Hal's men waited, bright-eyed with anticipation, until the signal; then they topped the rise and struck. The slope of the land favored them, and the momentum of the battle was theirs from the start. First the archers showered the enemy with a deadly rain of arrows; then the mounted men charged, hewing like woodcutters. In their wake followed a swarm of foot soldiers and variously armed peasants, chopping like butchers. Within minutes the ranks of the enemy were decimated and forced back toward the river. But their scattered horsemen rallied, banding together at the center of their line. Into this group Hal plunged, for it was essential that they be split apart.

In a moment he was at the vortex of a seething, tumbling caldron of men and horses. Behind him and to the sides, Hal saw, his men were picking off the enemy warriors that had turned their attention his way. Still, he always faced several foes, and Night Storm turned to each threat, scarcely needing Hal's guidance. "*Bec wilndas,*" Hal murmured to him. "Good friend!" Though surrounded on all sides, they were hardly scratched, and through their concentration and teamwork they had stalled an enemy charge.

But suddenly Night Storm reared so high that Hal was catapulted off the steed. Dazed, Hal realized that an upraised enemy sword had an instant before been aimed at his own neck. Stormy feinted at the wielder with lightning forehooves. But the blade sank into the horse's throat, and Stormy crashed to the ground.

Not the first time he has saved my life, Hal thought hazily. *I'm sorry, Rafe. . . .* But there was no time for grief; hooves were bearing down on him from all directions. Hal struggled to his feet and looked wildly about him for some refuge. In this extremity Robin should have come to him; but it was Derek who appeared by his side. "Your back to mine, my King," Derek urged, and Hal obeyed him gratefully.

Derek stood almost a head taller than Hal, and protected him admirably. But Derek was not skilled with the sword; he had spent most of his life working with even grimmer implements. Hal was able to fend off his opponents with his long reach, to pink them in the belly or the thigh. But he was painfully aware that, behind his back, Derek was taking hard blows. He told him what nothing had ever made him say before.

"Kill the horses under them, Derek!" Hal shouted.

Derek scarcely heard the words, lost in the battle din around him. A red curtain swam in front of his eyes; he dimly realized that it was his own blood. He swung his sword at random. He cared little for his own life, but urgency pounded in him like a pulse: "My King—my King —my King—" Then pain pierced him to the vitals, and blackness blotted out the blood-red tide.

Hal felt him fall, and bit his lip in helplessness. But at that moment, like a fog being swept away by the wind, the struggling mass of men and horses disappeared from around him. Panting, Hal found himself staring at Alan's anxious face.

"Are you hurt!" Alan demanded.

"Hardly a scratch. Alan, finish it for me, pray. . . ." As Alan cantered off, Hal sank to his knees beside Derek, feeling for life. The mangled form stirred under his hands, and Derek opened his eyes, whispering, "Good my lord, you are well?"

Hal nodded, scarcely able to speak. He forced words out against the tightness of his chest. "Derek, the debt is paid in full, and over. For my life I thank you."

But Derek's eyes stared peaceful and unseeing at the blue sky. Hal closed the lids. Beyond him, the battle was nearing an end. Hal rose and trudged heavily off to find Rafe.

"The news travels across the land almost faster than mortals can convey it," Alan said. "It is as if there is a power in the air. Everyone in Isle knows that something wonderful is happening."

"The end of the Age is approaching," Hal quietly agreed, "and all things are spinning quickly to a close. The people feel it, though perhaps they do not understand."

Hal and Alan, with Rosemary, Rafe and Craig, sat together in council the day after the battle.

"The people of Welas understand," Alan replied. "Legends have come to life for them, and they accept it with fierce joy. I believe there is not a man or boy of Welandais birth who has failed to turn his hand against the oppressors. The companies of Torre and Adaoun swept across the countryside like fire in a field of dry grass. Before I left Laueroc, I heard they were already in Welden. Folk told of a giant white horse, gold-winged, that flew above the armies, directing their movements to best advantage. They spoke also of a tall, fair race of mountain warriors who struck terror into the hearts of their adversaries, and of their horses, lovelier than dreams, who fought as fiercely as their masters. And these things were said fearlessly, with admiration and joy."

Rosemary was puzzled, for she knew nothing of the elves, but Rafe's eyes sparkled.

Alan continued more slowly. "Hal, I also heard that Torre and Galin both died at the taking of Welden."

Hal bowed his head in pain for a moment, and Rosemary reached out to inquiringly touch his hand. "My grandfather," he explained, "and my uncle, my mother's only living brother. I had so wished to see them again. . . ."

"Torre was ready," Alan said. "They say he was splendid. They say he fought with greater force than strong young men, that his face shone as he struck down the foes that had dishonored him. He shouted your name as his battle cry, Hal, and his army took it up. He received his death blow in the heat of the struggle, but he lasted long enough to see the battle won. Somehow he knew that Galin had been killed, and he named you as his heir. You are now the last of that line, Hal," Alan added gently, "and I know Galin would not begrudge you that crown."

Hal kept silence. After a pause Rafe inquired, "Any other news, Alan?"

"Pelys still had not taken Gaunt, when last I heard," he answered, "but it was said it must soon fall to him. All of the peasants and half the soldiers had made away with arms and supplies, later to join with your father, my lady. I heard also that the warlords fight against Arrok as one body, for a wonder. His doom will not be long in coming."

"Lord Roran has defeated Gar of Whitewater," said Rosemary softly, "and he will soon be here, and very glad, I am sure, to find Robin safe. And Ket had no difficulty taking Lee, with Nabon's garrison weakened by his raid. Why, Hal, it sounds as if it is all settled. You have nothing to worry you anymore."

"Nay," said Hal somberly, "nothing to do but bury the dead."

Chapter Three

Alan badly wanted to talk to Hal. But the time was never right. For days after the battle, Hal was silent and moody, taking shovel alongside his men to rid the battlefield of its grisly load. Only when he was with Rosemary did his face brighten, so Alan was careful to leave them alone.

By the time they departed for Nemeton, Hal was in better spirits. Swift messengers had come to him from all parts of Isle, each one bringing news of victory. Hal sent the couriers back to their masters with news of his conquest, and other news of which Alan knew nothing. There was a gleam in Hal's eye as he and Rosemary rode side by side into Nemeton.

The greeting he received there took away his breath, and replaced the gleam with a tremble of wonder. The streets were lined ten deep with people smiling and calling his name, each bearing the bounty of summer's flowers. Rosemary wore only a borrowed frock, and Hal was tattered and stained with weeks in the field. But before they reached the first crossroad they shone brighter than the gods of legend, laden with as many blossoms as they could carry. Wreath upon wreath decked the horses' necks, and trumpet vines entwined their ears. Rosemary held a huge bundle of roses in her arms, and daisy crowns

adorned her head and Hal's. Petals sprinkled them from
head to foot. Alan had fallen back a few paces, grinning;
great chains of flowers draped his neck and Alfie's. Rafe
and his soldiers, Robin and Cory, Craig and his men—all
were beset by swarms of happy folk, and those who could
not reach them threw their bouquets into their path or
pelted them with the blossoms. Hal and Alan were
amazed to see many whom they knew, peasants and cottagers whom they had aided or who had aided them. In
the center of town they met Roran and his company. He
embraced Robin, and the crowd cheered them; the noise
was deafening.

At last they all came to the castle. The courtyard was
filled with servitors and guards, and hundreds of towns-
people thronged in as well. The air trembled with their
happy chatter. But when Hal ascended to the platform
and turned to greet his people, one voice cut through
them all, clear as a trumpet call. "See where he stands,
the King of Isle!" Alan knelt with hand raised in salute.
Rosemary, and all of Hal's men, and hundreds more knelt
before him and joined Alan's salute with a great shout.
Hal was speechless.

Rosemary gazed at him with smiling, adoring eyes.
Alan faced him tenderly but almost defiantly. "I told you
once," he said, "that I would kneel before you someday,
and you would know why. Do you?"

Hal looked deeply into Alan's eyes, and saw shame
there, along with a glimmer of the love he had missed for
so long. "Ay," he said roughly, "I know. So much for it.
Now *will* you get up!"

He took Alan and Rosemary each by one hand, and
urged them to their feet. Wordlessly he presented them
to the multitude in the courtyard; then he turned and led
them into his castle.

That afternoon, Alan once more tried to make occasion to speak with Hal, but he was missing. The old
nurse Nana had taken him aside. "I have something for
you," she told him, "something your mother left you." She
led Hal to a sealed and forgotten garret where there stood
a small chest. He was startled to see, emblazoned on its
lid, the emblem of the half-sun. "I do not know what is
in it," the old woman said as she handed him the key. "I
confess I tried to open it once, but it stung my fingers.
Yet I know your mother opened it often. She was always

careful to keep it from the King and from you, so I have done the same until I was certain you were quite grown. It came from Welas, with your uncle Gildur," Nana added.

"Gildur!"

"Ay. He stayed here in great secrecy for almost a year and a half after the capture of Weldon. He whiled away the hours by teaching music to your mother. 'Tis a strange thing, but I could almost swear that your instrument is the one he played. . . . In the end, of course, the King caught wind of him, and he had to flee. This was all before your birth." The ancient woman paused thoughtfully. "There is a great deal I should explain to you, my child, now that you are King. But perhaps something in that chest will tell it better than I can. I shall leave you with it now. But if you wish to speak with me, call me back."

He did call her back after several hours, and sent her out again after a long talk. Alan and Rosemary grew anxious when he missed the evening meal, and went to wait for him on the garret steps. It was almost dark when he emerged, but they could see that his face was pale and distraught. "Alan," he said abruptly, "will you ride with me in the morning? Rosemary, love, I need time to be alone and think. Do not be troubled for me. I shall see you tomorrow." He strode off into the twilight, leaving them puzzled and worried.

The next day, Hal and Alan rode at random over the rolling wealds that surrounded Nemeton. Hal seemed to be in no hurry to reveal his concern, and Alan had decided to postpone his own difficulty until Hal's was done. Their talk was as wandering as their track. They spoke of people they had known, of fun they had shared in the years past, and of the troubles they had shared, too. But those hard days were over now; the goal was attained. They felt a vague sorrow, and did not know how to comfort each other.

In time, the talk turned to Blain. "I was blood-blind and crazed with rage," Alan said. "But when my fury calmed, I was full of doubt. I knew what I had to do, and yet I felt like a murderer."

"You did me a great service," Hal told him, "which I might not have had the strength to do for myself."

"I did not feel strong, but weak and helpless," Alan

muttered. "My bloodthirst is cured, Hal. Never again will I reproach you for squeamishness."

Hal startled Arundel by banging his fist into the saddle, gesticulating wildly. "Mother of mercy, Alan!" he cried, "you did not have to say that! Time was, when . . ." He choked back his words.

"When a glance would- have been enough." Alan finished the thought with his heart in his voice, and looked up with aching eyes. "Hal—"

How he had longed for that warmth. But Hal could not yet bear to hear what Alan had to say. Staring straight ahead, he cut him off with a crisp statement. "Alan, we leave for Laueroc on the morrow. For the wedding and coronation."

"Laueroc!" gasped Alan, startled. "But why?"

"Ten hundred years ago, the Very King Bevan took his beloved that way, and perhaps wedded her on a Midsummer's Eve, as I will mine. Folk will be there from throughout the realm." His hesitation was barely perceptible, but Alan, who knew him well, sensed it at once. "The elves will meet us there, though I would never ask them to come all the way to Nemeton. Adaoun is performing the ceremonies." Hal looked at his gaping brother in carefully affected anxiety. "You do not begrudge me the use of your town, I hope?"

But Alan was not fooled. "You have laid a trap for me," he said, and his voice was low and dangerous.

"Destiny is no trap, but most often a blessing," Hal replied. "The course of our lives was set, Alan, long before either of us was born."

"Destiny be damned!" Alan shouted. "I will not go!"

"You shall go!" Hal commanded icily. He faced Alan with gray eyes gone cold and hard, gleaming eerily with elfin power. Alan's blue eyes blazed just as bright with mortal wrath, and did not waver for an instant. For a full minute the two wills clashed with all the force of physical combat. On a hilltop the horses stood rigid as statues, the young men sitting them silent as the wealds all around; but legend was to remember the flash of bright metal and the ring of steel in the air.

Slowly, like the soft dusk of dawn, Hal smiled, and the shining steel of his gaze turned to glowing love, a love welling up from so deep in his soul that Alan continued to stare, lost in a trance of astonishment. "Your power is the equal of mine," Hal murmured. "It is well."

"Name of Aene," Alan whispered. Suddenly he realized that Hal was aged beyond his years, battered and agonized by the death he had dealt, tired and sad; yet his back was straight and his face filled with honest joy.

"It is well," he repeated. "Alan, if you love me—"

"Hal!" pleaded Alan wretchedly.

"Nay," he continued, as if agreeing with something Alan had said, "you are right. I will not do that. Once you made me swear an oath that nearly tore my heart to shreds, for my own sake. But I will bind you by no such oath. I know you, Alan of Laueroc, and I know that you do not need my bidding to keep the law that springs from love. Farewell, Alan. Let your heart guide you well." He wheeled Arundel and sped away toward Nemeton.

"Hal!" Alan called after him. "Hal! Wait—" But Hal had disappeared over a rise of the rolling wealds, and Alan got no answer except the lonesome cries of straying sea birds.

Chapter Four

"He was not back all night," Rafe told Hal the next morning.

"I expected as much," he answered. "Well, let us go."

It did not take them long to make ready, for they were all accustomed to traveling light. For the first time since Rosemary had known him, however, Hal needed a pack horse to carry something he wished to take along.

They were all saddled and waiting when Cory appeared, looking distressed. "I cannot find Alan anywhere!" he exclaimed.

"Alan will be coming later, I dare say," Hal replied. "We must go on without him."

"I will wait for him here," Cory decided.

Hal shook his head. "You shall come with us. He must make his journey alone." The youth gaped in startled protest, but Hal shot him a glance that made him quickly take his place in line. For the first time in their acquaintance, Hal had chosen to command.

The castle folk merrily wished the company a good journey and great happiness. Nevertheless, it was a silent cavalcade which made its way out from Nemeton toward Laueroc. There were Hal and Rosemary, Cory, Robin and Roran, Craig and Rafe and a few maids. Not a word was spoken among them; they all felt the presence of the unseen watcher on the wealds.

That night Robin came to Hal. Concern for his tow-headed friend blotted out fear of Hal's wrath. "Hal, whatever is the matter? You must tell Cory something. He is so miserable."

Hal sighed. "I cannot tell Cory what is happening," he explained, "or you, or anyone else—not even my lady. For, if Alan's journey does not go as I expect, no one must ever know." He shook his head fretfully. "Tell Cory that Alan is in no danger or hardship. He knows that Alan can take care of himself. Tell him—I miss him, too. . . ."

"Are you quarreling?" Robin asked gently.

"His quarrel is more with himself than with me. Robin, what more can I say? I know him well; he will fight dragons, if need be, to—to come to me. All will be well."

Robin returned to Cory with these words of dubious comfort. But if Hal's reassurances sounded confident, his restless sleep that night belied him. There had been a time when he thought he knew Alan's heart. But his brother had been distant for so long, and he did not know why. . . .

Still, it was impossible for Hal to remain unhappy for long with Rosemary. He was on his way to his wedding, at long last! Within a few days, the spirits of the entire party had lifted. They traveled in easy stages, taking pleasure in the journey. In each village the excited folk called greetings and good wishes, pelting them with flowers.

When they came to Laueroc at last, a great throng awaited them, not only townsfolk but many old friends. One of the first they saw was Pelys in his litter. Rosemary ran to him and embraced him, whispering, "Father, pardon." But Pelys answered gently, "Tush, tush, daughter, I expected you would be off," and kissed her absently.

Will was not with Pelys. He had been killed at Gaunt; Rafe sorrowed to hear it. The warlords were not present either, for already they were fighting among themselves. But old Margerie was there, cackling in coquettish shock as Hal kissed her. The King of the Gypsies was there, a tiny man, gnarled as an ancient thorn tree, and stone blind. His hands traced Hal's face reverently, as if he touched the carved features of an idol. Ket was there too, his blazing hair still out of control under a leather cap. His brown eyes glowed warmly when Rosemary greeted him. Then, like everyone else, he asked Hal, "Where is Alan?"

"Thinking," Hal grumbled. "Say no more about it, Ket."

And then there was Adaoun, with all the People of Peace. It was indeed the closing of the Age, and perhaps the hearts of men had been purged for the new beginning to follow. Whatever the reason, they greeted their earth-brothers the elves with joyful wonder, though they could not communicate their gladness with words. But Rosemary trembled when she faced Adaoun, even though she was not afraid, and Hal put his arms around her. Adaoun gazed deeply into her unflinching eyes and set kindly hands on each side of her head.

He spoke to her softly, *"Laifrita thae, Kellea,"* which is to say, "Greetings, Kellea." Her elfin name meant "the faithful one." Rosemary responded in the Ancient Tongue, *"Laifrita thae, Adaoun."* ["Fair peace to thee, Elf-Father."] With the Old Language, there came to her the understanding of many mysteries, so that she looked at Hal and saw that he was Mireldeyn. He gazed at her with loving pride, and she answered with happy tears; at last she knew him entirely.

"She is the one," Adaoun told Hal.

"Did you ever doubt it?"

A spark of light glowed deep in Adaoun's ancient, youthful eyes as he shook his head.

"Where is Elwyndas?" asked Lysse.

"Wrestling with his pride," Hal replied. "And yet, he may hardly know with what he fights. There are many things he does not fully understand, and the very thoughts of his mind take arms against him. But I depend on his great heart to bring him here in time."

"I will go out and wait for him until he comes," said Lysse, and in a moment she was gone.

Cory and Rafe searched the crowd for the elf they knew, but did not find him. Soon Hal brought them confirmation of their fears: Anwyl had been killed at Welden. "He was one of only a few of us who fell," Adaoun explained, "for most of the lordsmen fled from us rather than fighting us. But Anwyl was overbold for your sake, Hal, eager to wrest Veran's treasure from the ancient hold of Welden, and he met with men to whom the panic had not yet spread. He was not afraid to die, but it grieves me that we did not find what he sought."

"I have it with me!" Unbuckling the canvas of his pack beast's load, Hal exposed a small, strongly built chest, plain except for the half-sun emblem shining from its metal top. "Torre's youngest son, Gildur, brought it to my mother's keeping before I was born. I knew nothing of it until three weeks ago, when my old nurse showed it to me."

"Let us see," Adaoun said in a hushed voice.

The chest seemed to open itself to Hal's touch, so quick and silent was the task. He stood aside, and Adaoun stooped and reverently took from it a crown of shining silver, beautifully simple and unadorned, the bright metal molded in graceful pointed shafts like the rays of a sunburst. "This is the ancient crown of Eburacon," Adaoun explained softly. "Veran brought it with him when he came to us over the waves of the Western Sea. It was all he had left of that former Age of greatness."

Next he took from the chest a crown of gleaming gold, pure and graceful of design as the first. "This he fashioned like the first, out of gold freely taken from the streams of our mountain valley, and in a mold newly made by his own hands, to signify the dawning of the new Age."

Then he brought forth a velvet pouch, and carefully shook from it two golden rings, plain and unadorned, but of a brightness that almost pulsed. "These rings, also, Veran made from the gold of the Eagle Valley, and with them he and my daughter Claefe plighted their troth."

Once more Adaoun stooped, and he removed from the chest a leather-bound tome of parchment pages, ancient, but with golden fastenings and tooled scarlet designs still glowing. Adaoun held it aloft, and the light flashed on strange golden runes for all to see. "And this," he said vibrantly, "is *The Book of Suns*. In the time of our despair,

the One offered us words of prophecy and comfort. They
are written in this book, by Veran's hand, and almost
all are now come to pass."

Each of these statements Hal had relayed to the awed
multitude that had gathered around. But now Adaoun
said something he kept to himself. "If you have read this,"
he remarked with mindful pity, "you know many things."

"I have read it." Hal turned to Rosemary. "And so
shall you, my love, and know everything that is in it:
the secrets of the elves, and of the elfin part of me. But
not yet. Not for a few days." He turned and locked the
crowns, the rings and the Book once again in their chest.

The following days were spent in feasting, merriment
and much talk. Hal was able to check on the welfare of
his entire kingdom, and the news was good. Most of the
spring planting had been done before Iscovar's death,
and Hal's throne had been secured so swiftly that the
rhythm of work was scarcely interrupted. Famine, the
specter that so often stalks in the wake of war, was not
likely to be seen—especially since half of each lord's
holding of land had been divided among the peasants.
The same had been done with the enormous stockpiles
of grain and other supplies, and with each lord's hoard
of treasure and gold. Such a spirit of peace lay upon the
land that there had been no quarreling over fair shares;
the countryfolk rejoiced in their unexpected prosperity.
In most of the manors a man who had been a leader
among the people was elevated to the position of responsibility, with the assurance of help and advice from
the King and his liegemen. Hal offered Ket the manor
of Lee, but he refused it, saying he would rather stay by
Hal as one of his officers. So Rafe was prevailed upon
to accept Lee, and Craig took management of Whitewater, since Margerie said she was too old for such nonsense.

As the wedding day drew near, neither Lysse nor Alan
had been seen. From time to time, Hal raised the hope
that they were together, but in his heart he knew they
would have come to him if it were so. In his mind's eye
he envisioned Lysse as indeed she was: a patient figure
waiting and watching the road by a lonely campfire. But
try as he might, Hal could not envision Alan. By the eve of

the Midsummer festival, the Feast of Bowers, Hal's low
spirits had influenced the entire camp. Rosemary could
have wept at the despair in his eyes, and only her generous heart kept her from cursing Alan as a graceless, selfish,
thick-skulled mule, he who had spoiled what ought to
be the happiest time of Hal's life.

For two full weeks Alan lay in the sun on the upland
hills, waiting for some unknown succor, foraging for food
when he felt the need, seeing no living being except the
birds and the furry beasts. After the first few days he
gave up consciously struggling with his problem. Its dull
ache rose with him in the morning, lived with him through
the day, went to bed with him at night. His dreams were
colored cruelly with pain and sorrow, leaving him as
fatigued as if he had fought a long and losing battle.

On the last day when he could leave and hope to reach
Laueroc in time, he rose and saddled Alfie, scarcely
knowing how or when he had decided to go. Then the
dull ache in his heart was replaced by sharper pangs of
fear that he might miss Hal's great day. He set his course
as straight as an arrow toward Laueroc, and Alfie ran
with all the urgency his master felt. At least there was no
longer any fear of lordsmen. Alan sped through the days,
rested only a few hours each night, and ate as he rode.

As the afternoon before the Midsummer festival drew
on, Alan sighed thankfully and slackened his pace somewhat at last. Laueroc was only a few miles away. *I shall
be there in time for the late meal,* he thought, *and that
will give me the evening to set things to rights.* Under the
golden light of a low sun, he was cantering up the last
slope outside of town, smiling with relief, when he looked
up and saw the one person who was the cause of all his
heart's commotion.

Lysse sat still upon a filly of the *elwedeyn* breed, and
she wore a dress of the same dark, sun-flecked green as
her eyes. Golden sunset rays made a halo of her golden
hair. No amount of resolve could have prepared Alan
for this moment. His eyes fastened upon her, and slowly,
scarcely knowing what he was doing, he took her hand
and held it pressed to his cheek.

"Wherever have you been!" she asked in her sweet,
melodious voice. "I have awaited you these many days."

The sound of the Ancient Tongue shocked him out of his trance, and he dropped her hand. "I have come to see my brother, Lysee," he declared hoarsely, "to bring him something that belongs to him and to wish him joy on his wedding day. I must go to him now." Dazed, he lifted the reins, but for the first time in years Alfie balked. The horse rolled his eyes until the whites showed, and flapped his ears, ogling impudently. But Alan did not notice; his gaze was caught on Lysse. The pain in her eyes was pitiful. Yet she was an elf, and should not know such heartfelt pain. . . .

"Alan," she whispered, "by the mighty Wheel, tell me now, truly: do you love me still, or not?"

The cruel lie, rehearsed a thousand times, came to Alan's mind, but wrestle with it as he might, it would not leave his tongue. For a breathless moment he struggled, shaken to the roots of his being; then the answer exploded from him. "Ay!" he shouted, and the hills of his native land rang with it. "Sweet Lysse, I do!" Shaking, his voice subsided to a whisper. "Oh, Lysse, I am so sorry. . . ."

"Why?" She placed gentle hands upon his bowed shoulders. "For you know I love you, too, Alan of Laueroc."

"Because I cannot have you." He spoke decidedly, with the perfect calm of longstanding pain. "I will not doom you to death, you whom I love, or tear you from your people. Go, Lysse, sail to fair Elwestrand which is your birthright, you and your brothers and sisters. Live there long after I am dead and turned to dust. I cannot kill you, Lysse!"

"I will not go," she told him with dogged patience, as if she must explain to him the clearest facts of his life, even the rising and setting of the sun. "Nor will my father ask me to; he knows I must be with you. If you ride away from me I will follow, and if my horse fails me I will walk, winter or summer, to be by your side. I love you. Is so simple a thing so difficult for you to accept?" In her eyes, to the deepest reaches of her soul, there was no hint of faltering or sorrow.

Alan gazed into those incredible eyes, and saw there a love as marvelous to him as it was incomprehensible, for he scarcely felt deserving. Breathlessly, he sensed the deepest strength of his soul stirring within him, surrendering foolish pride and false honor to the love that rules the heart. With tears of relief flowing freely down his cheeks, Alan took Lysse's chin in his hand and kissed her deeply on the lips. All the jagged pieces of his life fell into place, and he was finally at peace with himself and with his world.

Chapter Five

On that last night before the fateful day, the strong stone walls of Laueroc Castle seemed to choke Hal, so that he felt he must move out of doors, under the stars and the full moon. With Arundel for company, he built a little fire in a copse of trees on the town common. Sitting beside it, he bowed his head and thought of Alan, wishing that his thoughts could draw him there.

Lysse and Alan were still deep in talk. "Silly," she was chiding him fondly. "To think that any good could come to me, without you! My immortal life would have become a curse, for the Ages of the elves are at an end. My brothers and sisters, like me, will find mortal love in Elwestrand, and will die happy that their ancient loneliness is ended. And perhaps a finer race will come out of it all."

"Why did you not tell me!" he cried. "You or Hal . . ."

"The choice had to be yours, without telling. Though I know Hal has suffered with you."

"Dear Hal," he murmured, holding her close against him. "For months I have been longing to speak to him."

"Come, let us go to him. The night moves on apace." He still held her and sighed, but she laughed at him tenderly. "You shall have me the rest of your life!"

They found Hal with his head on his knees beside a dwindling campfire, keeping a dozing vigil, as Alan had often known him to do in times of wounds or sickness. The silver circlet on his head had slipped rakishly over one ear, and Alan knelt to gently straighten it. Hal looked up, scarcely daring to believe he was in the world of the waking, whispering, "Alan!" He reached out to embrace him, but his arms stopped in midair as he remembered that, lately, Alan did not care to be touched.

Alan groaned to himself with aching heart, realizing what distance he had put between them. Lysse kissed Hal on the cheek, then kissed Alan squarely on the lips. "I shall see you on the morrow," she said, and disappeared into the night. Alan still knelt before Hal, meeting his eyes. He reached into his tunic.

"I have something that belongs to you," Alan said, "that I have been longing to give you." He drew out the silver ring he had taken from his father's skeletal hand. He had not worn it since returning to Celydon from Laueroc almost a year before, but evidently he had often polished it; the tiny circle shone brightly even in the moonlight. Alan handed it to Hal, warm from his body heat, and looked at the ground, searching for words.

"I know," Hal whispered, saying for him the unspeakable. "I know, my brother. I watched my father die in torment on my account, in the Dark Tower."

Alan's head snapped up. "How long have you known?" he gasped.

"Since two days before we left. It was written in *The Book of Suns,* which my old nurse showed to me that afternoon in the garret. But you have known since you went to Laueroc, that first time."

"Ay. My father left a letter for me."

"Then it is that which has been hidden in your eyes since then?"

"Ay."

"Nothing more?"

"Nay. At least, not at first."

Hal was impatient, and his voice echoed the pain of ten months of needless misery. "Oh, Alan, Alan, why did you not tell me?"

"Because of the seven generations," Alan explained

earnestly. "Because of—of that by which I made you swear. You have often told me that, if you were not the son of that fiendish King, no power on earth could make you seek the throne—that you wanted nothing from life but peace and a little love. For the sake of all the poor folk in this oppressed land, I could not tell you, Hal! You were the only one who could save them!"

Hal shook his head. "No power on earth, nay. But an even heavier burden found me after I said that, Alan— heavier, but somehow easier to bear: the burden of prophecy." A tiny smile played around the corners of his lips. "It was not only your mighty oath that saved my life. It was a song Rosemary sang to me that reminded me of the other burden that came with my birth. *'Bearing balm of Veran's flower, Man born blest with elfin dower.'* Adaoun's image came to my mind, and his eyes upon me compelled me to live until you came with Veran's comfort."

"You mean," asked Alan with a dry mouth, "that I could have told you?"

"By my wounds, I wish you had!" declared Hal with a bitterness that struck Alan to the heart.

"May I die for it, Hal, I didn't know," Alan choked, and then he broke and wept like a child with the frustration of almost a year of estrangement. "I didn't know," he moaned.

Hal's arms went around his shoulders; the brothers clutched each other tightly. "Of course you didn't know," Hal said fiercely, hating himself. "You did what you felt you must. Oh, Alan, I am sorry. Why did I tell you that!"

"Small blame to you," Alan gulped, still struggling for breath. "The way I've been acting, I'll warrant you had forgotten I could care." He flung his head up and faced Hal with a tear-streaked face in which the whole of his soul showed plain and unashamed. "Hal, I love you so. . . . I had to put some distance between us, or the secret in my heart would have driven me mad." His head dropped wearily to Hal's shoulder, and Hal held him in silence, swallowing at the lump in his throat.

"I knew my father was unfaithful," said Alan at last, sitting up and wiping his face with his sleeve. "We quarreled about it. He had married my mother in policy, not in passion, but she was a good, gentle woman, and I loved her deeply. Now I know that your mother was his

mendor, and he was fated to love her, despite loss of
honor—despite the shadow of death. . . . But then I
blamed him bitterly. Still, when I first knew you, I
hoped—I wished like a boy—that you might be my
brother. When you told me you were the King's son, it
nearly broke my heart, for who could have dreamed that
Leuin's lover, all those years, had been the Queen herself? And then to find that my dream had come true,
and not to be able to tell you!"

"Did Iscovar know, I wonder?" murmured Hal, changing the subject, for Alan was still close to tears.

"He knew. My father—our father—says in his letter
that Iscovar was unable to beget children, due to the same
disease of lust by which he died. He knew you were
Laueroc's son, but his need of an heir constrained him
to keep the secret. For a long time, my father's—our
father's—power was great enough to protect himself, the
Queen, and you. But little by little, by means too foul to
be answered in kind, the King weakened Laueroc, until
at long last he had his horrible revenge."

"Horrible, indeed. But no wonder he hated me," Hal
muttered. "The more so because he could not do away
with me. . . . Did you tell anyone else, Alan? Cory perhaps?"

"Nay, no one. I kept my peace most obstinately. But
if I had known the needless pain it would cost you, I
would never have done it. Dear Hal, I wish you would
kick me! It would make me feel so much better."

Hal threw back his head and laughed. The two of them
were walking at random now, arms around each other's
shoulders, as they had at other happy times. "Poor Alan!
I believe I begin to understand. All that crustiness. . . ."

"Was the only way I could hide the longing in my
heart from you. If I had let myself show love for you, my
secret would have popped out in an instant. Then I was
vexed that I could manage it no better, and being vexed
with myself I grew vexed with you and the whole world.
But even that is not the worst of it."

"Nay," agreed Hal wryly, "on top of all that, your eyes
caught the glitter of this pretty bauble I wear on my
head."

Alan winced as if he had been struck. "By my troth,

you know me better than I knew myself," he whispered.

"But why, Alan? You were not really planning to seize the throne from me."

"Nay, of course not! But in spite of my best intentions, the thought would nag at the back of my mind, and it nearly drove me mad with shame and frustration. To add to my shame, I knew that I had only to ask you, and you would have given me your crown as freely as you give your love! But of course I could not ask any such thing. If only I could have come to you, talked to you—but to explain my malady would have been to explain the cause."

"That, by birth, you have as much right to the throne as I do."

"Ay. Such nonsense. Your right to the throne has always gone far beyond the right of birth, and I have always known it."

"Do you still desire it?" asked Hal quietly.

"Nay! Mothers, nay. Blain cured me of that."

"Then you shall have it, Alan." Hal faced him, smiling, with warm affection in his voice. "You fought for me, I know. . . . But I fought, in large measure, for you."

"You are babbling nonsense, Hal!" Alan exclaimed. "You know I can't take your crown!"

"Who said anything about *my* crown!" Hal teased. "Think more of *your* crown!" He took Alan by the shoulders, his eyes bright with joy and mischief. "What, Sunrise King, do you not yet know yourself? Just as I am the last of the line of Veran, the sunset of the Age, so are you the sunrise of the new Age, the first of the Liege Kings of Laueroc! Do you not think that two brothers such as we can rule together? Our capital is to be in Laueroc, centered between east and west—though you know I shall look most often to Welas. After my death, the two peoples shall be united under you and your heirs, as they ought to be. And the blood of the elves shall enrich your line, as it did the Blessed Kings before you. By all that is lovely, you shall be a bright dawning for this land after a long, dark night."

"You are serious!" Alan whispered.

"Quite serious. It is written in *The Book of Suns*, though I knew it long ago. Torre let it slip, and you, modest soul that you are, soon forgot it."

"But how can I rule? You are Mireldeyn."

"And you alone are Elwyndas. Your power is equal to mine—remember? Is it so hard to accept?"

Alan shook his head, stunned. "But Hal, what of your heirs?"

"I shall have none." The joy went out of his voice. "I am to be the last of the line of Veran, the last of those Very Kings—though there will be others, Alan, mark it. But Rosemary and I will have no children. That is the prophecy."

"Oh, Hal, I am sorry." Alan gently touched his shoulder.

"That is the advantage of prophecy, you see, Alan." Hal tried to smile. "If I had not known this, your crown would have been obliged to wait until my death. But now we can both be crowned and wed to our ladies together, on the morrow." He faced Alan whimsically, brushing the ever-unruly hair from his brother's brow. "Have children, Alan—my second self—and I shall love them as my own. It is for Rosemary that I mind it most. I do not know what comfort to give her."

"You yourself are her best comfort. So you plan to tell her?"

"Ay. If there is one thing I have learned in the past year, it is not to keep a secret from a loved one. Secrecy breeds fresh sorrow, but sharing is joy in itself. Still, I have not told her yet. I did not wish to mar her wedding day."

For an hour Hal and Alan walked together, voicing random thoughts, reluctant to give up their rediscovered companionship on this last night of their single lives. "It is past midnight," Hal finally said. "Let us get some sleep. It will not do for us to be tired, not tomorrow."

They returned to Hal's fire, in embers now, and laid out their blankets. Nearby, Alfie and Arundel peacefully grazed.

"We could go inside, you know," Hal remarked. "There is no need to sleep out."

Alan laughed quietly into the darkness. "Strange. So many times we camped together, each longing for a warm room and a soft bed; and now . . ."

"Ay. One last time. . . . Well, good night."

"Good night."

In her castle chamber, Rosemary lay still and miserable on her canopied bed. There was scarcely a rustle, but like a green-and-golden spirit of summer Lysse stood beside her.

"Sleep, my sister," she said. "Be content. Alan is here, and all will be well."

Rosemary sat bolt upright. "Oh, has he come at last!" she cried.

"Ay, that he has." Lysse smiled a secret smile.

"And—are we to be sisters, truly?" asked Rosemary more calmly.

"Indeed, we are."

"Oh, Lysse, I am so happy," said Rosemary softly. Lysse looked into her eyes for just an instant; then with all her heart she embraced this generous mortal woman, her first and lifelong friend in the strange race she was fated to join.

The next morning, Cory slept late, for even in his dreams some dejected part of his brain told him there was little use in waking up. A rough shaking roused him at last.

"Alan!" he cried, dazed with joy and surprise.

"Come on, you sleepyhead!" shouted Alan, grinning with delight. "This is my wedding day, and you must be my best man. Aren't you going to help me make myself presentable?"

"Your wedding day!" Corin sat up, squeezing his head in disbelief. "But who?"

"Lysse."

Corin thrashed his way out of bed, shaking his head. "Lysse!" he sputtered. "You lucky dog! You lucky, lucky dog!" Hastily he dressed, muttering to himself in bemused happiness. "Confound it, is that what you and Hal were quarreling about?" he finally demanded.

"Well, after a fashion, ay."

"It was! But why?"

"Because I was a dolt, forsooth!" Alan retorted cheerfully. "But come on, we have lots to do. I'll tell you about it later." He strode out, and Corin trotted after him, still shaking his head.

A few hours later, Robin and Cory stood waiting in the castle courtyard, smiling at each other from time to time.

Already their eyes were glazed from the events of the day. They wore tunics of finest fawn-colored wool, gifts from Adaoun, and they held the reins of his other gifts: steeds of the *elwedeyn* breed. Cory's was creamy gold in color, and Robin's a gray so dark as to be almost black. These had never known saddle or bridle, but at Adaoun's gentle command they now bore intricately woven blankets. The youths led them by soft hackamores, such as were worn by Alfie and Arundel beside them.

As the sun reached its height, Hal and Alan came out and mounted. They carried no weapons or warlike gear, except their swords, suspended from the chain-link belts Roran had given them years before. They wore shirts of pure-white wool, delicately embroidered in multicolor designs of every living thing. Bright cloaks fell back from their shoulders. Their heads were bare and high. On his right hand, Hal wore a large, dark gem set in silver, with a strange glow emanating from its heart. Alan no longer tucked the green Elfstone beneath his shirt, but proudly centered it on his chest. From time to time, he and Hal glanced at each other in silent, sober affection—men with the look of eagles, great in stature beyond their physical size, regarded with awe by poor and prosperous alike, each other's equal in power and valor. They waited together for their destiny.

Soon, Rosemary and Lysse rode out with glowing eyes, in gowns of a simplicity which set off their beauty as no jewels and laces ever could: long, sweeping dresses of purest white, somehow made without a seam. Their hair swung long and free, crowned and intertwined with roses of soft pink, yellow and creamy white. Flowers of the same hues adorned pretty little Asfala and Lysse's darkly golden Faen. They sat sideways on blankets of summer green, and their white skirts trailed down below their feet. Hal took Rosemary by the hand, and Alan clasped hands with Lysse, and they rode four abreast through the town, with the rest of the company following. The townsfolk, and countryfolk from miles around, watched them pass with quiet joy, then fell in line and followed after.

On a green, tree-crowned hill outside of town, a hill Alan remembered from his earliest years, Adaoun waited for them. He was to perform the ceremonies by greater right than any priest of any god, for he, sung in the First

Song, had not forgotten Aene. He needed no temple except the blue sky above, which had always been his roof.

The weddings were simple and eloquent. Each loved one and each lover stated their devotion in the words which best came to mind; then they vowed troth, honor, and duty until death. Hal and Rosemary exchanged the rings that had been worn by Torre and Megolyn, sent to him at Torre's dying request. Alan and Lysse exchanged the rings that had wed Veran and Claefe. Each couple joined hands to seal their promises, and the crowd stirred and murmured in pleasure.

From the little chest at his feet, Adaoun reverently took up *The Book of Suns*. From this he read in the Ancient Tongue, the only language he knew. Rafe translated for the sake of the witnesses: "And it shall come to pass that a truly great lord of the land of Isle shall have two sons. One shall be by his *mendor,* a daughter of the house of Veran, and the other by a gentle lady to whom he shall be wed by chance of custom. And these two brothers shall not know each other, but shall grow in courage and goodness, each in his own way. Manhood shall be thrust early upon them, and great misfortune, and they shall meet strong enemies. In the course of their struggle they shall find and aid each other, and love one another as if they had been raised together from birth, though they shall not know of their bond. And the goals of their two lives shall become one."

Hal glanced at his bride and, seeing that she understood, smiled and pressed her hand.

"The son of Veran's line shall be he to whom all your dreams should turn, People of Peace. He shall be the means of your leaving to the land I have promised you; he shall be the savior of Isle and Welas, and the consummation of the Age. The blood of elves shall flow strong in him, giving him knowledge, power, and vision beyond those of other mortals; yet he shall know the love and pain of a mortal heart. Men shall stand in awe of him, and call him Healer, Ruler, Welandais Prince, and Sunset King. But your name for him shall be Mireldeyn—'Elf-Man.' And these shall be the signs: that he shall come to you, unbidden, on a steed of the elfin blood, with the marks of suffering on his body, and the Old Language on his tongue, and the vision of the legends in his eyes. His only magic and his only power shall reside in himself.

"But men's dreams shall find fulfillment in his brother, for he shall begin a new Age of peace for mortal men. A great-hearted man, like Veran before him, he also shall win the love of an elf maiden—"

Alan stood, scarcely listening, with his arm around Lysse.

"—so that his heirs may be blessed with elfin wisdom and vision. The knowledge of the Old Language, and of many mysteries, shall be his. Men shall love and honor him, calling him Elfstone, the Golden One, and Sunrise King. But your name for him shall be Elwyndas—'Elf-Friend.' And these shall be the signs to you: that the ash maiden shall find love for him in her heart, and intervene for his sake, and lead him to you; and he shall fearlessly find the knowledge of the Old Language and its secrets in her eyes."

Adaoun closed the Book, speaking now more slowly and thoughtfully. "This is called *The Book of Suns*. It tells of the rising and setting of many kinds of suns—the suns of all men's days, the suns of many men's lives, the suns of all the ages of history for both men and elves. But all of these are bound up and reach their culmination in the two sons who stand before you, sons of a truly noble man. From their first meeting, though they did not know each other, they loved each other as brothers, and now they find that they are brothers in truth. They were born on the same day, in the same hour; there is no thought of younger or elder between them. They are at one with each other, just as the sun which sets at night is the same sun which rises in the morning. In Mireldeyn, you see the splendid setting of the sun that rose with Veran. In Elwyndas, you see the splendid rising of the sun of a new Age, dawning, like the Age of Veran before him, in peace and love. Whether peace and love shall endure, mortal men, depends on each of you. . . .

"This is a moment of great weight in your history, folk of the Second Song. The One has said that, if you will it, the sun can set forever on the wreakers of war and oppression. The tide of their onslaught can be turned for all time, if this land of Isle stands strong in its path. Aene has given you two men, the likes of which you will never see again, for this, your time of need. He has given you two who are something more than men, who face the specters of pride and greed and dare them to do their worst. They have shared the chances of life and death. They have fulfilled all the prophecies of *The Book of Suns*, except this last one, and they shall fulfill that one also: that greed and pride shall have no dominion, but all men shall live in harmony. Long, prosperous, and peaceful shall be the reign of Laueroc!"

The people cheered. Hal smiled a tiny smile, thanking Adaoun for what he had not said.

"Therefore," continued Adaoun, and his voice was suddenly awesome in its majesty, "I say to you, mortal men, that it is meet that these two sons who have shared their peril and yours should also share the reward which means so much less to them than their love. For the first time in your annals or ours, I show to you Kings equal in power, goodness, stature and love—I show to you the Sons of Laueroc. I show to you the final Chapter of *The Book of Suns*—I show to you the Sun Kings!"

At the beckoning of Adaoun's imperious eyes, Hal and Alan stepped forward and stood before him. A roar went up from the crowd, echoing to the sky, and fell off all at once to a waiting silence. Hal and Alan dropped to one knee.

Adaoun placed the silver crown on Hal's head. "I crown you first, Mireldeyn," he murmured, "only because you are the child of the old Age, which came before the new."

He next placed on Alan's head the crown of gold. "All the blessings of Aene be on you both," he whispered, and raised them.

They stood before the multitudes of their people, their friends. They were crowned in rays of glory like the suns from which they took their titles. Thousands knelt before them with faces uplifted in glowing joy, with hands raised in greeting, with voices raised in shouts of praise. Hal and Alan stood, and their knees weakened before the adulation as they never had before hostile armies, and they turned to each other for support, only to see tears shining in each other's eyes. Almost laughing, they embraced in their grip of brotherhood, pummeling each other, and then they stretched out hands to their brides, holding them tight as the shouts of their people blended into a mighty chant of triumph.

Robin and Cory brought them their horses. As they rode toward their hilltop bowers, the crowd pressed around them, and flowers filled the air. Somewhere, music started, and feasting began. Their whole world rejoiced, for their happiness was the happiness of their people.

Epilogue

A week's gentle journeying brought them to the Bay of the Blessed. It was just the four of them—Hal, Rosemary, Alan and Lysse—with the entire race of elves. They had experienced one last whiff of eternity. The days of pleasant riding melted together in memory, leaving only an image of glowing days and balmy nights. The Kings did not wear the heavy crowns of Veran; Hal wore his plain circlet, and Alan a similar one of gold that Hal had given him. They rode with heads held high, and their wives regarded them with proud, loving eyes. In all those days, Rosemary did not ask the question reposing at the back of her mind. She knew, as simply as a mother with child knows, that the time was not yet.

They arrived in midmorning of the eighth day. For the past two days they had seen no one but themselves, for this was a forbidden place, protected by the spirits of the legendary gods. The Bay of the Blessed shimmered silver-gray between shale shores and shadowy evergreens. At the mouth of the Gleaming River rode three gray ships at anchor, silent as ghosts.

"Veran prepared them for us," Adaoun explained, "when the prophecies became known to him."

"They have stayed whole all these years?" Rosemary gasped.

"They have stayed whole. There is power in living wood, and there was great power in his hands."

There were no supplies needed for the voyage to Elwestrand, nor any sails, for that is a singular journey. The elves lingered a while, talking with their friends, and ate a last meal before they embarked. The horses, all except Wynnda, had been given as gifts to Hal and Alan and the House of Laueroc.

"We closed the valley," Adaoun explained. "We blocked the entry with great rocks, and Wynnda flew us out. It comforts us to know that the creatures will always live there, the great eagles and the shy deer, without fear of men. We know you would have done what you could, Mireldeyn and Elwyndas, but a mortal's span is but short. . . ."

"We understand," Hal replied quietly.

After a while there was nothing more to say, and the elves slowly boarded. The four stood silently on the shore as, swimming like swans, the gray ships slid away with a lapping of ripples against their wooden flanks. Everyone waved. Hal held Rosemary's hand. Alan put an arm around Lysse's waist as she watched her brothers, sisters and loving father slip away from her, bound for Elwestrand across the Western Sea. Her eyes held a strange, sad joy.

"Farewell—farewell!" cried the elves, until their cries became one with the salt cries of the sea birds. Adaoun, at the prow of the largest ship, was soon only a dark post against the silver sea.

They watched until the ships became birdlike shapes against the setting sun, disappearing into its embrace. Then the sun sank, and they could see the ships no more. Rosemary broke silence at last, for she felt the trembling of Hal's hand and heard the straining of his heart.

"You wish you were going with them," she said gently, "do you not?"

He turned to her, his gray eyes awash with the mystery of the gray sea. "Ay," he whispered. "Ay. But there is so much healing to be done, in Isle. . . . I am fated to be left behind to carry on."

Hal and Rosemary, Alan and Lysse camped on the shore that night, with the lapping of the waves and the crying of the sea birds in their ears. When the new day dawned, they turned their faces to the rising sun and rode back toward the world of green meadows and mortal men.

So the battle's won, the consummation
Now at hand, the living sweet;
And still the Wheel is every turning,
Year by year the hill fires burning;
Vision flits upon the moonlit waters.
So if ever I should lose the love of men
And choose to walk again
My own fey, lonely way,
Do not grieve, Love, but say
That once, a summer day,
You held me in the meadow sunlight,
Kissed me in the meadow sun,
And in that sunlit meadow closed my eyes.

—a song of Hervoyel

Fantasy Novels
from
POCKET BOOKS